SARITA

SARITA

A NOVEL

NATALIE MUSGRAVE DOSSETT

atmosphere press

Published by Atmosphere Press

Cover design by Ronaldo Alves. Cover image by Wojciech Kwiatkowski.

Atmospherepress.com

For Dad
"Never Give Up"

"The manufacture, sale, or transportation of intoxicating liquors imported or exported from the United States is prohibited."

The Eighteenth Amendment went into effect at midnight on January 16, 1920. Seldom has a law been so extraordinarily difficult to enforce or so flagrantly violated.

CHAPTER 1

Sunlight shifted through the oak canopy above, golden rays glistening on my fingers, slick with blood and gloved in small brown and gray feathers. I picked up another quail from the pile at my feet, popping the head off and snapping the fragile wing bones. As I plucked it clean, small tufts of down sailed away like dandelion seeds, floating with the buzz of locusts and grasshoppers on the summer breeze. The lazy sound reminded me of childhood naps in the shade of the big live oak behind our house, of waking up in a hazy sweat to Mama's dinner call. My mother lay buried under that tree now, and everything had changed.

Holding the bird's stiff feet in one hand, I pinched the film of skin around its thigh and peeled it away from the shiny meat underneath. A triangle of shotgun pellets pocked the rose-tinted breast, tiny copper cannonballs that had folded the bird mid-flight and sent it diving to the ground. I picked them out and turned the headless body over to scoop up the wormy intestines, dropping them onto a small mound of guts on the ground. Coyotes were probably circling already, nosing the wind.

I finished cleaning all the birds, shoved them into a burlap sack, and wiped my hands on the back of my canvas trousers, already soiled from a full day of ranch chores. Gathering my gear, I walked over to Buster. The horse had wandered to the edge of a watering hole, grazing on sparse stalks of buffalo grass not yet burnt crisp by the July sun.

As I pushed the .410 shotgun into the saddle scabbard, I paused, sensing a subtle change in the air. The insects had fallen silent; even the chortling of the white-winged doves roosting in the high branches had stopped. The hair on the back of my neck prickled. Buster raised his head, ears swiveling.

Turning in a circle, I searched the heat-wobbled horizon. The surrounding mesquite thicket stood waist-high, not tall enough to hide a horsebacker, but several nearby oak motts, like the one I stood in, could provide plenty of cover for someone wanting to keep out of sight. A chill ran down my arms despite the near hundred-degree temperature, the four miles to our house seeming to grow longer.

A minute or so passed before the insect noise stutter-started back up. Buster let out a snort, nudging my hip. He was ready to head home to the bucket of oats waiting in the barn. Whatever had caused the hush—a bobcat, a fox—must've passed.

I shoved the bird sack into the saddlebags, threw the reins over Buster's head, and swung up onto his back. Tapping my heels against his sides, we moved out of the tree cover toward the road home. I tried to shake the feeling of being watched. On his morning rounds, Papa had discovered four cut fences and a butchered heifer way up at the north pens, which had me jumpy. He'd taken some ranch hands there to mend the holes and round up the straying cattle. Barbwire might have put an end to the open range for livestock, but trespassers only needed a good pair of wire cutters.

There'd been a surge in activity over the past several months, news of some sort of trouble arriving like the hot gulf breeze, unwanted and inevitable. The threats of cattle rustlers, bandits, and thieves had always existed, but since Prohibition had gone into effect, *tequila* smugglers had been added to the mix. They seemed particularly brazen, taking what they wanted as they crossed ranches north of the Rio Grande, heading to San Diego to sell their loads.

I urged Buster into a gallop, zigzagging through the scrub. As we came over a small rise, my breath caught. A rider was leading an extra horse down the middle of the road. I yanked the reins back, reaching automatically for my gun—then got a better look and settled back in the saddle.

My younger brother sat astride a little dapple-gray horse he was breaking in. When he saw me, he pulled up.

"Hey, Sarita," JJ called.

His colt pranced impatiently at the end of a lead rope attached to his saddle horn. Twister had been JJ's payment for working a *remuda* of wild mustangs for the neighboring Arrowhead Ranch. He didn't go anywhere without him; he'd have let Twister sleep by his bed if Papa would've allowed it.

"You headed home?" I asked, trotting up beside him.

"Not yet. I need to work her a while longer," JJ replied, referring to the young mare he rode. "They want her ready for round-up next week, and she's still pretty squirrelly."

As if to prove him right, the mustang skipped sideways, throwing her head up and down like an impatient child.

"Woah, there, Bluebird," he soothed, patting her neck.

We'd both been riding since almost before we could walk, but JJ had a way with horses; some even called it a gift. He'd earned quite a reputation breaking wild mustangs and busting broncos even grown men had given up on. The problem was that all JJ ever wanted to do was work horses. Our father didn't mind the extra money it brought in, so long as JJ's ranch work got done—which it never did. At least, not by him. His gift was my curse.

"You better be back before Papa gets home," I said. "You've got chores and I'm done covering for you."

"Yeah, I know." His eyes fell on the top of the bird sack sticking out of my saddlebag. "How many did you get?"

"Twelve shots, twelve birds."

"Guess that's supper then," he said.

JJ leaned over to scratch the white star marking the colt's forehead as Twister nibbled at his leg.

"You treat that horse like an overgrown puppy," I remarked.

JJ grinned. "He's a hundred times better than any dumb old dog."

Despite myself, his love for Twister touched my heart. He'd smiled more in the two weeks since he'd brought the colt home than he had in the whole two years since Mama had died.

"Must be nice messing around with ponies all day," I teased, slapping the flap of my saddlebag closed. "I, on the other hand, have to get home and do some real work."

"You got no idea what you're talking about." JJ's blue eyes scowled at me from under his dove-gray Stetson. "Saddle-breaking mustangs is real work."

"Real or not," I shot back, "training other people's horses has got nothing to do with our ranch, which is what you should be concerning yourself with."

He rolled his eyes, as sick of this argument as I was. In my heart, I wished my father would give in and teach me the cattle operation. I was better suited to it than JJ, and Papa needed the help. He'd had two more bad spells over the last several months. Dr. Andrew had told him his heart was getting weak and he needed to cut back, but he was too damn stubborn to listen.

"Sooner or later, you're going to have to learn how to run La Barroneña like Papa wants," I said. "You're thirteen already, and he can't work as hard as he used to."

JJ sighed and yanked off his hat, running a hand through sweat-damp hair that had grown so long it curled below his ears.

"You're pissed no matter what I do; you been mad ever since Jackson left," he said, not looking me in the eye. "It ain't my fault he cut and run."

Anger crept up my neck. Jackson had vanished about a year ago. Two weeks after he'd asked me to marry him. No one had heard from him since. For a while, it had been good fodder for gossip—did something happen to him? Did he get cold feet? Eventually people found other things to talk about. In spite of all my efforts, it still hurt.

"It's 'isn't' not 'ain't,' and you need a haircut before people mistake you for a girl," I snapped, glaring until a frown pulled at his mouth. "See, I can say hurtful things too."

"Sorry," he mumbled.

Bluebird bounced forward like she was playing hopscotch. JJ shoved his Stetson on and pulled the reins in. "We done? She's getting antsy."

"Guess so. Don't go too far off, and don't be late."

"Yes, ma'am, Miss Sarita," he smirked in a singsong voice.

Ignoring his taunt, I kicked Buster into a canter. I didn't enjoy bossing JJ around any more than he liked me doing it, but Mama's death had put me in charge of running the house and raising him—whether either of us wanted it that way or not.

I reached the house pasture and unhooked the latch to the wooden gate. It swung open, old rusty hinges groaning the way Papa did first thing in the morning. I didn't bother to dismount and drag the gate closed since JJ should be back soon. Buster made a beeline for the big oak doors of the barn, which stood open like two arms waiting to embrace the smallest breath of air.

After dismounting, I pulled the shotgun out of its scabbard, leaning it against the wall, then yanked the birds out of the saddlebags. A pack of black horseflies appeared as soon as I set the bag down, circling like miniature buzzards. I rolled the top of the burlap tighter, then unsaddled Buster and put the rig away in the tack room. After he ate a handful of oats, I walked him out to the corral. He nickered a greeting to the other cowpony in the pen on his way to the water trough. As

I dragged the gate closed, several loose boards shook along the bottom. Fixing them was on JJ's to-do list.

I glanced down the road past the gate, surprised to see dust boiling up in front of the brush line less than half a mile away. Maybe JJ would actually be home in time to get some work done. I stepped up on a stump, shading my eyes to get a better look.

Bluebird materialized in front of the dirt cloud, galloping flat-out. JJ bobbed in the saddle with her motion, reins held high. Twister sprinted behind them, long, slender legs flying, loose lead rope sailing next to him. JJ never worked a green-broke horse that hard, and running the colt down the uneven, gravelled road could damage his young bones. JJ slapped Bluebird's hip with the end of the reins, urging her even faster. Alarm snaked around my chest as the screen of dust behind them parted and two riders charged out. JJ wasn't running; he was being chased.

I raced for the barn, grabbed the .410, and thumbed off the safety. The riders thundered through the open gate as I came out. I raised the shotgun to my shoulder and pointed it at the strangers. They were more than twenty yards away, but they caught sight of the gun and pulled back.

JJ rode up next to me and yanked hard on the reins. The mare skidded to a stop, hooves spraying pebbles as Twister crashed into her backside.

"*Tequileros!*" he yelled, leaping out of the saddle.

A tremble ran the length of my spine. I gripped the gun tighter.

"Get behind me," I said, fighting to keep my voice even. JJ balked and reached for the .410, but I swung it away from him. "For once, do as I say."

Chest heaving, he grabbed Bluebird's reins then reached out to catch the lead dangling from Twister's halter. The excited colt stamped his feet, throwing his head up and down, nostrils flaring.

"*Buenas tardes, señorita,*" one of the smugglers called out. "You can put the gun down. We just want the horses."

Amusement tinged his deep voice, but his hand rested on a revolver holstered at his hip. A black cowboy hat sat pushed back on his head, exposing a hard, lean face. Thick stubble covering his chin matched the red color of the hair sticking out from under his hat. It was his eyes that held my attention, though, glowing pale and cold, like a coyote's did in the moonlight.

The straw *sombrero* the other man wore cast a shadow down to the fringe of his bleached-out mustache. A tangled white beard fluttered to his waist. His slender body leaned over the saddle horn, making him seem old and frail compared to his partner, but the gun belt and revolver on his waist made him just as dangerous.

I sucked in air and placed a finger on the trigger.

"Go away or I'll shoot," I said.

"Ah, *señorita,* for such a pretty girl, you are not very polite," sneered the man in the black hat. "We will leave, I assure you, but we are taking the horses."

"I told you, mister," JJ blurted out, "you ain't taking my horse!"

The red-haired smuggler slid his revolver out in one smooth gesture, aiming it at JJ. I swallowed hard. I'd lost my advantage in a split second, no longer the only one pointing a gun.

"It has been entertaining chasing you around, *niño,*" he said, "but I have no more time for this."

The *tequilero* urged his horse a step toward us. The instinct to back away was so strong I had to concentrate to keep my feet planted.

"As for you, *señorita,*" he continued, aiming his stare at me, "if you do not put the gun down, I will shoot the boy. I promise, I can kill him before you pull that trigger."

I held the gun steady as I weighed his words. He didn't look like a man who bluffed.

"If not, my partner will kill you both." He shrugged, the gesture terrifying in its casualness. "Are the horses worth it?"

The air thickened, fighting my lungs. The old man could draw any moment. Between the two of them, they had up to twelve bullets loaded. I had two. I was a good shot, but I couldn't kill them both at once. Trying to shoot one then the other could throw my aim off, and then I'd just pepper them with birdshot. The .410 was useless at that distance against a pair of six-shooters; I might as well have been holding a broomstick.

I lowered the gun a few inches.

"*Bueno.*" The bandit rested the revolver on his thigh, eyes glittering. "We have a deal: the horses for the boy's life. Tomás, *ándele.*"

"*Sí,* Javier."

Tomás swung his wiry body out of the saddle and walked over to the horses. He took Bluebird's reins, then tugged Twister's lead out of JJ's fist. As he turned, pulling the horses away, JJ's face burst open. A bellow exploded from his mouth as he jumped Tomás from behind.

Tomás lurched sideways, his sombrero flying off, a long, white braid tumbling down his back. Panic and anger seeped into my veins. This wasn't a schoolyard squabble. JJ was risking his life over a horse.

"Stop it!" I yelled.

JJ paid no attention. He grabbed Tomás's hair like it was the tail of a calf he meant to wrestle to the ground. The old man dropped the leads but held his own, the two of them scuffling around in a circle. As Twister and Bluebird shied away, I jerked my eyes to Javier. He'd moved closer, pointing the gun as if waiting for a clean shot.

I held the .410 by the stock and rushed at JJ. Grabbing his arm with my free hand, I yanked as hard as I could. He stumbled and let go of Tomás's hair. The old man leapt out of reach then turned back to face JJ.

"*Qué pasó, m'ijo?* Please, give us the horses," he begged, arms outstretched. "*Lo vas a enojar!*"

"I ain't your son, and I don't give a shit if he gets mad!" JJ shouted. He walked over to Twister and grabbed his lead. "You can't use my horse to haul your goddamn *tequila*. He ain't old enough. You'll break his back."

The click of the revolver hit my gut like a punch.

"Do not make me kill you, *niño*," Javier growled.

"*Javier, por favor.*" Alarm rang through Tomás's voice.

"Give him the horses, JJ," I said through clenched teeth. "Now."

JJ's entire face contorted, his lips pressing together in a struggle to hold back tears. Twister was the first thing he'd loved since Mama died, but acting like a child hanging on to his favorite toy was going to get him shot.

"Do it!" I shouted.

To my horror, Javier nodded at me, as if we were on the same side. Then his coyote eyes slid down my body and a new fear sliced through me, one that had been hovering just outside my thoughts.

JJ strode to Bluebird.

"Here, take this one," he said, holding the mare's reins out. "Load all the *tequila* you want on her." He pointed at the corral. "There's two more in there. Leave the colt here and you can have them all."

Javier's face darkened.

"I will take whatever I want, *gringo*. I do not need your permission." No humor left in his tone, his glare moved to JJ's waist. "*Ahorita*, I want the horses, all of the horses, and that belt buckle."

"What the hell?" JJ placed his hand over the silver buckle, but Javier's focus had turned back to me.

"Maybe I want the pretty girl, too," he said. "I am fond of the blondes, *las rubias*."

His voice rumbled through the thick heat like a boulder sliding downhill. My stomach knotted, stories banging around in my head of kidnapped girls—raped, mutilated, sold into slavery, beaten until nothing remained but empty shells. Ghost girls better off dead.

JJ's hand fell from his waist.

"Don't touch my sister." The bravado had drained from his voice, leaving it raw with fear—fear that boomeranged through me.

Tomás took a tentative step forward.

"*Por favor*," he pleaded to Javier, "*solomente los caballos, no?*"

"All that long, yellow hair, Tomás," Javier mused, narrowed eyes groping every inch of my body. "She would be worth more than the horses."

JJ threw a chastened look at me, his face the color of caliche dust. He led both horses over to Tomás.

"Take them," he said. "Leave her alone. Please."

My fingers tingled as I gripped the shotgun. Javier was closer now. Maybe I'd hurt him enough to buy us time to run to the house.

"Get the other horses from the pen, *viejo*," Javier said to Tomás.

The old man hesitated for a moment, squinting up at Javier like he was trying to discern his next move. Would he stay put and wait, or shoot JJ and grab me?

"*Date prisa*," Javier barked.

Tomás handed over the leads and shuffled to the corral.

"Hey, *niño*." Javier gestured at JJ's waist with his gun. "You forget something?"

"Give him the buckle," I said.

The smile slid back onto Javier's face.

"You like to tell little boys what to do, *rubia*?" His suggestive tone, the crawl of those eyes across my skin, sent a frozen stone barreling through my gut. "Wouldn't you prefer a man to take charge?"

Breathe. If you shoot, aim at his face.

"Look, I'm getting it for you." A quake shook JJ's words,

fingers fumbling to undo his belt.

Tomás came out of the corral with Buster and the other cowpony. As the horses approached, Twister let out an excited whinny. If JJ heard it, he didn't react. Yanking the large, silver rectangle free, he walked toward Javier.

"No, no," Javier said. "I want *you* to bring it to me, *rubia*."

His cold eyes repelled me like flaming torches. I couldn't move.

"Come on," he teased, beckoning me with a jerk of his chin. "I won't bite."

I stayed still, arm twitching with the weight of the gun.

"So brave before. Now you are being shy, *como una virgen*." He cackled—the harsh caw of a green jay. "Has no one been between those white thighs of yours yet? I could be your first. You will not have to tell me what to do, *gringa*."

"Go to hell, you piece of shit!"

JJ hurled the buckle. It flew at Javier like a spear, striking his face with a sharp crack.

"*Pendejo!*" Javier exclaimed, touching the blood already welling up on his cheekbone. "I told you not to make me kill you."

Javier aimed his revolver.

"*No!*" Tomás yelled.

"Get down!" I screamed, lunging for JJ.

The explosion ripped through the air, slamming into my ears, stopping me as if I'd smacked into a wall. JJ shuddered, stumbling backward. He tried to steady himself, but his legs folded. He sank to the ground, wide eyes fastening on mine before he pitched back. His head landed in the loose dirt with a thud, the Stetson lifting from his scalp like a half-open lid.

The earth stopped spinning.

Get up, JJ!

He'd scramble to his feet any second. I'd have to stop him from rushing at Javier like a crazed bull. But he didn't move. My vision darkened. The outline of his body, sprawled on the ground, grew fuzzy. The harder I stared, the less I could see. Everything funneled into the dark spot growing on his chest.

"*Ay, Dios mío!*"

Tomás's cry snapped the world into focus. JJ's wet gasps cut through the ringing in my ears. I dropped to my knees at his side, terrified by the crimson circle widening across his shirt. *Too much blood, too fast.* I pressed both hands against his chest, trying to staunch the flow. A coughing fit shook his body, red mist spraying across my face and neck.

"It's okay, it's okay," I whispered. "You'll be okay."

Dusty boots appeared by JJ's head. I looked up into Tomás's watery eyes.

"Help me!" I pleaded. "I have to stop the bleeding."

"*Señorita, no se que puedo hacer.*" The old man raised his arms, a pained look deepening the creases in his face.

"*Basta,* Tomás," Javier snarled from behind him. "*Vámanos!*"

"*Pero, el muchacho?*" the old man said, a quiver in his voice.

"*No le hace,* the world will not miss another goddamn *gringo.*" Javier spat the words out like venom, then pointed the revolver at me. "Bring her."

My throat closed with terror, but I kept my hands clamped over JJ's chest. If Javier wanted me, he'd have to rip me off my brother.

"The Rangers could be nearby," Tomás said in Spanish, shaking his head. "They might have heard the gun."

Javier paused, scoping the horizon for a moment. Rangers passed through our ranch often. They, or anyone else within a few miles, could have heard the gunshot and be racing this way to investigate. Javier had time to get away with the horses, but trying to wrestle me onto a saddle would be a big risk.

"*Basta.* This has taken too much of my time already." Javier exhaled in a long, exaggerated hiss. "Get the goddamn buckle. Let's go, *viejo.*"

Javier holstered his gun and reined toward the gate, yanking Twister and the other three horses after him. Tomás risked one more furtive glance my way before retrieving the buckle and his hat. He climbed onto his saddle and galloped after Javier.

The drumbeat of retreating hooves was soon lost in the cries I could no longer hold in. I looked down at the pool of thick, dark blood stretching out from under JJ, bile pricking the insides of my cheeks. The bullet had gone all the way through his chest. The chances it had not punctured a lung were few. It sounded like he was drowning because he was.

"Hang on, JJ." I moved my head close to his. "You hear me?"

His eyes fluttered open. A flicker of hope lit my heart as he tried to focus on my face.

"I know I'm always bossing you around," I said, forcing a grin, "but this time I mean it."

A smile tugged at his lips, blood trickling from the corner of his mouth. I wiped it away, leaving my hand on his cheek. "You know I love you, right?"

"Yeah ... I know," he wheezed. "Is ... he gone?"

"Yes. He's gone. You're safe."

JJ's head lolled from side to side.

"Couldn't let him ... take you," he mumbled between gasps. "Papa said ... I'm supposed to watch out for you."

A small hand slipped through my ribs and grabbed my heart.

"Twister?" His lips barely moved.

"He'll be just fine. We're both okay," I choked out. "You did good, JJ."

I bent, pushing the corona of curls off his forehead to kiss him. As my lips met his cool, damp skin, his labored breathing calmed. Encouraged, I raised my head, only to find a look of frightened bewilderment hovering on his face.

"JJ?"

His crystal-blue gaze sharpened for a moment, then his eyes rolled back. A loud gush of air escaped his mouth, and his body went limp.

"No!" I shook his shoulders. More blood welled up from the hole in his chest. "Breathe, damnit!"

Why couldn't he ever do what he was told? I pressed my ear to his breast. *Is that my heart pounding or his?* I grabbed his wrist, feeling for a pulse the way Mama had done with her patients. There was nothing, not the slightest tap. I sat back on my heels, hot tears racing down my face.

The .410 wavered on the ground in my blurred vision. I scrambled to my feet and snatched it up, aiming blindly, pulling the trigger. Pellets rained down in front of me. I fired again, knowing it was futile, craving the slap of the butt against my collarbone, the explosion in my ears—anything to rid me of the helplessness coiled around my throat. I blinked my eyes clear. The *tequileros* had disappeared into the thick brush, leaving nothing behind, as if they'd never existed.

The caliche road leading away from the house glimmered in the fading light. For a fleeting moment, I wanted to run down it, to disappear forever into the endless sea of mesquite.

I forced myself to look at JJ's face. His innocent expression made him look even younger than he was. I lowered myself to the ground next to him, reaching out to caress the dirt and blood and my own tears off his face. He'd been so proud of the recent growth of peach fuzz above his top lip, dancing around as he'd informed me that he'd soon be shaving like Papa.

Papa. Thinking about him was like touching hot coal; I couldn't bear it for more than a second.

With trembling fingers, I pressed JJ's lids closed. His blood was everywhere—caking in the grooves of my knuckles, drenching my clothes, speckling my forearms. It glued my hair to my face and neck, tightening my skin as it dried. The raw stench of it drew the horseflies from the barn. They began to circle, the sound growing louder and louder, filling my head with an unrelenting drone. I swatted until my arms grew weak, but it made no difference; insects crawled over the ruin of my brother.

A void opened within me; a chasm I knew would never close. I pulled JJ's body into my lap, holding him as I'd done in the days after Mama had died, rocking back and forth while the thirsty soil around us faded from bright ruby red to dull reddish gray.

He was trying to save me.

Time froze, holding me prisoner until the first whispers of evening blew across my slick skin. I'd begun to shiver by the time I heard Papa's Ford sputtering in the distance. The noise grew louder. The truck came through the gate, brakes squealing as it lurched to a stop by the barn. Papa climbed out of the cab, a ghostly silhouette in the twilight. He let the tailgate down and started pulling his tools out.

I opened my mouth, forcing sound from my lips.

"Papa?"

His eyes searched the dimness until they found us. The post digger he held dropped to the ground. He stumbled forward, stopping at the edge of the stained circle of dirt, his low-pitched cry slugging me in the chest.

"My god! What have you done?"

CHAPTER 2

The house was still and quiet inside; a time capsule I couldn't make sense of. Clean dishes sat by the kitchen sink, prairie coneflowers bloomed in a vase on the table, laundry hung on a drying rack by the open window. As if nothing had changed since I'd walked out that afternoon. As if JJ weren't lying dead in his bedroom. I wanted to tear it all apart, rip off the mask, make the house match the wreckage in my mind. Instead, I hurried to the bathing room off the kitchen, desperate to wash away my brother's blood.

Two buckets I'd filled at the windmill that morning sat next to the white enameled bathtub. Not bothering to heat the water, I emptied one into the tub and began to peel off my clothing, flinching as the dried-stiff fabric pulled at the fine hairs on my arms and torso. Naked and shivering, I sank into the shallow, lukewarm water, hugging my knees close to my chest, trying to hold myself together.

When my shaking calmed, I picked up the coarse wash-cloth hanging on the rim and scrubbed. Clouds of pink swirled through the water, my skin soon red and stinging. I lifted the other bucket from the floor and dumped it over my head, running my fingers through my hair. The bathwater blushed darker—a diluted pool of JJ's blood. Sickened by the image, I scrambled over the side of the bath, landing on the Saltillo tile floor in a wet heap.

By the time I dried off and made it to my room, all I wanted was to curl up in a ball and give in to sorrow. I doubted that luxury would be mine. When Mama had died, I'd barely had time to check my tears, much less mourn. No matter what happened, work on a ranch never stopped. Horses had to be fed, eggs had to be gathered, butter had to be churned, and clothes had to be washed and mended. Breakfast, lunch, and supper had to be cooked.

My thoughts plowed to a stop. Those meals had to be cooked for whom? Papa and I were the only ones left. As a timeline of family meals unreeled through my mind, all the way back to one-year-old JJ throwing peas and refusing to use a fork, I couldn't imagine ever sitting at that table again, staring at two empty places.

I shook the images away. After we'd carried JJ's body inside, Papa had driven to town for help. He'd expect me to be dressed and ready to tell the sheriff what had happened when he returned. I took a deep breath and picked up my brush, dragging it through my hair. A metallic odor wafted from the still-damp strands. There was no water left to rinse it again. I swallowed the lump in my throat and tied it back with a ribbon.

I pulled on a green and blue calico skirt, numb fingers struggling to button the waistband, then threaded my arms into the sleeves of a white blouse with a dainty lace collar that had been my mother's. What would Mama have done in this moment? She would have been heartbroken, of course, but would she have been able to rise above it, trying to stay strong for Papa and me?

In the other room, the front door creaked open, then banged shut, shattering the quiet. Papa's heavy steps thumped across the floor of the parlor into the kitchen. I forced my grief down and shoved my feet into a pair of house shoes. As my hand rested on the door handle, I felt the shift of time. From now on there would be before and after. I pulled the door open and walked out to face my father.

A lantern on the sideboard cast dancing shadows across the walls of the kitchen, as if an audience had gathered to watch. Papa, his clothes marked with russet stains, sat slumped in his old stuffed chair, staring into the bare fireplace. I picked up the matchbox from the kitchen counter and walked over to light the kerosene lamp on the table next to him.

"One squeeze of the trigger," he muttered, as if to himself. "Like he was of no consequence."

A tear worked its way through the worn-leather grooves of his face. I'd never seen him cry, not even when Mama passed away. He'd had his first spell the day after her death, but if he'd shed a tear, it had been in private. I reached out to place a hand on his shoulder, wanting to comfort him, but drew back.

"He wasn't here long enough to leave anything behind." His voice was dry and rough. "He'll just fade away, like a vision that's gone before you figure out what it meant."

"JJ will always be a part of us, Papa," I protested.

His head swung up, as if he'd just realized I was there.

"What's it all been for?" he asked with a searching look. "My father, dead twenty years after getting this land; my mother, bit by a rabid dog. I lost two brothers, one killed in an Indian raid, one suffocated at the bottom of a well. I've seen babies not make it to their first birthdays. Two wives dead, and now ... it's all gone."

Pain cut into his pale face, etchings on cracked glass.

"All the toiling, and the sickness, and the dying," he went on. "For what? To have it end with my boy shot down like a stray dog?"

My blood ran cold. He was looking at me, but he was seeing the end of his dreams.

"What am I to do with this place?" He lowered his head onto his hand. "I'm old and worn out. I've got no help."

Self-pity was not characteristic of my father. His hopelessness bore a hole right through me, but he was wrong. He wasn't alone. He might feel all was lost, but that was grief casting a shadow over the future. As hard as it would be, we could survive; the ranch could survive. We could get to the other side of JJ's death together. We had to.

"I'm still here, Papa," I said, my voice just above a whisper.

He looked at me and shrugged.

"What's a girl going to do without a man to help her?"

His words hit me like scattershot. From the moment he'd been born, JJ had been the chosen one. The late-in-life surprise baby boy who would pass on the family name and preserve our heritage. John Junior had only been six years old when Papa handed him a shotgun and put him in the truck to help check the fences and hunt for game—a job that had been mine until then.

Mama had known I was unhappy. With her encouragement, I'd been accepted to a boarding school in San Antonio, a hundred and fifty miles north and a world away. Unlike many of the girls at Saint Mary's Hall, though, I hadn't yearned for a life off the ranch. If I could've been a part of La Barroneña the way I wanted to, I'd have never left.

I'd done well in school, and particularly enjoyed writing for our school paper. I wasn't afraid to ask questions—sometimes too many—and I liked investigating a story, digging up details and putting facts together. The headmistress had sent some of my articles to the *San Antonio Light* newspaper. They'd published two of them and asked me to write more. In the city library, I'd read all I could about Nellie Bly and other women journalists who'd reported from the front lines of the war in Europe. Their lives seemed exciting and their work worthwhile. I'd decided that after I graduated and had more experience, I wanted to try to write for bigger newspapers, maybe even the *New York Times* one day.

Then Mama had died, and so had my plans. I'd been so close to graduating, but there hadn't really been a choice, much less a conversation. Papa had expected me to stay home, and I did.

I respected my mother more than any person I knew. Her knowledge as a midwife had helped people from all over the Nueces Strip, but home and family had been her priority. I tried my best to emulate her. I just couldn't find pleasure in running the house. I itched to saddle up every morning and ride with the cowboys, to feel the warmth of the rising sun on my face, to smell the buffalo grass before the dew dried, to trot through the thorn scrub tracking lost cattle.

No matter how often I offered to help, Papa always declined. Over and over, he made it clear he didn't think I could be anything other than a rancher's wife, and now he'd reminded me even that possibility was in doubt. My immediate chance at marriage had vanished with Jackson.

"Maude Langley has been running La Retama for almost ten years," I blurted, "and Henrietta King has overseen the King Ranch for longer than that."

"There's a big difference between a girl not even twenty years old and full-grown widows," Papa replied.

"I could help more than you let me," I said. "I like working the ranch."

"It's not about what you like or don't." Papa shook his head. "There's more to it than that, Sarita."

I opened my mouth, but loss caught in the back of my throat. We should be grieving together, consoling one another, not arguing.

A loud knock on the door startled me.

"That'll be Sheriff Nolan," said Papa.

But when I opened the door, it was the deputy sheriff who stood on the dark stoop. I'd forgotten how much he and his younger brother resembled each other. Clyde and Jackson were both tall and broad-shouldered; they could be mistaken for one another in the dim light. As I looked at Clyde, the prick of Jackson's absence sunk deeper. At that moment, regardless of everything, he was the only person I wanted to talk to.

"Evening, Sarita," said Clyde, his expression a mix of concern and something like embarrassment. "I haven't really had a chance to talk to you much since—"

"Let's not bother with that now," I interrupted.

"All right. It's just ..." He paused, shaking his head. "Well, this must've been a terrible thing for you. I'm sorry."

He was talking about JJ now, not Jackson, but the tears stinging the corners of my eyes were for both. What if Jackson was dead too? I blinked the thought away and led Clyde into the kitchen.

"Can I get you anything?" I asked. "A cup of water?"

"No, thank you."

"Where's the sheriff?" Papa rasped. He'd shrunk into the back of his chair, chest bouncing with each breath.

"His brother Zeb's place was attacked last night," Clyde explained, running the brim of his hat through his fingers. "A gang came through and killed the foreman. They tried to kidnap Zeb's two little girls, too."

The word "kidnap" felt like a shallow bruise, a reminder of something that could have been worse. If Javier had taken me, my life would never have been the same. Even if I'd survived, even if—by some miracle—I hadn't been raped or traded to the Indians, people would never have looked at me the same. I'd have worn a brand as undeniable as the marks the Mohave tribe had tattooed on Olive Oatman's face.

I'd been lucky to have escaped unscathed, but at what cost? Wanting JJ to step up and take more responsibility had not meant I expected him to protect me. Never would I have traded his life for mine.

"Whole family's pretty shook up," Clyde continued. "Zeb's wife, Sally, wasn't expecting the baby for another few weeks but seems it's coming early now."

Papa sat forward and glared at Clyde.

"Are you trying to tell me the sheriff's too busy to see about my boy's murder?"

"No, sir, of course not," Clyde answered quickly. "He had me go to the Ranger station over on Los Ojuelos before coming out here. I caught Captain Wright just in time. His company's riding to Laredo tonight, but they're going to stop here on the way. Shouldn't be too far behind me."

The prospect of the Texas Rangers' help seemed to quell Papa's frustration. When the loud clatter of hooves galloping up the road filled the house, he struggled out of his chair and went to the front door, pulling it open before anyone could knock.

A short, square man strode up the steps. His bespectacled face resembled a minister's more than a rough and ready lawman's. He was dressed like a Ranger, though, in a white shirt, a loose black tie, and a brown leather vest. His thick chaps had deep creases at the crotch from hours of sitting in a saddle. A pearl-handled Colt .45 sat on his hip.

"Mr. Gibson?" he asked.

"That's right," replied Papa. "Who're you?"

"Captain Miller Wright, Company D."

He took his white Stetson off, revealing a receding hairline, and shook Papa's hand. A teenaged boy stepped into the house behind him. He had a smooth face and long, black hair tied with a strip of leather. His plaid shirt fit snug, tucked neatly into the waist of worn leather leggings. He looked just about ready to burst into manhood.

"Your other men coming in?" asked Papa, looking out at the silhouettes of the rest of the company, still mounted on their horses in the moonlit yard.

"No, sir," Wright answered.

Papa pushed the door shut and led the way into the kitchen.

"Deputy Cage." Captain Wright acknowledged Clyde then gave me a sharp nod. "Miss."

"Should I put some coffee on?" I asked.

"No, thank you, ma'am, we haven't much time," Wright

replied. "Mr. Gibson, I hear you had trouble with some *tequila* smugglers."

"You could call it that," Papa said gruffly. "They killed my boy."

"I was sorry to hear that, sir." Wright paused for a moment in what I assumed to be a show of respect. "Deputy Cage tells me you saw the men who did it."

"My daughter did," said Papa.

The two Rangers turned to me.

"All right then, miss," said Captain Wright in a softer tone. "Do you think you could tell us what happened?"

I hesitated for a moment, put off by having to describe my nightmare to strangers.

"There were two of them. They chased my brother into the house yard," I said, pushing through the catch in my voice. "JJ argued with one of them, and the man shot him."

"What'd they look like?" asked Wright. "Height, weight, age? Anything distinctive you remember would be helpful."

"I don't know the shooter's height, he never got out of the saddle," I answered. "He was of average build, probably in his late forties. He had unusual coloring for a Mexican, though, dark red hair and light eyes. Maybe blue or green."

"Blue or green eyes?" Wright repeated. "You sure?"

"Yes, sir." I could still feel the crawl of those eyes down my body, I'd never forget them. "The other man was older, maybe in his sixties. He called the redheaded man Javier."

The rangers looked at each other, communicating something the rest of us weren't privy to. I waited, hoping one of them would say my description meant something.

"I've heard my grandfather talk about a gang of red-haired bandits," said Clyde, breaking the short silence. "He ran into them during the Bandit and the Border Wars. He might have some useful information."

"Captain Cage retired, didn't he?" asked Wright.

"He did, as you know." Clyde's tone soured a bit. "But he

tries to stay informed, especially since Jackson went missing."

"Of course. Well, I'll let you know if we need his input." Wright turned his attention back to me. "Were you armed, miss?"

I nodded.

"Did you fire on them?" he asked. "Either of them wounded?"

It had happened so fast. When was I supposed to have shot?

"She didn't pull the trigger," Papa interjected. "I guarantee you those bastards would be full of buckshot if I'd been here."

He might as well have punched me.

What have you done?

"Yes, sir." Wright nodded. "They take any horses?"

"Four," said Papa. "One's just a colt."

"Sounds about right. These *mezcaleros* steal anything they can pack *tequila* on," said Wright. "Are the horses branded, Mr. Gibson?"

"Three have our Lazy L Bar," Papa answered. "One belongs to the Arrowhead. Theirs is a Rocking A."

"Anything else stolen?"

They all turned back to me. My pulse quickened, the slow interrogation eating at my patience. I'd described who'd shot JJ, even given them his name. Why weren't they racing out the door to track him?

"What difference does it make what they took?" I snapped.

"It helps to identify them," Clyde said in the even tone a teacher might use to explain basic addition. "We see a man on a horse with your brand, or someone in possession of your property, we know to question him."

I sucked in air, trying to resign myself to letting the lawmen do their job.

"They took JJ's belt buckle," I said. "It looks just like my father's."

Papa had given JJ the buckle a few months ago on his thirteenth birthday. A smooth silver rectangle with our brand shining in gold at the center, a replica of the one Papa had worn every day I could remember. My stomach had churned with resentment the minute JJ pulled it from its felt pouch. He'd put it on right away, the two of them laughing at how much bigger it looked on him than on Papa. I'd walked out of the room without either of them noticing.

"He might try to sell that for metal weight; I'll add it to the list," said Wright. "I can't give you any guarantees, but we'll do what we can to recover the property," he continued. "Your neighbors lost ten horses, five hundred dollars, and a gold wedding ring. Could've been worse."

"Worse?!" The word burst out of Papa's mouth as if he were a kettle that had finally boiled. "What could be worse than having your only son shot dead in your own goddamn yard?"

Wright's cheeks colored. "I only meant—"

"That son of a bitch took my boy away!"

Papa's hands fisted into hard knots. He rocked forward like he might take a swing at Wright. Alarm surged through me. His last spell had happened after a ranch hand ran a Hereford bull through a barbwire fence, slashing its legs to shreds. In the middle of bawling the cowboy out, Papa had clutched his chest and fallen in the dirt.

I rushed over, placing a hand on his arm. "Please. Try to calm down, Papa."

He shook me off and jabbed a finger into Wright's sternum. His mouth opened, but instead of yelling, he closed it, drawing his hand back and placing it on his own chest. His eyes misted over, his face crumpling before he caught himself and smoothed his expression.

"Justice," he said, almost in a whisper. "That's all I want. My son deserves that much."

Wright's face softened.

"I have to be honest with you, sir," he said in a solemn tone. "We're more than short-manned thanks to all Prohibition has thrown at us. There's a war going on down here, and the truth is, I can't spare the men right now to chase after your boy's killer."

"It's your sworn duty." Papa's voice had regained some tenor, but I could hear the torn edge of it.

"Yes, sir, it is, and I'm not saying we won't be looking for him," Wright replied, "but it wouldn't be right to mislead you into thinking we can deliver some sort of swift resolution."

He reached out and clutched Papa's shoulder in a fraternal manner.

"The cost of evil and wrongdoing does not long go unpaid, Mr. Gibson," he said, meeting Papa's weary gaze. "Try to be patient."

How could anyone look at my father's bloodstained clothes, his grief-stricken face, and preach to him about patience?

"There's a whole pack of Rangers sitting out there in our yard," I said, struggling not to sound disrespectful. "Can't you spare a few of them?"

"I'm sorry I can't offer more," said Wright, putting his hat on.

"That's it then?" asked Papa. "You're leaving?"

"We've got to meet with the border inspector in Laredo about a shipment of overhauled guns that never arrived at Camp Bullis from the San Antonio Arsenal."

All business again, Wright conveyed the information as if the gravity of his task would make us understand why it was more important than our family tragedy. He didn't wait for a response. He tipped his hat, spurs jangling in the stunned silence as he marched out of the house.

The young man followed him but paused at the door.

"I'm real sorry for your loss," he said.

They were the only words he'd spoken the entire time. He looked right at me, but I was too dismayed by the whole encounter to respond. When he closed the door, I stared at the barrier between us and the possibility of help. What had happened to the famous slogan, "One riot, One Ranger"? Where was our one Ranger?

I flung the door back open and charged outside. Captain Wright was already in the saddle, reining his horse around. Without a glance my way, he spurred into a gallop, the other men close behind.

"Wait!" I shouted, running down the steps into the churned-up dust.

The young man was the only one who pulled up his horse.

"Miss Gibson?" he asked. "What is it?"

"What's your name?" I demanded as the rest of his company swarmed through the gate.

He touched his hat brim.

"Wagley Phillips, ma'am, at your service."

I'd been too polite, too flabbergasted, to argue with Captain Wright, but Wagley was just a kid.

"At my service? You've done nothing to help, not one damn thing," I said. "How can it take an entire company of Texas Rangers to chase down a few old guns?"

"Five hundred Colt .45s ain't a few," replied Wagley. "Old or not, put bullets in them and they work. Whoever stole them could arm every bandit from here to Mexico City."

I stared at him. He twitched in his saddle, turning his head longingly toward the other riders as they got farther away.

"These are good men, Miss Gibson. It ain't that they don't care," he said after a moment. "It's like Captain Wright said, they're overrun with lawbreaking and can't drop all to go after one bandit. That's pretty much the long and short of it." He lowered his gaze, a sad smile pushing his mouth sideways. "I realize that's not much comfort to you."

"What do you know?" I retorted. "You don't even look old enough to be a Ranger."

"I'm more than sixteen already," he said, sitting straighter in his saddle, "but I'm not a Ranger; I track for them."

"You're a guide?" I squinted up at him with new interest.

"Yes, ma'am," he answered with some pride. "My grandfather was captured as a boy and raised by the Kiowa up north.

The militia rescued him when he was eighteen. He taught me how to look for sign the way the Indians had taught him. I'm pretty good at it, I guess."

"You ought to be able to hunt down the man who killed my brother then."

I meant it as a challenge. Even if he was young, he was better than no one.

"Well, no, I can't. I mean, I could, but ..." Wagley peered from under his hat brim with the same I-wish-things-were-different look that Clyde wore. "It wouldn't be right to go off on my own, Miss Gibson."

"Then leave," I said, waving him away.

Wagley caught my glare, his bright blue eyes so much like JJ's it hurt. "I know what it's like to lose someone. I am sorry."

I turned my back on him, disappointment nipping at me when I heard the *thwump* of his heels. I walked back to the house as he raced off to catch up with the others, dragging my hope after him. When I entered the front door, Papa took a step forward like he thought Wright might have changed his mind. He saw I was alone and turned to Clyde.

"What about the sheriff, or you?" he asked.

Clyde looked down at the floor like he wished it would open up and swallow him.

"Sheriff Nolan's already left for Zapata, tracking the gang that crossed his brother's place. He told me to go over to Alice and muster up recruits, then head down there to help him. I'm obliged to follow his orders, sir."

"That's bullshit and you know it!" Papa's anger had returned, his chest rattling with each breath.

"Papa," I said. "It's not good for you to get so worked up."

He spun in a shaky half-circle to face me, perspiration glistening on his forehead.

"Don't you understand what's happening here?" he seethed. "The damn Rangers have more important things to do than hunt a murderer, and the sheriff's too busy chasing the men who harassed his brother to go after the one who killed yours. That bastard is going to get away."

I couldn't argue with him. What was the use of all these lawmen coming to our house only to say they could do nothing? I wanted to yell at Clyde, too. I wanted to pound on his chest until he agreed to help.

"Harassing Clyde's not going to change any of that," I said. "You need to get some rest."

I braced for his rebuttal, for him to throw his anger at me. Instead, he let out a deep groan and doubled over, clutching at his arm as he sank to the ground.

CHAPTER 3

The first light of morning pushed through the wooden shutters, casting a pale ladder across Papa's bedroom floor. I hadn't meant to fall asleep, but exhaustion had finally won. I stood, stiff from sitting in a chair next to the bed all night, and studied my father's ashen face. He'd been out for several hours. His breathing had steadied, but his pulse still banged against my fingers when I placed them on the inside of his wrist.

After he'd collapsed, Clyde had scooped him up, carrying him into the bedroom and placing him on the big iron bed. I'd covered him with the quilt my grandmother had made as a wedding gift for my parents. It was sewn from brightly colored scraps of fabric in a design called *colchas bordadas*. JJ and I had both been swaddled in it when we were babies. Later, we'd snuggled under its warmth while Mama read to us. Most recently, though, it had covered my mother's feverish body as she'd died of influenza.

Passing out had given Papa a reprieve, but when he woke, I'd have nothing new to offer him. All we had was the vague guarantee that the Rangers would look for Javier—the way cowboys kept an eye out for snakes, happy to shoot one if it crossed their path.

Clyde had promised to send Dr. Andrew and the undertaker before he headed to Alice. Then he'd left, leaving me to wait. Wait on the doctor to help Papa. Wait on Mr. Mortimer to take JJ. Wait on the Rangers to find Javier. Wait on Jackson to come back. Wait on my father to decide my fate.

Papa stirred. I placed a cool rag on his forehead. After several slow blinks, his eyes opened.

"What happened?" he asked.

"You had another spell."

"No." His head brushed across the pillow. "How did he kill my son?"

Ice crept along the walls of my chest. Did he want details, or was he asking how I'd let it happen? I'd spent most of the hours he'd been unconscious playing it over and over in my mind, scenes flashing before me like a macabre version of the tiny flipbooks in JJ's boxes of Cracker Jacks. Where had that moment been? The one that could have changed everything?

Before I could answer him, Papa sat up.

"What are you doing?" I asked.

"Going for help."

"Where?" Had he forgotten Captain Wright had already stopped by?

"Laredo." He swung his legs over the side of the bed. "I'm going to go to the frontline of this so-called war and badger those goddamn Rangers into doing their job. If they won't, I'll find the son of a bitch myself."

"Papa, the doctor is on his way. Please lie back down."

He stood, legs wobbling under him.

"What'd you do with my boots?"

I moved to block him, placing a hand on his forearm.

"Listen to me, please. You can't go to Laredo."

"You can't tell me what to do," he barked, trying to push past me.

Papa had been strong and vital his whole life. I knew even now he didn't think of himself as ill or weak.

"Your heart is not strong enough," I said, intent on making him understand. "You'll never see justice for JJ if you kill yourself trying to get it."

He looked stunned, either by my words or the truth of them. After a moment, he sank onto the bed.

"You're awful pale," I said. "I think you should lie down."

He swung his legs up with some effort, then settled against the pillow, staring at the ceiling with an air of resignation that scared me more than his attempt to leave. As I watched the rapid rise and fall of his rib cage, a jolt of anger tore through me. Why hadn't JJ cooperated? Why hadn't he just handed Twister over when Javier first asked? There were plenty of other colts in the world. His decision to fight for that one had cost him his life and had maybe cost our family everything.

My thoughts were interrupted by the jingle of tack and rumble of wheels. Through the open window, I saw two burly quarter horses pulling Sam Mortimer's hearse toward the house. A shiny pickup followed close behind. I quickly closed the window against the noise and slipped out of Papa's room, praying he'd stay put, worried what watching his son carried away would do to him.

I straightened my rumpled skirt and blouse as best I could, then let Mr. Mortimer and his assistant in, walking them to the entrance of JJ's room. When I went back to close the front door, I saw the truck had pulled up next to the hearse and someone was getting out of it. Despite the already warm day, the man wore a black knee-length wool coat over Levi's, which he'd tucked into a pair of showy lizard boots—not the sort of boots cowboys wore. With a thud of dismay, I realized who he was.

"Morning, Miss Gibson."

Burleson Archer strode up the front steps, ten-gallon in hand. He'd slicked his thick brown hair back from his temples, gray roots framing a creased forehead. Each time he'd visited before, Papa had asked him to leave before he had time to take his hat off; without it he looked closer to fifty than I'd guessed him to be.

"Mr. Archer."

"Please, call me Burr."

His smile caught me off guard; wide and friendly, full of white teeth. I almost smiled back before I noticed the warmth of it didn't reach his steel-gray eyes.

"Allow me to say how very sorry I am for your loss."

His words had a practiced rhythm to them, but I nodded in acknowledgment.

"I followed Sam out here to offer my condolences to your father," he continued, "and see if there's anything I can do."

"My father is resting," I said.

"No, I'm not."

I turned to find Papa standing outside the door to his room. He'd changed into clean clothes and combed his hair, but he still looked tattered and worn. He seemed to have aged ten years.

"Let him in."

Papa walked into the kitchen and sat down in his chair by the fireplace.

"My thoughts have been with you, John," Burr said, pulling one of the kitchen chairs over next to Papa. "I just can't imagine losing your only son that way. Your mind must be spinning fast as a windmill in a norther."

Burr sat down. For a moment, I thought he might take Papa's hand in his.

"I just had to come," he went on, his Texas accent seeming to thicken with every word. "I wanted you to rest assured that my offer still stands. I hope that's some comfort to you," he glanced my way, "and to your daughter, of course."

I watched my father. Burr hadn't come to offer comfort, and Papa knew it. He'd come to take advantage of the situation. After some success wildcatting for oil in Mexico, he was trying to do the same in South Texas. He needed land, a lot of land.

"I'll keep it in mind," Papa muttered.

"Well, good." A smile threatened to crack Burr's mask of

concern. "I'd be happy to have my lawyers in Houston draw up a formal offer. Would that suit you?"

Papa sat still. I silently pleaded with him to turn Burr down flat like he had every other time.

"I'd take a look at it," he replied. "Same price as before?"

A weight pressed on my chest.

"Oh, well, sure, John," said Burr, waving his hand like he was granting a wish. "I think prices have come down some since we last spoke, but in light of what you've been through, I'd be willing to let it stand."

Prices had not come down; anyone who read the newspaper knew that. Every man with the means was buying up land and prospecting for oil. I watched Papa for some sign of disgust, some clue that he was just letting Burr waste his breath. All I saw on his face was defeat.

"I've got some traveling to do," Burr continued, "but I'll be back in a week or two. I can come out then with the paperwork. All you'll have to do is sign it, John. Easy as that."

His words were flowing fast, a snake oil salesman making a deal.

"In the meantime, you just holler if you get to feeling overwhelmed," he said. "My boys would be glad to come down here and lend a hand. Just say the word."

I flinched at the mention of his "boys." How could he exploit my father's loss so callously, and so shrewdly? It was as if he'd heard Papa's lament.

Sam Mortimer stepped tentatively out of JJ's room and cleared his throat. The three of us looked at him as if he were a forgotten houseguest.

"Excuse me, Mr. Gibson," he said from the doorway. "What would you like us to take to attire the boy in? For the service?"

Papa's eyes fell on me.

"Let her decide."

Leaving Papa alone with Burr Archer would be like leaving a rat to gnaw at a wounded dog. My father didn't need any more reminders of how difficult life on the ranch would be; he'd known it the minute he'd looked down at JJ's lifeless body.

"Mr. Archer," I said. "I think my father's had enough."

Burr's mouth twitched in annoyance.

"Of course." He stood, sticking his hand out to shake Papa's. "I'll keep you in my prayers, John."

He put the kitchen chair back at the table then turned to me.

"Let me know if I can help with anything, Sarita."

The Cheshire cat grin was back. His eyes traveled down my neck, stopping just shy of going too far. My nose crinkled with revulsion. He caught my look and turned away.

"See you back in town, Sam," Burr called out.

As soon as he crossed the threshold, Papa withered. There were so many questions in my head, but I didn't have the heart to ask them. With some effort, he shoved himself out of the chair and shuffled to his bedroom, closing the door behind him.

Sam Mortimer was waiting. I started toward him but stopped short when I looked down. A line of crimson drops trailed across the floor, presumably left when we'd carried JJ's body to his room. Someone had walked through them, smearing the blood, leaving partial footprints on the tile. It could have been anyone—Clyde, Captain Wright, the undertaker—but a chill ran through me at the thought of Burr Archer carrying my brother's blood around on the soles of his lizard boots.

I shook my head clear and walked into JJ's room. Not so long ago, I'd taken Mama's white button-up boots and her favorite gingham dress from the cedar trunk where she'd kept her treasures: a copy of *Little Women*, a gold locket that had been my grandmother's, a photograph of her and Papa on their wedding day. It had been almost unbearable, even though her body hadn't been in the room. JJ's was still on his bed.

"It's all right, miss, he's covered up," said Mr. Mortimer, as if reading my mind.

JJ's cowboy boots lay in the middle of the floor. I walked around them to the tall chest on the far wall. Pulling the top drawer open, I took out his favorite wheat-colored shirt and a pair of brown cotton pants. I'd laundered the clothes just a few days ago, never imagining JJ would be wearing them to his own funeral instead of to Sunday school.

I stooped to find his necktie and suspenders in the bottom drawer. When I turned to hand the items to Sam, my eyes caught on the bed. I'd sat on the edge of it every night for two weeks after Mama's death, holding JJ while he'd cried himself to sleep. He'd never need me like that again; a lifeless, shrouded form had replaced him.

My lungs locked up. I shoved the clothes at the undertaker and dove out of the room, out of the house. Outside, I hurried past the funeral wagon and ducked into the refuge of the oak's low-hanging limbs. Gulping dewy morning air, I stumbled to Mama's grave marker at the base of the tree. It looked achingly new, protected from the sun and rain by the thick branches and leaves.

Roses had been my mother's favorite flower. They didn't grow very well in South Texas, shriveling up in the pounding heat, but Papa had given her some that would last, carving dainty rosebuds into the yellow oak of her cross. I sank to the ground in front of it, tracing the petals with my fingers. I missed her all the time, but right then, I needed her. I tried to picture her sitting with me, but the image was as blurry as the sun shining through the thick morning fog.

As desperately as I wanted to hold on to Mama, she was fading from my memory. The scents of rose petals and lavender still reminded me of her, but I couldn't remember her smell. I caught myself using her phrases, but I couldn't hear her voice. I tried to make decisions the way she would have, but I couldn't be sure. People often commented on how much

I resembled her. My straight blonde hair, the gold flecks in my brown eyes, the long, athletic build. I could catch a glimpse of my mother in the mirror, but how long would that last?

JJ had Mama's flaxen hair but Papa's curls and blue eyes. What would that mustache have looked like? Would his long, lanky body have filled out, or stayed slim and angular? I tried to picture him as an adult, but I couldn't. Maybe Papa was right; our memories would dim until only a fleeting glimpse of what might have been remained.

I heard heavy feet trudging down the steps from the front door then shuffling through the dirt, followed by the sound of fabric brushing across the wooden bed of the hearse. I refused to look, staring instead across the pasture. By the time the wagon's wheels began grinding down the road, the sun had burned away the mist, peeking over the line of trees along *Los Animas* Creek. I dropped my head into my hands, picturing JJ galloping off on a horse.

Why had I so resented mothering him? Already, I longed to see the flash of mischief in his grin, to argue with him about bedtime and cleaning the barn. I ached to hear the thrill in his voice when he talked about horses, to see the joy dance across his face when he looked at Twister.

Over and over, I'd prayed for things to be different. Those prayers had been answered, but not in a way I would ever have wanted. I'd never imagined a life without my brother or a world in which my father gave up.

CHAPTER 4

The red Ford roadster barreled through the open gate, skidding to a stop next to our front steps, its nose planted in a clump of low huisache. Maude Langley, dressed as always in a man's shirt and cotton twill pants, heaved herself out of the automobile. I left the shelter of the oak to meet her as she bustled over, bundling me up in a hug.

"Oh, sugar," she murmured. "It's just plain awful."

I let myself soften into her. Maude had a reputation as a life-hardened widow who spit nails if a person crossed her, but I knew the size of her heart matched the rest of her.

The passenger door opened. Dr. Andrew's tall frame unfolded from the seat. Reluctantly, I disentangled myself from Maude's embrace and walked over to greet him. We all went inside, and Dr. Andrew disappeared into Papa's room.

"Thank you for bringing him out," I said to Maude.

"We were both over at the Nolans' place helping Sally. Her little chickabiddy got scared out before he was quite done cooking." Maude shook her head. "I don't mind saying your mama's skills were sorely missed. That woman could make delivering babies look as easy as pulling turnips from a garden."

Mama had helped hundreds of women bring their children into the world. I was grateful she hadn't had to watch her own child leave it.

Maude glanced at Papa's door.

"Women are just better at taking care of women. Especially in matters where men have zero personal experience, if you catch my drift," she said with a wink, "but the nearest midwife is that *patera* all the way over in Laredo, so poor Sally got stuck with Doc."

"I don't remember how far along Sally was," I said.

"She had less than a month to go," said Maude. "This is her third, you know. Girl's as fertile as a prize sow. She'll end up with a baker's dozen at this rate."

"Is the baby all right?"

"He's a wrinkled little peanut of a thing, but he'll pull through," Maude said, her expression dimming. "Anyway, Clyde showed up looking for the doctor. He told us about JJ and said your pa had passed out. Doc's still got that old nag pulling his wagon, would've taken him an age to get here. So, I loaded him and his black bag up, and we rushed over."

She followed me to the kitchen, lowering herself onto a chair at the table. I opened the hatch on the stove and lit the wood to heat some coffee.

"I just can't fathom what your poor father's going through," Maude said. "Losing a child that way would knock anybody down."

I took two cups and saucers out of the corner cabinet, turning to find her studying me.

"He's going to need you more than ever, Sarita," she said.

I set the cups on the table.

"I know," I said quietly, irritated by the prickling in my eyes. "It's just ..."

"Come on, now," Maude prompted. "Speak your mind."

I sank into the chair across the table from her.

"Lately, I'd been thinking about looking for a job in San Antonio. Maybe at the newspaper."

"You wouldn't be happy away from here," Maude scoffed. "This ranch is sprinkled through your cells like caliche dust;

you'd never sweep it all out."

I gazed through the window, watching a pair of scissor-tails maneuver across the sky, long tail streamers flaring as they chased bugs and flies.

"It's not that I wanted to leave," I said after a moment, "it's just that JJ was getting old enough to take care of himself. I didn't want him to depend on me so much." I hesitated, then went on. "The ranch was going to be his to run one day, and, after Jackson disappeared, there really wasn't anything left for me here."

"Well, that's all changed now," said Maude. "The reason is a damn travesty, but the result is that your father has to let you help him. He's got no choice."

"He does have a choice."

Maude cocked her head.

"Burr Archer was here earlier," I said. "I think Papa's going to sell. If he does, we'll probably move to Hebbronville, or maybe Corpus, depending on his health. He'll need me to take care of him."

"For the love of Pete, don't let that happen!" A line burrowed into Maude's forehead. "John's got no reason to sell. You're smart as they come and you're a hard worker. You can learn to manage La Barroneña."

Maude had been stopping by a few times a month since my mother died. Instead of sewing, cooking, and childrearing, her visits focused on what she called 'ranch learning'—fixing a flat tire, shoeing a horse, butchering a hog, and scorching the spines off cactus with a pear burner. I looked forward to those lessons; birds and other wildlife seemed to be the only things my father still cared to teach me about.

"Papa doesn't think of me like that," I argued, "like someone who could run the ranch."

Maude leaned in, thick auburn hair framing her face like a mane.

"Then prove him wrong, sugar," she said. "When Mr. Langley

passed, there wasn't anybody to teach me what to do. They were all too busy betting against me. Folks wagered I'd be on the next train back to Kansas City, or on the prowl for a new husband. Man-Trap Maude, they called me. But I knew to the very center of my soul that I could take care of La Retama better than anybody. Even the cheating bastard who left it to me."

One of the things I admired most about Maude was her confidence. She was like a steamship; when she got moving, you didn't want to be in her way.

"And here's another thing," she went on. "Screw that scoundrel, Jackson Cage!"

My face warmed. I'd had the same sentiment, just maybe not the same words. I couldn't get my feelings about Jackson ironed out. Part of me was scared something terrible had happened to him, but the rest of me was mad as hell that he'd left with no explanation.

I'd known Jackson growing up. He was only a year older, and his reputation had made him a bit of a legend. Once he'd set a fifteen-foot Blue Indigo snake loose in the classroom to get out of an arithmetic test. The prank had become a favorite town tale.

While I'd been away at school, I hadn't seen much of him. Following the death of his father, Jackson's mother had taken off with a traveling salesman. By the time we got reacquainted, shortly after my mother's death, he and Clyde had been in the care of their grandfather for a few years. I'd thought losing both parents and living with a tough Ranger captain had changed him. Maybe I'd thought wrong.

"You don't need him," Maude went on, "or any of the other tomcats who'll be sniffing around trying to convince you that it isn't proper for a lady to deal with certain things, like banking and breeding. What a pile of horse feathers!" She slapped her hand on the table. "As if talk of numbers and animal husbandry might muddle our feeble brains and offend our fragile sensibilities!"

Her face shone pink under the freckles sprinkled across the bridge of her nose. Her eyes sparkled like topaz.

"Don't get me wrong, a cattle ranch is a big operation. Running one isn't for the weak of mind, body, or spirit," she said, "but anybody who claims you can't do it is dead wrong."

"I don't think Papa will ever have as much faith in me as you do," I said with a sad smile.

"Well, he's not going to put a big, fat bow on this place and hand it to you. I had to prove myself, too. It took some time for people to see me as a rancher, not just a woman." She paused, glancing at Papa's closed bedroom door. "It's natural for your father to see his little girl when he looks at you. What you've got to do is make him see a successor. Someone who's not only going to take care of the livestock and the land, but who's also going to look out for the future. Legacy is a big responsibility."

I weighed her encouragement. Her passion was hard to resist, but one thing stuck in my heart like a thorn. My brother's death was the only reason I'd have the chance to run La Barroneña. He'd died on my watch. I'd failed to protect him, and in doing so, I'd caused my father to consider giving up. Instead of looking after it, I'd put the future of the ranch, of our family, at stake.

"Papa left me in charge and his only son got killed."

Maude pulled herself to the edge of the chair, reaching across the table to grab my hands.

"You got no cause to feel responsible for that. What happened to JJ was terrible, but it sure as hell wasn't your fault."

"I had a gun," I said.

"Shooting a person is no easy thing, especially in those circumstances," she said, squeezing my fingers. "Hindsight is an advantage we don't have until it's too late. You couldn't have known how things would play out."

But I knew now, and so did my father.

The kettle gurgled to a whistle. I pushed away from the

table and grabbed the handle with a hot pad. As I poured coffee into the cups, Papa's door opened, and Dr. Andrew walked out.

"I've given him some sleeping salts and a tonic he needs to take every day," he said, walking into the kitchen. He peered at me as he stuffed a stethoscope into his black bag. "He needs rest; a great deal of rest."

"Will he be all right?" I asked.

"Hard to know without some tests, but he's refusing to go to Corpus to have them," the doctor replied. "One thing is certain; his heart won't continue to survive these episodes. Sooner or later, they'll cause enough damage to be fatal."

Maude scowled at Dr. Andrew, but I appreciated his bluntness.

"I'm hoping he'll feel better in a few days," he went on in a less brusque manner, "but keep him calm, Sarita. His body needs a chance to recover from the stress and shock of all this. It's going to take a while."

Papa had already tried to go after the Rangers. How was I going to keep him quiet? Strap him down? He'd never been one to sit still. Maybe the only advantage of selling the ranch would be that he'd no longer have a reason to work so hard—but what would he do then? He'd be lost without the structure of a workday.

"He should sleep through the night. I'll check on him tomorrow." Dr. Andrew headed for the door. "I need to fetch my buggy, if you don't mind, Mrs. Langley."

Maude stood and placed a callused hand on my back.

"I'll come back out with some supper," she said. "Meantime, you think about what I said. Things like this either shut you down or push you forward." She gave my shoulder a squeeze. "Choose the latter, sugar."

I walked her out. The doctor had already settled into the Ford's passenger seat. Maude got in and fumbled around with the levers until she got the engine started, then she backed up and turned toward the gate. As I watched the roadster speed away, her words flew through my mind the way those scissor-tails had swooped through the air.

Maude was right. This dusty, thorny place was part of me; I couldn't let it go any easier than I could run away from it. Our land meant nothing to Burr Archer, other than the money it could make for him. It was everything to us. Three generations had sacrificed to keep it. My ancestors and my mother were buried in it; my brother's blood was mixed into its soil.

Papa's faith in the future of La Barroneña had to be restored before he gave up or, worse, died from hopeless grief. If I ended up with the ranch because the stress of my brother's murder killed my father, it would be nothing but a guilt-ridden reminder of failure. I needed Papa's blessing. That wasn't going to happen by proving I could rope a calf or fix a windmill—we had cowboys and workhands to do those things. He had to believe his legacy could continue through me, but any sliver of confidence he'd had in that had been destroyed. That was what I had to rectify.

My father wanted justice; our family, what was left of it, deserved justice. A few years ago, Papa would not have rested until his son's murderer paid. Now he'd been sentenced to bed by a frail heart. He was too weak to chase after moral rectitude. But I wasn't. It wouldn't bring JJ back, but if there was no retribution for his death, another wrong would be committed. I could at least prevent that. I could step into my father's shoes and do what was right for our family.

I changed clothes then walked into JJ's room. It seemed unfair that he was gone, but his scent, an earthy mix of saddle soap and leather, still lingered. I picked up his blood-splattered cowboy boots and sat down on the bed, wiping them clean with a damp rag. They were loose when I pulled them on, even over two pairs of socks, but more practical than my knee-high riding boots. I tucked my brush pants into them. His brown leather vest was hanging on the footboard of his bed. I slipped it over my cotton work shirt, stuffing the milk money I'd saved into the inner pocket.

When I turned to leave, I noticed his dove-gray Stetson sitting on a chair. The hatband had fallen off in the scuffle with Tomás, exposing a white-capped sweat ring around the crown. I picked the hat up, tracing the marking with my finger, then pushed it on my head.

I would never have considered wearing my brother's clothing or his sweaty hat before, but I wanted to be taken seriously. Maude was the one woman I knew who everyone took seriously, and she never wore a skirt or a dress. There was something more. All that was left of JJ were his things. In a strange way, wearing them made me feel like he was with me.

In the kitchen, I wrote Maude a note telling her I was going to Laredo to petition the Rangers again for help—after I paid Gus Cage a visit. Maude referred to Captain Cage as a stove-up old moss head, but Clyde had said his grandfather might have information about Javier. Maybe he could tell me something that would convince Wright to take action.

I left the note on the table. The .410 was leaning against the wall by the fireplace. I picked it up and grabbed a bag of shells from the gun cabinet next to it. On my way out, I peeked into Papa's room. He was sleeping peacefully, his breathing deep and regular. I was grateful Dr. Andrew's medicine had knocked him out. It had allowed him to get some rest and saved me from trying to explain what I was doing, and why. I paused, worried about leaving him, but the doctor had said he'd sleep through the night, and Maude would arrive soon. I could trust her to take care of my father until I returned.

After a few tries with the crank, I got the truck started and climbed in. The remains of the lunch I'd packed Papa yesterday sat on the front seat with his work gloves and canvas duck jacket. Life had been normal just a day ago. I drove out of the yard and down the main road to the nondescript entrance of La Barroneña. Once through the front gate, I shifted gears and headed south.

CHAPTER 5

I arrived in Hebbronville on Smith Street, the quiet of my near hour-long drive ending abruptly. The town vibrated with the roar of motorcars and jangle of wagons. The constant bellowing of the cattle penned up at the stockyards nearby rumbled through the air. I rolled the window up to dampen the noise and keep out the town's smell—a dusty sachet of manure, gasoline, and wastewater.

I slowed to a crawl to avoid hitting anyone as I drove past the courthouse, a white stucco rectangle with columns marching across the front. It overlooked a busy central square. Commerce and the railroad had made Hebbronville one of the largest livestock shipping centers in Texas. Cattlemen stood in crowded clumps, bartering sale prices, arguing over the cost of feed, and arranging shipments across the country. I could picture Maude among them, holding her own. Could I see myself there?

Mixed in with the cattlemen was the new population of landmen and prospectors, set apart by their briefcases full of contracts. They'd been drawn to Jim Hogg County by reports that an oil well in nearby Thompsonville was about to come in big. They wanted to talk area ranchers out of their land or into drilling leases. I thought of Burr Archer's greedy white teeth and drove a little faster.

Papa had been one of the few ranchers to resist punching

holes in his land. He'd said most of the wells turned out dry, so why destroy the ground and poison the water? Maude kept encouraging me to change his mind about drilling, and about modern conveniences like electricity, but it wasn't my place to make changes. It might never be.

I turned west at Hotel Viggo. Our family had stayed there several years ago; the first time we'd ever stayed in a hotel. It was shortly after Pancho Villa had attacked Columbus, New Mexico. His army had killed over twenty people and left the town in flames. Rumors of an attack in our area had been circulating among ranchers, and a group of them decided to use the three-story limestone building as a kind of fortress.

To JJ and me, the stay had been a big adventure. We'd spent hours playing hide-and-seek in the stairwells and stealing sweets from the kitchen. On the way home, though, a thick silence had permeated the truck. Villa's men had indeed invaded a local ranch. The Texas Rangers had chased the *insurrectos* back across the border, but no one was certain whether additional gangs had hit other ranches. My parents had been nervous they'd find our livestock slaughtered and our homestead burned out, but La Barroneña had been spared.

A sharp whistle startled me. I slammed my foot on the brake, forgetting to engage the clutch. The truck jolted to a stop as the motor quit. A train engine steamed down the tracks in front of me, thick black plumes billowing from its smokestack. Through the windows of the passenger cars, I caught glimpses of nondescript faces staring out like storefront mannequins. I'd been one of those faces as I'd headed to and from San Antonio, transported between two worlds, neither of which I was sure I belonged in.

I hopped out of the truck and arm-wrestled the crank until the engine sparked to life. Sweat rolled down my face as I got back in and drove across the tracks. A couple miles later, I arrived at the wide, iron gate to Stillwater Wash, ten thousand acres Captain Gus Cage had bought from J.R. Hebbron himself, a fact Jackson had been proud of.

The ranch resembled most of the surrounding properties—mile after mile of thick, thorny brush and low mesquite. If ever a plant had a hold of a place, it was the grip mesquite had on South Texas. It wasn't native; the seeds had arrived and spread in the manure of cattle brought up from Mexico. It was hard to imagine how different it must have looked when Papa was a boy and grassy plains had covered the Nueces Strip.

As I drove down the bumpy road to the house, I noticed several fence posts that needed to be replaced and wondered how well Gus was managing without Jackson. I'd once believed Jackson and I would run his place together. He'd said he wanted me to help him, words that had spoken directly to my heart. Maybe he'd just been telling me what I wanted to hear, but what would have been the purpose of that? There was no reason to ask me to marry him if he didn't love me. It wasn't as if I came with a dowry. The only thing of value my family possessed, the ranch, would have belonged to my brother one day.

A long, white adobe with a red tile roof came into view. I hadn't been to the house since we'd told Gus we were engaged. He'd offered curt congratulations then spent the rest of the meal discussing cattle, weather, and grass with Jackson.

I parked the truck, pulled on the brake, and climbed out. Forcing the rusty wrought iron gate open, I hurried down the overgrown path and up three steps to a wide porch running the length of the house. I took a deep breath as I stood at the front door. I hadn't talked to Gus since he'd come to our house to tell me Jackson was gone. Not on a hunting trip, not off buying cattle, just gone.

Music swelled from inside. It was a combination of sounds I'd never heard before—piano notes dueling with brass instruments in quick tempo. Encouraged by the upbeat noise, I gave the door a hard knock, sending flecks of paint swirling to the ground. The music screeched to a stop as if the phonograph needle had been lifted abruptly. Uneven footsteps approached and the door swung open.

"Sarita Gibson," Gus announced in a gravelled voice. "What're you doing here?"

His mood didn't match the spirit of the music. I decided to skip basic pleasantries.

"*Tequila* smugglers killed my brother yesterday."

"I heard," he replied, regarding me warily. "Don't explain what you're doing on my veranda."

"I've come to ask for your help."

"You want me to ride off after them?" His laugh came out in a snort. "Case you hadn't heard, my Ranger days are done."

"No, that's not what I want." I rushed to explain before he decided to slam the door in my face. "Clyde said you might know who one of them is. A red-haired Mexican with light eyes."

A flinch tugged Gus's cheek.

"Javier isn't Mexican," he said after a moment. "He's *Tejano*."

The name of JJ's murderer echoed through my head. I was relieved to hear Gus confirm it but disturbed by the raw images it brought forward.

Gus limped out onto the porch, leaning on a cane fashioned from a gnarled oak limb. He sat down on the dusty rope-seat of a rocker and laid the stick across his lap. A couple years ago, he'd taken a bullet in the thigh chasing cattle rustlers. By the time he'd seen a doctor, the wound had festered. The resulting falter in his step might suggest feebleness, but his body was fit, his eyes bright and clear. His age was hard to guess. There was hardly any gray in his hair, but the lines crisscrossing his face ran deep, as if the trails he'd spent his whole life following had mapped themselves there.

"Wright already been out to your place?" he asked.

"Yes, sir."

Gus took a pouch and a small tin box out of his shirt pocket. He flicked the box open with his thumbnail and removed a square piece of paper. Questions spun round my head like a ball of moccasins, but I bit my lip as he slowly sprinkled a line of tobacco down the middle of the wrapping.

"What difference do you think talking to me is going to make?" he finally asked, carefully rolling a cigarette.

"I thought you might have some information about Javier I could pass on to Captain Wright."

"Huh," Gus huffed. "Whatever I might tell you, it's not going to make Wright jump up and run after him for killing your brother."

"How can the Rangers just refuse to help?"

"You've got no idea what those men are up against," he replied, placing the smoke between his lips. "Your trouble seems like the biggest trouble there is, but trust me, to others it ain't."

Captain Wright had made it clear they were preoccupied, and Wagley had driven the point home. I understood it, but still had a hard time accepting that their full plate meant a murderer got to go free.

"Maybe I should find Javier myself." As the unvetted words left my mouth, my stomach clutched like I'd just let go of a rope swing over a deep hole.

Gus's brow sunk over one eye. He glanced up at me sideways, stuffing his mixins box back into his pocket. "You just light on that idea, gal?"

"Well, there's no one else to do it," I said, gathering determination as I spoke. "My father's too sick and Clyde's off helping the sheriff."

"Who do you think you are?" He scoffed. "Annie Oakley?"

I ignored the quip. Gus studied me for a moment, like a sergeant sizing up a recruit, then shook his head.

"It isn't a woman's place to take off after outlaws," he said. "You best leave it alone."

As he spoke, the unlit cigarette waggled around under his mustache. I fought the urge to slap it out of his mouth.

"Leave it alone?!" I barked. "My brother was murdered for no good reason. He bled to death in my arms. Would you leave it alone, or would you be looking for justice?"

"Justice," he said, "that's what you want?"

"Yes."

He rocked forward, staring straight into my eyes.

"You willing to risk your life chasing it?"

He wasn't posing an idle question. It was one thing to try to talk the Rangers into going after Javier—it was quite another to do it myself. Danger was more than a possibility; it was probable, and death might not be the worst of it. Dying meant you left others behind to grieve. There were far more terrifying fates. Horrors I didn't dare imagine.

No one expected me to do anything. I considered jumping off the porch, climbing into the Model T and scurrying back home. Then Papa's demoralized face floated up in front of me. This was my chance to change the way he thought of me.

"Getting justice for my family is the only way I'll have a life," I said.

The captain's gaze flicked to the skyline. He didn't move for several minutes then his gray-flecked mustache twitched, as if crank starting his mouth.

"He's part of the Salsito de Ortega family. *Los Diablos Pelirrojos*, the red-haired devils," Gus said, pinching the unlit cigarette from his lips. "They joined the *Seditionistas* during the raids. My company lost a number of good men fighting them."

He stopped talking, his jaw clenching. Jackson's father had been killed while serving in Gus's company during the Border Wars. I'd just witnessed firsthand the devastation wrought by that kind of loss. Gus was a tough old bird, but he was also a father. He'd lost his son to war, and now his grandson was missing. He must have been as troubled by Jackson's disappearance as I was. He'd been abrupt, almost cold, when he'd delivered the news, but maybe that had been his way of trying to cover his grief.

"Your campaign was successful," I said, trying to move the conversation forward. "The Border Wars are over."

"They might be over, but they ain't hardly forgot," said Gus, swiveling my way, his moment of sorrow passing. "One thing leads to another. Governor Ferguson's man, Ransom, with his 'scorched earth' campaign, did as much damage trying to quell the unrest as the rebels did causing it. A lot of people were killed, some of whom had it coming, some of whom were minding their own business on their own land." Gus shook his head. "Ground a load of salt into old wounds. Especially when it came to the *Tejanos*."

"My grandmother was *Tejano*," I said. *Abuela* had been my namesake; Sarita meant 'little Sara.' She'd been tall and proud and tough. Whenever I'd mistakenly spoken to her in English, a foreign language she found ugly and coarse, she'd pretended not to understand me.

"Your family's history and Javier's are different. Your father's father was an honest Irishman. He purchased your ranch fair and square. Your mother's land became part of La Barroneña when your parents married," replied Gus. "The King of Spain granted Spanish settlers large *porciones* north of the Rio Grande. They lived on them for near a century. When the Nueces Strip became part of Texas, a wave of crooked Anglos migrated here and stole the land right out from under people like the Salsito de Ortegas. The Border Wars were a campaign to get back what the *Tejanos* rightfully considered theirs," Gus continued. "Instead, they watched even more of their people cheated, lynched, and chased into Mexico. They got reason enough to hate Anglos."

"Are you saying their actions are justified?" I asked.

"I'm saying nothing of the sort," Gus replied stiffly. "They're cold-blooded killers."

He stuck the cigarette back in his mouth then removed it.

"You asked me to tell you about Javier. I'm trying to explain how he and *Los Pelirrojos* came to be as ruthless and spiteful as they are. Rule number one of understanding someone is knowing what drives them." Gus rolled the cigarette between his thumb and forefinger. "You say you want justice; those men gave up on justice years ago. They want revenge, and they don't care who they take it from."

Javier's voice echoed in my ears: *The world will not miss another goddamn gringo.*

Gus stared at me. "You still think you want to tangle with them?"

"Javier had no right to ruin my family because of what happened to his."

"That's a true statement." He paused, looking thoughtful, as he rubbed his lame leg. "Irony of it is they're probably making more money bootlegging than their land grant was worth."

"How do they get that much *tequila* across the border?"

"Call it what you want," Gus smirked, "but the Rio Grande is just a river. There are hundreds of places to cross—law can't cover the whole of it. Guns and money go one way; drugs and liquor go the other. Livestock goes both ways. It's been a problem since the Treaty of Hidalgo and I expect it always will be, long as one side's got something the other side wants."

"What use is Prohibition if people are going to get liquor anyway?" I asked.

"None, in my opinion," he said. "Making something illegal won't ever stop people from getting it. A man can make more money in one successful liquor run than in a whole year of ranching. Government fools opened a gold mine for those who don't mind breaking the law and caused a whole lot of trouble for those sworn to uphold it."

"Javier is a smuggler and a murderer," I stated. "Why won't the Rangers uphold the law and go after him?"

"This conversation has come full circle," Gus retorted. "You think you can do better than the Rangers? What talents have you got other than frying up supper?"

A touch of sincerity swirled through his sarcasm, as if he were challenging me. I wanted to tell him I could outride most men in the county, track game as good as any scout, gut a deer in eight minutes flat, and shoot him between the eyes before he knew what was coming. But those claims held no merit. When it had mattered, I'd done nothing.

"Like you said, JJ's just another casualty to the Rangers, but he meant the world to me and my father," I said. "I don't have any other missions. I just have this one."

Gus grew very still, deep in thought for a moment.

"One thing's for certain—no one would expect a girl like you to come looking for them," he said, as if talking to himself.

"Where would I go to find Javier?" I asked.

A shadow crossed Gus's face. He flicked his unlit cigarette into the wild lantana growing along the porch.

"Finding Javier will only get you a grave marker next to your brother's."

"What do you suggest then?" I asked. "So far all you've done is tell me what won't work."

My tone was more curt than I'd intended, but instead of angering Gus, it seemed to focus him.

"If you want the Rangers to target Javier, you need to find out if *Los Diablos Pelirrojos* are up to something bigger than trafficking a few hundred bottles of *tequila*," he said. "That's information Wright needs. He's not going put a dent in border banditry picking off one *bandito* at a time, but if he can take down a whole gang, a whole family, put an end to a criminal ring, well, that's a different story."

The journalist in me perked up, but how was I supposed to investigate Javier? I couldn't exactly interview his friends and colleagues.

"How do I figure out something like that?"

"You ever been to Villa Hidalgo?" he asked. "It's just on the other side of the border."

"I went there with my father and brother several years ago," I said, "after trapping wild mustangs on *La Isla Grande*."

"There's a *cantina* there, *El Conejo Loco*, The Mad Rabbit," said Gus. "The barkeep is a man called Mozo. The crooked mayor is his uncle, but Mozo's one of the few honest men in the whole town. Talk to him. Be careful no one notices you, though. If Javier gets wind of it, you won't last long."

"What exactly do you think Javier is doing?"

"If I knew, would I be telling you to find out?" Gus picked up his cane, stabbing the wood floor with the tip. "I'd go myself, but ..."

"Did you have to retire because of your leg?" I asked.

"I could still be useful. Rangers use automobiles and aeroplanes these days," Gus said, "but by the time I'd healed up, they said I was too old."

"Must be frustrating to be told you can't do something because you're old."

"It is." Gus banged the floor with his cane again.

"Sort of like being told you can't do something because you're a woman."

A wry smile stretched across his face. "I don't know about your shooting skills, but you sure can hit a target with that tongue."

I grinned back at him despite myself.

"Jackson told me you had grit." Something close to warmth crossed Gus's face, but only for an instant. "Hidalgo's always had its share of saloons, desperados, and whorehouses, but the rot has spread deeper since Prohibition. You know anyone who lives there?"

"Alicia Polanco, a friend from grammar school," I answered. "She moved there a few years ago after her father died."

"Good," he said. "Place is crawling with vermin. You're going to need someone who knows what's what, someone you can trust."

Nervous energy tumbled through me. In the last few minutes, the decision had been made that I was going to Hidalgo to dig up information on Javier and his family. Had I decided it, or had Gus?

Gus pointed at Papa's truck. "You plan to drive that Tin Lizzie across the border bridge?"

"Yes, sir."

"What about a gun?"

"I've got a .410."

He let out a disapproving grunt as he used the stick to push himself out of the rocker.

"First off, border patrol is not going to let a white girl, even Annie Oakley, drive into Mexico alone. Second, even if you were able to talk your way across, those tires wouldn't get you more than a couple miles into the chaparral. And lastly, you need a revolver, not a child's bird gun."

"All right?" I wasn't going to argue with him. If he had a point, or a solution, I wanted to hear it.

Gus turned to survey the patchy acres of gray-green. A red-tailed hawk glided by, head bobbing, sharp eyes hunting for mice or rabbits. As he watched the bird, he exhaled, his body losing a little of its rigidness. He'd made up his mind about something.

"I'll make you a deal," he said. "I'll loan you a horse and a gun on the condition you deliver a message for me."

I felt a zing of adrenaline.

"To Mozo?" I asked.

He kept watching the hawk.

"To Jackson."

The porch tipped sideways under my feet. I backed up against the closest post to steady my legs, an irregular thud beating in my chest. Jackson was alive? Could I let go of the dark image of him rotting under a layer of dirt? He was in Mexico? If Gus had found out something, why hadn't he told me? By all intents and purposes, I was still Jackson's fiancée. Had Gus been lying all along? Outrage sped through my veins, a rabid dog looking for something to bite. I pushed away from the post and grabbed Gus's arm, my face inches from his.

"You've known where he was this whole time?" I hissed.

His eyes narrowed, but there was something soft floating in them, a forlornness that resonated with me, sucking some of the heat out of my anger.

"No," Gus answered softly, "but I've had my suspicions."

"I've spent months not knowing whether to be worried or mad," I said. "I deserve a straight answer."

"You do." He placed his hand over mine, loosening my grip with roughened fingers. "But not from me."

Tears needled my eyes, but I blinked them back.

"Your grandson left me with no explanation," I said, trying to keep my voice from breaking. "Do you have any idea what that's like?"

"I do."

The answer stopped me. Jackson had left all of us. Me and my family; his grandfather and his brother. Until facing Gus, I hadn't considered the consequences of his disappearance on anyone but myself. As if reading my thoughts, Gus's face slammed shut like the gate on a cattle chute.

"That's all I'm going to say on the matter," he stated. "Day's getting on. Villa Hidalgo's not a place you want to ride into after dark. We have an agreement?"

I did need Gus's help. If the border patrol turned me away, I'd be stuck in Laredo, wasting time searching for another way across the river. If I managed to get across the bridge, a flat tire would leave me stranded in the Chihuahuan Desert with a .410 and a bag of birdshot. I'd already experienced how inferior the shotgun was to a revolver.

The thought of seeing Jackson sent an undeniable prickle of anticipation down my arms, but I could not let him distract me. What I had to do was about JJ and my father.

"I want to be sure we understand each other," I said. "I am not going to Villa Hidalgo to look for Jackson, but if I happen to see him, you want me to give him a message."

"Correct."

Gus reached his hand out and I shook it. There was a lot he wasn't telling me, but he was giving me a way forward.

"Tell him I understand," he said, "but it's time to come home."

CHAPTER 6

The Rio Grande meandered like a giant brown serpent through the low, rugged bluffs ahead. Thick foam lathered the neck of the big bay Gus had loaned me, his rib cage rising and falling beneath me as he stood trying to catch his breath. Gus had called him Rat, dubbing him the finest horse he'd ever met—high praise from a Texas Ranger. So far, the horse had lived up to the boast. We'd ridden hard to reach the river with plenty daylight left. Rat had dodged through the thorny scrub and prickly pear cactus with ease. We'd come across a few other riders and a transport wagon full of oranges as we'd followed the Texas-Mexican railway west. But there hadn't been another soul since we'd veered north to avoid the border patrol near Laredo.

I'd stuck Gus's Colt .45 in my waistband. It rubbed against the small of my back with every stride Rat took. I found the irritation comforting. I could reach around, grasp the pearl handle, and yank it out whenever I needed. As an extra bonus, Gus had thrown in a Bowie knife. It was hidden inside my boot, its leather sheath pressing into my calf. I'd only need it if all else failed. No matter my level of skill, a knife wasn't nearly as effective as a gun. An attacker had to be within arm's length to land a meaningful stab.

I reined Rat down a short embankment, his hooves sliding in the gravel, and headed toward a sandy area south of the island. I'd crossed there before with Papa and JJ. Despite being called The Big Island, *La Isla Grande* only consisted of a few acres. It sat in the middle of the river like an overgrown turtle sunning its back. Wild mustangs migrated up through Mexico each spring, swimming to *La Isla* to breed, and to be caught by cowboys and *vaqueros*. The last time we'd been there, JJ's face had glowed with joy as he'd watched the horses running free across the rocky berms. When it had been time to round up the ones we'd selected for the ranch, he'd hesitated, a sullen frown on his face.

"I wish we could just let them be," he'd said. *"Once you put a saddle on them, they're never the same."*

Rat stopped a few yards from the wide, muddy bank. I scoped the river, but it was too murky to see the bottom or tell its depth at any particular place. Crossing water was always a gamble. Floods and droughts changed rivers, digging out some places and building up others. I headed for a spot with the narrowest distance—still a quarter mile or so—across to Mexico. As we got closer to the edge, Rat's pace slowed, his head nodding up and down. I nudged him on with my heels. He took a few steps but stopped when his hooves hit the water.

"Don't be stubborn." I kicked him harder.

He splashed in but tried to turn back as soon as the water reached his knees. Yanking on the reins, I pulled his head around, but he stood stock-still, refusing to go farther. What was wrong with him? The water barely licked the soles of my boots, and even if it got deeper, horses were good swimmers. I didn't have time for bullheadedness. The border patrol, or someone worse, could show up. We were vulnerable standing out in the water.

"Get on!" I shouted, impatience driving my heels into his ribs.

He rocked forward but didn't take a step. I reached back and slapped his hip hard enough to make my hand sting. The loud smack reverberated off the high bank behind us, amplifying the sound. Rat jumped like a scared rabbit, my stomach lurching with him as he bounded through the water.

I pulled the reins in, trying to gain control before he could throw me off or break his leg hopping blindly across the riverbed. It was no use; I'd startled him into a reckless frenzy. He stumbled, sliding sideways, losing his footing. His body pitched forward, the momentum launching me onto his neck. The saddle horn punched my stomach like a hard fist, knocking the air out of me. I grappled for something to hold on to, fingers clutching handfuls of his mane. With a massive push, I shoved myself back into the saddle, strands of hair slicing my palms then slipping through my fingers as Rat jerked up, rearing all the way onto his hind legs, dumping me backward into the river.

Water wrapped around me like a heavy cloak. The current was stronger than it had appeared, quickly pushing me downstream. My head broke the surface, and I sucked in air, struggling against the flow. Finally, I got my feet planted in the soft, muddy bottom and stood. Blinking water out of my eyes, I saw Rat crawfishing away.

"No you don't, you goddamn horse!"

I yanked my feet free of the mud, lunging through the waist-deep water to catch hold of Rat's reins. JJ's Stetson had fallen off when I fell and was floating nearby. Without thinking, I snatched it up and slapped it across Rat's nose. His head pulled away. Nostrils flaring with quick breaths, he looked at me sideways, his ears flattened against his neck.

My ire dwindled. Rat might have feared the water, but now he feared me. I shouldn't have hit him. JJ would never have let his emotions get the best of him like that. He'd had unlimited patience when it came to horses. He would've tried to calm Rat, to reassure him everything would be all right. He would have gained his trust.

Holding the reins taut, I stuffed the hat into one of my saddlebags then stroked Rat's neck.

"I'm sorry, boy."

I forced myself to wait for him to settle. Something hard and slimy wriggled against my leg. I cringed, imagining all kinds of things lurking under the water ready to bite or suck or sting, but I didn't dare risk exciting Rat again. After a few minutes, his stance relaxed, and he let me rub his forehead.

"Good boy."

I took a few steps backward and he came along easily. Turning, I pulled him with firm, steady pressure through the water toward Mexico. Mud sucked at my feet. I clenched my toes to keep from stepping out of JJ's boots as I trudged forward, not looking back at Rat.

A good horse isn't led; he follows.

If I'd remembered that bit of JJ's advice when Rat had first balked, it would have saved a lot of time. The horse was behaving now, and we were more than halfway across the Rio Grande. Locating the sun, I measured its distance from the horizon. I could still get to Hidalgo before dusk, which wasn't until eight-thirty or nine o'clock in midsummer.

I pushed on, trying to go faster, panting from the effort of moving across the current and through the sticky muck. Thinking longer strides would shorten the number of steps to shore, I wrenched my foot from the sludge, swung my leg forward as far as it would reach—and plunged underwater.

The current caught me like a giant, sweeping hand. I clung to Rat's reins, using him as an anchor, hauling my head up, gasping for air. I tried to find a foothold, but the riverbed had disappeared. The reins slackened. Rat gave in to the tug of my weight and moved forward, plummeting into the deep wash, rushing at me like a freight train, the whites of his eyes shining, his legs thrashing wildly. If I let go, I'd lose him; if I didn't, he'd drown me. I kicked out of the way, his hoof clipping my shin as he surged past.

I strained to keep my head above the surface, paddling with all my might, but the weight of my clothing and water-filled boots dragged me under. Scissoring my legs hard, I popped up, gulping in air and water. The shoreline whisked by. I tried to swim, but the gulch sucked me under like the mouth of some horrible beast. Muscles burning, I clawed and kicked against the undertow, only to sink deeper, the river rushing faster. The boots were drowning me. Loose when I'd slogged through the mud, now they clung to my feet like fists of cement. I tried to kick them off, but they only slid halfway down my heel then stuck. Resisting the impulse to breathe was almost impossible. My chest convulsed, thousands of needles stabbing at my lungs.

I willed my knees to bend, my hands to reach for my feet to get the damn boots off, but my limbs had turned to rubber. I couldn't make them respond. My body was wilting, water penetrating my bones, making them too soft to support my muscles. Tired, I was so tired. The desire to give up, to glide down the sunken slide, was almost overwhelming.

Let the current carry you, relax into the flow.

I'd been crossing water since I'd learned to ride. I'd never thought to be afraid of it, but the Rio Grande had swallowed me whole. Muted sounds gurgled above the pounding pulse in my ears. A faraway part of my brain screamed to keep fighting, to wrestle my way to the surface, but it was disconnected, easy to ignore. A calm peacefulness spread through my body, lulling my will away.

Had JJ felt this peace before he died?

No!

JJ had not been peaceful in death. His face had brimmed with confusion and fear. He'd had no chance; his life had been taken, running out of him like sand through a funnel. He had died trying to save me. I couldn't give up so easily. I would not make his sacrifice worthless by being washed out to the Gulf of Mexico like a helpless ragdoll.

I opened my eyes, determined to fight. Blurred shapes passed by. Someone called to me, but I couldn't make out the words. The voice grew louder, screaming. I was screaming, my mouth wide open, precious air escaping, the sound reverberating in my head.

Swim, damnit!

I forced my legs to move, kicking my feet and sculling my hands back and forth. The surface shone above me but drew no closer. Hunger for air sucked at my chest. I slammed into something hard. Bubbles shot from my mouth and nose, a bolt of white-hot pain exploding in my shoulder. I clutched at it. I'd hit a boulder. Digging my fingers into its shell of dirt and slime, I clawed my way up, one hand reaching over the other, until finally my head burst out of the water.

Choking down air, I shoved off the rock before the river could yank me back in. A patch of more boulders sat near the bank a few feet away. I kicked toward them, my knee smashing against the gravelled riverbed. Nausea zipped up my throat. I reached down and felt the bottom. I'd hurtled onto a shallow rock bed as suddenly as I'd dropped into the deep gulley.

Scrambling onto my hands and knees, I crawled out, collapsing face-first on the shore. I struggled to catch my breath, my lungs expelling water in hacking barks. When the coughing and gagging finally began to subside, I rolled onto my back. I'd never been so thankful to be on dry land. The damn horse had nearly done me in.

Rat. Where was Rat?

I struggled to my feet, wincing against the pain in my shoulder and knee, and raked my eyes across the water. No sign of him anywhere. I staggered up the stair-stepped bank to get a better vantage point, my exhausted legs quivering like a newborn foal's.

What sort of horse was afraid of water? Rat was a Texas Ranger's horse; he must have had to ford plenty of rivers in his career. He might have sensed the sudden drop-off, but he'd spooked before we'd reached it. Where had he gone? He should've been able to get to shore once he stopped panicking, but on which side and how far away? Was he already galloping back to his barn at Stillwater Wash? I could almost hear Gus Cage's smug snort at the sight of him. Surely Gus knew the horse had a problem with water. Why hadn't he warned me?

What would I do without a horse? The shaking in my limbs moved inward. Hidalgo was several miles away, a short, easy ride, but a long, hard walk. How far downriver was I? I looked upstream to a far-off bend. *La Isla Grande* was nowhere in sight. The only way I knew to get to Hidalgo was to follow the road that began across from the island.

The western sky was filling in with pink and orange. I'd never make it to the town before sundown if I had to walk, and it would be dangerous, only my worn-out legs to get me away from predators—animal or human. But searching for Rat would use up even more valuable daylight.

I sat down on a flat rock and pulled JJ's boots off, dumping water out. I was grateful now that they had not come off. My feet would've been a bloody mess within a few yards if I'd had to walk in only my socks. I tightened the leather ties holding the knife sheath to my calf and tugged the boots back on.

My knee stung and throbbed. I chose not to examine the damage through the tear in my pants. There wasn't anything to be done about it. I squeezed water from the vest and reached back to tuck my shirt in. My fingers brushed across the spot on my lower back rubbed raw by Gus's .45, and my stomach seized. The gun was gone.

I leapt up, scouring the ground. I ran back to the water and splashed into the shallows of the rock bed, peering through the murky brown ripples for a glint of metal. I shoved piles of gravel aside with my foot, praying to feel the solid weight of the gun. When water surged over the tops of my boots, I jumped back, shying from the tricky river.

I'll die like a stupid, helpless girl out here without a gun.

No horse. No weapon. No way to protect myself, no way to escape from a threat except to run. All I had was the Bowie knife strapped around my shin. When had I lost the gun?

When Rat first ditched me? When I'd been whisked into the deep gulley? I peered upriver. I'd never find the exact place. Even if I did, what were the chances the gun had sunk straight to the bottom? The fingers of the current could have carried it anywhere.

I'm easy prey; a fawn at a watering hole.

Black bears were known to fish along the Rio Grande. One could drag me off to its den, feasting little by little on my undead body for days. The very *tequileros* I was looking for could find me first. Would Javier recognize me? His evil eyes, the smirk on his mouth, the innuendo in his words—he'd be only too pleased to carry out his not-so-veiled threat.

Dread spun through me. Would it be safer to go back to Texas? The wide, undulating ribbon shimmered, slanted sun-rays catching on its ripples. If I could get back across without drowning, I'd still have to walk to Laredo. Perils existed whether I was in Texas or Mexico.

I stepped out of the water, an insignificant speck on the wild landscape. The bank, the chapparal, the horizon expanded away, stretching into infinity. Crossing my arms, I held my breath, squelching the sobs threatening to erupt. I'd barely made it onto Mexican soil and already I'd lost the two things that made survival possible. If a river could beat me up, how would I fare against bandits and cutthroats? If I died out here, eaten by a ravenous mountain lion, would anyone ever know what had happened? Would anyone come searching? Or would I just be the foolish girl who took off after her brother was murdered?

What's a girl going to do without a man?

Had I proved Papa's point yet again? Why had he ever left me alone with JJ if I was so useless? Why hadn't he been there to fill Javier with buckshot? As much as it hurt, his disregard enflamed the part of me that wanted so badly to prove him wrong.

A flock of white egrets circled overhead. The birds landed

in the shallows in front of me, stabbing at minnows with orange beaks. Moments later, they all rose, alighting in a nearby cottonwood to roost for the night. I couldn't fly up to a safe spot and wait out the dark. I needed to get moving.

Laredo was more familiar than Hidalgo. I'd been to the stockyards with my father countless times. I could try to prod the sheriff there into helping me. Or buy a train ticket home. I felt the weight of disappointment, but going on would be as impractical as Papa trying to drive to Laredo.

I started walking, following the river south, looking for a place to cross. My knee throbbed and the boot's shaft hammered my bruised shin. Half a mile or so later, I spotted an outcropping of land lined with tall reeds of Carrizo cane. It jutted all the way out to the middle of the river. The distance to the other bank would not be far to swim, even if the surface hid another swift channel.

I sat on the ground, letting my tears flow, and yanked the boots off my feet. I did not want to be hobbled by them again, or risk losing them. Removing my belt, I started to thread it through the finger holes in both sides of the boot shafts but stopped, the hair on my arms standing up. Behind me, the grinding sound of steps rose above the rush of the river.

I yanked the bowie knife from its sheath and leapt to my feet, spinning around, ready to plunge the point into whatever was coming. Instead, my mouth dropped open. I straightened, watching Rat jog across the spit of land. He slowed to a walk as he got close, then stopped by my side. I reached out to touch him, afraid he was a mirage. His solid forehead was warm from exertion, and very real. I stared in wonder. I'd had the tiniest hope of finding him, but I'd never expected him to find me.

He bent his head to nuzzle my shoulder. I stroked his neck, breathing in his sweet, grassy smell, longing for JJ. He'd have had all sorts of theories on why Rat had lost his head in the river and how on earth he'd found me. Had JJ sent Rat to my rescue? The thought made me smile and glance up at the sky.

I squinted across the Rio Grande as the sun met the horizon behind me. Going back to Texas might still be the easiest path, but Maude's voice whispered in my ear: "*Nothing worthwhile lands in your lap dipped in honey, sugar—you got to charge ahead and grab it.*"

"You don't want to get back in that water, do you, boy?"

I patted Rat's neck, then unbound the boots, put them on and shoved my foot into the stirrup. Ignoring the aches and pains, I pulled myself onto the sodden saddle and reined Rat toward *La Isla Grande*.

CHAPTER 7

The last scrap of daylight dropped over the horizon, pulling darkness down with it like a shade. I shivered in the cooling air, still shaken and damp from my fight with the Rio Grande. We'd left the noise of the river behind a while ago, the night growing very quiet beyond the steady clop of Rat's hooves. In the dark, I could barely see his head in front of me and had no choice but to trust him to stay on the road to Hidalgo.

Eventually, the quarter moon rose high enough to light the stars. I could make out bushes and trees flanking the narrow road as we rode by. I wasn't accustomed to traveling at night—it made the surroundings feel alien, even though I knew the landscape was not dissimilar to home.

As I scanned the distance for signs of town, I thought I saw something move in the brush ahead. I glued my eyes to the spot. When we trotted closer, I saw tufts of grass bend sideways, accompanied by a rustling sound, sending a dart of fear through my stomach. Rat slowed, raising his head in the direction of the noise. He let out a short snort, which was answered with more stirring through the undergrowth.

I urged Rat on. As we passed, a pair of glowing eyes peered out of the brush. I drove my heels down harder, an itch spreading between my shoulder blades as I imagined Javier stepping out behind us, aiming his revolver at my back. I turned in the saddle to look, but the road appeared empty.

Rat kept sprinting until the domed glow of Hidalgo rose from the desert. The sounds of laughter and music met us at the outskirts, the dirt road soon giving way to cement. Rat's shoes clanked on the new pavement as we followed the unnatural glimmer of electric lights into the heart of town. A crowd of people was gathered in the main plaza where a quartet of *mariachis* played, their trumpets and guitars accompanied by singing and shouting, both in English and Spanish. I stayed in the shadows along the side of the road.

I hardly recognized Hidalgo. Instead of the traditional adobe structures I remembered, wooden buildings bordered the street, electrical lines hanging between their eaves like Christmas garland. The air seemed saturated with scents of new money—fresh paint, paving tar, automobile exhaust, and cigar smoke.

We passed rows of shiny motorcars and pickup trucks parked in front of places with names like *Cantina Americano* and Last Stop Saloon. The Mad Rabbit could be nearby, but as people spilled in and out of the bars, I knew I'd missed my chance to find Mozo that night. I'd wait for the sobriety of daylight to look for both him and my friend, Alicia. Gus's warning that Hidalgo had become a modern-day Sodom and Gomorrah was fresh in my mind. I felt an urgent need to get off the street and find a place to stay.

The Lucky Texian anchored the next block. Over the entrance hung a sign written in English offering special nightly rates. A group of men bantered loudly in the doorway. I wasn't sure how to tell the difference between a hotel and a brothel. I'd once seen printed cards from a bordello in New Orleans featuring photos of scantily clad women on red velvet chaise lounges trimmed in gold fringe. My friend, Amié, had swiped the cards from her older brother, passing them around school until the headmistress confiscated them. How could you tell from the outside of a building if there was red velvet inside?

I turned down the next side street, hoping to find a small,

quiet inn. Most places off the main square seemed to have closed for the night. I rode past a market, a hardware store, and a post office, their dark windows watching me go by. The cement petered out, the road becoming gravelled dirt. I'd begun to wish I'd chosen a different way when a glowing lamppost appeared at the end of the block.

Behind its small circle of light stood a two-story adobe building, a leftover from the Hidalgo I remembered. The plaque at the front entrance read, *La Fonda, est. 1890*. No motorcars lined the front of the inn, no groups of men stood blocking its entry. There was a large corral behind the building, a big white mule its only occupant. I tied Rat to the hitching post in front and walked through the open door.

Two electric wall sconces lit the small lobby. The only other décor was a woolen tapestry of a howling wolf hanging on the wall—no red velvet or gold fringe. There was a single staircase on the left leading to the second floor. At the back of the reception area, a woman with thick black hair streaked with gray stood behind a tall desk. Only her head and the tops of her shoulders were visible.

"*Buenas noches.*"

Her voice was deep but welcoming. She peered at me like a curious owl, and I realized what a mess I must appear. My clothes were soggy and dirty, my hands tinged brown from river mud, fingernails torn from clinging to the rocks, and my hair was a nest of tangles.

"Good evening, *señora*," I replied in Spanish, smiling. I hoped she wouldn't ask questions. She might be skeptical about letting me stay if she knew I'd swum across the river instead of crossing the bridge like most people did. "I'd like a room, please, and a place for my horse?"

She nodded and swooped around the desk while I silently sighed with relief. As I followed her, I realized that not only was she small but also bent. Under the embroidered yoke of her purple blouse, her back curled over her shoulders, forcing her to look up to see straight ahead.

Outside, the innkeeper untied Rat, leading him around the building to the corral, where she shoved the gate open with her foot. She walked him in, uncinched his girth, then pulled him close to the fence. Hiking up her long black skirt, she climbed up two rungs so she could reach to remove his saddle, blanket, and bridle. The sodden tack easily outweighed her, but the old woman showed no signs of exertion as she dropped each piece to the ground. I didn't even have a chance to offer help before she'd finished.

"*Ven*," she said, hopping down and motioning for me to follow.

"Where should I put the saddle?" I asked. I looked around for a barn, but all I saw was an open shed housing a wagon.

"In your room," she replied matter-of-factly.

I didn't relish the thought of sleeping next to the rig, which smelled of worn leather, horse sweat, and the fishy Rio Grande, but the innkeeper strode out of the pen without another word.

As I hauled everything into my arms, a sound erupted behind me. Rat stood with his legs spread apart, shimmying back and forth. I smiled; my spirits lifted by the sight of him shaking off the river like a huge dog. The horse was starting to grow on me, again.

I lugged the load up the narrow flight of stairs. There were three rooms on each side of a hallway. The innkeeper stopped at the last one on the right, unlocking it with an iron key. Instead of electric lights, an oil lantern hung from a bracket just inside the door. She pulled a box of matches from her skirt pocket and lit it.

The room was modest but clean. A red-and-brown-striped *serape* covered the cot-sized bed. It was a bit threadbare, but it would do on a warm night. The only other furnishings were a washstand with a bowl, pitcher, and washcloths sitting on it, and a ladder-back chair. A sash window faced the corral. The innkeeper parted the gauzy white curtains and opened it a crack then shuffled off to fill the water pitcher. I dumped the tack in the corner farthest from the bed.

"*Medicina?*" asked the innkeeper when she returned, pointing at my torn pants.

Through the ragged hole, I saw the chewed-up flesh of my knee. It started to sting the minute I looked at it.

"Yes, *gracias*," I said.

She left for several minutes, handing me a small glass jar of ointment when she came back.

"*Cinco pesos por el cuarto y el caballo*," she said.

"I only have dollars," I replied.

"*Sí, un dólar.*"

I pulled my money pouch out of the vest pocket, handing her a silver dollar. She left, and I locked the door behind her. An empty feeling came over me as the room went quiet. I'd never stayed in a hotel alone before. Craving the comfort of a friend, I suddenly wished I'd tried to find Alicia. Home felt far away. Hispanic culture so infused South Texas that Villa Hidalgo hadn't felt foreign when I'd visited before, but things had changed. It was as if someone had applied a varnish of Americanism to it, ironically making the town seem less familiar. It felt edgier, almost wild.

I pushed my loneliness away. Through the slim opening in the window, I could still hear muted noises from the square, even though it had to be close to midnight. It was good that I wasn't wading into the boisterous crowd. I'd find Alicia and Mozo in the morning.

As I relaxed, every inch of my body began to complain. I undressed and inspected the damage. A peach-sized welt covered my left shoulder and angry bruises spotted both arms. A contusion stuck out like a deep-purple plum on my left hip, which I didn't even remember hitting. My right shin bulged unnaturally in the middle. My knee, which resembled ground sausage imbedded with little chunks of gravel, was worst of all.

I poured water into the bowl on the washstand, washed my hands, then picked up a cloth and soaked it. I gently wiped the blood and dirt away, the cool water burning like alcohol. I clamped my teeth closed and kept at it, worried about infection if I didn't get the wound clean. It took forever to pick out all the grit, but I finally patted my knee dry, pressing lightly until the bleeding stopped.

I unscrewed the top of the innkeeper's jar and sniffed. The thick salve smelled of peppermint, lavender, and something earthy-sweet I couldn't identify. Scooping out a fingerful, I held my breath and spread it on, expecting it to sting. Instead, a warm, tingling sensation spread across the area before it went numb. Encouraged, I smeared some on my shoulder, hip, and shin. I would have dipped my entire body in it if I could have.

After undressing, I wrapped myself up in the blanket. I pulled Papa's duck jacket out of the saddlebags and laid it, along with my moist, soiled clothes, across the wooden chair. Next, I took out JJ's crumpled Stetson, smoothing out the creases and working it back into shape. I set it on the floor then opened the window fully, letting the night air in to dry everything and diffuse the odor of the saddle and blanket.

The sounds of the square poured into the room, along with savory smells from the food carts I'd noticed. My stomach growled like an angry cat. I'd brought Papa's lunch leftovers—an apple, a hunk of bread, and a wedge of yellow cheese. The bread was a doughy glob, the cheese slimy, but the apple was only bruised. I bit into it and limped over to the bed. My whole being begged to lie down.

The rope frame sagged, crunchy straw poking through the thin mattress cover, but my aching muscles twitched with relief as I settled in. Closing my eyes, I tried to focus on the fact that I'd made it to Hidalgo, but Javier kept invading my mind. He'd terrorized me in my own homeland; I shuddered to think what he could do in his.

CHAPTER 8

The dank, musty odor registered first. I lay still, eyes heavy, wondering if I'd fallen asleep in the hayloft. Somewhere in the distance, people laughed, and music played, as if a barn dance were in full swing. I forced my lids open and stared into the gray light of an unfamiliar space, my brain idling, as if I'd taken a twenty-year nap like Rip Van Winkle.

Looking around the small room, I noticed the saddle, bridle, and blanket piled in the corner. Clarity bloomed, details rushing in to fill the empty spaces. *JJ, Papa, Javier.* How long had I slept cocooned in the thin blanket? The soft light was such that it could have been dawn or dusk.

My body felt like it had rusted tight. I pushed up to a sitting position, pain shooting through my shoulder. When I threw my feet over the side of the bed, the gouges in my knee flared. The apple I'd taken one bite of before falling asleep clunked to the floor and rolled under the chair. I rocked up onto my feet, muscles quivering. I put a hand on the mattress for balance, bent over like the old innkeeper.

The noise billowing through the open window mounted, and my heart sank. It must be dusk. If it were dawn the town would be quiet. An entire day lost to sleep. Now what? Waste even more hours waiting for morning? I needed to find Alicia and Mozo to make any sort of headway.

I'd seen Hidalgo after dark as I'd ridden through town the

night before. The revelry had been intimidating, but it had been much later in the evening. Also, I'd been exhausted and raw from nearly drowning. Maybe now that I was rested, it wouldn't seem as bad. There were too many thoughts crowding my head to go back to sleep. Staying in the room with nothing to do but stare at the walls would drive me insane.

Papa could be getting worse, growing weaker by the minute. Maude had said she'd come back to our house, and I trusted her word. She would have seen my note when she got there. I knew she'd make sure Papa was cared for, but she couldn't stop his heart from failing. I needed to get back to him as quickly as I could.

I smeared the innkeeper's salve on my bruises and wounds, and hobbled over to the chair, picking up my camisole and underwear. They were a dingy gray color now, but dry. I'd worn my only pair of trousers yesterday, but I'd brought a pair of JJ's thick woven pants and his tan calico shirt. I pulled the shirt over my head, my heart filling as I breathed in a note of honey—a JJ smell, probably from the beeswax in the saddle soap he'd used.

I buttoned the band collar and slipped on the pants. They were snug around my waist, but the length was good. I put my socks on and shoved my feet into the boots, then picked up the Stetson. It held its original shape, except for a few crimps in the brim. A smile pulled at my lips as I ran a finger around the crown. The Rio Grande had not washed away JJ's sweat halo. Thinking of a perspiration stain as part of my brother was ridiculous, but I did. I twisted my hair into a messy braid and tucked it into the hat.

At the bottom of the staircase, I rounded the corner and scooted outside without seeing anyone. Daylight had just melted away, but activity hummed through the Saturday night air. I smashed the hat down farther on my head. With my face mostly hidden, and wearing JJ's clothes, I hoped people would assume I was a boy, not a young woman on her own. I crossed the road and headed for the square as the electric streetlights blinked on, casting their odd glow over everything.

I hesitated on the edge of the pool of people in the *centro*, not wanting to get caught up in the *fiesta* but not certain which way to go. My stomach rumbled. It had been two days since my last real meal. I scanned the surrounding buildings for a café where I could get some food and ask about Alicia.

My eye caught on a wooden sign hanging over the entrance to a one-story building with a rusted tin roof. Carved into the top of the sign was an exaggerated rabbit face, pointed ears sticking out sideways, black eyes squinting, mouth baring enlarged teeth. The cartoonish image was enough to give children Peter Rabbit nightmares. Below it, big block letters spelled out *El Conejo Loco*. The Mad Rabbit.

The sign swung back and forth in the breeze, as if beckoning me. Before I could change my mind, I wove through the revelers and hurried up the front steps of the *cantina*. Lively chatter and piano music swelled through a pair of hinged doors. I pushed them open cautiously and slipped into a cloud of cigar smoke.

I'd never been in a bar. I peered out from under my hat brim, trying to get my bearings. The room was the size of an average barn. Eight to ten round wooden tables crowded the cement floor. A large oil-fueled chandelier made of wrought iron hung overhead, but its light was dim and sooty. Staring glassily from the wood-paneled wall on my right were three mounted deer heads sporting oversized antlers. On the left side, a bald man dressed in black was playing an upright piano, fingers moving across the keys with enthusiasm.

As I looked around, I realized with a start that there were only three other women in the entire place. Two leaned against the wall next to the piano, both wearing off-the-shoulder dresses and bored expressions as they watched several men arguing over a card game. The other woman, however, was quite animated. Attired in a strapless dress of bright yellow satin with black lace trim, she sat at a table in the middle of the room with three men, her voluminous bosom bouncing as she laughed.

A patron at a table in the front looked my way with curiosity. Unease crawled over me. No respectable woman in Hebbronville would go into a place like this, especially not alone; even Maude would have taken an escort. The urge to turn and walk away grew as more people began to take notice. I needed to find Mozo or leave.

A polished mahogany bar ran across the back of the *cantina.* I scanned the length of it, looking for the bartender, but saw no one. Another sweep of the room was also fruitless. I started to head back to the entrance when a door behind the bar swung open and a heavyset man walked out carrying a clay urn.

"Mozo!" someone sitting on a barstool called to him. "*Más cerveza.*"

Relief ran through me. I kept my head down, skirted the crowded tables, and slid onto an empty stool at the end of the long counter. Mozo approached from the other side after a few minutes. He had jet-black hair that curled down his neck and round cheeks that glowed above a very full beard. He wore a red and black plaid shirt, suspenders stretching over his belly, and a white apron tied around his waist. He reminded me of Santa Claus.

"*Qué quieres?*" he asked in a deep, friendly voice.

I thought of Gus's warning to be discreet. The man next to me sat so close our shoulders almost touched. Even through the din of the *cantina,* he'd easily hear our conversation.

"Can I get something to eat?" I asked. "*Comida?*"

"Oh! You are *una señorita!*" said Mozo in English, smiling broadly. "I did not see you come in and only noticed the *sombrero.* I just brought out some *frijoles y chorizo* and *tortillas de masa, está bien?*"

"Yes, *muchas gracias,*" I said, my mouth watering.

He turned to the clay urn he'd put on the ledge behind him and ladled some red beans into a bowl, setting it in front of me with a spoon.

"Thank you," I managed to say, before shoveling a huge spoonful into my mouth.

As I chewed, the tender *frijoles* exploded with flavors of serrano peppers, cilantro, onion, and smoked sausage. Mozo pulled a round straw basket out from under the bar and placed it next to the bowl. It was full of flat, warm circles of buttered corn flour. Tugging a *tortilla* from the basket, I used it to push more beans onto the spoon. I finished the whole serving in a few huge bites, sopping up the remaining juice at the bottom with another *tortilla*.

Mozo chuckled. "I am not sure I have ever seen *una señorita* eat *más rápido*."

"Those are the best *frijoles* I've ever tasted," I said, swallowing the last bite.

"*Es la verdad!* I am always telling this to my cook," he said. His grin tapered as a crease appeared between his full brows. "Tell me, *señorita*, what are you doing in here?"

I peered into his face, gauging the question—merely friendly curiosity or more? The customer next to me was staring at the dark liquid in his glass. I couldn't tell if he was paying attention to us, but it still seemed safer to wait to talk about Javier.

"I'm trying to find a friend," I answered softly, my tone casual. "Maybe you know her? Alicia Polanco?"

"She is my cook!" Mozo exclaimed, belly rolling with laughter.

"Really?" I laughed too, his joviality lightening my mood. "She's here?"

"*Pues no,* Alicia does the cooking at her home," he answered.

Of course, Alicia wouldn't work in a *cantina* at night. Why was she cooking for Mozo at all? Why hadn't she gone back to school? She'd been so proud that she would be the first in her family to graduate. She'd wanted to be a teacher, not a cook.

"I'd really like to find her tonight," I said. "Can you tell me where she lives?"

"How do you know Alicia?" Mozo asked, still friendly but maybe a little reluctant to give a stranger his cook's address.

"We went to school together in Hebbronville," I answered. "We were very good friends, but I haven't seen her since her father died and she moved here with her mother and brother."

He nodded, the details seeming to reassure him.

"Yes, very sad about her *papá*," he said. "It would be good for her to see a friend from home. She is living with her grandmother over on the west side. You have been to Hidalgo before?"

"A few years ago," I said. "I don't really know my way around, though."

Glasses banged on the counter, several customers summoning Mozo.

"I need to serve the next rounds," he said, clearing away the bowl, spoon, and basket. "Then I will get some paper from the back and draw you a map."

There was a small commotion at the front of the *cantina*. Mozo hesitated, looking past me. His face darkened. I turned, glimpsing a group of men walking in.

"I will not be long," he said. "Stay right here."

I was so close to finding Alicia, I could almost feel her warm embrace. Gus had been right; it would be good to be with a friend who knew how to navigate Hidalgo. As I tapped the toe of my boot impatiently on the brass footrail, the guy next to me pushed away from the counter and left. I relaxed a bit, hoping now I'd have enough privacy to bring up Javier with Mozo, but the seat wasn't empty for long.

One of the men Mozo had watched enter the *cantina*—a short, thick man with long, snuff-colored hair—shoved himself onto the seat. He grabbed the lip of the bar as the stool tilted sideways, managing to gain his balance before toppling over. Irritated by his presence, I looked around him to see if Mozo was almost done. My new neighbor swayed closer and fish-eyed my hat.

"What the hell, *hombre*?" he slurred, his English mixed with a German-Mexican accent. "I would offer to buy a gentleman a drink, but if you was one you would not have on that goddamn Stetson."

His attitude caught me by surprise. Was it considered rude to wear a hat in a bar? I took a quick survey of the room, surmising that at least half the patrons wore some sort of headgear. He was just drunk. Instinct told me to ignore him, but I was unfamiliar with bar etiquette. He leaned in, clearly expecting a response.

"I just came in to get something to eat," I said, smiling to be polite. He squinted, then his face lit up like a match, and I knew I'd made a mistake.

"I'll be damned. You are a fucking girl!" he exclaimed as if he'd solved a mystery. "I think maybe a good-looking one, yes? Take that bullshit Stetson off so I can tell. I will buy you some *mescal*. You can repay me later."

He winked in a way that made the beans I'd eaten clump in my stomach.

"No, thank you, I'm done. I'm just waiting to pay."

I dug into my vest pocket for some money, wanting to get away from the drunk, but wavered. Mozo was only a few feet away, holding a half-full mug under the beer tap. He'd said it wouldn't take him long; he'd said to stay put. Without his directions to Alicia's, I'd be facing another long night by myself at the inn, having made no headway at all.

"Mozo, two *mescales*!" the drunk exclaimed.

Mozo looked over and set the mug down.

"*Señor* Hank—" he began, frowning.

"*Ándele!*" Hank growled.

Mozo sighed and filled two small glasses with *tequila*, sliding them down the smooth, polished bar. Hank pushed one my way then lifted the other one, swiveling to face me full-on. I stifled a gasp. A fiery scar twisted from his brow, through an empty eye socket, and down the right side of his cheek. It ended in a puckered period at his jaw. I quickly averted my eyes.

"*Vas?* Too ugly for you?" he barked. "Fine, we toast to you not running into the wrong end of an Injun's scalping knife. *Prost!*"

He raised his glass higher in my direction and downed the pale gold liquid in one swallow. He called out for more. Two glasses clinked to a stop in front of him. He threw another shot of *mescal* into his mouth. A drop trickled off his stubbled chin as he scowled at my untouched drinks. Swiping one up, he held it out to me.

"*Ahorita,*" he growled, *tequila*-laced spittle spraying my neck.

Hank had started out irritated, but now he seemed to be getting angry. How much longer would Mozo be? If Hank got any louder, the whole place would notice. If Hidalgo was like Hebbronville, stories of an Anglo woman causing trouble in a *cantina* would drone through the town like a swarm of mosquitoes. If Javier was anywhere nearby, he'd hear about it.

I ignored the shot in Hank's hand and put my money on the counter.

"Who the hell do you think you are?" Hank seethed, slamming the glass down, *tequila* splashing across his knuckles.

I couldn't wait any longer. I jumped off the stool, crashing into a chair behind me as I backed away. The man sitting in it cursed in surprise. Hank stood, hand shooting out, meaty fingers locking around my upper arm like a steel trap. Heart pounding, I looked for Mozo. To my dismay, he'd disappeared.

"I paid for that." Hank's scar glowed; a crack lava might flow from. "Sit back down, take off that fucking hat, and drink it."

Think. Take away his rough appearance and language, and he was just a bully, and bullies were best dealt with by standing up to them.

"I don't drink," I spat back, trying to jerk out of his grasp.

"Then what the hell are you doing in *der cantina*?" he demanded, a lopsided sneer revealing the nubs of a few yellowing teeth. "Looking for something else, yes? *Vas?* I am not pretty enough? My money is not good enough?"

His putrid breath swam up my nose, my full stomach roiling. Did he think I was a prostitute?

"I told you; I just came in to eat," I said. If I couldn't get out of his grasp, maybe I did want to draw attention. "Let me go or I'll scream."

"Scream your bloody head off," he scoffed, pulling me against his leg. "Nobody here is going to give a shit."

I scanned the room, searching for an ally, but most of the men either weren't paying attention or appeared amused. The two women by the piano avoided my eyes, the one in the yellow dress no longer laughing.

"You need to learn to be grateful," said Hank. "I have a mind to turn you over this barstool, *fräulein*, and teach you a lesson."

Was he crazy enough to spank me? Or was he implying something worse? Suddenly his free hand slammed onto the back of my neck, fingers digging into my skin as he wrestled me around to face the stool I'd been sitting on. With the strength of a bulldog, he shoved my head down, trying to force me to bend at the waist.

"*Señor* Hank!"

Mozo's voice boomed over the bar as he came out of the back room holding something in his hand. The piano music stopped abruptly. A hush fell over the *cantina*. The men lining the counter rocked back and forth for a good view.

"I do not want any trouble with you, Mr. Hank." Mozo's voice cut the air like a machete. He lifted his arm just enough to show the wooden bat he held. "Let go of the *señorita*, *por favor*, and I will pour you another *tequila*, on the house."

Hank dropped the hand from my neck but tightened his

grip on my arm as I straightened. Mozo came around the counter, marching toward us, but two men stepped in front of him, blocking his path. Chair legs squealed across the concrete floor as people stood, gawking like they were watching a sideshow. Hank turned. He had an audience now.

"Not only does she refuse my *mescal*, she won't take off that goddamn hat." He batted the front brim, knocking the Stetson off my head. Exclamations and catcalls rang out as the loose braid tumbled down my shoulder. I held my chin up, realizing with deepening terror how quickly Hank had managed to win over the crowd. I looked at Mozo. He was struggling against the two men who held his arms. A third was holding his bat. I squirmed, but Hank's fingers only drilled in deeper. If I could have, I would've gnawed my arm off like a snared fox.

People began goading Hank on. He grabbed my braid, using it like a tether to pull me even closer. An image of JJ holding on to Tomás's hair flashed through my mind.

"Let's see what else the whore is hiding!" Hank shouted.

On a wave of encouraging jeers, he seized the collar of my shirt, jerking me forward. Before I knew what was happening, he ripped it open, buttons flying off as his thick hand plunged in. Skin crawling under his groping fingers, I cried out, clawing at his arm, but he dug in farther.

"Guess what I have found?!" he announced, clutching my breast.

I heard cheers as my knees buckled. I sank through myself, wanting to leave my body and disappear. The room spun, my eyes welling with humiliation. This would never have happened at home; Hank would've been dragged outside and shot before he had a chance to go so far. Faces whirled around me, mouths gaping, spewing filthy taunts. What sort of men egged on an assault? If he decided to rape me, would they all watch?

A rush of indignation and disgust rose from my gut like a buoy. I'd seen enough ranch hands horse around to know the one place all men were vulnerable. Gathering my strength, I drove my knee as hard as I could into Hank's groin. He let out a high-pitched bellow, his nails scraping across my chest as his hand jerked away. He folded over, cupping his manhood as if it were about to burst.

Finally free, I tried to run, but rough hands grabbed me. The circle of men squeezed in, yelling slurs, words I'd never heard. I was suffocating.

Hank lifted his head, snarling like a crazed dog.

"You fucking cunt!"

He stood up, cocking his fist back. I couldn't get away, they were all over me, pawing at my chest, trying to shove their hands down my pants, holding me in place. All I could do was turn my head. I screwed my lids shut, already feeling Hank's blow, part of me hoping it would knock me out so I wouldn't know what happened next.

A splintering thud exploded. My eyes flew open. Hank's head snapped sideways. He staggered into the crowd. Several men caught him, propping him up.

"What the hell!" he yelled, wiping his bleeding mouth on his forearm.

"Leave her alone."

I thought Mozo must have broken away from his guards, but the deep, calm voice wasn't his. The sound of it resonated through my body, lighting a dormant spark. I struggled harder.

"Fuck you!" Hank swung his fist, hitting only air as his target ducked away.

Hank's assailant stood with his back to me, his body poised like a boxer's. I took in the width of his shoulders, the strength of his arms. His hand shot out, the punch landing square on Hank's nose with a sickening crunch. The next cracked his jaw, Hank's worn teeth crashing into each other like battering rams. His eyes rolled back, and he dropped to the floor.

Groans and exclamations rose from the spectators. The men let go of me, jockeying to get a look at Hank sprawled on the ground. I yanked my shirt together over my thin camisole. My mother was the only person who'd seen—touched—more of my flesh than these strangers. Like vultures their heads bobbed, eyes bouncing from Hank's limp body to the man who'd knocked him out. Then they looked back at me.

Fresh fear rained down. My single defender would be overpowered if they all jumped me at once. I took a deep, shaky breath, and began to shove through the pack, prepared to fight like a wildcat if anyone tried to stop me.

"Move aside, damnit." That solid, steady voice rose above the mayhem. "Let her pass."

A hand pressed against the small of my back in a familiar way, pushing me forward with gentle strength. Turning to acknowledge his help, I raised my eyes to meet his, as blue-green as the sea. My mouth opened, but months of pushing the name from my head and my heart kept me from saying it out loud.

CHAPTER 9

My body refused to function. Jackson half-pushed, half-carried me through The Mad Rabbit. As if in a nightmare, I registered open mouths and flashing teeth as we shoved past. Disembodied hands tore at my ruined shirt and yanked my braid, jerking my head back so hard I thought my neck would snap. The *cantina* had stretched into a never-ending corridor, a twisted funhouse tunnel. Taunting shouts followed us, muffled by the shell-shocked roar in my ears and Jackson's name reverberating in my head.

Finally, the swinging doors appeared, slapping my arms as we broke out onto the porch. Jackson plowed ahead, but I stumbled, dizzy and disoriented, as if I'd leapt out of a tornado. He steered me over to the outside wall of the *cantina*.

"Get your feet under you," he said. "I can't carry you through town. We don't need any more attention."

I leaned against the rough-hewn wood, holding the ends of my shirt in a wad at my ribs, gulping air. A couple walked by. They were laughing and flirting as if they hadn't a care in the world. The woman glanced sideways at me, her eyes lingering on my torn top. Could she tell I'd been molested on the other side of the wall now holding me up? I turned away, feeling the sting of shame.

"Got your breath yet?" Jackson asked. "We need to go."

Before he could tow me away, increased shouting and the

sound of splintering glass burst from The Mad Rabbit. Two men spilled noisily out of the swinging doors, tumbling into us.

"What the f—well look at that," one of them declared. "That whore's still here!"

I'd never thought a word like that would be hurled at me so many times. I opened my mouth to defend myself but froze. Jackson grabbed my elbow and drew me to his side. He glared at the men until they backed off, grumbling a few more insults as they staggered away.

The air in the plaza was heavy with smells—body odor, *marijuana* smoke, roasting goat from a *cabrito* stand. Jackson led me through the throng of people like a rudderless boat. I clasped my arms tight across my chest and kept my head down. I wanted to make myself small, invisible, but I felt my long blonde hair glowing like a beacon.

As I tucked in behind him, I studied Jackson. He'd changed. His sun-bleached hair had grown long, brushing the tops of his shoulders, and a thick beard covered his jawline. He looked more like a full-grown man than I remembered. He'd always carried himself with a don't-mess-with-me air, but there seemed to be more purpose behind it. People parted as he strode forward. I hastened to keep up with his long strides, trying to ignore the sharp jabs in my knee.

"You limping?" he asked, giving me a swift once-over.

"It's nothing."

The first words I'd spoken to him in a year. Not, "I can't believe you're alive," or "why did you leave," but "it's nothing."

"I assume it's you that's got Rat penned up at *La Fonda*," he stated, clearly not expecting an answer.

At last, we turned off the main street and our path cleared. I recognized the road to the inn, and the banging in my chest began to slow. Thankfully, the reception desk was vacant when we entered, and we didn't have to explain my appearance or why we were together. I followed Jackson up the staircase.

"Which room's yours?" he asked when we reached the landing.

His familiarity made a prickle of irritation skitter down my neck. I was grateful he'd stopped Hank, but now that I was safe, my mixed emotions about him bubbled right back up.

"Don't presume I'm going to let you in my room," I said.

"You walked into a bar full of drunk strangers," he scoffed, "and you're worried about being alone with me?"

Before I could form a response, the chink of metal spurs rang out from below as someone walked across the lobby's Saltillo tile. A man's voice floated up the stairs, calling out for assistance.

"We could've been followed," whispered Jackson, glowering at the stairwell like he expected someone to charge up it any minute. "We'd be a hell of a lot safer behind a closed door."

The contorted faces in the *cantina* rose before me, chilling my desire to prove some useless point to him. I led him down the hallway and unlocked my door. As soon as it shut behind us, his chin jutted out the way it always had when he was mad.

"What the hell were you doing in there, Sarita?"

"You'd know if you hadn't run away," I snapped.

"What's me leaving got to do with you wandering into a *cantina* alone?" he asked. "You had no business doing something so reckless. Did you lose your mind over the past year?"

The smug look on his face filled my vision. Something in my chest released like a wound-up spring. I drew my hand back and slapped him with twelve months' worth of resentment, sorrow, and worry. He jerked away, bumping into the door behind him, as a red imprint of my fingers surfaced on his face.

"I guess I should've expected that from you," he said, reaching up to touch the mark with a grin. "I probably deserve it."

His smile taunted me. I wanted to yell at him, to tell him what I'd been through since he'd gone. I wanted a fight.

Instead, Jackson walked over to the water pitcher, picked up the washcloth, and soaked a corner of it.

"You're bleeding," he said, gesturing at my chest.

I looked down. A flare of embarrassment traveled across my cheeks. I'd forgotten about the shredded shirt. It was hanging open from my shoulders to my waist, blood seeping into the top of my camisole from four long gouges in my chest.

Jackson came to stand in front of me. He gently wiped the scratches, his face softening. Even through the damp cloth, his touch sent goosebumps down my arms. He was barely a breath away. I'd thought I might never be this close to him again. We'd shared our first kiss when he'd proposed, the warmth and softness of it dwelling in my heart even after he'd left. It would be so easy to lift my chin and press my lips to his. I moved away before desire overwhelmed me, and tugged the shirt closed, tying the ends together.

"I'll do it." I took the washcloth from him and placed it over the cuts.

"You should have the old woman downstairs, Griselda, look at those," he said. "She's a healer."

I didn't want his advice; I wanted his apology.

"Just because you got me away from some drunk who was a little out of control doesn't mean you don't owe me an explanation."

"A little out of control?" Jackson's hands sat on his hips, his chin pointing at me again. "Hank would've done whatever he wanted if I hadn't stepped in. He's the mayor's strong arm; no one would have stopped him. They would have watched or joined in. Going in that bar was foolish. It was irresponsible."

"You've got no right to scold me." I brushed the rag too hard across my chest, the sting reminding me that he did have a point. I had been stupid to walk into that bar. I was lucky he'd been there, but there were a lot of things I wanted to express to him other than gratitude. "You left, Jackson. You abandoned me and your family. You're the one who's irresponsible."

His shoulders slumped.

"It's not like that," he said, his voice lowering.

"What is it like, then?"

He paused, then walked over to the window, drawing the curtain aside to look out, his reticence reminding me of his grandfather.

"I am sorry for leaving the way I did, Sarita," he said, looking up at the stars instead of at me. "It couldn't be helped."

"If that's your apology, it's the sorriest one I ever heard," I replied. "You owe me some answers. Start with why you're in Hidalgo."

"I could ask you the same thing." He turned to meet my glare. "Did you come here looking for me?"

"I gave up on you months ago," I said. "I figured you'd either run away like a coward, or you were dead."

His brow furrowed, the wisp of hurt in his eyes pleasing me.

"Did my grandfather send you?" he asked after a beat. "Is that why you've got his horse?"

I shook my head.

"Then what the hell possessed you to come to Mexico?" he demanded.

The reason floated over me, trailing grief behind it like a kite tail. There was no way to tell Jackson about JJ without being vulnerable, but at least then he'd understand why I was in Hidalgo. I sat down heavily on the edge of the bed.

"What's happened, Sarita?" The honest care that had seeped into his voice almost undid me. I kept my eyes on the floor. I'd dissolve if I looked at him.

"Two *tequileros* came through our ranch. They wanted horses," I said. "One of them killed JJ."

He sat down next to me, pulling me into his arms. A sob elbowed its way up my throat, and I couldn't stop the tears.

I started to wipe them away, to try to stuff down my emotions as I had with everyone else, but it was Jackson. I'd spoken freely to him about running the ranch, about how unfair it was that I had to care for JJ, about Papa's refusal to see me as anything other than a cook and caregiver. If anyone could understand how JJ's death affected me—the anguish and regret and guilt—it was Jackson. My resolve gave way like snow in the sun, and the past three days poured out of me, soaking the front of his shirt.

"My God, Sarita," he said, when I got myself under control.

I pulled away and searched his face, relieved to see tears and real sadness.

"Nobody would do anything," I said. "The sheriff's off after a different gang. Your brother had to go with him. Clyde brought the Rangers out before he left, but they're too busy to help."

"I can't imagine what this has done to your father."

"He had another spell. Dr. Andrew says he should get some tests done, but Papa won't go."

"That doesn't surprise me," said Jackson with a sad smile. "He's as strong-willed as he is tough."

"He wanted to chase Captain Wright to Laredo, even though he could barely stand," I said. "I had to do something before he kills himself trying to get help, or else decides to give it all up."

"Give all what up?"

"The ranch," I said. "Burr Archer's been coming around trying to buy it."

Clouds scudded across Jackson's face.

"When was Burr last at La Barroneña?"

"Two days ago, after he heard about JJ," I replied. "He wanted Papa to know his purchase offer still stands."

"Damn bastard," Jackson hissed. "Don't ever let Burr Archer in your house again, Sarita."

He'd taken on a protective tone. Normally, I would've stiffened at it, but nothing about the last few days had been normal. In that moment, his concern felt reassuring, like someone finally understood my side.

"Papa's always turned Burr down flat before, but now that JJ's gone ..." I looked up at him. "Papa has never believed I could run the ranch. I need to prove him wrong before Burr comes back. That's why I'm here. To show my father he can count on me."

"I'm not following you," Jackson said.

"I need to make sure JJ's murderer doesn't get away; to make sure he faces justice."

He grew so still he seemed to stop breathing.

"Who killed JJ?" he asked.

"Javier Salsito de Ortega."

Jackson recoiled like he'd been stung by a wasp. He bounced off the bed and strode back to the window, taking the familiar sense of closeness with him.

"What makes you think it was him?" His voice sounded thin and strained.

"He shot JJ right in front of me," I said, the scene floating through my head like black smoke. "Clyde told me your grandfather knew who Javier was, so I went to talk to him, to get his advice. He lent me his horse and told me to come here."

"The Captain is not the advice-giving, horse-loaning type," Jackson said. "Why would he agree to help you?"

I didn't want to tell him about the deal, fearing it would water down my motives, but Gus and I had shaken on it.

"He wanted me to give you a message ... if I saw you."

Jackson let out a short, miffed chuckle.

"Well, now the pieces are falling together," he said. "Whether you realize it or not, you were sent here to find me."

"I was clear with Gus that I wasn't going to look for you."

"When the cork-pullers clear out, this town's got more stray dogs and goats than people. He knew we'd run into each other," he said. "I suspect my grandfather was more interested in using you as bait to get me home than in helping you find Javier."

A chill flushed through me. Had Gus set me up? Had he thought Jackson would feel duty-bound to take me home? Had he sent me to The Mad Rabbit hoping—knowing—there would be trouble, betting on Jackson having to rescue me? If so, I'd played right into his 'damsel in distress' scheme.

"I can see that mind of yours churning," said Jackson, sitting down on the chair. "What's his message?"

I stared at him, the self-satisfied look on his face evaporating any attraction I'd felt earlier. If he was right, I'd accepted Gus's deal under false pretenses, but I'd keep my end of the bargain—if only to watch it irritate Jackson.

"'I understand, but it's time to come home.'"

As I repeated the words, Jackson's assumption seemed even more likely.

"Goddamn it." The color in his bronzed cheeks deepened as he shook his head. "He had no right to put you at risk, Sarita."

"He didn't *put* me at risk. I came here of my own accord."

"Well, you can't stay," he said. "This town is no place for a woman, especially a white woman poking around asking questions."

I forced myself not to react, to stay still and think for a moment. Maybe it was true that Gus had his own motives, but he hadn't lied to me. The Mad Rabbit was a real place. Mozo really was the bartender there, and it was plausible he knew something useful about Javier.

"I'm not going, and I won't be 'poking around,'" I said. "Give me some credit and stop acting like being a woman is a handicap."

"It is," Jackson stated. "Did you learn nothing from what just happened? You might have more brains than most men, but it's not about how smart you are. It's not about your ability to shoot or hunt or ride, either. It's about plain physical facts. Most men here don't care about social niceties. They think women are only good for one thing, and they'll damn well prove it if they have to."

As his words sank in, I knew they were valid. I wanted to think I could've fought Hank off, but physically I'd been no match for him or the other men. Brute strength wasn't on my side, especially when outnumbered.

"You've got no idea what's going on here," continued Jackson, the veins in his neck pulsing. "You need to leave, for your own good and the good of others. Trust me."

"Trust you?" His self-righteousness was getting to me; my voice sounded shrill. I jumped to my feet, stabbing a finger at him. "You made promises; we made plans. You asked me to marry you then vanished like a ghost. Why would I trust you?"

"Keep your voice down," Jackson said, glancing at the closed door as if someone might be listening on the other side. "I don't need any more trouble before you leave."

"I am not leaving." I planted both feet on the ground and crossed my arms.

"Good God, Sarita, this is no time to be stubborn."

"Stubborn?" The word stung. "That's what you think I'm being?"

My arms dropped to my sides.

"I held JJ while he bled to death, Jackson." I looked into his face, searching for the compassion I'd seen there earlier. "My father is in such deep despair he's considering selling the one thing that's ever mattered to him. He's sick, his heart is literally broken. He's clinging to the hope he'll see retribution for his son's death. I am that hope. There will be no justice for my family if I give up."

Jackson stood and walked over to me, resting a hand gently on my waist.

"I understand better than you might think," he said softly, "but I'm begging you to get on Rat at daybreak and go home."

His touch no longer gave me butterflies; it prickled like nettles. I shrugged away from him.

"Why aren't you offering to help me?"

He looked down at the floor briefly. When he lifted his head, his jaw was set firm.

"I'd best go if I can't convince you to." He took several steps backward toward the door. "We shouldn't be seen together."

"We've already been seen together." I smirked. "You cold-cocked a drunk and dragged me through a mob."

He bent his arm to look at the swollen, purple knuckles of his right hand.

"That might've been a mistake," he muttered.

My mouth dropped open. He'd gotten me out of The Mad Rabbit with most of my virtue intact, and he regretted it? The more he said, the closer I came to disliking him. Maybe I'd been better off thinking he might be dead.

"You told me those men only wanted one thing, which, by the way, I don't need you to spell out for me. Now you wish you'd just stood by and let it happen?"

"Of course not!" Jackson drew back like I'd bitten him. "That's not what I meant. You know me, Sarita."

The green of his eyes had deepened to the color of summer storm clouds. Had I gone too far? As much as I'd been raised to protect my honor, he'd been raised to defend it. His reaction allowed me another glimpse of the old Jackson, but it was brief. I still had so many questions.

"I'm not sure I do know you," I said.

He let out a frustrated sigh.

"Whether you know me or not, or trust me or not, you should listen to me," he said. "If it had been Javier in that bar, you'd be dead or wish you were. Steer clear of him."

"I can't let him get away with killing my brother."

"Suit yourself," he said, head hanging like a worn-out steer, "but you should know this: Villa Hidalgo is made up of two types of people: the ones with money and power, and the ones who work for them. Whichever they are, they protect their own self-interest at all costs. You're not in Hebbronville anymore," he went on. "The lines between good and bad are merely suggestions here. If you stay long enough, you'll find yourself crossing those lines in ways you've never imagined."

Without another look, he yanked the door open and strode out, leaving me to wonder what lines Jackson himself had crossed.

CHAPTER 10

The room brightened as the sun rose. I had not slept well, every sound reminding me of Jackson's concern that we'd been followed. I'd kept imagining a figure—one of the men from the bar— climbing through the open window. I'd finally closed it, then I spent the rest of the night in a sticky film of sweat.

I sat up on the side of the cot, trying to push Jackson and all his warnings from my mind. If Gus had sent me to Hidalgo to retrieve his grandson, his plan had failed. Jackson had told me to go home, but not once had he offered to escort me there. He hadn't offered to help me at all. I thought he'd cared about JJ and Papa. Once upon a time they would have been his in-laws, but he'd only fleetingly acknowledged the tragedy that had befallen my family.

There were fresh stains along the top of my camisole. The deep scratches had barely started to scab. They pulsed; red and hot. I could only imagine what lived beneath Hank's fingernails. When I stood, the muscles in my legs threatened to cramp. I walked over to the washstand, picking up Griselda's ointment. I smeared some on my chest then rubbed it into my neck, which was sore and stiff from being whipped back and forth by the men in the bar, and certainly bruised where Hank had squeezed it. His fingers had also left a deep purple bracelet around my upper arm.

I shuffled to the window, drew the curtain aside, and pushed the sash up. A cool breeze flowed in. As I looked down at Rat lazing under a live oak in the corral below, a sense of comfort twirled through me. When I'd been in grade school, the schoolhouse had burned down. After it had been rebuilt, our teacher told us we should always have an exit plan in case another emergency arose. Rat was my exit plan. Despite insisting to Jackson that I wouldn't leave, as long as I had a horse, I could.

I tilted my ear to the open window. The town was quiet except for the soft *hoo-hoo* of mourning doves and the distant crowing of a few roosters. Sunday mornings came early at home, getting chores done so we could arrive at church on time. Papa often found a reason not to go—busted windmill pipe, renegade bull, an errand in another town. He claimed he didn't need to be in a building to pray. I'd made JJ go with me, though it had been a struggle. I hoped God had recognized him when he got to Heaven. I wanted to believe in the image of a kindly grandfather embracing his children.

I'd put on a good show for Jackson, but I had no idea what to do next. I'd been in Hidalgo for three days and made no progress. In fact, I'd accomplished the opposite of progress. I couldn't go back to The Mad Rabbit to talk to Mozo. I wasn't even sure I could leave the room without being recognized. I clearly needed the guidance of someone familiar with Hidalgo, but I hadn't made contact with Alicia yet, either. On top of all that, I was a mess. I'd been sore, hurt, and tired after the river, but I was worse off now. Even the back of my head was tender from Hank and his *compadres* using my braid like a leash.

I looked at my faint reflection in the glass of the window. My unbound hair fluttered around my arms like a veil, but instead of concealing me, it made me more noticeable. I plaited the long strands and walked to the chair where the buck knife—uselessly strapped to my leg while I'd been attacked—lay. I picked it up and unsheathed it. Pulling the braid tight, I placed the blade at the top of it, near the nape of my neck, and began sawing back and forth. My eyes watered as it snagged on knotted strands, pain prickling across my bruised scalp. It was more difficult than expected—I had to stop several times to uncramp my hand—but finally the thick blonde cord separated and fell to the floor.

My remaining hair settled just below my ears in a sort of jagged bob. It felt strange as I ran my fingers through it, shivering slightly when a gentle gust blew across the back of my now naked neck. I expected a surge of regret. Instead, I felt lighter.

A knock on the door startled me and I dropped the knife. Had Hank come to finish what he'd started? I felt a surge of adrenaline and looked out the window. How far was it to the ground? Could I jump out?

"*Señorita?*"

The male voice didn't sound threatening, but I kept quiet.

"It is me, Mozo."

I relaxed a bit, though surprised he was there. Maybe he wanted to chastise me for causing problems in his bar.

"What do you want?" I asked.

"I have your hat," he said. "*Señora* Griselda told me which room was yours."

I pulled on my pants and shirt, then picked up the knife. I opened the door a crack. Mozo stood in the dusky hallway alone, holding JJ's Stetson.

"I wanted to be sure you are all right, *señorita*," he said. "Is it okay if I come in?"

Several thoughts ran through my head. Gus trusted Mozo— although I wasn't sure I still trusted Gus. Would Griselda have told him which one was my room if he were a bad man? Lastly, I still needed his help locating Alicia.

I pulled the door wider for him to enter.

"I am Enrique, by the way," he said as he walked in, "but

everyone calls me Mozo."

"I'm Sarita."

"*Con mucho gusto.*" He bowed his head as if meeting me for the first time. When he lifted it, I noted a purple welt under one eye. I also noticed he was wearing a gun belt around his waist instead of an apron.

"I'm so sorry about last night," I said. "I understand if you're upset with me."

"*Pues,* fights in the *cantina* are nothing new," he said. "If those men want to beat each other, I do not stand in the way, but what they try to do to you ... *Dios mío* ... that was not right, and it was not your fault."

I took a deep breath. Jackson had chastised me for even walking into the *cantina,* as if I'd deserved what had happened. It was true I'd made a mistake, but Mozo's sympathy was refreshing.

"What happened to your long hair?" he asked.

I looked down at the knife I still held. "I cut it off."

His kind eyes dropped from my hair to the bruises on my neck, then to the top of the scratches visible at the neckline of my shirt.

"I have been feeling very bad. I could not stop them," Mozo said, his voice a little shaky. "Hank's men, they—"

"I know you tried, Mozo," I said. "Thank you."

He nodded, handing me the hat. I set it down on the bed, along with the knife.

"It is good Jackson arrived when he did," he said with a spreading smile. "He is young and strong; I am old and fat!"

I peered at him with renewed interest. He knew Jackson's name. Jackson had said that without the visitors, Hidalgo was not very big. Everybody probably knew everybody. Would Jackson have to explain why he'd knocked Hank out instead of joining in like the rest of the men? Is that what he'd meant about making a mistake?

"How long have you known Jackson?" I asked.

"He came here sometimes with his father and grandfather when he was a boy," said Mozo. "You know him from Hebbronville?"

Something about Mozo made me want to open up. A degree of thoughtful shrewdness lay behind his cheery expression; I suspected it would be difficult to hide things from him. His concern for my welfare seemed sincere, and I didn't feel I could ask for his help without being honest.

"Jackson and I were supposed to get married about a year ago," I said. "Before you ask, I didn't come here to find him."

"*Pues*," he chuckled, "it is lucky he found you!"

I smiled at him. I appreciated his making light of what had happened instead of dwelling on how much worse it could have been.

"Do you know what Jackson is doing in Hidalgo?" I asked.

"Getting rich like *todo el mundo*." Mozo shrugged his shoulders as if this were too common to have to explain. Then he squinted at me. "Tell me, why did you choose *El Conejo Loco* if you did not know Alicia was my cook and you were not looking for Jackson? There are quieter places to eat."

"I was looking for you," I said.

Mozo's bushy brows floated up briefly. He paused, glancing out the window as the light shifted.

"On Sundays, I serve *cabrito*," he said.

"The *cantina* is open on Sundays?" I asked, wondering what the menu had to do with our conversation.

"Of course, but not until afternoon." He winked. "People are extra hungry after a morning of church."

I smiled at his humor, assuming he meant after sleeping off their Saturday night.

"I am on my way to Alicia's to finish the meat and help with the rest of the food. The kitchen in the *cantina* is really just a fireplace," he said. "You come with me. You can tell me what you need on the way, then you can have a reunion with your friend."

Eager to find out if Gus had sent me on a wild goose chase or not, and longing to see Alicia, I quickly finished dressing. I was grateful to have the Stetson back. I'd changed the length of my hair, but I couldn't change the color.

"I left the kids with *Señora* Griselda," Mozo said as we walked down the stairs.

I had a vision of us herding baby goats through town, which would not be a good way to stay unnoticed, but Griselda was waiting in the lobby with a large burlap sack. Juice dripped from the bottom, and it smelled like smoke. Mozo must have already grilled the hind quarters of the goats for his *cabrito*. I was grateful he hadn't brought the messy bag up to my room.

After Griselda handed the sack to Mozo, she looked me over. Noticing the raw scratches, she made a tsking sound with her tongue.

"*Espérame.*" She went into a room behind the desk and came back with a yellowish-brown tincture in a glass vial. "*Para infección.*"

She turned me around so my back was to Mozo. In the matter-of-fact manner I'd noticed before, she unbuttoned my shirt and swabbed the anti-infection medicine onto my chest with a soft cloth. Its bite was sharp, making me inhale. She pursed her lips and blew on the area. The act startled me, but I reminded myself that she was used to helping people. It was probably something my mother would have done. After a few seconds the sting lessened, and she stopped.

"*Muchas gracias.*" As I buttoned my shirt back up, I noticed the tincture had stained the skin on my chest a golden-brown.

She stared at the ragged ends of my hair. I wondered what she must think of me. I'd shown up alone, battered, and smelling like the bottom of the river. Now my hair had been chopped off, I sported fresh bruises and wounds, and I was leaving with Mozo and his bag of goats. More than likely, she knew what had happened in The Mad Rabbit. Her keen eyes and the shiny tufts of gray in her black hair reminded me of a titmouse—spry and watchful. I doubted there was much she missed.

She held the vial out to me. When I took it, she wrapped my hand in hers.

"*Ten mucho cuidado, señorita*," she said. Her tone was not menacing. She was telling me to be careful out of concern, not delivering a warning. Again, I wondered what she knew.

The humid air outside smelled fresh, as if it had been laundered overnight. The town hadn't been so free of people since I'd arrived. It was a little eerie, like walking into an abandoned house or a vacant theater. I was grateful not to have to deal with the stares of strangers, but still glad to have Mozo and his gun by my side.

We crossed the paved main street into the plaza. The *centro* lay open like an empty jewel box, its border of orange trees shimmering with dew. It was still very early, but whatever trash had been left the night before had already been cleaned up. Without the nocturnal zoo, the square appeared quaint and welcoming. Hidalgo must have been a lovely *pueblo* before Prohibition brought in prosperity and all its chaos.

Mozo cleared his throat.

"What is it I can do for you, Sarita?"

I took a deep breath and explained why Captain Cage had told me to find him. When I finished, Mozo raised his face to the sky, as if searching for guidance. I found myself willing him to know something useful and praying he would tell me.

"*Pues, El Capitán* might be right," Mozo said finally, "lately the *tequileros* have been stirred up about something. I am not sure what, something *más grande*."

A tingle sped through me.

"Could it be drugs?" I asked. "My mother told me a lot of veterans became addicted to the cocaine in pain medicines and can't get it legally anymore."

"*Sí*," he said with a nod, "but the *contrabandistas* have already been taking *marijuana, coca, y opio* across the river with the *tequila*."

Mozo threw the bag of kids over his shoulder.

"No, this is new," he continued. "The mood in the *cantina* has been much more *tenso*."

We reached the other side of the plaza. I located The Mad Rabbit a block away. In the fresh morning light, it looked like any old building, although the image on the sign made me twitch. It could be a blunt characterization of the men who'd been there the night before. Were all the patrons of the bar bandits and smugglers?

"Do you own the *cantina*?" I asked.

"My father left it to me," he said. "He started it as a small store. *Papá* used to hide *tequila*, sugar, and fabric in his wagon, so he did not have to pay taxes when he went back and forth over the border. No one cared, he was not hurting anybody, and he sold it for cheaper that way. Now, after the revolution and the war, things are much more serious. Whatever Javier is doing, he must think it is worth the risk."

We turned off the main street and entered a maze of narrow roads. A church bell began to ring, echoing through the quiet neighborhood.

"Does Javier come into the bar often?" I asked.

"Mostly only when he comes through town on his way to their *campo*," Mozo said.

"Where is their camp?"

"*La Sierra Madre*," he said. "In the foothills above *La Villa de Múzquiz*, a little town near Sabinas. No one is supposed to know it is there, but the *tequileros* forget I have ears when they are drinking. Whisky makes the brain quiet and the mouth loud."

"Do they make the *tequila* there?"

"No, no. You need *agave* plants; they grow in the south. The *mezcalistas* make it and bring it to the camp. Then the *tequileros* take it across the *Rio Bravo* to *Tejas* where *los gringos* buy it." Mozo chuckled. "Everybody is working together!"

As we traveled farther from the square, the buildings

became sparser and more rustic. After a few blocks, we entered a quarter of small adobe homes lining both sides of a dusty lane. The path had so many bumps and potholes I doubted an automobile could drive down it. Most of the houses had been decorated and painted in hues of red, yellow, or blue, the colors starting to fade. Their flat roofs were thatch mixed with clay, though some were made only of rusted metal. Chickens roamed freely around us; dogs lifted their heads as we walked past.

Mozo's gaze roved over the surroundings as a few people—mostly women and children—began to appear, perhaps making their way to the church. He shifted the bag to his other shoulder.

"It is hard to see things changing here," he said. "People like Javier are a plague on this town. We are all infected by him. Even my uncle, the mayor. My father would be very sad."

It was difficult to imagine Mozo, with his resemblance to Saint Nick, had a relative who would associate with men like Javier and Hank.

"Are you close to your uncle?"

"I was like his son growing up," he said. "When he became mayor, he changed. I understand he must make hard choices—he can work with Javier and his kind or be threatened by them—but there is more he could do to protect people. He is not strong enough. He likes *la requeza* too much."

We stopped in front of a tan house with a wooden door painted turquoise. I reached out and placed a hand on Mozo's arm, certain he knew more than he'd told me so far.

"I think you would like to be rid of Javier, too," I said. "Can you help me?"

"I do not know you, Sarita," he said, not unkindly, "but I know *El Capitán*. Gus Cage would not send you to me without considering the risk. Make no mistake, though, you need to be very cautious."

"I understand."

Mozo glanced around.

"This is what I can tell you; there is an old mission in Villa de Múzquiz, Santa Rosa de Lima," he said in a hushed voice. "I think Javier is hiding something there."

Before he could say another word, the blue door flew open.

CHAPTER 11

Alicia stormed out of the house, chickens scattering in front of her. She marched up to Mozo, big, inky eyes flashing, her thick chestnut-colored hair hanging down to her waist in a disheveled mass of curls. One side of her long brown dress was tucked into a leather belt at her waist. Beneath the hem, chalky dust covered the rounded toes of knee-high black boots. She didn't even glance at me, her gaze locked on Mozo.

"Where is my brother?" she demanded. "He didn't come home last night."

"I don't know about last night," replied Mozo, "but he is supposed to be cleaning the *cantina* this morning."

"I was just there," Alicia said. "The *Conejo* is a mess, and Carlos is nowhere to be seen."

"That boy," Mozo said with a sigh. "His good intentions have led him to bad choices."

"I don't care about his intentions," she snapped. "I need to know where he is."

"You do know, Alicia," said Mozo somberly. "I am sorry, I have tried to keep him busy, but once the taste of real money crosses the tongue, it is hard not to want more."

Alicia put her hands on her round hips. I thought she'd throw out more curt words, but she started to cry instead.

"He has fancy new boots, Mozo. We had another fight," she said between sobs. "He's going to get caught. He's going to rot in jail. When I try to talk to him, he says all I do is complain."

Mozo put a comforting arm around her shoulders.

"I know you are scared for him, *m'ija*," he said, then gestured my way. "Look, I brought someone I think will cheer you up."

Alicia finally looked closely at me.

"Sarita?!" She grabbed my waist in a surprisingly strong embrace for her petite frame. We squeezed each other for a few seconds, then she studied me at arm's length. "What happened to your hair? And why are you dressed like a boy? You are all bruised and scratched. Have you been in a fight?"

A smile tugged at my lips. I'd almost forgotten her rapid-fire way of speaking, especially when excited.

"There is a lot to tell you," I said, my smile dimming.

"Let's get inside and start the cooking," Mozo interrupted. "I need to get to the *cantina* to clean if Carlos is not coming."

"When I find him, I'm going to tie him up so he can't go anywhere," Alicia announced. "He can live in the closet. I'll bring him food and water. At least then he'll be safe."

"I tell her to stay out of it," Mozo said to me, "but she does not listen."

"He's my responsibility," Alicia said. "What am I supposed to do?"

Carlos was only a couple years older than JJ. I knew what a burden feeling responsible for your younger brother could be. I'd give anything to have the weight of it back.

I reached out to take the burlap sack from Mozo.

"I can carve the meat and help Alicia with the rest of the food," I said. "Go put your *cantina* back together. It's the least I can do since I'm the reason it's such a wreck."

"What's she talking about?" Alicia asked Mozo.

"Hank and his men," Mozo replied.

"That explains your shiner," said Alicia. She raised one

brow and waved at my neck and chest. "Did they do all that?"

I nodded.

"What is wrong with the stupid men in this town?" she exclaimed. "Mozo, you are the only decent one. Even my brother has gone bad."

Mozo left and I followed Alicia through a cozy main room with a kiva fireplace in the corner. I saw two bedrooms down a short hallway on my right. As far as I knew there were four people living there: Alicia and Carlos, and their mother and grandmother. The kitchen was in the back. It was large for the size of the house. A table and four stools were on the left. On the far wall was a door, which opened into a small courtyard. A cast iron stove sat next to the exit, its chimney pipe sticking out through a hole in the ceiling.

Along the other side of the room was a narrow wooden counter with two drawers and an attached shelf below. A water bucket had been placed in a hole at one end, so the opening was flush with the surface. Piles of tomatoes, onions, garlic, avocados, *jalapeños*, and bunches of fresh cilantro covered the countertop. There was also a big bowl of corn soaking in water with slices of lime floating on top.

I pulled the three hind quarters from the bag and set them on the counter as the smell of grilled meat and mesquite filled the room. Alicia lifted a large carving knife out of a drawer and handed it to me.

"I remember watching you clean a goat at your house," she said with a grin.

"I remember watching you throw up."

We both laughed.

"Well, it had been a pet just the day before," Alicia said.

"Are you going to be sick now?" I asked.

"Those are already cooked," she said with a shrug. "It's the blood and guts that get me."

I placed one of the goats flat on the surface and began

cutting the meat off the bones.

Alicia bent to take a basalt mortar and pestle—a *molcajete* and *tejolote*—off the shelf. She placed them at the end of the table near the water bucket and soaking corn. The meat was warm and juicy, and the drippings began streaming off the table as I sliced, splashing onto the concrete floor. Alicia handed me a towel to clean it up with, then placed handfuls of soaked corn into the *molcajete*. We worked in silence for a few minutes, but the air felt heavy, as if we both had much to say but neither knew where to start.

"What is Carlos doing?" I asked finally.

She let out a long sigh, but she stayed focused on her task.

"He is working for a gang of *tequileros*," she said, as she ground corn with the *tejolote*. "Smugglers, led by a very evil redhead."

"Javier?" I asked.

She froze then looked at me. "How do you know him?"

As I told her about JJ's murder and all that happened since, Alicia wept quietly. Our families had been close, and she'd always had a tender spot for JJ, but I suspected concern about Carlos was making her even more sensitive. Her brother wasn't messing around with a bunch of teenagers making a few extra *pesos* by carting *tequila* over the border; he was involved in organized crime. I put the knife down and hugged her.

"I should be comforting you," she said when we parted. She picked up a clean kitchen towel and wiped her face.

"You've got good reason to be worried about Carlos," I said.

The next thought that entered my head turned my stomach. Alicia's brother worked for the man who'd murdered mine. No direct connection likely existed between Carlos and JJ's death, but even that he spoke to Javier, or did his bidding, or took his filthy, ill-gotten money made me queasy.

"Why would Carlos do something so foolhardy?" I asked.

"Isn't he smart enough to know better?"

Alicia's small hand wrapped around the *tejolote* so tightly that her knuckles glowed white.

"My mother has consumption," she said after a pause. "She hid it for months. By the time we took her to the doctor in Nuevo Laredo she had become very ill. He said we needed to send her to the sanatorium in El Paso, but they wanted three months of payment in advance. We didn't even have enough money to buy her the train ticket. We brought her home, hoping the doctor was wrong and she'd get better.

"The coughing was terrible," she went on. "She could barely breathe. Carlos couldn't stand it. He kept yelling at my grandmother and me to do something." Alicia paused, drying her tears again. "One morning, he stormed out of the house before daylight. When he returned that night, he had enough money to pay for the train ticket and the whole treatment."

I felt her words in my soul. Watching my mother suffer with influenza had torn me apart. I'd felt helpless as she'd shivered through the night with fever, only to soak the sheets in sweat by noon. I'd tried to keep her comfortable—bathing her, feeding her. I'd read to her for hours to take her mind off the pain. I'd begged Dr. Andrew for a miracle, but there had been no place to send her, no cure that could save her. I would have done anything for her if I'd had the chance.

I had judged Carlos too harshly. Like him, I'd chosen to act now that Papa was ill, instead of having to watch him slowly die as Mama had.

"I understand taking chances to help people you love," I said.

"I was grateful at first," Alicia said, "but we sent *Mamá* to El Paso more than a month ago. Since then, Carlos has been disappearing for days at a time with no explanation." She let out a frustrated huff. "Mozo finally told me what he's doing."

"What exactly?" I couldn't imagine a job the *tequileros* would entrust to a fifteen-year-old, or how Carlos could work with such dangerous men. Even Tomás, as old and wizened as he'd appeared, had cowed as he'd followed Javier's orders.

"Among other things, he packs *tequila* then leads a string of loaded mules and burros to the river, where he transfers the bottles onto rafts and floats them across," Alicia explained. "Then he swims the animals over, reloads them on the other side, and takes them to his contact."

"He could drown." I'd barely gotten across the river with Rat, never mind a mule train and several rafts weighed down with *tequila* bottles. "He could get caught by the border patrol."

"I know," said Alicia, her chin trembling. "If *Mamá* comes home only to find her son has been locked up in jail, or something worse, it will devastate her. I should never have let him do this."

"He didn't ask your permission," I replied, even though I knew it wouldn't lesson her guilt. I hadn't asked JJ to protect me, but still felt responsible for what had happened to him. "You didn't know what he was doing."

"I knew the money was tainted," she admitted, color seeping into her cheeks. "No one gets that much that quickly in an honest way, but I thought it was a onetime thing. I thought he'd done whatever he had to do to help our mother, and that was it. Never did I imagine he'd traded his whole life away to become a *contrabandista*." Alicia clunked the stone against the counter. "He's just a stupid kid. They can't really force him to be a bootlegger forever, can they?"

I wanted to say no, to go down that trail of hope with her, to tell her everything would be all right, but that would be a lie. Carlos owed a man who didn't play by the rules. The *tequileros* probably needed all the manpower they could wrangle to transport contraband—men, women, children; they wouldn't care who they used. The more they moved, the more money they made. Carlos was a young, strong boy who'd indebted himself to the wrong people.

"Those men are capable of anything," I said. "JJ was only

thirteen, and Javier murdered him over a horse."

As soon as the words were out, I wished I hadn't been so direct. The gusto Alicia had worked up evaporated, her small frame caving in. I'd forgotten for a moment that behind those flashing eyes was a scared sister.

"I don't mean to frighten you."

"No, you're right." Her voice was just above a whisper. "I knew Carlos was in even more danger than I'd thought the minute you said Javier had killed JJ."

She sat down on a stool.

"They aren't just using him to move their contraband; they are changing his thinking. They have convinced him that *Papá* was a fool. That he did the right thing his whole life for nothing," she said. "Carlos claims that the rich *gringos'* cattle trampled our father into the ground then they kicked us out of the country with nothing." Alicia shook her head. "I know *Tejano* and Mexican families have been taken advantage of, but that's not what happened to us. Carlos and I were born in Hebbronville; we are citizens. We came to Mexico because *Mamá* needed her family. Then she got sick, and we had to stay. He talks like all Americans are out to get us."

"A common enemy creates strange bonds," I said, thinking how chickens and hawks will fight off a snake together.

"How am I going to get him away from them?" she asked. "Mozo says they gain loyalty with favors and money, but also with threats. They won't let him just walk away; it would be a bad example. I need help, but I don't know who to turn to, who I can trust. I tried talking to Jackson, but that was a dead end."

"Jackson?" I asked, sitting on the stool across from her. "What's he got to do with the *tequileros*?"

Alicia paused, frowning. I felt a tug in my gut.

"In the last letter you sent me, you wrote that you two were engaged," she said, sitting up straighter. "Then Jackson showed up in Hidalgo alone. I didn't think it would take this long for you to come get him."

"I didn't come here to get him," I stated firmly. Would I be repeating that forever? "I had no idea where he was until last night."

"*Pendejo*," Alicia snapped, her spark returning. "I wanted to write and ask what was going on, but then I saw how he acted, and I was glad you weren't here. He's in the *cantina* all the time, drinking and smoking cigars with the *contrabandistas*, his new *compadres*."

"Why would he befriend a bunch of bandits?"

"Most likely because he's one of them."

Alicia made the statement as if it were a natural conclusion, just as Mozo had theorized that Jackson was in Hidalgo to get rich.

"That doesn't make sense," I countered. "His father and grandfather were Texas Rangers; his brother is a deputy sheriff. He comes from a family of men who uphold the law, not break it."

"Don't you remember what a rabble-rouser he was when we were younger?" she asserted. "There was that snake, and the fire? He was always causing trouble."

"He settled down after he went to live with his grandfather," I argued. "Gus needs Jackson to run Stillwater Wash, especially since Clyde is the deputy sheriff now. Why would Jackson give up a good future to become a smuggler?"

"You just can't see past his pretty face." Alicia smirked. "Maybe he's like Carlos, seduced by their talk and all their cash. It's not only Mexicans running *tequila*, you know. Plenty of Anglos turn a blind eye when mule trains cross their land. They put hidden openings in their own fences for a payoff. Some even start selling *tequila* themselves. I see them in town, making deals with the smugglers. Money makes people stupid."

Something niggled at the back of my mind. I'd seen the state of Stillwater Wash when I'd gone to talk to Gus. Jackson had planned to make improvements to the land and the structures, to invest in windmills and machinery, and build up the cattle herd. How would he pay for those things?

Did Jackson need cash? Not for the sake of being rich, but to invest in his family's ranch? Gus's medical bills had to have been significant, and then he'd had to retire. At the time, Jackson had been at the University of Texas in Austin. He'd come home after one semester because college came with expenses, and Gus had needed him. Were the Cages in debt? Maybe Jackson was afraid they'd have to sell the ranch. Maybe that's what Gus's message meant.

"After Jackson disappeared, I racked my brain for something I'd missed," I said. "Some hint he'd inadvertently dropped that would explain it, but I couldn't come up with anything. He talked about taking over Stillwater all the time. We made plans for a future there. He never mentioned needing money."

"He never mentioned he was leaving either," Alicia shot back.

It smarted, but she was right. Could Jackson really be working with Javier? Doing what? Helping the *tequileros* cross South Texas? I'd never have agreed with such a thing, even before JJ was killed. Was that why he left without an explanation? Even now he wouldn't tell me what he was doing.

I thought of his reaction when I'd told him about JJ and who had killed him. He'd immediately become more distant. Was Jackson concerned Javier would find out about his actions in The Mad Rabbit? A cold finger slid down my back. If Javier did hear, how long would it take him to put it all together? Would he come after me?

"I told Jackson what happened to JJ," I said. "I thought he'd help me, but he just told me to go home."

"I asked him to convince the *tequileros* that Carlos was too young to do something so risky," Alicia said. "He acted like he had no idea what I was talking about."

None of this sounded like the man I'd agreed to share a

life with. It was as if some strange bug had bitten him, poisoning his entire personality.

I finished carving the *cabrito* and started dicing the vegetables and herbs to make *pico de gallo*. I looked over at Alicia, my eyes burning from the onions. She was mixing water into the ground corn in a bowl, a distracted look on her face.

"Mozo said you know where Carlos is?" I asked.

"Probably with the *tequileros* on their way to pack the mules." Alicia started rolling the *masa* into balls. "I should go to that camp and drag my idiot brother home before he ends up dead—"

Her hand flew up to cover her mouth, but I knew the rest of the sentence. *Like JJ.*

"I'm sorry," she said.

Alicia and I had a common enemy. We both needed to stop Javier. She needed to stop him from killing her brother; I needed to stop him because he'd already killed mine.

"Mozo said the hideout is near a town called Múzquiz," I said. "Have you heard of it?"

"My great-aunt goes there several times a year," she replied. "She's a healer, *una curandera*. There's no medical care for the small villages between here and the mountains. Many of the people are too poor or too sick to get to Nuevo Laredo. They gather in churches and missions, or sometimes in homes, and wait for her visits. She's sort of famous."

"Are you talking about Griselda?" I asked. "I'm staying at *La Fonda*. She gave me some ointment."

"Yes, she's one of my grandmother's sisters. My cousins own the inn. She stays there when she's in town gathering supplies," Alicia said. "There's a corral for her mule and a shed big enough for her wagon. She likes to help out in exchange, even though they tell her it's an honor to have her there."

"She moves as if she has no deformity," I said. "Has her back always been crooked?"

"She was born that way." Alicia smiled with affection.

"It's her trademark; everyone knows *la Curandera Jorobada*, the Hunchback Healer."

"Would she tell me how to get to Múzquiz?" I asked.

"Why do you want to go there?"

"Javier's gang is doing more than smuggling *tequila*," I said. "Mozo thinks they're hiding something in an old mission there. If I can find out what, maybe the Texas Rangers will go after them."

"There's a desert between here and Múzquiz, *amiga*," said Alicia, shaking her head. "It's too dangerous to cross by yourself. You'd get eaten by a puma or defiled by a desperado. Why don't you just tell the Rangers what Mozo said?"

"Hearsay is not enough to get their attention," I replied. "Besides, what if Mozo's wrong? What if there's nothing there?"

"Then none of it matters," she said. "Why take such a risk?"

"Because if he's right, it would change everything."

Alicia went quiet for a few minutes, smooshing *masa* balls into flat circles.

"When he's not being a complete ass, I can tell how afraid Carlos is," she said. "I told him to go to Laredo and turn himself in. I thought he could tell the lawmen what he knows in exchange for his freedom." She rolled her eyes. "He called me an idiot and said they'd just arrest him for smuggling. Then Javier would know Carlos had betrayed him, and we would all be in danger."

"If I find something, we can figure out how to get your family somewhere safe before I go to the Rangers," I said. "Right now, it probably is best for Carlos to keep his head down and not raise suspicion."

"What will raise suspicion is a white woman showing up in Múzquiz," Alicia jested. "Cutting off your blonde hair doesn't make you look Mexican, or really that much like a boy now that I'm used to it."

The tolling of the church bell rang through the open back door.

"It's already noon," Alicia said. "We need to hurry so I can pack everything and take it to the *Conejo*. I don't like to be there when it gets busy."

I quickly peeled the avocadoes and cut them up. I placed the chunks in the *molcajete* Alicia had used earlier, mashing them with the *tejolote* then mixing in diced onions, garlic, *jalepeños*, cilantro, and a squeeze of lime juice. The irony of helping Alicia prepare food for my attackers was not lost on me. As I made the *guacamole*, I was tempted to spit in it more than once.

Alicia stood in front of the stove, cooking the *tortillas* on a griddle with her back to me.

"If you really want to go to Múzquiz," she said. "There might be a way."

"I do want to go," I replied.

She flipped the discs over with a wooden spatula, then turned around, eyes glinting.

"*Curanderas* are considered sacred, blessed with a gift from the Holy Mother," she said. "In all her years of traveling, *Tía Griselda* has never been harmed. She's always wanted me to go with her so I can learn to be a healer. She thinks I'd make a good one." Alicia laughed. "She underestimates my issues with blood."

I'd first become aware of Alicia's "issue" when we were only six years old. We'd been jumping from the loft in the barn into a huge pile of hay. I'd landed on a hidden coil of baling wire and sliced my calf open. Blood had gushed from the deep cut. Alicia had taken one look and passed out. I'd ended up running to get help for her instead of the other way around.

"In any case," she went on, "we could travel with her as apprentices. It would give us a believable reason for going to Múzquiz. *Tía* knows the way well, and we'd be safe with her."

Excitement thrummed in my chest, but one word she'd said worried me.

"We?"

"You think I'd let you go without me? She's my *tía abuela*, not yours." Alicia smiled, the dimples in her cheeks showing for the first time. Those dimples had been well known in Hebbronville when her life had been simpler. It was nice to catch a glimpse of them again.

"Our goals are no different," she said, the grin retreating. "We're like sisters, both wanting to do the right thing for our family. You want justice for JJ; I want freedom for Carlos."

"You don't have to go," I said. "If I find something at the mission, it will help both of us."

"No, Carlos is right," she replied. "Worrying is of no use if I'm not willing to do something about it."

I looked at her earnest expression, trying to quell my reservations. I had no more right to tell her what to do than Jackson had to tell me. Also, she had a point about going by myself. So far traveling alone had not gone well. As Jackson had pointed out, I was in a foreign land where the rules were very different. It would be nice to have a 'gang' of my own. I pushed aside my doubts and reached out.

"*Hermanas en sufrimiento*," she said, grasping my hands in hers.

Sisters in suffering.

CHAPTER 12

The mule-drawn wagon trundled behind me at the speed of a tortoise, Griselda and Alicia jostling about on its bench seat. If I encouraged Rat to go much faster than a slow trot, I quickly left them in the dust. It felt like we'd been heading west for days, but we were barely into our journey.

Griselda had been reluctant at first when Alicia told her our plan. She'd eventually agreed out of concern for Carlos. With no offspring of her own, she loved Alicia and Carlos as if they were her grandchildren. She'd already been packing her wagon with supplies for her upcoming trip to Múzquiz. Gathering the rest of what she needed had not taken long, and we'd left by midafternoon. She'd told us the trek would be over a hundred miles. I'd mistakenly assumed we'd cover a lot of territory by sundown. I soon realized miles had little to do with hours. I was certain Carlos and the *tequileros* would already be bedded down in their mountain hideout by the time we reached the small *pueblo* of Sinta, where we would stay the first night.

With every mile, a new sore joined the injuries I'd already collected. Pain gnawed at my nerves as the road in front of us went on and on, an undulating line to the curve of the horizon, making Santa Rosa seem as if it existed beyond the end of the earth. The view offered little diversion, waist-high chaparral interrupted occasionally by tall clumps of feathery retama bushes, their yellow flowers buzzing with bees. I'd watched the white tail of a deer bobbing over some devil cholla cactus earlier, but the blazing sun had baked everything else into place.

I glanced back, struck by what an odd trio we made. Griselda steered the wagon with experience, hunched over the reins as if in prayer. Even if she hadn't been known by her deformity, she would have been recognized by her getup. On her head was a yellow calico bonnet with a tiny rosebud pattern. She'd secured it with a bow under her chin. It had a wide visor like those worn by frontier women a century ago.

The neckline of her loose linen tunic was embroidered with a green garland. A matching skirt skimmed the tops of beautifully beaded ankle-high moccasins. It all worked together in a peculiar mix of styles. I found myself coveting the cool comfort of her clothing as my back sweltered beneath JJ's leather vest. The only weapon Griselda appeared to carry was a bone-handled knife, sheathed and hanging next to the huge turquoise and silver buckle of her belt.

We rode into Sinta a little after dusk and were welcomed by Griselda's friends with a light meal. They had an extra bedroom for Griselda to use and a loft for Alicia and me. I was so exhausted that I hardly said a word beyond thanking the couple before climbing up the ladder and falling asleep. Before dawn, we were on the road again. The few hours of sleep had not been enough for any kind of recovery. The morning passed in a blur as I tried to concentrate on anything other than my aching body.

"Do you want to ride in here for a while?" asked Alicia, catching me stretching my legs. "We can take turns so you don't get saddle-sore."

The aged wagon bench didn't look much more comfortable than my saddle, but at least it would be a change. Griselda pulled to a stop. Alicia hopped to the ground, dust puffing up around the ankles of her tall boots. She wore a pair of Carlos's Levi's that she'd altered to fit her shorter legs and full shape. I dismounted and she handed me her straw hat, then stretched her hand up for the saddle horn.

Even on tiptoe, it was inches beyond her reach. Undeterred, she grabbed hold of the side of the cantle with one hand and the cinch strap with the other, hoisting herself off the ground. I felt a bubble of amusement rise in my throat. She looked like a tick trying to crawl up a wet wall as she stabbed blindly at the stirrup with the toe of her boot. Eventually, the leather *latigo* slipped out of her hand and she dropped to the ground, landing with a thud on her fanny.

"Damnit! Why do you have a giant horse?" Alicia exclaimed, floundering around in the dirt. "I need a ladder to get on him."

Laughter erupted from my mouth. Then Griselda, who'd said next to nothing since leaving Hidalgo, started to cackle, the front of her bonnet shaking. As Alicia plucked sticker burrs from the seat of her jeans and slapped off dust, we both laughed harder. It felt good to forget for a moment that we were on a journey that scared me more than I dared admit.

"Oh, you two think it's funny?" asked Alicia, her dimples giving her away. She stomped to the back of the wagon and climbed in. "Bring him closer. I can step on the side rail and—"

"*Alguien viene*," Griselda interrupted.

The rhythm of hoof beats rose behind us. I looked down the road at three riders galloping our way. We'd seen a few other travelers, but these weren't ranch hands or goat herders. Riding in a triangle formation, they looked like men on a mission, their pace as steady as a train steaming down the tracks.

As they closed in, I noted the bullet-lined bandoliers crisscrossing their chests, the guns glinting on their hips, and the rifle butts sticking out of their saddle scabbards. The amusement I'd felt just seconds ago dried up as fast as the saliva in my mouth. Only men expecting a battle, or preparing for a massacre, would need so much firepower.

"Who are they?" I asked.

"*Villistas*," said Griselda.

Sweat gathered under my arms. To some Mexicans, Pancho Villa was a Robin Hood, but to most Anglo Americans he was a menacing threat. Last summer a rancher in Monterrey had told Papa he could no longer buy our cattle. Pancho Villa had forbidden Mexicans from doing business with Americans after the U.S. Army had intervened in his attack on Ciudad Jaurez across the border from El Paso. Villa had lost over a hundred men in the skirmish, along with horses, guns, and ammo. He'd told his remaining army to kill any and all Americans they encountered. *Los Villistas* carried out his orders with legendary brutality.

"How did they get so many guns?" I asked, keeping my voice low. "I thought it was illegal for citizens to bring them into Mexico?"

"It has been since the Revolution began. The government is afraid they'll be used by the rebels." Alicia scoffed. "As a result, it's only the rebels who have them."

I wished I'd never gotten off Rat. I felt small and defenseless on the ground, but I didn't want to call attention to myself by scrambling back into the saddle.

"Push your hat down and don't say anything." Alicia's words came out clipped and fast as she put her own hat on and slunk onto the bench seat next to Griselda. "They're revolutionaries, not bandits. They probably won't bother us unless they get a good look at you."

I shoved the Stetson over my ears, relieved the blonde braid no longer hung down my back. Luckily, the pale skin of my arms wasn't showing. I'd left my long sleeves unrolled for protection from the sun. I leaned into Rat's side and fiddled with the saddle. The galloping horses parted without missing a stride. One passed on my left, the other two on the right side of the wagon.

I stared at the riders' backs, willing them to keep going, but one lagged behind then stopped. His rein hand jerked sideways. As he brought his horse around to face us, I held my breath, clutching Rat's reins, nails biting into my palm.

The *Villista* trotted back our way. Had he noticed my coloring? There were light-skinned Hispanics and *Tejanos*, like my grandmother. Even Javier had red hair and light eyes. Would the rebel ask questions? Would my Spanish be fluent enough to fool him?

I felt a tiny bit of relief when he did not ride up to me. Instead, he stopped next to the opposite side of the wagon, leaning over in his saddle to examine the contents in the back. He wore some sort of disheveled uniform—a matching jacket and pants made of olive-green khaki with a faded tricolor armband. The felt brim of his *sombrero* had been stitched with intricate gold curlicues. A prayer card featuring the Madonna and Child stuck out of his hatband.

His holster held a pearl-handled revolver similar to the one Gus had given me. The rifle sticking out of his scabbard made me inhale in surprise. Not long ago, a veteran of the war in Europe had traded my father a German Mauser 1898 for two cows. The soldier had been desperate to feed his starving family. Papa had made the trade because he'd felt sorry for the man. He'd locked the rifle up in the gun case and never used it. With a five-round internal clip and a firing range of over five hundred yards, it was too powerful for hunting. It was a weapon of war.

"*Estas la curandera jorobada?*" the *Villista* asked Griselda.

"*Sí, soy.*" Griselda nodded.

I looked down the road at the other two rebels. They'd stopped and turned their mounts around.

"*Ándele, Álvaro!*" one of them called out, perturbed. "*Qué pasó?*"

"*Espérame, Ramón.*" Álvaro told him to wait, his gaze sliding from Griselda to Alicia, then sticking on me.

"Who is she?" he asked in Spanish, pointing his grizzled chin in my direction.

"My goddaughter," Griselda lied.

I dropped my eyes, my chest drumming so hard I was certain he could hear it.

"*Señora Curandera*, your goddaughter looks very much like a *gringa*," Álvaro replied.

His horse started moving. My stomach twisted tighter with each step. I could smell the tangy odor of the metal strapped across his chest. He could slaughter us all, including the horses, and still have plenty of bullets left.

"What do you need, *m'ijo*?" asked Griselda. "A cure? Medicine?"

Álvaro stopped next to where Alicia sat on the bench. He squinted at me, then glanced up the road at his partners, who waved impatiently.

"*Señorita*," he said, addressing Alicia in polite Spanish. "Please, would you leave the wagon and allow me to speak with the *curandera*?"

Alicia climbed down. As she walked away, Álvaro's eyes fell on her pant-clad backside. The indigo-blue fabric was still chalky with dust from her fall, which seemed to accentuate the sway of her hips.

I'd been envious of the cotton jeans; they looked cooler than my heavy brush pants, and much easier to move around in than women's clothing. Now I wished she'd worn a full-length skirt, or a traditional, formless *puebla* dress—anything that better hid her figure. Mexico was even more conservative than Texas; the snug pants could be mistaken for an invitation.

I glanced at Álvaro's *compadres*, the taunting faces in The Mad Rabbit looming in my mind. Alicia came around the front of the mule and headed toward me, in clear view of the other two *Villistas*. I braced for the crude gestures and vulgar words I was sure would come, but they continued talking to each other.

When Alicia was close enough, I grabbed her arm and pulled her around behind me. Álvaro had watched her entire short journey. He opened his mouth as if he were going to say something, but Griselda cleared her throat and he turned to her instead.

"Are you sick?" she asked.

He beckoned her closer, and she slid across the bench. He spoke in a quiet voice.

Griselda asked a few questions then climbed into the back of the wagon. While she rummaged through her supplies, I silently begged her to hurry; the sooner the men left, the better. Alicia's breath hitched behind me. I looked down the road. Ramón and the other *Villista* were riding our way.

"*Miras, Leandró,*" Ramón said to his companion when they got close. "*Es la curandera famosa.*"

"The famous Hunchback Healer! Are you asking for help with your ugly penis, *amigo*?" Leandró called out, his Spanish not as polite or as formal as Álvaro's. "*La sífilis* is the real price of fucking so many whores!"

Leandró and Ramón continued their banter, guffawing loudly. They were joking about the possibility of Álvaro's member falling off like a dead tree limb when a sharp blast cracked the air.

Rat shied, reins jerking my hand sideways. Alicia cried out, clutching my arm.

"*Cállate!*" shouted Álvaro. A wisp of smoke twirled from the end of his revolver. He'd pointed at the sky, not the hecklers, but the shot had killed their laughter.

"What are you thinking using such foul language? This is an honorable woman, gifted by the Holy Mother!" said Álvaro, gesturing at Griselda. "What if you or your family need her services one day? Do you think she will not remember your disrespect?"

The two men looked at each other briefly, then at Griselda, chagrined expressions on both of their faces.

"*Lo siento, Señora Curandera.*" Ramón apologized, turned his horse around, and headed up the road. Leandró followed suit.

Griselda continued searching through the boxes and bags.

She'd folded the brim of her sunbonnet back, but I couldn't see her face well enough to know if the *Villistas'* behavior had rattled her.

"*Aquí está todo,*" she announced, the curve of her spine rising. She offered Álvaro a small pouch. He pulled the drawstring open and peered inside.

"*Qué es?*" he asked, removing a pinch of the contents and holding it to his nose.

"Special herbs to make a tea. Drink it twice a day," Griselda told him. "And this is made from the root and some berries," she added, holding out a jar. "Put it on the sores."

Álvaro placed both items into his saddlebags as if they were made of eggshells. To my dismay, his focus returned to Alicia. She backed away, his glare pushing her into Rat's side.

"I must tell you, *señorita,*" he said. "There are men who would see your clothing as immoral. I am sure you are too young to know better, but you should heed my warning. Wear something more proper."

Álvaro glanced at his *compadres*, who were about to disappear around a bend.

"*Señora*, would you honor me with a blessing?" he asked.

Griselda acquiesced, entreating the Holy Mother to watch over him. Álvaro reached into his jacket for a leather billfold, plucked out a paper note, and handed it to Griselda.

"*Vaya con Dios,*" he said, before spurring his horse.

Sweat rolled down my neck as he disappeared around the curve in the road. Alicia stood plastered in place.

"Are you all right?" I asked, noticing the pumping of her chest under her white cotton shirt.

"Who the hell does that *pendejo* think he is?" she demanded, stepping out of Rat's shadow. "How dare he lecture me like I'm some *puta*, or stupid little girl who doesn't know better? It's not as if I'm walking around naked!"

I should have known she'd resort to anger.

"He's the one who has syphilis, for God's sake!" Her

cheeks glowed. "You know the only reason women have to cover up? Because men are too damn weak to control themselves. Heaven forbid we tempt them, because of course it's our fault when they behave like dirty pigs!"

I thought of Jackson's implication that simply by walking into the *cantina* I'd somehow brought Hank's assault upon myself. Alicia was right, it wasn't fair, but Maude was one of the few women I knew who could flaunt social norms and get away with it. I wanted to be as offended for womankind as Alicia was, but I was too relieved the *Villistas* were gone.

I got on Rat, happy to be up in the saddle again. Alicia climbed into the wagon, still grumbling to herself. Griselda tucked her things back into place, then crumpled the money Álvaro had given her into a ball and tossed it in a tin can.

"Don't you want his money?" I asked. "Couldn't you use it to buy more medicine or provisions?"

"That is only good for fire starter," Alicia said. "Pancho Villa had his own currency printed back when he had more power. He forced people to trade in their gold for worthless paper. Then he used the gold to fund his raids. This is what powerful men do, they make up their own rules."

Griselda scuttled onto the bench, unfolded the front of her hat, and took up the reins. My limbs still tingled with adrenalin, but the old woman appeared calm and collected. She patted her great-niece's leg with a bony hand.

"What did you give him?" I asked her. My mother had said mercury was the only cure for syphilis, and its side effects were brutal—drooling, blue moods, tooth loss, even death.

"*Tobaco Indio y el saúco*," Griselda answered, slapping the reins against the mule's back.

A smile flitted around Alicia's mouth.

"Tea made from Indian tobacco leaf will drive the infection out if he's not too far gone, but he'll throw his guts up for a few days," explained Alicia. "The ointment is made from the plant root mixed with elderberries. It will soothe his blisters." She let out a chuckle. "And dye his penis purple."

I smiled. There were small victories to be had.

CHAPTER 13

A boy squatted like a watchdog on a flat rock outside of Sabinas. As we drew closer, he stood, holding a shotgun almost as tall as himself.

"*La Señora Jorobada!*" he proclaimed.

He slung his gun across his back, secured with a strap, hopped on a fat little burro, and hurried away.

I pushed my hat off, letting it hang down my back by the chin cord, hoping for a breeze to dry my sweat-pasted hair. My eyes smarted from staring into the sun, and my neck had grown as stiff as a rod.

The encounter with the *Villistas* had set me on edge, the way finding a black widow in the house made you check all the shoes and sheets. I hadn't been looking for rebels, but now that we'd seen some, I couldn't stop searching for more. Alicia had finally stopped grousing about Álvaro's censure. Griselda appeared unfazed, though her reserve was hard to interpret. I was eager to leave the exposure of the road and blend into a town.

"The inn is on the far side of the main square," Griselda said as we entered the village.

I groaned quietly. The promise of a bed was the only thing keeping me from melting off Rat into a puddle on the ground. Griselda had given me some dried leaves to chew. They tasted mildewy and made my tongue numb, but they had dulled the discomfort.

Sabinas appeared to be smaller than Hidalgo and lacked its modernization. Instead of the hubbub I'd expected, the main street was quiet, and the rows of old adobe buildings looked empty. At home, people took advantage of the long, cool summer twilight to stroll in the parks or visit stores that stayed open late. We continued down the main dirt road without seeing anyone; even the boy who'd announced Griselda's arrival had disappeared.

"Where is everyone?" I asked as we passed a deserted train station.

"*Muy extraño,*" Griselda replied. "Usually, families are here meeting the men returning from the coal mines."

As we approached the *centro*, animated voices broke through the stillness. I looked across the square to a *cantina* named *La Estacada*. A large crowd began spilling out of its open doorway; mostly men covered in patches of black coal dust and carrying picks or shovels. Through the bar's arched windows, I could see more people jostling around inside. A few began shaking their fists in the air as a chant started up.

"*Somos fuertes solos! Somos fuertes solos!*" We are strong alone.

Shouts of disagreement rang out in response. Griselda pulled the wagon up, a frown on her face. As I looked around for a way to bypass the throng starting to flow into the road, I spotted the boy, still astride his donkey. He was leading a man on horseback up a side street.

"*Señora Griselda!*" called the man, urgency lifting his voice.

He sat tall in the saddle, his light brown hair swept back from a handsome, earnest face with a neatly trimmed beard. Clean, fitted clothing set him apart from the villagers I'd seen so far.

"*Buenas noches, Lancero,*" Griselda greeted him warmly.

"*Buenas noches,*" he replied. "Please, follow me."

Lancero led us away from the protestors. After several

blocks, we came to a wide, tree-lined river spanned by a timber and steel truss bridge. I worried how Rat would react, given our trouble crossing the Rio Grande, but he clopped across without hesitation.

"Where are we going?" asked Griselda as the noise from the crowd faded.

"Ah, I am sorry for not explaining. I would like you all to be my guests," Lancero said. Then his pleasant smile faded. "It is not safe in town. The people who are in need of your help have gone on to Múzquiz."

Griselda introduced us to the man and his son, Aldo. Lancero's gaze lingered a moment on my face and hair, but he did not comment. As he steered his horse between me and the wagon, I noticed a lever-action rifle in his scabbard.

"Sabinas is normally peaceful," said Griselda when we reached the other side of the river.

"There has been much turmoil lately. We heard that Pancho Villa is gathering the remains of his followers," Lancero said. "Some of his *Dorados*, his most loyal men, have already crossed the Chihuahuan Desert. I think they are looking for recruits and replenishing their store of arms and provisions."

"We met some *Villistas* on the way," Griselda told him as she removed her sunbonnet. "I do not often run into such men."

"Yes, several have passed by our *hacienda*," said Lancero. "They must be meeting nearby."

The skin on the back of my scalp tightened. I scanned the vast desert, wondering how many eyes were watching.

"Why are they coming here?" asked Alicia.

"I believe they are preparing to attack Sabinas," said Lancero. "They will seize the town and choose a *hacienda* to take over as their base, a nice place for *El Centaur* to stay while he holds us captive."

"Why Sabinas?" I asked.

"As a show of strength," he answered. "Since his defeat at

Juarez and President Carranza's assassination, Villa has been trying to negotiate a peace treaty with the provisional president."

A high, barbwire fence line started up next to the road. Lancero watched some lights flickering across the pasture near the shape of a two-story house.

"My beautiful country has been embattled for more than ten years," he said, "but for whatever reason, this state has been spared the recent guerilla warfare and looting. The towns are prosperous, the *haciendas* rich with crops, cattle, and horses. If Pancho Villa takes Sabinas and threatens other villages in Coahuila, he could force Adolfo de la Huerta into an agreement. The government would not want to lose our resources, or the contributions our coalfields and steel plants make to the economy. De la Huerta will not want to appear weak to the United States, either. He needs to show he can restore order to Mexico."

"Shouldn't you all be preparing?" I asked, remembering how the people in my area had reacted when warned Pancho Villa was coming.

"A few people want to send for troops," Lancero replied, "but most do not want the government involved. There are some rebel sympathizers—maybe paid off by the *Villistas*— and some pacifists who feel we should surrender and not risk fighting. The rest think Villa's march across the desert is just rumor. They believe he is a has-been with a skeleton army who represents no real threat now that the revolution is winding down."

Griselda looked intently at Lancero, moonlight playing in the silver strands of her hair. "And you; what do you think?"

"They all underestimate him," he said. "I have witnessed his fierce drive. Unrest in this country is far from over. Pancho Villa can easily recruit more men to do his bidding." He shook his head. "While my neighbors quarrel, our town sits like a powder keg awaiting a match."

Griselda glanced at Alicia and then me. Her shoulders seemed to slump lower.

"Here we are." A pair of yuccas the size of pickup trucks flanked the wide gate of Lancero's *hacienda*. The name, *El Lago Vista*, was burned into a wooden arch stretching overhead. The smell of cigarette smoke tainted the air as an armed man stepped out of the shadows.

"*Buenas noches, Patrón*," he said to Lancero, dropping his cigarette on the ground and grinding it with his bootheel.

"You have a guard?" asked Alicia.

"I have several," Lancero replied.

The guard unlocked the iron gate and swung it open for us. We passed through and headed down a lane lined with young walnut and apple trees, their spindly trunks tied to stakes to keep them straight. A cotton field on our right looked almost ready to harvest, bolls glowing like scattered popcorn. Beyond the field, the river we'd crossed shimmered between thick cypress and cottonwood trees. A narrow tributary fed a small lake behind the house, giving the *hacienda*—Lake View—its name. Without the irrigation supplied by the river and dammed lake, Lancero's property would probably have been nothing but fenced dirt.

On La Barroneña, massive live oaks, wild persimmon bushes full of purple berries, and *guajillo* trees with butter-colored blooms grew along the creek beds, while twenty yards away the earth barely supported prairie cactus and mesquite. We didn't have a surface water source big enough to irrigate, but our windmills pumped enough water out of deep underground channels to support both humans and livestock. Those veins kept the ranch alive.

Unlike the old adobe buildings in town, Lancero's home was a large, unpainted clapboard with a pitched roof. A row of four windows on both stories shone with soft light from within. They had long, double shutters that could be closed against dust and heat or, perhaps, bullets. Despite the expensive glass, the house had a thrown-together feel to it, as if there hadn't been time to add a coat of paint, or plant a flowerbed, or set a stone walkway.

"*Bienvenido a mi casa.*" Lancero welcomed us as we pulled up to the front porch.

"This is a beautiful place," said Alicia. "How long have you owned it?"

"My grandfather bought it long ago, but never did anything with it. We have been here less than two years. It takes time to erect buildings, plant crops, and breed livestock. There is still much to do." He sounded almost apologetic as he went on. "We have no electricity or indoor plumbing yet, but you will be safer here than in town. As the drinking and arguing continue, weapons are inevitably drawn. If Pancho Villa waits long enough, our people will kill each other."

Lancero went inside to let his wife know we'd arrived. Aldo led us around the back of the house to a corral. Next to it was a four-stall barn, also built of barely weathered wood. We untacked Rat and the mule, letting them loose in the pen. Then we pushed the wagon into an empty stall and took turns using the outhouse a few yards away.

There was a well near the back door of the house. I pumped water from it into a bucket. Cupping my hands in the coolness, I splashed my face, combing my fingers through my hair. The mineral odor of damp dust rose from my skin and scalp, mixing with dried sweat and the pungent smell of horse. I needed a bath and a clean set of clothes.

Alicia soon joined me. I dumped out the bucket and started pumping fresh water for her.

"*Tía* is concerned," she said.

"You told me she's never had any trouble."

"She hasn't," said Alicia, "but the climate here is something new."

"Does she want to go back to Hidalgo?"

"She didn't say, but I can tell she's worried."

Aldo appeared just as a woman wearing a red blouse with ruffled sleeves and a chambray skirt pushed the screen door open.

"*La cena está lista, m'ijo*," she said to the boy.

"*Si, Mamá*," he answered, leading Alicia and me into the house for supper.

Several gas light fixtures lit the white walls of the kitchen, making the room bright and cheery. A large slab of beef roasted on a spit in the open fireplace, and something simmered in a cast iron cauldron on the woodburning stove.

Griselda came into the kitchen from a different room in the house.

"*Mi salvador!*" exclaimed Lancero's wife, giving Griselda a warm embrace then turning to Alicia. "This must be the great-niece you speak of so often."

"Yes," Griselda said, "and this is my goddaughter. Sarita, Alicia, this is Josefina."

"*Con mucho gusto*," I said.

Josefina's eyes were the golden-brown color of falcon feathers. They took measure of me with one swift glance.

"You are American," she replied in English, her tone just shy of accusatory.

I felt a desire to explain my heritage, to lay claim to my grandmother's *Tejano* and Spanish lineage. I wanted to say that Alicia and I were born in the same town; she was just as American as I was, but these facts were not the issue.

"I live east of Laredo," I said.

"Well, I'm even more relieved now that you are all staying here." Josefina turned to Griselda, giving her a look that in my mind said, "This is maybe not the best time to be traveling with your *gringa* 'goddaughter.'" Instead of a rebuke, though, she gave her arm a friendly squeeze.

"Wait until you see Margarita!" she said, switching back to Spanish. She hurried from the kitchen, returning with a sleepy toddler in her arms. "Look how big and strong she is growing. All thanks to you."

Griselda cupped the child's full cheeks in her worn hands, smiling in such a warm manner it surprised me. I might have thought the child would have been scared by the wrinkled old woman with the wild hair and hunched back, but Margarita seemed entranced as Griselda babbled and chirruped to her.

"Margarita was only three weeks old when we left our home in Chihuahua," Josefina explained to Alicia and me. "We traveled in wagons through the *Bolsón de Mapimí*, miles and miles of desert and mountains. She became sick with pneumonia, and very dehydrated." Her voice hitched and she squeezed the little girl to her chest. "We were fortunate that *Señora* Griselda came through Sabinas the day after we arrived."

Lancero had walked in, catching the end of Josefina's story.

"Margarita is fine, José," he said with an indulgent smile. "One day you will have to stop telling the story of her near demise. Although, I agree, we will always hold a special place in our hearts for *Señora* Griselda."

"Sarita lives near Laredo," Josefina remarked, handing Margarita to him. "She is American."

Although Josefina almost sounded as if she were scolding him, Lancero's face registered no surprise or concern. He led Griselda and me into a separate dining room while Alicia stayed in the kitchen to help.

Aldo already sat at a long trestle table made of burled mesquite. He'd washed up and dressed for dinner in linen shorts and a blue cotton shirt, his creamy-brown hair neatly parted and combed away from a face that resembled his father's. He looked younger than he had before, maybe only nine or ten years old.

After plunking Margarita down in a high chair, Lancero walked to the head of the table, pulling out the chair between Aldo and himself for Griselda and inviting me to sit on the other side. Griselda turned her attention to the boy and the carved wooden horse he was galloping across the table in front of him.

"Where is your home?" Lancero asked.

"About twelve miles north of Hebbronville."

"I know the area," he said. "I sold some of my cattle to the Arrowhead Ranch. My *vaqueros* and I drove them up there."

"We share a fence line with the Arrowhead. My brother works ..." I paused, swallowing the barb in my windpipe. "My brother used to break horses for them. The owner is a friend of my father's."

"A very fair man," said Lancero. "He paid me a good price, even though he knew I was desperate due to our move and the ban on doing business with Americans."

I glanced around. A cabinet took up most of the wall at the end of the room. It was made of polished walnut with drawers in the bottom half and shelves on the top. The shelves displayed bone china dishes, so fine they looked translucent in the candlelight cast by a crystal chandelier hanging over the table.

"Why did you move?" I wanted to ask a barrage of questions but made myself stop at one. I knew from the interviews I'd done that people shut down if you overwhelm them with an interrogation.

"We had no choice," said Lancero, his hazel eyes darkening. "After several unsuccessful battles, the *Villistas* needed money to replace supplies. They started ransacking homes and businesses, taking anything of value. Pancho Villa began demanding bigger and bigger payments from the *hacendados* in return for our safety, which is to say, to protect our ranches and families from his own rebels. When I ran out of cash, he started taking my cattle. I could watch the herd disappear, along with our livelihood, or leave, sell most of it, and start over."

I thought of Burr Archer's constant pressure on Papa to surrender the ranch. There is a limit to everything, a drop that finally breaks the dam.

Alicia and Josefina came in carrying platters of sliced beef, *calabaza* squash boiled with potatoes and peppers, and a basket of pan-fried bread. After putting the dishes on the table, Josefina went to the china cabinet and removed the dinner plates. She placed one in front of each of the grown-ups then finished setting the table with shiny silver flatware from one of the drawers. Everything in the room looked expensive. If this was just what they'd been able to pack in a wagon, I wondered what they'd left behind.

"It must have been hard to leave," I said as savory smells filled the air.

"It broke my heart."

Lancero's voice was so full I forgot my hunger. I thought sadness might cause him to stop talking, but he gestured at a portrait hanging on the wall across from him. A scowling man peered out from the canvas, wavy dark hair to his shoulders, his beard shaped into a point at his chin.

"My grandfather maintained our *haciendo* in Chihuahua through the rule of Maximillian, and my father expanded it during Diaz's years of economic growth, but sadly, the Revolution plagued my tenure. Villa, Carranza, and Zapata sent their troops across the countryside, burning and pillaging, forcing ranchers to 'restore' land to the people."

"They took some of your property?" I asked.

A short sigh escaped Lancero's lips. He looked down, finger tracing his knife.

"I deeded more than half the acreage to the *peones* who had worked and lived on our *hacienda* for generations. I gave them horses and tools, and cows to feed their families. I only wanted to hold on to the house and enough livestock and land to make a living, but even that became impossible."

Josefina sat down at the other end of the table and cleared her throat.

"Ah, my lovely wife is reminding me not to bore you with our troubles," Lancero said with a wry smile. He reached out to Griselda and then to me. We all held hands around the table and bowed our heads. "Let us thank God for this bounty and remember what we have earned and what we have been given."

After amens were said, the dishes of food were passed around. No one spoke for a while as we enjoyed the meal. Aldo's clay plate was full, but he lost a few pieces of meat over the side of the table as he tried to wield his knife and fork. Griselda started to get up.

"No, no, *señora*," said Josefina. "Aldo, you pick it up, please."

"We need to go back and get *Pato*," the boy said as he scooched out of his chair. "He always cleaned the floor."

Josefina grimaced at her husband across the table.

"I told you, *hijo*," said Lancero. "When you are old enough, we will get you a new puppy."

"I don't want a new one," Aldo complained from under the table. "Can I be excused, please?"

"Yes, go do your reading." Lancero shook his head as his son collected his plate and stomped to the kitchen.

"If Pancho Villa does invade Sabinas," I asked, "will you move again?"

"No, not again, we have lost too much already." Lancero ran a hand over his beard. He glanced at Margarita, bouncing in her high chair while Alicia spooned mashed-up food from a bowl into her mouth. "This is all I have left to pass on. I do not have the resources to start over again. This is *la herencia de mi familia* and I will do whatever necessary to assure its future."

Margarita let out a hair-raising screech.

"I don't know what happened," said Alicia, leaning away and covering her ear.

"Don't worry." Josefina left her seat and lifted the toddler out of the high chair. "She is getting a new molar."

She carried Margarita out of the room, the screaming getting fainter as she moved deeper into the house.

"*Señora* Griselda has told me about your troubles with Javier," Lancero said. "I only know his reputation. He is not a man to tangle with."

Alicia's face filled with worry I knew was for Carlos.

"Do you think Javier is helping the *Villistas*?" I asked, remembering Gus saying the Salsito de Ortegas had joined the *insurrectos* before.

"It is possible," said Lancero.

"Could the rebels be gathering in Múzquiz?" I asked. "In the mission there?"

"I doubt it," he said. "I've heard Villa obtained property near here where he plans to build his own community. There must be a camp there they are using as a headquarters. It is closer than Múzquiz, easier to raid Sabinas from."

"Do you think we will be safe going on to Santa Rosa?" asked Griselda. "Many people are waiting for me there."

"I cannot say for sure, *señora*. I do not think the *Villistas* will bother you," Lancero said. "They are preoccupied with political issues, and, whatever else they are, they are not cutthroats. I can make no predictions about Javier, however. He is a different sort of menace." He leaned his head my way. "Your 'niece,' on the other hand, needs to be very discreet. The death edict on Americans was made by Pancho Villa, but it is carried out by anyone who resents Anglos, and there are many who do."

My chest buzzed, as if a hundred hornets were circling through it. I'd accepted the threat Javier represented, but the presence of the *Villistas* magnified the danger. Javier had his *tequileros*, while Villa, according to Lancero, still had a formidable force at his beck and call. Both were killers, and both hated Anglos. Together they were the difference between a severe storm and a hurricane.

CHAPTER 14

We left Sabinas early the next morning, the sun swimming up behind us as we headed into the rough, uneven landscape of the foothills. Rat dodged dagger-like rocks jutting out along the road and sidestepped shallow trenches in the ground. The mule, however, caught his foot on every stone and slid down every ditch, even with Griselda deftly handling the reins. Alicia marked each misstep with a squeak of surprise.

I tried to concentrate on helping Rat navigate the path but couldn't lose the pang of unease. Lancero's talk of Pancho Villa and Javier had chewed at me all night. When Griselda, Alicia and I had talked in private before going to sleep, each of us had sounded sure about continuing. I hoped the day would restore my confidence.

While the thought of encountering *Villistas* was more than disquieting, I was eager to catch my first glimpse of the mountains. I'd seen photographs and read accounts of what lay within the Sierras—abandoned gold and silver mines, deep coal shafts, caves full of buried treasure, fearless Indians, and wild desperados. The raw, untamed range seemed the perfect place for bandits, *tequileros*, and rebels to hide.

The wagon's wheels screaked against a rocky ledge.

"I'm going to call this mule 'Grace,'" stated Alicia.

"I thought mules were supposed to be more sure-footed than horses," I said.

"Well, Grace is a clumsy ox compared to your *ratón*," Alicia complained, "and this so-called road is winding around enough to make me seasick."

"How much farther is it?" I asked.

"We will arrive after noon," Griselda answered from the depths of her sunbonnet.

I'd stuck a small wad of Griselda's mulch in my cheek when we left. The bitter taste was beginning to make me nauseous, or maybe it was the twisty road, as Alicia had said. I leaned over to spit it out just as the rhythm of Rat's hooves stopped, pushing me forward in the saddle. The slimy plug rolled down my chin. I wiped it off with the back of my hand and clucked my tongue, urging Rat forward. He threw his head around and held his ground.

Griselda pulled the wagon up next to me.

"*Qué pasó?*" she asked.

"I hope he hasn't gone lame," I said.

Dismounting, I lifted each foot to check his hooves. They looked fine, no loose nails or rocks caught in his metal shoes, no cuts or bruises marking the tender middle frogs of his feet. I patted his neck, leading him on while I walked backward to watch his stride. He followed until we reached the top of a rise, where he planted his feet like a two-year-old about to throw a tantrum.

I turned around. The problem drifted across the road in front of us—a wide swath of clear water, bordered on each side with bald cypress and river oaks. What lay beyond the stream nearly took my breath away.

Stretching across the entire horizon was the ragged blue outline of the mountains. How could something so massive spring up out of nowhere? They were beautiful, rising dark and majestic into the sky. I stood slack-jawed for several moments, trying to identify the emotion surging through me. Something timeless and forbidding resided in their unmovable presence—ancient giants standing guard, feet embedded in the center of the earth. The term "awe-inspiring" floated out of my subconscious, as if the mountains were the very definition of the term.

"*Los Sierras*," Alicia announced from the wagon.

"They're incredible," I said, my voice deep with admiration for God, or Mother Nature, or whatever force had formed them.

"Yes, and dangerous," she replied. "Why is your *ratón* refusing to go on?"

I rolled my eyes. "It's the stream. He's not fond of water."

"Are you kidding me?" Alicia snorted. "Maybe he's more like a baby mouse than a giant rat!"

Sore, tired, and unsure about what awaited us in Múzquiz, my reserves sat on empty. I yanked the reins hard enough to pull Rat's chin and tried to drag him onward.

"*No, no*," Griselda chided.

I knew better. JJ would've chastised me as well.

As soon as I thought of him, I felt my brother. Not in a physical way, but as a presence within and around. I stopped tugging the reins and stood still, allowing myself to embrace the notion. As I did, I realized Papa was wrong. JJ was everywhere—in Rat's stubborn stare, in the mountains JJ would have been astounded by, in the cool air that would've made him whoop with glee.

"It's okay, boy," I said, patting Rat's cheek and looking into his eyes. "We can do this together."

I heard the slap of Griselda's reins and watched Grace splash into the stream. At the deepest point, the water only covered the bottom half of the wagon's wheels.

"See, Rat," I said, talking to him as if he were a small child instead of a twelve-hundred-pound gelding. "Come on, this'll be a piece of cake."

His head bobbed, but I took hold of the reins and started walking, JJ's voice whispering in my head: "*A good horse isn't led; he follows.*"

My breath caught as water poured over the tops of my boots, chilling my feet to the bone. I'd never felt anything so cold. I glanced back at Rat. He was lifting his feet high with each step as if he too found the temperature uncomfortable. Had he known it would be?

The tension of the reins slackened, and Rat trudged behind me to the other side without any more drama. We stopped by the wagon, which Griselda had pulled up near a huge tree. A shiver shook down Rat's mane. Alicia put her hands next to her mouth in an imitation of paws and squeaked. Her jests were beginning to irritate me.

"That's the tallest cypress I've ever seen," I announced to change the subject.

She stopped pretending to be a mouse and looked up into the lacework of limbs and featherlike leaves.

"We call them *Ahuehuetes*," she said. "Old men of the river."

The tree stood at least fifty feet tall. Its trunk looked as if it were made of separate logs leaning together vertically in a tall bonfire shape. Its thick roots squirmed in and out of the ground around the base like a nest of huge worms. Suddenly, a long snout poked out of a split in the trunk.

"Oh!" exclaimed Alicia. "There's a javelina in there."

The animal's whole head appeared, beady little eyes giving us a once-over. Apparently deciding we were no threat, it walked out of the tree house, dappled sunlight sinking into its coarse black hair. It turned back, letting out a short snort, and three reddish-brown babies trotted out, bleating like lambs.

"*Oler mal*," Griselda said, waving a hand in front of her nose as a strong, musky smell wafted over us.

"What cute little pigs!" said Alicia, clapping her hands.

"All baby things are cute," I replied, still a little grouchy as I took my boots off to pour the water out. "They're peccaries, not pigs."

"I know, smarty-pants. I think it would be fun to have one as a pet," Alicia remarked. "Except for the skunky smell."

"The adults can be mean as hell," I said. "A couple of our cow dogs chased a pack into a dry creek bed once. The javelinas turned and ripped the dogs to shreds with their tusks."

"That's awful," said Alicia with a look of disgust. "Did your father shoot them?"

"They were just defending themselves," I replied. "Can't blame an animal for doing what's in its nature."

Papa had a deep love and respect for wildlife. He hunted for food or preservation, not for sport. A new ranch hand had once shot a whole family of bobcats—a mama and three babies. He'd bragged about it until he realized how angry my father was. Then he'd claimed they'd dropped out of a tree on him while he'd been taking a *siesta*. Papa had fired him on the spot. If he was scared of some kittens, he wasn't man enough for the job.

Why would a person kill something just because he could? The way Javier had killed JJ. Maybe killing had been cured into him, but he was a man, not an animal. Human beings had the gift of reason. Wasn't that what separated us from beasts? Javier chose to ignore his humanity in order to feed the hungry ghosts of his past. Would they ever be satisfied? How much trauma did it take to become a vessel of anger and revenge? What would it take for me to turn away from my nature; to become something other?

The javelinas trotted off into the scrub. I threw the reins over Rat's ears. When I stuck my boot into the stirrup, he bent his neck around and nuzzled my shoulder.

"He's apologizing for being such a chicken," said Alicia, getting in one more dig.

Maybe she was right. Rat had done the same thing after the Rio Grande, but this water crossing had gone much more smoothly. I pulled up into the saddle and leaned forward to scratch between his ears, feeling as if we'd passed some sort of test.

My eyes hardly left the outline of the mountains as we

continued. The closer we got to them, the more impressive they became. I'd gazed across acres and acres of brushland, sensing its endless bounty. The Sierras seemed like a vertical version of that. By the time we reached Múzquiz, they blocked two-thirds of the horizon, their ridged peaks thrusting up into a cloudless sky.

My apprehension had continued to rise with the altitude. Smaller than Sabinas, the town square of Múzquiz was bordered by a single row of adobe and rock buildings. People milled about, taking care of daily tasks. True to Lancero's prediction, I saw no sign that the town had been overtaken by *Villistas*. On the mountain side of the plaza, a large church, almost big enough to call a cathedral, sat nestled in a lush thicket of fir and juniper trees. Twin *campanarios* rose from its stone façade, their cast iron bells hanging silent. What a lovely sound must fill the town when they rang, echoing off the rocky backdrop.

"The missionaries named it *Santa Rosa de Lima* for the patron saint of the native people," said Alicia, "but it's also what this part of the mountain range is called, *Los Sierras Santa Rosa*."

Even through the patches of cement stuck across the limestone like plaster bandages, the mission's original beauty was evident. I couldn't imagine the resources it must have taken to build it in such a remote part of the country.

"They must have been pretty confident they could coax the natives and Indians out of the mountains and convert them," I said.

"They failed to convince most of them," said Alicia, "but at least the abandoned mission is being used for good."

Having now seen the mountains, I could understand how someone could find their spirituality in them and never choose to leave.

Villagers, humming with excitement, began to follow us as we made our way around the *centro*.

"*La Curandera!*"

"*Que ha venido!*"

"*La Curandera Jorobada está aquí!*"

We turned the corner onto the road fronting the church, steering around various forms of transportation parked willy-nilly. I spotted mule-drawn wagons and carts, horses with travois poles attached to their sides, a tattered covered wagon, burros wearing rope halters and *serape* saddles, a dented pickup truck, a bicycle, and even a rusty red wagon like the one I'd pulled JJ around in when he was little.

A tall pair of wooden doors stood open at the entrance to Santa Rosa, the low din of conversation emanating from them, punctuated by an occasional cry or wail. I followed Griselda past the front to a long water trough on the east side. She and Alicia climbed down from the wagon. They had untethered Grace and tied him to a hitching post so he could drink by the time I managed to ease my rigid body off Rat.

"*Señora* Griselda!"

An Anglo woman wearing a long dress of plain black wool swooped out of the front doors. Our group of followers parted to let her through.

"We heard you were headed our way," she said.

The spring in her step, her neat waist, and the sunny highlights in her long hair gave her a youthful air, but something about her face didn't seem right. As she came closer, I realized what.

CHAPTER 15

A puckered circle of scar tissue formed an "O" underneath the woman's pale blue eyes. The part of the nose that usually protrudes from a person's face was missing. What was left was a hole the size of a quarter, overexposing her nostrils and the line of cartilage separating them. The only comparison I could draw, although it was a poor one, was to the surface of a pig's snout.

"You're Dove." Alicia sounded a little awed.

"And who are you?" asked Dove. Her voice was soft and airy, as if too much of her breath escaped though her nasal passage when she spoke.

"My great-niece, Alicia," said Griselda, "and my goddaughter, Sarita. They are my apprentices."

"You two are lucky to be learning from such a skilled healer," said Dove.

Try as I might, I couldn't stop staring at the hole in her face. The irregular border told me she had not been born that way. Something had happened. Though well-healed, the raw, purple color and shiny texture of the scarring meant it hadn't happened very long ago.

Her light pink lips were full and perfectly shaped, although scar tissue lifted the upper one just enough that they didn't quite meet when she closed her mouth. The skin around the frame of her face, her neck and collarbone, was as flawless as a cup of cream. She must have been beautiful.

"So, let's get this out of the way right off," she said as Alicia and I stood dumb before her. "Yes, I can breathe just fine, and no, it isn't painful, just tender. Hurt like hell when it happened. I thought I'd die, then I wanted to die, but *Señora* Griselda nursed me back to health. So, stare until you're used to it, then let's move on. There's a bunch of people way worse off than me waiting inside."

I smiled sheepishly at her.

"It's nice to meet you, Dove," I said, forcing my eyes to meet hers.

"Yes, it's a pleasure," said Alicia. "*Tía* has told me a lot about you and the wonderful work you're doing here."

"She taught me, like she's teaching you, and I'm grateful." Dove patted Griselda's arm. "I'll help you carry your supplies in. We were already busy, but soon as word went out you were on your way, people started arriving by the cartful."

The three of them gathered armloads from the back of the wagon and walked into the church. I stayed behind to loosen Rat's girth and lead him to the trough. As I approached the big church doors minutes later, Alicia came flying out, hand clamped over her mouth. She fled around the corner of the building. The unmistakable sounds of retching soon followed. I walked over to check on her, but she held up a hand, stopping me from coming too close.

"Are you all right?" I asked.

"I had no idea how awful it would be," she gasped, wiping her mouth on her sleeve. "So many ailing, injured people."

"Luckily, you actually want to be a teacher, not a nurse," I teased.

"Very funny," she said with a fleeting smile. "I really do want to help *Tia*, but ..."

"It's okay," I said. "Just do what you can."

"I wish I was more like you," she replied. "You don't fret and hesitate. You're so much braver than me. I never seem to be able to do anything that makes a difference."

I didn't feel brave, and when it had really mattered, when I could have saved my brother, I had hesitated.

"You're here, aren't you?" I replied. "That took courage."

"I'm a wimp with a weak stomach," she answered. "All those poor suffering people in there, and I'm the one out here throwing up."

"Can I get you some water?" I asked.

"I'll get myself together. Go ahead, *Tía* and Dove need help."

I walked into the dusky mission. The smell hit me first, the sour stench of suffering I knew too well. Even after scrubbing the floors and walls, and washing the linens over and over, it had taken months for my mother's room to lose that odor.

Hand over my nose, I took in the cavernous room, my eyes adjusting to the murky light seeping through a row of narrow, dusty windows on each side of the nave. There were no pews. Instead, people were draped over chairs or sitting on the ground. Some leaned against the thick walls; others lay on pallets scattered across the stone floor. Seemingly undaunted by the number of people, Griselda was busy at the back of the church near the altar, which stood on a raised wooden area resembling a stage.

For a moment, I wasn't sure what to do—make my way to Griselda or flee as Alicia had? I'd never seen so many different maladies in one place. From red, damp faces full of fever, to bones poking out of flesh, to festering sores, the sheer diversity was overwhelming. One second, I felt disgusted by an oozing cut, the next touched by a naked child shivering on her mother's lap. Other than some healthy children running about in a game of tag, it was truly a picture of misery.

How could Javier hide anything in Santa Rosa with so many people around? He had a commanding presence; he'd be noticed if he marched in. They might not dare question him directly, but curiosity would prompt speculation. Then again, maybe the mission was the perfect place to stash something, specifically because there was so much activity. Perhaps the people who came here were too miserable to care what a red-haired bandit was up to.

I briefly thought about asking some of them if they'd seen Javier but remembered Jackson's warning about probing. I needed to be careful, for myself and others.

"Vengas aquí, Sarita."

Griselda's voice carried across the nave, amplified by the domed ceiling above her. Sunshine streamed through a round window set high on the back wall of the mission. Its light cast a semicircle over the area where Griselda was setting up her makeshift clinic. I wound my way through people to the steps, walking up to the altar. It was the width and length of a casket and made from a slab of worn oak. Four sturdy turned legs held it up. A couple of boxes and a large crate underneath caught my eye. They could be full of ... something.

I helped Griselda cover the oak top with a heavy piece of burlap, which draped to the floor like a tablecloth. I wondered if it was sacrilegious to use an altar for anything other than communion. When Dove and another woman brought in more containers, Griselda placed her creams, ointments, salves, and pouches of plants and herbs on the retable as if it were no more sacred than a kitchen counter.

The undercurrent of conversation in the mission softened and a polite line began to form. As Griselda started examining patients, I looked around for places Javier could hide things. Like most Catholic churches, Santa Rosa had been built in the shape of a cross with two short wings expanding from either side of the apse. At first, I thought Dove must use the side transepts for storage, but as I focused, the contents registered.

The floors of both areas were littered with wooden crutches, along with an array of canes and walking sticks, even a few rusty wheelchairs. It was as if their owners had regained the ability to walk right in that spot and left them behind.

All sorts of bandages and splints lay in mounded piles on the floor. Eye patches, hearing funnels, and reading glasses hung among dried flowers and notes nailed into the adobe walls. Had Griselda cured all the people who'd left these things? Or were they tributes to the patron saint?

"*Ayúdame, por favor*," Griselda said, snapping my attention back to her.

She'd stitched together a jagged gash on a man's forearm. Handing me a jar of ointment, she pointed to a roll of bandages before turning to help the next person.

The man's muscles quivered at my touch.

"*Muchas gracias, señorita*," he said as I wrapped a strip of muslin around his arm.

As soon as he stepped away, another person stood before me, and it became apparent that, although she knew the real reason I was there, Griselda expected me to continue assisting her. She had pulled a thorn from my next patient's eyelid. I told him to lean over so I could rinse it with water from a pail. He winced as I applied some of the multi-purpose ointment.

"*Lo siento*," I said, apologizing.

"*No, está bien*," he replied, a forced smile stretching his mouth. "*Sigue haciendo lo que quieras.*"

I smiled back, wondering if he'd be so anxious to trust me if he knew the limits of my healing experience.

"Keep it covered so it doesn't get infected," I told him in Spanish, securing a bandage around his head.

In rapid succession, I treated a woman's infected toe, splinted a girl's broken finger, and lanced a silver-dollar-sized blister full of green pus on an old man's heel. I had no idea if what I was doing or saying was medically correct, but I'd picked up a few things helping Papa with the animals and Mama with her patients. Two legs or four, common sense seemed to be the main ingredient to any treatment.

As each person expressed their gratitude, some with tears in their eyes, a kernel of satisfaction grew in my chest, along with a new depth of understanding for my mother. Once, in a fit of self-pity, I'd accused her of caring more about the people she helped than her own children. I'd bristled at being left with JJ and the housework while she'd disappeared for hours to deliver a baby. Even then I'd known my reaction was unfair; those people needed her, and she'd never come close to neglecting us.

What I hadn't taken time to realize was what working as a midwife must have meant to her personally. Since her death, I'd come to understand that the daily routine of caring for a family offered few immediate rewards. As soon as the housework was done, it was time to do it again. Raising a child never ended ... unless in tragedy. My mother must have felt a sense of fulfillment in providing care to people, seeing the fear and pain lift from their faces, delivering a baby they'd waited nine months to meet. I felt grateful that she'd had that.

She'd have been amused to see me administering care—something I'd adamantly claimed to dislike—but not surprised. I had been her nurse, after all. I regretted my impatience with her when she'd been well. I should have been more supportive. I would have loved to tell her I understood now why her work had been so important to her, but that was yet another conversation we would never have.

Griselda walked down the steps to a man whose leg was bent at an unnatural angle. Two young men had dragged him on a blanket across the stone floor to the front while he bellowed in pain. As I waited to see if she'd call me over, the naked little girl I'd noticed when I first walked into the nave stepped in front of me, guided by her mother's firm grasp on her shoulders. The child couldn't have been more than four or five years old. Her gaze darted around before settling on my face. I smiled, and the little girl's lips turned up for a second before she shyly looked away, scratching under her arm like a kitten with fleas.

"*Cómo te llamas?*" I asked.

"Her name is Esmé," the mother replied. Her Spanish had an inflection I'd never heard before, perhaps a local accent. "I am Eudora."

"*Hola, Esmé*," I crooned, squatting down to her eye level. "*Cómo estas?*"

I kept my tone light and friendly, attempting to win Esmé's trust. She stopped digging at her skin and wrapped her arms around her mother's leg.

"*Déjame*," Eudora said, ordering her to let go.

Esmé's skinny little arms tightened. Eudora huffed and roughly pried her daughter off, holding her arms up so I could get a good look at the angry red blotches covering her torso. I glanced over at Griselda, who was busy splinting the man's leg, and decided to go on with the exam. The more people I saw, the faster I could go on to other things, like searching the two transepts. Javier could have concealed plenty of stuff under all those piles.

Eudora spun her daughter around so I could see her back, which was also covered with the flat, red rash. Smallpox? There had been an outbreak at school once, and eight of my classmates had come down with it. I'd been vaccinated and hadn't gotten sick. Mama had still made me take cod liver oil, just in case. I dug through one of Griselda's baskets until I found a bottle of the thick yellowish liquid.

"I need to give her some of this," I said to Eudora, pouring out a tablespoon.

Esmé turned to me but refused to open her mouth. She pursed her lips together, reminding me of myself. I hated the goop; the taste and texture made me think of dead pollywogs. Eudora grabbed Esmé's chin, pinching it hard. A surge of emotion squeezed my chest. The child was so young and obviously miserable; it was all I could do not to intervene.

Esmé's jaw released, and I dumped the medicine into her mouth before she could slam it shut. She swallowed then erupted in a fit of gagging. Instead of gentle pats on her back,

Eudora thumped her hard with a closed fist. Esmé's eyes welled up and she unleashed a loud, sputtering cry. I'd had enough. I reached out to comfort the child, but Griselda pounced out of nowhere, slapping my hands away.

"*Sarampión!*" she said, shaking a big-knuckled finger at me.

Measles, not smallpox. Instinctively, I drew back. There was no vaccine for measles, which was deadly and highly contagious. My heart filled with even more sympathy for the child. At least I'd gotten the treatment right. Griselda handed Eudora the cod liver oil, telling her that they both must take a swallow twice a day. She advised them to stay indoors, away from other people. If the rash didn't go away in a few days, or if the fever got worse, they were to return right away. Griselda handed her a jar of the cure-all ointment to help with itching.

As the pair walked away, Esmé bawling like a lost calf, I gazed down the line of people still waiting. It had doubled in length, and another large group was coming through the front doors. At this rate, it would be hours, even days, before I was free to explore.

What if the *tequileros* showed up? Worse yet, what if Javier himself appeared? What if there was nothing here, and I'd wasted all this time chasing a hunch instead of taking care of my father?

Alicia had not come back in. I felt a twinge of resentment. She could at least try to help; maybe being busy would quell her nausea. I looked around for Dove, hoping she'd take my place for a while, but she was moving through the nave like a triage nurse on a battlefield, dividing people into groups by the seriousness of their complaints. Her care seemed genuine and deep. She was very much in control of Santa Rosa; if Javier was keeping something there, certainly she would know.

"*Tía!* Hurry!"

Alicia's shout ricocheted off the thick walls. People waiting in line turned toward the entrance. Dove was closer to the front than Griselda. She hurried outside after Alicia, returning moments later.

"It's a girl," she called breathlessly. "She's bleeding out, and I think she's in labor."

CHAPTER 16

A high-pitched howl punched through the open doors, splitting the thick air in two. I hurried behind Griselda, hot water from a bucket she'd told me to bring sloshing down my legs. As we slammed into the bright outdoors, I blinked my eyes clear and searched for Alicia.

Face void of color, she held the halter of a burro tethered to a two-wheeled cart, the type used to haul dirt or hay. A woman sat in it, facing the back, bent over and sobbing. Dove stood behind the cart, facing the woman. She moved aside as Griselda and I rushed over, both of us seeing the horror at the same time.

A young girl lay sprawled across a blood-soaked pallet, groaning in agony, her head rolling from side to side in the woman's lap. The bucket slipped from my fingers as I was dragged back to JJ gasping in a dark red circle. The smell, the sounds, the ache in my heart—all flooded in.

"*Dios mío,*" whispered Griselda.

I grabbed the side of the cart to steady myself and took several deep breaths. That girl was not JJ, and I was not going to stand by helplessly and watch her die.

"How can I help?" I asked.

Griselda handed me some towels. I dunked them into the bucket, which had landed upright, and gave them back to her. She searched the girl's body, as if looking for a place to start.

Slick blood covered the girl's bare arms and legs. Her torn muslin nightgown glistened as she writhed in the cart like a partially slaughtered lamb, so much gore her wounds were indiscernible.

The woman holding her removed a sodden rag she'd been pressing to the girl's neck, revealing a deep gash from her jawbone almost down to her clavicle. Whatever cut her must have been a hair's breadth away from slicing an artery. I handed the woman a clean cloth.

"*Santa María, Madre de Dios!*" she implored in Spanish, tears streaming down her face. "Please, please don't let my daughter die!"

The girl exhaled a deep howl, raising a clawed hand to her mother's arm. Her whole body spasmed, the drenched gown pulling tight across her swollen abdomen. Dove had been right; the girl was in labor. Griselda stopped wiping her limbs and lay her hands on her belly.

"What happened?" I asked Dove. "Who did this to her?"

"Her mother said a man attacked her with a knife," Dove answered. "Some bastard called *El Lobo*."

"Why?"

"I gave up asking why a while back," Dove replied, her voice thick.

I didn't know what she'd gone through, but I felt the resigned sorrow in Dove's tone.

"She can't be more than a child," I said.

"Esperanza, her mother, said she's twelve," Dove replied. "Her name is Flora."

Flora's contraction ended, her wails ebbing to whimpers.

"I need more water—hot water—and my suturing kit," said Griselda. "I want to try to close some of her wounds before the next contraction. She is bleeding too much."

Dove ran to pump more water and boil it. I dug through the supply basket and found the suturing kit, handing it to Griselda. She cleaned a deep laceration on Flora's calf and started to stitch the edges together, but Flora jerked away with a growl.

"Hold her tighter," Griselda said.

Esperanza gathered Flora up, wrapping her arms around her.

"Listen to me, *hija*," she crooned in Spanish, rocking back and forth. "Please, please, you have to be still and let them help you."

Flora's lips pulled back from her teeth in a horrible silent scream as another contraction set in. She lurched out of her mother's grasp, grabbing at her stomach with both hands. I'd seen some of Mama's patients go through labor, but never under such horrendous circumstances. Those women had been in their own beds, surrounded by family and friends, enduring the pain of childbirth for an outcome they'd planned for and wanted.

"I need to see how far along her labor is," Griselda told Esperanza when the contraction had passed.

Esperanza hugged Flora to her. Griselda lifted the tattered gown, gently pushing Flora's knees apart, but as soon as she reached in to check the baby's progress, Flora kicked her legs closed, catching Griselda's chin with her foot.

Griselda would never be able to stitch the girl up, much less help her birth the baby, with Flora flailing around like a cornered animal. It had only taken minutes for JJ to bleed out, and Flora was so much smaller. She had to calm down. I grabbed a pile of clean gauze and some wet cloths and crawled into the cart. Crouching next to the girl, I took my hat off, dropping it over the side, and leaned in close, hoping she wouldn't try to scratch my eyes out.

"It's okay, Flora," I said in a hushed voice.

The sun was behind me. She squinted against the bright light, her stare holding the same gleam of terror I'd seen in the eyes of a mangled bobcat kitten I'd tried to pry out of a steel-toothed trap.

"I know you're scared, but you're safe now," I said.

Her keening stopped and she stilled, seeming momentarily entranced.

"You ... glow," she whispered in Spanish. "Are you an angel?"

I wondered if she'd ever seen a fair-skinned woman before.

"No," I said, "but I am here to take care of you."

As her mother rocked her, I took advantage of the lull and carefully wiped blood away from the gash down Flora's neck. Esperanza needed both hands to hold her daughter still. Without the pressure of the rag, thick blood was streaming down Flora's chest and shoulder. I gently cleaned the area then wrapped a strip of gauze around it.

"It's going to be all right," I said as I swabbed her body hurriedly with the warm cloth.

Each time I discovered a laceration, I quickly cleaned it and applied a dressing. I found one on her shoulder, three on her arms, and two on her hands. The respite ended when Griselda crawled into the cart and perched between the girl's legs. Flora started kicking like a deer fighting for its life.

I jumped to the ground. She was small, but if she kept pummeling Griselda, she'd eventually do some damage. Also, she was making it nearly impossible for Griselda to help her. Leaning into the back of the cart, I grabbed hold of her twig-like leg just above the ankle. I reached around behind Griselda and caught the other leg. Their circumferences were so small my fingers wrapped all the way around.

"*Bueno!* Hang on to her, both of you," said Griselda.

Esperanza tightened her hold, locking the girl's arms at her sides. I clamped my hands like vises, my arms jerking with Flora's attempts to break loose. Holding her like that felt wrong, but there was no other choice. Flora's labor would progress no matter what else happened.

Griselda reached out to feel for the baby's head.

"It's coming," she said.

Flora screamed, bucking her hips with another contraction.

"*Empuje!*" Griselda instructed, pressing on the top of her stomach to help her push.

Flora's blood-smeared face contorted. She let out a deep, feral moan. Esperanza leaned forward with her, Flora's chest pressing into her belly, the primal urge to expel the baby taking over, her raw screech piercing my ears as she bore down.

"*Empuje!*" Griselda shouted encouragingly, working to guide the baby's head and shoulders out.

Suddenly, Flora's legs flopped open as if every ounce of fight had drained from her body. The screaming stopped just as abruptly, its echo reverberating through my head in the silence.

I peeked around Griselda. Flora looked almost peaceful with her eyes closed and mouth slack. I let go of her ankles and stepped away, grateful for all of us that she'd passed out.

"*Es una niña,*" Griselda announced, pulling a puny, slime-covered baby into her arms.

A girl. I waited breathlessly, but no shrill newborn cries rang out. Griselda quickly wiped the baby's face. She cleared the white, cheesy matter from her tiny nose and mouth, then turned her over and softly thumped her back three times. Nothing happened. The baby's eyes didn't open, her body didn't move.

"*Por favor, sigue intentándolo,*" Esperanza cried, begging Griselda to keep trying.

Cradling her in one arm, Griselda rubbed the length of the baby's limbs, then rolled her small arms and legs between her fingers. Papa had saved a newborn puppy once by massaging it to get its blood circulating, but Flora's baby did not respond. Griselda pinched her nose closed, covering the tiny mouth with her own, blowing quick bursts of air into it, as if she were trying to breathe for her. With each attempt, I strained to see movement, but the baby's limbs remained draped over Griselda's arm as if full of sawdust instead of muscle and bone.

"*Lo siento.*" Griselda shook her head, tears spilling from her sage eyes. "There's nothing more I can do."

"*Dios mío, pobrecito.*" Esperanza bowed over her daughter's unconscious body in prayer. "*Reloj de Dios sobre este niño inocente.*"

"What's wrong?" asked Dove, arriving with the hot water and clean towels.

"The baby came too early," replied Griselda.

Dove nodded, seeming to take the death in stride. She climbed into the cart and knelt next to Flora, removing my bandages to try to sew up the multitude of wounds before the girl awoke.

Griselda tied off the baby's umbilical cord with string then cut it. She set her knife down on the floor of the cart and turned to me, holding out the small, lifeless form. I shrank away. I didn't want to touch the dead child. I could still feel the cold weight of JJ in my arms. Griselda pushed the baby closer until I finally reached out. My stomach roiled as the warm body, still covered in waxy white goo, slipped into my arms.

Tamping down my distress, I forced myself to look. Under all the mess, she had ten tiny fingers and ten tiny toes. A tuft of wet, dark hair with just a shimmer of auburn sat like a cap above her closed eyes and button nose. Other than the unnaturally quiet repose and bruised tint of her skin, she was perfect—a little wren nesting in my arms.

I'd been so excited the first time Mama had let me hold JJ, and so scared that I would drop him. A chubby, pink-faced, squirmy thing, he'd been nothing like the motionless, pale-blue infant in my arms now. I had no connection to this child, but tears rolled down my face anyway. Little Wren was lost to the world, just like JJ. Neither would grow old, the promise of life snatched away too soon.

Griselda delivered the afterbirth, dumping it over the side of the cart before she took out her suturing needle. Even though Wren had been premature, she'd been big enough to cause damage to Flora's young body. Mama had said it was a rare woman who didn't rip like tissue paper during childbirth, a notion that made the whole idea even less palatable. How unfair for Flora to go through all the risk and pain of pregnancy and labor, only to carry the scars and bury the child.

I looked around the churchyard, reconnecting with my surroundings as if waking from a terrible dream. Alicia no longer held the donkey tethered to Esperanza's cart. It had been tied to a tree trunk with a long rope. I heard a steady undercurrent of voices and turned to find a semicircle of people standing around the back of the cart. They kept their distance, but whispered as their eyes traveled from Griselda and Dove, who were both still working on Flora, to the dead baby in my arms.

A flare of anger shot through me. How dare they intrude? This was not a public spectacle to be observed and discussed. Flora's labor had taken place in the open only because there hadn't been time for privacy. All at once, I was overwhelmed by a desire to protect the dead child. I wrapped her tighter in my arms and leaned over to Dove.

"People are staring," I said. "What should I do with the baby?"

"Find something to put her in," she answered sensibly. "Esperanza and Flora can decide about a proper burial later."

Dove went back to concentrating on Flora's neck. As she stitched with slow determination, my heart warmed to her. There wasn't anything to be done for Wren, but Dove could help Flora heal, maybe more than physically.

I walked over to Griselda's wagon in search of something appropriate to put Wren in. The featherlight weight of her in my arms, the loose movement of her limbs with my steps, felt odd. It didn't seem right to put her in a box like a doll no one wanted to play with, but I did want to shield her.

All the larger cartons containing Griselda's supplies had been taken into the church, but I found some clean pieces of cloth stacked under the bench seat. Sitting cross-legged in the wagon bed, I propped Wren against my thigh and wiped away the pink streaks of birth matter. Then I swaddled her as I would have done for a living baby, leaving her little face exposed. Flora could see what her daughter looked like if she wanted to.

Clean and not quite so vulnerable, I carried Wren into the church, walking to the altar where Griselda's supplies had been placed. There were a couple of cardboard containers, but they were either full of stuff or too flimsy to hold even Wren's slight weight. I remembered the boxes I'd seen earlier under the altar. My next thought caused a pinch of guilt.

I had an acceptable reason to search through the boxes. I glanced down at Wren, apologizing silently for using her as an excuse, then reached under the burlap cloth with my free hand. My fingers landed on the corner of something. I dragged out a crate. *Nelson's Fine Peaches* was stamped in bright orange letters on the side, along with a cartoon of an impish, smiling peach. Inside were a stack of folded towels and several rolls of cotton. I pushed the crate back and pulled out the next box. Stored in it were green army blankets like the ones I'd seen covering some of the patients in the nave. The last box was very heavy; I had to lay Wren on the ground and tug with both hands. Lifting the top, my heart sank a little when I saw canned food and condensed milk. Nothing unusual. I was replacing the lid when footsteps approached from behind.

"Qué necesitas, señorita?"

I turned to find the woman who'd helped Dove bring in the supplies standing over me. Her brow rose when she noticed Wren. I stooped down and picked the baby up, feeling my cheeks warm. I'd come into the church to do something respectful and had instead abandoned the dead child on the floor.

"The baby was stillborn," I explained. "Dove asked me to find something to put her in, for her family."

The woman gave me an understanding nod. I hesitated

for a moment, an internal tug-of-war happening between my intentions and my personal objectives. As my mother's daughter, I honestly wanted to do right by Wren, but I had an opportunity I might not have again. Dove was busy outside taking care of Flora, and I needed to search Santa Rosa.

"Those boxes are full," I said. "Is it all right if I look around for something else? I don't want her mother and grandmother to see her like this."

"*Sí, claro*," the woman said, waving her hand over the mission as if giving me free rein.

I silently promised to look for something proper to settle Wren in while at the same time searching for something to damn Javier with. I carried the baby down the wooden steps into the east transept, picking my way around discarded wheelchairs and crutches, looking for anything that appeared strange or out of place. I dug through cast-off medical devices, checked under chairs, even tapped on the stone floor in case something had been hidden underneath, but found nothing.

Crossing over to the other transept, I noticed an arched passageway off the back corner and ducked into it. At the end was a staircase. I walked down into a room carved into the rocky ground. The ceiling, hovering only inches over my head, was the wooden floor of the sanctuary above. Two large square grates had been cut into it, allowing air and light to filter in. Still, it was more like a large cave than a room.

As my sight sharpened, I realized I was in the mission's crypt. An alcove had been carved into the stone-and-dirt wall next to me. It displayed a silver box with three glass sides. Inside the case sat a circle of dried roses, their brown-edged petals faded to a dusty pink. On a square of yellowing lace in the center of the crown lay a wooden figurine of baby Jesus. It was only about five inches long, but the sculptor had included fine details. The baby's face held a calm smile, his hand reaching out, two fingers extended. A shiver shook my shoulders as I imagined the Christ Child blessing Wren.

I turned, trying to make out the rest of the crypt in the low light. A couple of wooden boxes sat on the ground right in front of me. I squatted down and pushed the lid off one. The contents were nothing exciting—rolls of gauze and cotton swabs. I dug through the other box, but only found syringes, needles, iodine, catgut—everything needed to treat cuts and sew up lacerations.

Standing, I focused on the dark area behind the boxes, realizing it was crowded with whiskey barrels. Disappointment wiggled through me. Had I come all this way only to discover a store of alcohol? The Rangers knew Javier was smuggling liquor—what difference would it make if he was transporting whiskey instead of *tequila*?

Fearing I'd reached a dead end, I walked over. A familiar smoky-sweet smell surrounded me. *Jack Daniel's Distillery, Lynchburg, Tennessee*, had been burned into the sides and tops of the barrels. Maude had a penchant for Jack Daniel's. Over the years, she'd collected more than thirty barrels of Old No. 7, gathering them before the temperance movement and Prohibition had halted whiskey production. To keep them cool, she stored them in a shallow hole she'd dug into the caliche and clay soil under her barn. She filled her own rectangular bottles from the barrels each Christmas, gluing on a label sporting her brand. She passed them out as gifts to business associates and friends. Papa kept his in the bottom drawer of his nightstand. He'd pour himself a swallow on certain occasions—celebrations, tragedies, cold nights that made his joints hurt.

Why would Javier smuggle whiskey all the way from Tennessee to Mexico? Were the barrels full of *tequila* instead of whiskey? Or did they hold something else? Old barrels made great storage containers. Whiskey and bourbon could only be aged in new barrels, that was why there were so many used ones around. Papa stored corn and feed in them. Maude cut her empty ones in two and used them as planters for her herbs.

I set Wren down and looked at the barrel closest to me. The lid had been removed, which was not easy. It took a special tool to dislodge the metal bands around the end of a barrel. Once the hoops were off, the oak staves could be pulled apart and the top circle of wood taken out. Papa would replace the bands, tightening the barrel up again, and file the edge of the lid so it could be taken on and off more easily.

I worked my fingers into the narrow groove, pleased when the top lifted off. The stale odor of charred oak and honey burst forth, but the container appeared to be empty. Why store a lot of empty barrels? I inspected the cask; something didn't seem right. I examined the exterior, then the interior, then reached in and knocked on the bottom. A hollow sound rang out. I pushed hard on one side. A thin circle of wood popped up and a thrill flushed through me. The barrel had a false bottom. I removed it and stared, disbelief swirling around me.

I'd prayed Mozo's suspicion had been right, and I'd find something at Santa Rosa to guarantee the Rangers would come after Javier, but what I'd found was more than I'd dared to hope for, and more than I'd thought to fear.

CHAPTER 17

At the bottom of the barrel, packed in shredded newspaper, were ten Colt .45s. I moved to another whiskey cask and lifted the lid. It too had a false bottom. Under it were ten more guns.

"Holy shit," I whispered.

I sank to the ground, so many implications flying at me I couldn't sort through them fast enough. I forced my brain to slow down. Journalists collected information, uncovered facts, then analyzed what they found. They didn't jump to conclusions.

What was the significance of the guns?

I got to my feet and counted the barrels. There were fifty of them. I reached into one I'd opened, my fingers closing around the grip of a revolver. I lifted it out gently, as if it might turn to dust. The stock wasn't fashioned from mother-of-pearl like Gus's had been. It was something cheaper, something man-made—like the Bakelite handles on our silverware. I tilted the gun toward the shafts of light coming from the ceiling vents. Several deep scratches marred the metal of the barrel and the cylinder. It wasn't a new gun.

I turned the Colt over in my hand. *SAA-1* had been stamped into the metal at the base of the barrel. I put it back and drew out another one, finding the same mark in the same place. SAA—San Antonio Arsenal?

Feeling lightheaded, I moved deeper into the crypt. There

were three medium-sized wooden crates stacked up in the back corner. The first one was too tightly secured to open without a screwdriver. I pushed it off the pile, struggling to guide its weight to the floor without dropping it. All four screws had been removed from the top of the second one. I yanked it off. It was packed with green cardboard cartons. The print on the top of each one read, *Remington Kleanbore .45 COLT smokeless cartridges, 50 count.*

Wagley Phillips's voice echoed through my head.

"Five hundred Colt .45s ain't a few. Old or not, put bullets in them and they work. Whoever stole them could arm every bandit from here to Mexico City."

Or fortify an army.

Javier didn't need an armed militia, but, according to Lancero, Pancho Villa did.

How had Javier managed to steal guns from the United States military? He'd had to snatch them from under the noses of armed soldiers and transport them more than two hundred miles south from San Antonio. Then he'd had to circumvent border patrol and get the load across the Rio Grande. Javier was a known outlaw. There was no way he could have done all that without help from someone who would draw less suspicion, someone who knew South Texas.

Someone like Jackson? Had he helped Javier transport the load to Mexico? He would've been the perfect accomplice. No one would believe Captain Gus Cage's grandson would help a *tequilero* run guns. Even I didn't believe it. Did I?

After crossing the river, the *tequileros* had managed to move the .45s over the Chihuahuan Desert to Múzquiz without getting caught by government troops. Once at Santa Rosa, it would have been impossible to carry fifty whiskey barrels through the mission without notice. They were large and heavy; it would've taken several trips by several men to get them all down into the crypt. Dove had to know what lay underneath the altar. Did she know what was stashed inside?

Why would she allow Javier to use the mission? Was her

role at Santa Rosa just a cover? Was she an outlaw and gun-runner, too? If so, her Clara Barton act had fooled me and, perhaps, Griselda. Maybe Javier had forced her to hide the barrels? Was he responsible for the damage to her face?

The thought chilled me. If Javier found out I'd discovered his stash, what would he do to me? I doubted mutilation would be enough. He'd want to make sure I couldn't tell anyone. He'd kill me. If he didn't, Pancho Villa surely would. What I'd discovered was lethal knowledge.

The .45 weighed heavy in my hand. I stared at the San Antonio Arsenal's stamp. The gun was more than evidence against Javier; holding the solid piece of metal gave me an undeniable sense of security. A gun changed the balance of power. Maybe I wasn't as strong as most men, but I could shoot. I needed to protect myself. I needed to protect Griselda and Alicia.

I needed to get the hell out of the crypt and race to Laredo.

I pushed the .45's cylinder open. As expected, it was empty. No one in their right mind would store loaded guns, but an empty revolver was just a showpiece. I squatted down and pulled a carton from the ammo box, took out five brass bullets and slid them into the Colt's chambers, leaving the one under the hammer empty so the gun couldn't fire accidentally. I closed the cylinder, then plucked five more bullets out and dropped them into my pants pocket. I wanted to stuff every pocket full of bullets, but the more I took, the more likely it would be that someone would notice.

I rearranged the cartons so that the one with the missing bullets was at the bottom of the crate, then shoved the revolver into the back of my waistband. A feeling of strength spread through me as it warmed to my body temperature.

As I stood, my gaze fell on the small cocoon shape of Wren. Guilt hit me like a gush of cold water. I had not yet kept my promise. I walked over to the first box I'd opened, the one that held the bandaging supplies. It might have been too small for a full-term baby, but Wren would fit. I fashioned a nest out of gauze and cotton squares, then settled her on it.

Faltering for a moment, I took in the only image Flora would ever have of her child—a tiny form with a pale blue face lying in a medical supply box. I couldn't fathom what a thing like that would do to a young girl, or to anyone. Would it be better never to have known a child, or to have known the child and then lost it? My guess was it didn't matter—loss was loss.

I put the extra supplies away and shoved the ammo boxes against the wall where I'd found them. After replacing the false bottoms, I set the lids of the barrels back in place, checking to be sure they were snug. Finally, I pulled my vest down over the Colt's grip, balanced the little coffin on my hip, and walked toward the stairs.

Before reaching the first step, I accidentally kicked a bottle of iodine I'd missed when repacking the boxes. It skittered across the uneven dirt floor, hitting the front wall below the relic alcove with a loud crack. Dark brown liquid leaked out as a sharp, metallic smell leeched into the closed air. I hurried over and began picking up the broken glass.

"What are you doing in here?"

I jumped, almost dropping Wren's box as I whipped around. Dove stood on the bottom stair.

"Damnit!" I said, chest pumping. "You scared me."

The half-light seeping through the ceiling vents played across her face, draining into the void in the middle.

"I asked you a question," she said, voice hard as stone.

As she stepped into the room, something in her hand, partially hidden by the folds of her skirt, glinted. She stopped and turned, her eyes brushing over the rest of the crypt, pausing on the whiskey barrels. When she swung back around to face me, her skirt separated. I saw what she held. Fear slithered down my neck as she lifted the knife.

CHAPTER 18

Dove stood like a pillar of salt, the point of her buck knife hovering inches from me. The temperature in the crypt plummeted, the warmth I'd felt for her earlier cut away by the sharp blade she held. I cleared my throat.

"I ... I came down here to find something to put the baby in." My voice sounded wobbly. "The woman upstairs said it would be all right to look around."

Dove's eyes slid from my face to the box under my arm, but the knife stayed steady.

"This box only had a few things in it. I thought it would be all right," I blurted, the need to explain now rushing my words. "I wanted something Flora and Esperanza could leave her in when they bury her. I thought it might be easier if they didn't have to touch the baby, but they could see her if they wanted to ... I guess that sounds silly."

"No," Dove said, voice cool with suspicion. "That sounds thoughtful."

She was still clutching the handle but lowered the knife to her side as she stepped down into the crypt. I took a deep breath, fighting the urge to run past her and up the stairway.

"I accidentally broke this." I held out the pieces of the bottle. "I can see if Griselda has one to replace it."

Dove didn't move. I couldn't decipher her expression. I'd always thought a person's eyes held the key to what he or she thought, but no matter how hard I tried to concentrate on her other features, Dove's missing nose threw me off. I set the shards down on top of a box.

Dove turned to look at the barrels again. I followed her gaze, my stomach cartwheeling when I saw what had caught her attention. Several clear boot prints marked the dirt in front of the closest one. The one I'd taken the gun out of.

"You looked in there," she stated.

I took a long, slow breath. If she didn't know what was hidden in the barrel, why would she care? I felt like she was playing chess. I decided to play along.

"What does it matter if I did?" I narrowed my eyes, mirroring her attitude. "Why did you come down here with a knife drawn?"

"I heard something," she replied calmly, glancing up at the grates in the ceiling. "I didn't know it was you."

She'd known by the time she'd pointed the knife at me.

"I just wanted to find something for the baby," I reiterated.

Her eyes flashed with some emotion. I had no idea what. She could break into relieved laughter or stab me in the chest.

"You weren't going to put the baby in a whiskey barrel," she remarked.

She was in a tough position. She knew I'd opened the barrel, but if I hadn't discovered the false bottom, she didn't want to let on that it held a secret. On the other hand, if I had found the guns, she'd have to decide what to do about it.

"How is it you know Griselda?" she asked.

Was she stalling? Trying to figure me out?

"Alicia and I have been friends since childhood. She invited me to come on this trip with her great-aunt to learn about being a healer," I said, adding, "My mother was a midwife. She passed away not too long ago."

Her head tilted. "You plan on following in your mother's footsteps?"

"She would have liked me to," I answered honestly. "I

guess that's why I feel protective of Flora's baby. I know Mama would've made sure she was cared for, even in death."

Dove reached out and tipped up the lid of the makeshift coffin. Her stance relaxed as she peered in at the nest I'd made for Wren. She let the lid drop, folding the knife closed with a metallic click.

"My mother died when I was about your age," she said softly. "Griselda's a good mentor; she can teach you a lot. I wish I'd met her sooner."

"When did you meet her?" I asked, relieved to be discussing any subject other than whiskey barrels.

"She cared for me ..." Dove passed a hand over her face.

I hesitated to ask more, figuring she'd tell me to mind my own business, but I felt like we'd made a small connection. I wanted to know how she'd found the strength to survive what she had been through.

"What happened?"

"Men don't think whores have the right to say no." She looked down at Wren's box, a shudder passing through her. "His voice wakes me up most nights."

She took several full breaths, as if bringing herself back to the present.

"I don't remember much about after," she went on. "I woke up in Griselda's room at *La Fonda*."

"Did the madam of the brothel take you to her?"

"Lord, no!" she scoffed. "If there hadn't been so many witnesses, she'd have loaded me up in a wagon and dumped me in the nearest hole. One of the customers took me."

"Why didn't he take you to a hospital?"

"They would've called the authorities," she said. "I did wonder why he took me to Griselda instead of leaving me somewhere to bleed to death or die of infection." A hard gleam shone in her eyes. "It wasn't out of pity for me. More than likely, he was trying to protect the Texan who did it. You can get away with raping a whore, but not murdering one."

"If you split a hare, you still end up with four feet and a tail."

I hadn't meant to say Maude's words out loud, but Dove let out a bitter laugh.

"You help so many people here," I said, attempting to continue lightening the mood. "It's fortunate for them the Texan didn't take your life."

"He took my only possession," Dove shot back. "I grew up dirt-poor. The one advantage I ever had was the way I looked. My body might've belonged to whoever was paying for it, but I owned my beauty. I wore it like a shield. In my world, it gave me power, over men and women."

Her lapis eyes scanned my face, the curve of a wry smile on her lips.

"Maybe you're too young to realize, but you've got it too," she said. "Natural, God-given beauty. Appreciate the gift, but don't ever wrap your self-worth up in one thing. When I lost it, I thought I'd lost everything."

I felt her heartache. With the stroke of a blade, the Texan had ended the life she'd known. It wasn't an equal comparison, but Papa could end mine with the stroke of a pen on a purchase agreement. Then who would I be?

"How did you move on?" I asked.

"Griselda told me about Saint Rose." Dove walked over to the alcove. "She was born beautiful, too, but hated it. She starved herself, rubbed lye and pepper on her face. She wanted the focus to be on the good works God did through her, not on the way she looked."

Dove trailed her fingers along the glass front of the relic box, the way you might trace the features of a loved one.

"She took a vow of chastity and devoted her life to baby Jesus, the healer. She raised money to care for the sick and injured by selling lacework and the flowers she grew in her garden. The only time she went out in public was to fight for the rights of the native people, especially the children."

Dove tapped the glass.

"Legend has it she wore this crown of roses over a circle of steel spikes that bit into her scalp." Dove's somber sigh floated through the cave. "I'll never match her self-sacrifice—wouldn't want to, she was crazy—but she brought me back from the dead. My life has more meaning now than it did before."

I stared at Dove's face. For the first time since meeting her, I saw past what was missing. The strength emanating from her wasn't from surviving a horrific ordeal; it was from finding her calling. I craved that feeling of fulfillment. I knew in my soul it lay in the broken heart of my father and the sandy dirt of La Barroneña. Who would have thought the path to two such familiar places would be so difficult?

"Stop looking at me like you've seen a goddamn angel," said Dove. "I'd do just about anything for the people here, but I'm no saint. If I come across the Texan again, he better hope I'm not holding this knife. To hell with it all."

The way her mouth twisted left no doubt in my mind that, to her, revenge would feel as satisfying as rain in the desert. Maybe her comment should've tainted my opinion of her, but instead, it gave me a sense of kinship. Seeking justice sounded better than wanting revenge, but the two were close cousins.

"You must be grateful to the man who helped you, no matter what his reasons were," I said, thinking at least someone had done the right thing. Because of him, she'd found Griselda and a new life. Or maybe I said it to test her ... because I thought I knew who her savior was.

"Grateful?" Dove scoffed. "That's not the word I'd use." Her breath whistled through the opening in her face as if her pulse had sped up. "The man who took me to Hidalgo is no hero, but I'm in his debt, for better or worse."

A dark thought occurred to me.

"Does he make you ..." I stumbled on my words, not wanting to offend her.

She'd started walking to the stairs but stopped, shaking her head.

"It's not what you're thinking," she said. "The things I do for him are unpleasant, dirty even, but not of an intimate nature. He brings medical supplies and offers protection from other bandits, who seem to think we're easy prey. So, I do what he asks."

Suddenly, the .45 pressing against my back felt like a hot iron. What would Javier do to her if he discovered a gun was missing? Above us, the thud and scrape of slow footsteps resounded, faint sounds of suffering falling through the ceiling grates. Who would care for all the sick and injured if something happened to Dove? Who would shield them from danger?

I glanced at the woman I barely knew. I respected her dedication, I was angered by the cruelty of her disfigurement, I envied her sense of purpose, but I had no real understanding of who she was. If I told her what I'd done and why, would she help me get the gun to the Rangers, hoping to be free from her obligation to Javier, or would she sink that blade into my chest to protect herself and her precious Santa Rosa?

I'd tucked the .45 into my waistband. I wasn't putting it back. Dove had made her choice, and so had I.

CHAPTER 19

I rushed out of the mission doors. The cart had been moved behind a tall piñon tree, its shaggy branches offering a light screen of privacy. Flora lay quietly on a blanket with her head in her mother's lap—a sleeping girl instead of a half-crazed wilding. Her wounds had been sewn up and bandaged, her bloody slip replaced with a clean cotton shift.

Griselda was wiping the last smears of gore off Flora's knobby knees. I needed to get her alone to tell her what I'd found and ask how soon we could leave. As I approached, Griselda leaned over to rinse her cloth out, then tipped the bucket sideways to empty it. Pink-tinged water poured out. A knot tried to crawl up my throat, but I swallowed hard, refusing to let the memory unfold.

Griselda set the pail down and stood, stretching her crooked back.

"Will Flora be all right?" I asked.

"The cuts will heal if they don't get infected, but she'll have terrible scars," Griselda replied in a hushed voice. "I don't know that she will be able to have more children. There was a lot of damage. She was molested, many times, by more than one man."

What would her future be like? Being raped, impregnated, stabbed, losing a baby—any one of those things would be traumatic enough on its own. Could she recover from all of it? At her age, my biggest concern had been whether Papa would leave me behind or let me ride the fences with him.

"The man she calls 'the wolf' kidnapped her over a year ago," Griselda continued. "Until last night, her mother didn't even know if she was alive."

I noticed Esperanza watching us. She leaned over and placed a hand on my arm.

"*La bebé está allí?*" she asked.

I nodded and held the crate out to her, an offering of her dead granddaughter. I had hoped Wren's condition would give her some peace of mind, but Esperanza did not lift the lid. She set the box next to her, resting a hand on it tentatively, as if touching it was almost too much to bear. I started to tell her I was sorry for her loss, then remembered how trivial those words had sounded when they'd been said to me.

To have your grandchild never breathe a single breath would be heartrending. Still, I wondered what would have happened if Wren had lived. Would Esperanza have been able to love her? Would Flora have been able to accept a baby who was the result of so much violence, the offspring of someone I assumed it would be impossible not to hate? None of it was the baby's fault, of course, but it would take a great deal of compassion to embrace such a child. Could I have done it with an open heart? JJ had not asked to be placed in my care, yet I'd resented him for it.

"Where is Alicia?" asked Griselda.

"I thought she was out here with you," I said, looking over behind the church where she'd gotten sick earlier. When had I last seen Alicia? I'd been so preoccupied I couldn't remember.

"She isn't in the mission?" asked Griselda.

"I didn't see her." Something squirmed in my gut. "I'll go look."

She'd probably managed to gain control of herself and gone inside to help. I could have missed her in my haste to talk to Griselda. I returned to the church, spotting Dove near the altar.

"Have you seen Alicia?" I called to her.

"Not in here," she replied, turning back to the young man she was bandaging.

I scanned the nave and the transepts, but Alicia wasn't there. Running back outside, I looked over at the wagon. It sat in the same spot. Rat was still tied to a nearby tree, his head lowered like he was taking a nap. I headed for the wagon to see if maybe Alicia was lying in the bed, then stopped in my tracks.

"Griselda!" I called out, stomach bubbling to a full boil. "Where's Grace?"

"Who?" she answered, turning from Flora to look at me.

"Your mule," I said. "Where is your mule?"

Griselda and I reached the wagon at the same time. It was surrounded by bags of fruit and vegetables, bouquets of wild-flowers, and baskets of baked goods wrapped in waxed paper. There were even two live chickens in a wire cage.

"What is all this?" I asked.

"Gifts from the people," said Griselda.

I circled the wagon then jogged down the road a ways to be sure Grace hadn't wandered off. When I got back, Griselda was rifling through the things in the back of the buckboard.

"The saddle and bridle are gone," she said finally. "Also, my knife and a water canteen."

Had Alicia saddled Grace and ridden off?

"Did she leave?" I asked.

"I don't know what else to think," said Griselda, climbing over to sit on the bench seat where silver crosses and *milagros*, small tin charms, sparkled like sequins.

"What was she doing the last time you saw her?"

Griselda thought for a moment.

"She was cleaning rags for me," she said. "She was pale, trying not to be sick. Flora had woken and was much calmer. Esperanza was asking questions; they were talking."

"Was it too much for her?" I asked. "Do you think she decided to go home?"

"Why would she do that without talking to us?" Griselda shook her head. "It is dangerous to ride these roads alone. She is a smart girl, she knows that."

Then what? I looked over at the cart. Flora was semiconscious, her eyes barely slits. Her mother was stroking her head, humming softly. I approached them, stopping a couple feet away so as not to frighten Flora. Esperanza looked up.

"*Cómo se siente?*" I asked.

"She is very weak and still has pain," she replied in Spanish, "but, by the grace of God, she is alive."

I knew I should walk away and let them have their time together. Flora had a long road of healing ahead of her; the sooner she started down it, the better, but maybe Alicia had said something to them that could help us. I glanced up at the sky. The sun was heading for the horizon; once it dropped below the mountain range, it would quickly grow cold and dark. Alicia was totally unprepared to be out in the wilderness on her own.

"Do you know where the other girl went?" I asked. "The one with the long dark hair?"

Esperanza looked around as if just noticing Alicia wasn't there.

"Did you send her to get something for you?" I tried again. "From your house maybe?"

"*No, señorita,*" she replied, a little defensively.

Flora let out a long, deep sigh. Esperanza bent over her, whispering in a calm voice, using her fingers to comb the girl's matted hair away from her face.

Griselda placed her hands on the side of the cart.

"I wanted to take you home in my wagon," she said. "It would be more comfortable for Flora, but it seems my great-niece has taken my mule, and my wagon is too heavy for your donkey."

Esperanza looked blankly from me to Griselda and back.

"Was Alicia talking with you and Flora earlier?" I asked.

"Maybe you said something?"

Esperanza's soft eyes drooped with hurt.

"I did not say anything to her, *señorita*," she replied. "I was only talking with my daughter."

"Of course, you didn't do anything wrong," I rushed to explain. "I meant maybe she was listening and overheard something that upset her."

"Oh, I see," said Esperanza.

Her gaze returned to Flora, but I pushed on.

"What were you talking about? When Alicia was here. Do you remember?"

Esperanza looked at Griselda as if pleading for help.

"Please," said Griselda. "She is not one to wander off."

"She could be in trouble," I added.

"You ... you are the angel."

Flora's voice was weak and strained, but her eyes were wide open, and she was staring at me. I was no angel, and not deserving of the awe in her expression, but I'd let it go if it meant she would talk.

"Do you remember, Flora?" I asked.

"We were talking about the camp," she said.

"Where *El Lobo* took you?" I asked.

"Yes," she answered. "Up the mountain trail behind the church. The *tequila* camp. I was telling *Mamá* it was like being in a haunted forest, hidden by big rocks and dark trees."

"What else were you telling your mother?" I prodded.

"What happened before *Viejo Jesús* saved me. How my stomach got so big, I thought it would split open."

Flora felt her abdomen, then seemed to remember the baby was no longer there. Her fingers traveled up to the bandage on her neck.

"How did you get hurt?" I asked.

"*Lobo* and *Jefe* got into a fight," she said. "*Lobo* wanted to bring me to Múzquiz to have the baby. *Jefe* said no, someone would ask questions. *Lobo* got mad. He said he didn't want his baby born in the woods like an animal." A quiver shook her voice, but she went on. "*Jefe* told him the baby probably wasn't his, it could belong to any of them, including him."

A child of twelve had lived through what I'd only been threatened with. I swallowed my repulsion and placed a hand on Flora's arm. She didn't flinch away, but I felt her tremble.

"That made *Lobo* crazy," she said.

Esperanza shot me a withering look. I forced myself to ignore it; I needed to find Alicia.

"What did he do?" I asked gently.

"He came after me with the knife. He was going to cut the baby out," she said, her eyes glistening. "The boy ran at *Lobo* to stop him, but *Jefe* grabbed him and threw him on the ground."

"The boy?" I asked, dread prickling under my skin. "Do you know his name?"

"Carlos."

I heard Griselda inhale next to me.

"What happened to Carlos?" I asked.

"He tried to get up, but *Jefe* punched him hard. He fell and hit his head on a rock. I saw blood." A tear rolled down Flora's cheek. "Carlos was nice. He always snuck me food. He wasn't like the rest of them. I wanted to help him, but I couldn't. I was trying to get away from the knife. I told *Mamá* I am very worried for him."

"There's nothing you could have done," I said, rubbing her arm. "Alicia heard you talking about this?"

"She ran behind the church," said Flora. "I didn't see her after that."

"*Dios mío*," whispered Griselda.

I pulled her several feet away from the cart.

"She has gone to the camp," she said.

Saving Carlos was one thing Alicia would risk her life to do. He was hurt and in danger. The *tequileros* would not take him to a doctor or get help for him. If his injuries were bad enough, they'd just leave him to suffer, or shoot him like a horse with a broken leg. Helping Dove had benefitted Javier, but there would be no benefit to getting medical care for Carlos, a boy who provided nothing more than manual labor. A boy who could tell the authorities all about the *tequila* operation and, maybe, the guns.

"I will go find Dove," said Griselda, heading for the mission. "She can help us."

I grabbed Griselda's arm.

"I don't think we should tell Dove."

"Why not?"

She wouldn't be asking if she knew about Dove's ongoing relationship with Javier.

"She does things for Javier in return for supplies and protection," I said. "Right now, she's hiding stolen guns in the crypt for him."

Griselda's face shriveled in anguish.

"I was afraid of something like this," she said. "The favors he does incur a big cost."

"You are familiar with Dove," I said. "What would she do if she knew the whole truth about why we came here?"

"I do not wish to put her in that position."

I wasn't surprised Griselda chose to protect Dove even though it made her own situation more difficult. What would she think of me if she knew I'd pushed aside the risk to Dove and her people in order to take the gun? I decided to spare her from that information, just as she was sparing Dove.

Griselda's exhale was almost a sob. Her posture was usually strong despite her deformity, but now she seemed to sink toward the ground.

"They are my family, my grandchildren."

I was desperate to get to Laredo, but Griselda wouldn't leave without Alicia, or without knowing if Carlos was all right, and I wouldn't ask her to. I could go on my own, but that would mean abandoning all three of them. Griselda had taken a big risk escorting me across the Chihuahuan Desert; I couldn't repay her by leaving her to deal with this alone.

"I'm going after them," I said, ignoring the sweat gathering at the nape of my neck.

Griselda looked up, her back rising a bit.

"How will you know where to go?" she asked.

"I'll find Alicia's trail. I can track her."

"No," Griselda said. "It is too dangerous. I cannot ask you to do this."

"You're not asking me," I replied. "Alicia is strong-willed. If she thinks Carlos is suffering, there will be no stopping her," a pained smile crossed my face, "no matter how many times she swoons or throws up."

Griselda looked up at the dark backdrop of mountains behind Santa Rosa.

"Alicia can't get Carlos out of there alone," I said.

"She should not have done this." A tear rolled down Griselda's nose.

"But she did," I said, "and she's my sister just as much as she's your granddaughter."

Griselda sighed in resignation, but concern dug deeper into her face.

"Tell Dove that Alicia and I went to Sabinas for supplies," I told her. "Depending on what happens, it might be too dangerous for us to come back here. If we don't show up by noon tomorrow, meet us in Laredo."

Griselda's wise eyes peered into mine.

"And if you do not make it to Laredo?"

"Find the Texas Rangers, ask for Captain Wright," I answered, grabbing her hand to be sure she understood. "Make him listen to you. Tell him everything, especially about the guns Javier's hiding in the mission."

Griselda nodded, her gnarled hand wrapping around mine.

"*Vaya con Dios, m'ija.*"

CHAPTER 20

I followed the mule's tracks from Santa Rosa in the direction of the foothills as low, purple clouds gathered like bruises along the ragged mountaintops. A clear moonlit night would have made the journey easier. As the sky darkened, I prayed it wouldn't rain and wash away Grace's hoofprints.

I understood why she'd done it, but I struggled not to be angry with Alicia. If she'd told me what she'd heard Flora say, I could have helped her come up with a plan. What did she think she was going to do when she got to the camp? Walk into a band of outlaws and demand they release her brother? She didn't even know how badly Carlos was hurt. What if he hadn't regained consciousness? What if ...

Her decision had been rash. She hadn't told me or Griselda because she hadn't wanted to be stopped. I kicked Rat into a gallop. If I could get to her before she made it to the hideout, maybe I could keep her from making matters worse.

Rat's ears stood up as the *swoosh* of running water rose in front of us. His chin lifted, and my frayed nerves wavered. The temperature was dropping; I did not want to jump into a cold mountain stream and drag Rat across it. I didn't have time for that. We stepped out of the trees, and I saw the river. It coursed through the dense pine-oak forest then plunged down a fifteen-foot drop. The pool below the waterfall was surrounded by tall cypress trees with finger-like roots clutching the bank.

Several lanterns hung from the trees' quilled branches, their glow making the waterhole glitter like a huge bowl of emeralds.

Rat held his head erect as we both regarded a group of children playing. They were shouting, "Marco," "Polo," at each other, splashing and swimming in and out of the waterfall. I'd played the same game at home with Alicia, Carlos, and JJ in the big round tank at the Macho Creek windmill. The water wasn't deep enough to swim in, so whoever was "It" closed their eyes and lunged around in the muck like Frankenstein's monster. JJ had hated being "It" and refused to say "Polo" in an effort not to get tagged. Carlos, however, had loved being "It" and would yell at the top of his lungs. Alicia and I had each blamed our own brother for ruining the game.

The bittersweet memory filled me with longing. Things had been so much simpler then, our brothers irritating us the way siblings did, before the responsibility for them had fallen squarely on our shoulders. I'd failed JJ, but Alicia might still have a chance to save Carlos. The thought smudged the edges of my irritation.

Nearby, a group of women sat on blankets around a fire amidst the remains of a picnic supper, keeping watch on the children.

"*Buenas noches.*" They looked up at my greeting, their happy chatter hushing as I went on in Spanish. "Did a young woman riding a white mule come by here?"

They glanced at each other.

"I need to find her," I said. "I'm worried about her being alone in the woods after dark."

There were nods of agreement around the group.

"She was here a while ago," one of them finally replied, "asking about the path up the mountain. We told her it is farther upstream, past the bend. We warned her not to go, but she still headed that way."

"She's looking for her younger brother," I said.

The women let out a series of "ohs" and "ahas" as if I'd given them the answer to a riddle. When several children ran up, complaining of the cold and demanding blankets, they quickly lost interest in me, and I rode on.

Rat seemed to keep one eye on the water as we cantered to the bend. When the wide, green river took a sharp turn, disappearing into the woods above, we stopped. The ground had become rocky, and the light was waning, making it harder and harder for me to find Grace's hoofprints. I scanned the ground for hints of the path the *tequileros* used. Wild game left tracks and droppings in the dirt, or tufts of fur caught on bushes, but most humans were less subtle. It was just a matter of seeing the signs.

Several yards past the turn of the river, I finally found something. An area of grass had been smashed flat in an oval shape at the base of an oak tree, as if a deer had bedded down there. I jumped off Rat for a closer look, my eye catching on a glint in the roots of the tree. I squatted down, pushing leaves aside to uncover a bottle wrapped in a casing made of blade-shaped leaves sewn together. My mother had called the shuck-like wrappers *tules*. She'd used them to protect the glass containers she packed food in for picnics. As I picked up the bottle, the astringent smell of *tequila* pierced my nostrils.

A few feet beyond the tree, I spotted a pile of fresh horse dung and found Grace's wide prints. Just past them was the mouth of the trail, camouflaged by a netting of juniper scrub. I stared at the twisting artery leading uphill to the *tequileros'* hideout.

"Not exactly a yellow brick road," I mumbled, jogging back to Rat.

I tried to imagine how Alicia must have felt as she'd headed up the path. We'd both heard Flora describe the camp as a place where nightmares came true. If it scared me, it must have terrified Alicia. Yet, she had not turned back; the hoofprints marched on.

I let Rat get a feel for the incline, then urged him faster. I didn't want him to injure himself, but I was still praying we'd find Alicia before she reached the camp. I felt under the back of my vest, fingers brushing across the butt of the .45. Like touching a good luck charm or clutching a teddy bear, it made me feel safer.

All Alicia had for protection was Griselda's knife. I doubted she had much experience using one outside of the kitchen. I was struck again by how impulsive she'd been. Were people at home thinking the same of me; chattering in the mercantile about how Sarita Gibson had taken off, leaving her sick father to grieve alone? If they knew the details, they'd surely think I'd lost my mind. Maybe love was the only emotion more powerful than fear. Or was it fear that pushed us forward? The fear of loss.

Air whistled through the forest, blowing away the last light. Chills spread down my arms. I tugged Papa's jacket out of the saddlebag. As I put it on, darkness fell, and my senses came to attention. I smelled the dankness of rain riding on the wind; I heard the rustling of leaves and the calls of hawks winging to their roosts; I felt every step Rat took as he deftly picked his way forward. How was Grace navigating the rocky path? He'd blundered over obstacles in broad daylight. What if he slipped and fell on Alicia, or sent them both tumbling downhill? I could ride past their broken bodies and never know it.

I pulled Rat to a stop and hopped down. Crouching until my head almost touched the ground, I searched until I finally saw a big C-shaped divot in a patch of dirt. Another one a few feet away reassured me that Grace had not taken them both over a cliff. Yet.

The shadowy vein of cypress trees petered out, and a vista opened to the riverbank's choppy contour. The busy water babbled like the voices of a hundred wood nymphs racing downhill, warning me to go back. Rock formations became mountain lions about to leap off boulders and sink their curved teeth into my flesh. Black bears were rare in South Texas, but not in the Sierras. A mama bear would tear apart anything she thought was threatening her cubs. When did bears give birth? In the spring? There could be hundreds of mother bears around with months-old cubs to protect.

"Stop it!" I growled to myself.

Rat huffed with exertion but trudged next to the stream without complaint, head up, ears forward in concentration. Perhaps dangers greater than water occupied his mind as well. I kept expecting some signal that we were gaining on Alicia. Rat would move much faster on the tricky trail than Grace, but I didn't know how big a lead they had.

The path took a hard right. As we left the gurgling stream behind, the surroundings hushed to the kind of undertone only the wilderness could hold. I'd never seen such tall trees. Trunks rose on both sides, blocking all but the hint of light. I had a slight fear of close spaces, but I wasn't often in them. As we continued, it seemed as if the woods were squeezing in tighter, making my chest heavy. When the path switch-backed to the left, I was relieved to be heading out of the cell of bark and leaves.

A sudden spate of flutters broke out in the branches above me. Heart skittering, I pulled Rat up and reached for the gun, my eyes following the noise. My head told me it was a bird, but my ramped-up nerves were convinced one of Javier's men was perched on a branch signaling our presence to the others. As I scanned the trees, the clouds broke apart and light leaked onto a bullet-shaped outline with glowing yellow eyes.

"*Whoot, whoot,*" the owl called out, announcing the emerging moon.

I sucked in air and tapped Rat's sides with my heels. He lifted his head, snorting dismissively.

"Yep," I whispered. "Just an owl."

I let go of the gun butt and dropped my gaze, catching a

glimmer in the brightening light. Several bottles like the one I'd found at the beginning of the trail had been tossed alongside the path like Hansel and Gretel's breadcrumbs. We must have been getting close; we'd been climbing for a while. Rat had begun to snort, a horse's way of panting. When I reached down to pat his neck, it was hot and damp. I'd never experienced ground higher than the hill country surrounding San Antonio. I'd always heard the air was thinner in the mountains. As pressure pushed against my lungs, I understood what that meant.

Rat came to a dead stop. I squawked in surprise, slamming my hand over my mouth, my cry already echoing through the woods. Rat turned his head uphill. The forest was now bathed in silvery-blue light. Had we caught up with Alicia? I checked for shapes or movement. I tilted my head and listened, half hoping to hear the grinding of hooves or the rustling of footsteps, half fearing it. An eagle's lonesome call was all I noticed over the sound of the brook and my own short breaths. Rat's ears swiveled back and forth like antennae trying to pick up a frequency. He nosed the air and nickered softly.

"What is it, boy?"

My senses vibrated, straining to see what he saw, hear what he heard, smell what he smelled. The wind swept by us in a cold current. Branches creaked. The murmuring stream grew louder. With a jolt, I realized the jumble of noise was human.

I let the reins fall loose, putting Rat in charge. He walked about twenty feet and stopped in a tight clearing. This time I didn't have to guess what he heard; the sounds had clearly organized into men's voices. Rat's nostrils flared and I caught the acrid smell of burning wood. I looked up, trepidation marching across my chest as I spotted a column of smoke rising from a stand of tall pines. I'd found the camp. Where was Alicia?

CHAPTER 21

I crept on foot through the woods, getting as close as I dared to the edge of the camp. The dead trunk of a felled tree lay across my path. I squatted behind it, the musty odor of rotting pine mingling with the smells of smoke and cooking meat that wafted from the *tequileros'* site.

Six men sat on logs and rocks around a crackling bonfire no more than forty feet away. Amber light bounced off glass bottles as they passed them around, each man taking long swigs. Three of them faced me, their features sinister in the shifting glow from the flames. I squinted until my eyes twitched but could not identify any of them as Javier.

The hideout was in the middle of an open space, about the size of a holding pen. It snugged up to a high wall of folded, lichen-covered rock on one side. The west side of the clearing opened out to the stream, but boulders and dense forest provided cover around the rest. Four tents had been pitched haphazardly near the firepit. Beyond them, I saw a pair of lean-tos with oilcloth tarps nailed across the sides. At the far edge of the camp, just inside the woods, a line of horses stood tethered to a stripped pine stand.

It felt eerily familiar, as if someone had built a stage to match Flora's description. She'd endured unspeakable torture in those tents and lean-tos, feet away from men who'd ignored her screams and pleas for help. I'd crawled right into her hell, yet an air of revelry hung over the camp. The *tequileros* gave the impression they'd gathered for nothing more than a cookout, tucked safely away in the bosom of the Sierra Madres.

"*Rojizo, cantas un corrido!*" someone called out.

One of the men lurched to his feet, hair swirling around his face as his slurred voice rose into the trees.

> *"El capitán de los rinches*
> *a Silvano se acercó,*
> *en unos cuantos segundos*
> *Silvano García murió.*
>
> *Los rinches son muy valientes,*
> *no se les puede quitar,*
> *los cazan como venados*
> *para poderlos matar.*
>
> *Ya con ésta ahí me despido*
> *en mi caballo Lucero,*
> *mataron tres gallos finos*
> *del pueblito de Guerrero."*

Rojizo finished his folk song about the heroism of *tequila* smugglers with a flourish, bowing so deep he lost his balance and stumbled through the edge of the fire. Sparks flew up, littering the air and catching in his unkempt hair. He screeched, batting at the tiny embers like an old lady swatting at spiders. Laughter exploded from the group, slamming against the rock wall and echoing down the mountain.

A slender man wearing a *sombrero* stood up, his back to me.

"*Silencio,*" he said. "Lower your voices. *El Jefe* will get mad."

The others made little attempt to heed his warning, chuckling loudly into their elbows like schoolboys. The man grouched at them as he walked closer to the fire.

"The old bloodhound is growling again," one of them joked.

To the side of the flames, a wheel-sized cast iron skillet rested on a grate perched on a pile of red-hot coals. The thin man lifted a long wooden fork and bent over to stir the contents of the pan, sending a balloon of steam into the air. It had a tangy smell, like venison or rabbit. He straightened, turning to return to his seat. Firelight flickered in his white, waist-length beard like gold tinsel, and my lips curled with loathing. Tomás. The man who'd had the chance to help me, to save my brother, but had chosen to do Javier's bidding instead.

Movement at the edge of the camp tore my attention away. A figure was limping toward the clearing from the fence where the horses were tethered. Even in the dim light, I recognized the compact build and thick chestnut hair, and felt a surge of relief. Carlos was alive. Was Alicia watching, hiding at the edge of the camp like I was? Grace's hoofprints had veered into the woods near the place I'd left Rat. I'd followed them on foot, but when they'd disappeared in a rocky area, I'd decided to get as close to the camp as I dared.

Carlos held the bail of a large wooden bucket in each hand. His shoulders hunched inward. Shadows darkened the hollows beneath his eyes, and a red slash shone across his forehead.

"You are not done with the horses yet, *huevón*?" groused a stout man, turning away from the fire to watch Carlos. A dark cowboy hat concealed most of the man's face, gray-streaked russet hair curling out from under it. Over his buckskin shirt he wore a chest-length necklace with some sort of decorations hanging from it.

"No, Danté," Carlos replied in a forced voice. "They need more water."

"You are as slow and stupid as an ass," jeered Danté. "*Tonto del culo!*"

The other men snickered; one started braying like a donkey.

Even beaten and battered, JJ would've had a hard time bit-ing his tongue in the face of such taunting, but Carlos just put his head down and continued toward the river. I considered following him. I could sneak up while he filled the buckets and let him know Alicia was there somewhere, that we wanted to help him. But the stream wasn't very far from the campfire; I was afraid the men might hear us.

The wooden pails clunked against some rocks a few times, then Carlos came back into the wavering glow of the fire, water splashing with each of his jerky strides. As he walked by, Danté threw his leg out in front of him, catching Carlos's feet. Carlos pitched forward. Unable to drop the buckets fast enough to get his hands out and break his fall, he landed face down on the rocky ground with a sickening smack. I winced at his sharp cry and scanned the boundary of the camp. The men yipped like a pack of excited coyotes. Where was Alicia? I slowly started backing out of my hiding place, feeling a dire need to find her.

"Shut the hell up!"

I froze. The shout had come from the area by the lean-tos.

"We've got two hours before we start loading up and I'd like some goddamn sleep." His voice was deep, his accent Anglo. "You're making so much noise they can probably hear you all the way to Laredo. You want to rot away in *una pinche celda*?"

A sick feeling slid through me. I rose high enough to look over the trunk. The man stood in the moon shadow of one of the lean-tos; a tall, square outline against the blue light. Recognition filtered into my mind, recognition I did not welcome. Before I could slam a door in front of it, someone stormed out of the other lean-to. A presence I had no trouble acknowledging.

The laughter quit as Javier swooped into the circle of light brandishing a revolver.

"I will shoot the next *coño* who makes a sound!" he snarled, firelight pulsing across his face, his red hair glinting like the embers.

The camp became so quiet I feared the men would hear the thrumming of my pulse. Only in rare moments since he'd killed JJ had Javier not occupied my thoughts. I'd imagined things I'd say to him, rehearsed a growing list of his crimes and abuses, pictured him swinging from the end of the hangman's rope. At that moment, though, all I wanted to do was pull out the .45 and shoot him. If not for the risk to Alicia and Carlos, I might have done it.

Javier twisted around, pointing his gun at each man, making sure they believed his threat. As his torso rotated toward me, the orange flames reflected off something. I squeezed my eyes shut and looked again, not wanting to believe what I'd seen.

At his waist was JJ's buckle, worn like a trophy won in battle, like the scalps of defeated foes the Comanche hung from their belts. Heat emanated from it like a branding iron, searing its shape onto my heart. I bit my tongue to keep from screaming. The tang of blood filled my mouth as hatred claimed even more of my soul.

A groan broke the moment. Javier's glare shifted to Carlos. "*Hijo de puta! Levántate.*"

Carlos raised his head, blood gleaming dark on his face. He tried to push his body off the ground but collapsed. Javier was on him in one long stride, kicking Carlos's side with such force the boy's whole body moved across the dirt. Carlos let out a strangled moan, then went still.

"*Ahorita!*" Javier bellowed.

Carlos didn't move.

"If you are not dead, *cabrón*, you will soon wish you were," Javier bent his leg, his boot thudding into Carlos like a hammer.

"*Por favor,*" Tomás implored.

"I've had enough of this *maldito embécil!* He has caused nothing but trouble!"

"Hey, *amigo!*" called the Anglo voice. "He can't help load the *tequila* if you kill him."

The man moved out of the dark toward Javier, my insides twisting with his every step. As light spilled onto his whiskered jaw, I could not deny who he was. The disjointed feeling of seeing someone out of context poured over me—the minister in plain clothes at a fair; the doctor playing baseball on a Saturday; Jackson standing in Javier's camp.

What was he doing there? Why did he seem so comfortable in the middle of a gang of outlaws? Why had he called my brother's murderer 'friend'? As my eyes swept over him, searching for a clue, I sensed a swift movement behind me, like a quail breaking cover.

I dove for her a second too late, watching in horror as Alicia scrambled over the dead trunk, running into the camp, Griselda's knife grasped in her hand.

CHAPTER 22

No one noticed her. Alicia soared, quick and quiet as an arrow. She was almost on top of Javier before he sensed her. Then, with the reflexes of a man who's been hunted his entire life, he lunged. Grabbing her arm, he wrested the knife out of her hand and spun her around. Arm across her chest, he pulled her backward, clutching her to him. Not a single second of uncertainty slowed him. He lifted the blade and jerked it hard across Alicia's throat. Her eyes opened wide, her lips parting in silent surprise.

I shoved a fist into my mouth, blocking my scream, as crimson tears began to weep from the slit in her neck. The ground beneath me spun. I crawled to the trunk, clinging to it, rotting bark crumbling in my clawed fingers. Confused shouts filled the night air. The *tequileros'* boots trampled over rocks as they ran. Tomás wailed.

I forced myself to look, praying it wasn't as bad as I thought. Javier held Alicia, who had folded over his arm. Jackson was running to them, yelling, his words lost in my silent, miserable shrieks.

She'd been so fast, so determined, her feet barely touching the ground. My beautiful friend, my sister. What had she done?

Jackson reached them. Javier looked down. Confusion rippled across his face. He flung his arms open, as if suddenly realizing what he held. Alicia sagged. Jackson caught her, sinking with her to the ground. She settled across his lap, her head lolling back, the dark gash in her throat gaping open, unfurling a veil of blood. My stomach heaved, bile burning a trench up my throat.

Alicia's eyes fixed on Jackson. Her lips began to move. He leaned closer, placing a hand across her neck. He seemed stunned as red streams seeped through his fingers. I knew there would be blood. So much blood. As it slithered from Jackson's hand, spreading down Alicia's white blouse, an irrational thought filled my head: *she's going to pass out when she sees all that blood.*

Her hands lifted, vibrating against an unseen weight, trying to hold death at bay. She gasped—the horrible, primal sounds of a battle to breathe. Sounds I still heard in my head. Then the noise stopped, her arms falling to the ground in surrender. She would never see the blood.

As her head drooped to one side, strands of hair spilling across her face, Jackson cupped her cheek, bowing his head over her. I couldn't stop staring at his bloody fingers. I wanted to leap over the trunk and snatch her away from him; I wanted to hold her in my arms until I had no tears left. I wanted to drive Griselda's knife deep into Javier's chest, twisting it slowly while he screamed in agony. I wanted to watch every drop of evil pour out of him until only a hard, empty shell remained.

I could do none of those things, held prisoner by so many emotions—shock, fear, dismay—and the instinct for self-preservation.

Alicia's attack had unsettled Javier. He crouched on high alert, clutching Griselda's knife, arms apart, half raised, ready for another assault. He'd kill me as quickly as he had Alicia if I dared to move.

My eyes swept over Carlos, unconscious on the ground, unaware that his sister had just lost her life trying to save him.

"*Qué carajo!*" Javier exclaimed after a few moments. "Is she dead?"

Jackson laid Alicia on the ground, gently pushing the hair from her face. Streaks of blood lined her cheeks; red pools gathered in her nostrils; her eyes stared at nothing. Agony swelled, trying to break out of my chest. I smothered it with both hands as Jackson placed two fingers on Alicia's wrist, feeling for a pulse.

"She's gone." He eased Alicia's eyelids closed.

"Who the hell is she?" Javier demanded, regaining his composure.

"His sister." An unmistakable rasp frayed Jackson's voice. He stood up, looking over at Carlos's motionless form only feet away. Then his eyes lifted, following the path Alicia had taken when she'd slipped, silent as mist, into the clearing.

Before I could duck, his gaze hit my face like the headlamps of a truck. I froze, cold panic leaking into my veins. The longer I stared at Jackson's face, the less familiar it became. The man standing there, covered in Alicia's blood, was a stranger.

Does he see me? Is he going to call me out? Will he let Javier kill me too?

After an endless moment, he looked away, giving no indication if he'd spotted me. Tremors broke loose, shaking my entire body.

Jackson turned to the other men. No one spoke. Shocked sober and dazed, they milled about as if wondering what they'd witnessed. A few of the men cast cautious glances at Javier, waiting for his wrath to explode. Even if they'd wanted to, though, there hadn't been time for any of them to protect him.

The burly man who'd tripped Carlos approached.

"You okay, *hermano*?" Danté asked Javier.

He'd removed his hat. Danté was heavier than Javier, but standing side by side their resemblance was unmistakable, although Danté's light-colored eyes did not glow with the intensity of his brother's.

"*La puta* came out of nowhere," said Javier.

A deep, pained grunt rose from the ground, filling me with foreboding. Carlos was regaining consciousness. Tomás hurried to him, but Carlos sat up before he got there. He turned his head, noticing the body on the ground next to him. I held my breath.

"Alicia?!"

His cracked voice reverberated over the camp. He struggled to his knees, holding his side, blood dripping off his chin. He reached for Alicia's body, but Tomás grabbed his arm, holding him back.

"*No, no, m'ijo,*" the old man chanted. "*No, no.*"

"Let me go!" Carlos wrenched his arm loose and crawled closer to his sister. His hand hovered over her for a moment then he slumped forward, head thumping on the ground.

Javier strode toward him. I dug my fingers deeper into the spongy, rotten wood, bracing for whatever would come next.

"Look at me."

Carlos didn't move.

"Now!" Javier shouted.

Carlos sat back on his heels, wrapping an arm around his waist, his face a twisted grimace.

"Did you tell her where we were?" Javier demanded.

Carlos shook his head.

Javier bent down. Still holding the grisly knife in one hand, he grabbed Carlos by the ear and placed the blade behind his lobe. A rivulet of cold sweat trickled down my back.

"What else have you been telling people?" he hissed.

"No ... nothing," Carlos said, his voice broken by sobs.

"She probably followed him here," Jackson cut in, moving closer to them.

"Do not lie to me, *cabrón,*" seethed Javier, his bared teeth an inch from Carlos's ear.

"I ... I said nothing," wailed Carlos. "Why would I want her to come here?"

Jackson squatted next to Javier, looking him in the eye.

"Even if he did tell her, he's clearly learned his lesson, *amigo*," Jackson said in a forced, calm voice. "Don't waste your time on a stupid kid. We've got more important concerns, like loading that *tequila* in time to get it to Santa Rosa by sunup."

My pulse sped up. Santa Rosa? My thoughts stumbled over each other as I tried to absorb it all.

Javier squinted at Jackson. I'd come to understand him well enough to know that Javier was not a man who liked to be told what to do, but something Jackson had said must have resonated. He withdrew the knife and let go of Carlos, shoving him sideways.

Carlos rolled on the ground, making no attempt to hide his grief. His raw, searing howls cut me to the quick.

"Take him away and shut him up. I will finish with him later," Javier said to Tomás, then turned to Danté. "You and Rojizo take the others and start packing the *tequila, ándele.* They want two hundred bottles."

Two hundred bottles? A lot of *tequila* to make Pancho Villa's rebels happy? And five hundred Colt .45s to make them deadly?

Danté, Rojizo, and the other three men headed across the camp in the direction of the tethered horses. Tomás bent over Carlos. He helped him into a crouching position then put a hand around his waist, whispering encouragements as he pulled him to his feet. Carlos wept quietly under his breath, but when he stood and looked at Alicia's body, he began bawling again like the heartbroken child he was. Tomás pulled him toward the tents.

Javier looked down at the crumpled, gory form on the ground.

"Who is going to take care of that?" he asked no one in particular, his tone as casual as if he were talking about a bag of garbage. "*Los lobos* will scatter pieces all over and make a smelly mess of the camp while we are gone."

An image of Alicia's lovely body torn apart by wolves, the parts not eaten left to rot, flashed through my mind. My stomach heaved. I dropped on all fours behind the trunk, inhaling through my nose, blowing air out of my mouth as quietly as I could, desperate not to give myself away by retching.

"There's a shovel in the lean-to," I heard Jackson say. "I'll take care of her."

Was he going to bury her? Although disgusted by Jackson's presence there, I felt a small curl of relief that he would be the one handling Alicia's body. He hadn't stopped Javier (had he tried? It was a blur), but he'd treated Alicia with care as she died.

I blinked back tears. The thought of Alicia spending eternity in that godforsaken camp repulsed me. I'd find a way to get her. This would not be her final resting place.

A loud yelp came from the tent that Tomás and Carlos had disappeared into. As much as I disliked him, I didn't believe Tomás was hurting Carlos. I chose, instead, to envision the old man trying to care for his wounds.

"*Cállate!*" Javier shouted, his footsteps heading off after Danté's group.

It was clear that Javier intended to continue his interrogation of Carlos when he had more time. What use would Carlos be to him then? Javier would surely kill him after he'd gotten whatever information he wanted. The boy was too shattered, both physically and emotionally, to help with loading or transporting the *tequila*.

Despite myself, I wondered why Javier hadn't already killed Carlos. Then it came to me. The guns. It wasn't the camp location Javier was worried about; it was the stolen Colt .45s in Santa Rosa's crypt. If Carlos knew about the guns, Javier needed to be sure he hadn't told anyone. He would cut Carlos apart, piece by piece, until he had no more questions. Or until Carlos could no longer answer them.

CHAPTER 23

I sprinted through the pine-oak forest, dragging my wretched heart behind me, to the spot where I'd tethered Rat. I stopped to catch my breath, misery quickly threatening to overwhelm me. If I let myself contemplate the enormity of what had just happened, I'd disintegrate into a thousand pieces. I could not change it; I had to focus on what I could do.

I had to save Carlos. I needed to get him into a saddle and out of the camp before Javier came back to interrogate him. I scanned the rock-strewn ground, locating the last set of Grace's hoofprints I'd seen. I followed them to where the tracks vanished in the rocks. I stopped looking down at the ground and started inspecting the bushes. The undergrowth was not nearly as thick as the thorn scrub at home, which caught on anything trying to push past, but Grace would have crashed through the woods like a charging bull.

Finally, I spotted broken branches on a small pine. Once I saw the first sign, the others became obvious, the way one jigsaw piece can be the key to the whole puzzle. I scrambled through the woods, following snapped boughs and bent leaves, tugging Rat along behind me. We didn't have to go far. Grace heard us approaching and let out a strange, muted whimper. We came around a huge black boulder and found him tied to a piñon tree.

I led Grace and Rat toward the camp. Grace seemed even more clumsy than before, stumbling over every twig and pebble. I winced with each thud, each scattering of stones, worried they'd hear us coming. I glanced behind me in irritation. Rat appeared to be floating over the same terrain that tripped up the mule—then I saw it.

Grace's right knee was the size of a large cantaloupe. He must have hurt it climbing the mountain path with Alicia. His muzzle was gray with age, and he'd probably never done anything more taxing than pull Griselda's wagon. Even Rat, who was in good shape, had struggled against the steep slope and the thin air. Going down the mountain would be harder, not easier. The ground would shift and slide under their hooves, gravity pulling them downhill. Grace would never make it with an injured knee.

I muffled a cry of frustration. How was I going to get Carlos away from the *tequileros* without another horse? We'd be too heavy if we both tried to ride Rat; the extra weight would make it impossible for him to keep his balance going down the mountain. If Carlos rode and I walked, we'd be too slow to stay ahead of whoever Javier sent after us when he realized Carlos had escaped.

Whatever I was going to do, it would not involve Grace. I looped his reins around a limb so he wouldn't follow us. I felt a twinge of guilt leaving him behind, but he could pull free if a predator started sniffing around. I had to keep moving. Javier could finish loading the *tequila* and return to torture Carlos any moment, then the question of how to get him down the trail safely wouldn't matter. And Alicia would have died for nothing.

Rat and I continued, skirting the bottom of the camp in the direction of the tent Tomás had taken Carlos into. Rat placed his hooves with care, moving as stealthily as a big gelding could. Through the trees ahead, I saw the tails of the *tequileros'* mounts twitching in the moonlight. I stopped and tied

Rat to a tree. As I snuck up to the horses, I noticed they were each already tacked up. It felt like a gift from the universe. If I could get Carlos on one of those horses, we might be able to get enough of a head start.

Danté and the other men had headed toward the horses to pack the *tequila*. I didn't see any of them now, but I didn't want to blunder into them. I moved between two horses to get a look at the campsite. I almost had a view when I stepped on a twig. It broke, the crack seeming as loud as thunder. One of the horses let out a surprised snuffle. I dropped to my knees, expecting a hot hand on my shoulder, the tight clamp of arms around me, but no one appeared, no one sounded an alarm. Where were they?

Before I began moving again, I heard noises.

Clink ... clunk, clunk ... clink.

Placing each foot on the ground as if it were covered with hot coals, I stepped to the heads of the horses and peered around them. Like bees working a hive, the *tequileros* were going in and out of a large cave. The men entered empty-handed and came out carrying several *tule*-wrapped bottles. With thin ropes they lashed the bottles onto the backs of donkeys and mules, spreading dried grass between the layers for further protection. Intent on their chore, no one spoke, not even Javier, who stacked his bottles with more speed and precision than the rest. The only sounds were the muffled chinks of glass and occasional huffs of the mules and burros as their burdens grew heavier.

One donkey had already been packed and stood apart. I tried to count how many bottles he carried, but it was hard to tell from a distance. Twenty-five, maybe, which meant the *tequileros* had about seven more mules to finish packing before reaching two hundred bottles.

I retraced my steps, stopping at the horse farthest from the *tequileros*, a smallish mare. Her ears twisted back and forth nervously as I untied the reins, but she came without a fuss. I led her over and tied her next to Rat, her soft steps and quiet demeanor reassuring me that leaving Grace behind had been the right decision.

With the two horses secured, I focused on locating Tomás, Carlos, and Jackson. Crawling to the bottom of a rock ledge at the border of the clearing, I prepared to swallow the emotion that would rise like vomit when I saw Alicia's body. I planted my hands in the loose pebbles on the top rim and lifted just enough to get a good view.

She wasn't there. Someone had moved her body. Was Jackson in the woods burying her? I felt a rush of relief, followed by a sucking wave of despair, thoughts of dirt and decay and worms filling my head. Alicia would hate being left in the dirt of the dark forest. I bit down on my cheek, the pain bringing me back to the task at hand. The most important thing I could do for her was save her brother.

I scanned the site for Jackson, peering into the trees along the far edge, but didn't see him anywhere. As I was looking, Tomás ducked out of a tent. He shambled slowly to the next one over, seeming even older and more haggard than he had before. He stooped down and did a slow-motion dive through the flap. I assumed Carlos had finally passed out and Tomás had decided to rest. I counted to fifty, then quietly climbed over the ledge and slid the gun out of my waistband.

The only noises were the cracks and pops of the dying bonfire and the distant clunking of *tequila* being packing. I crept forward, watching the ground for twigs that would creak or dried leaves that would crunch. Exposed in the open clearing, I thought of how a rabbit freezes instead of hiding when it senses danger, making it an easy target. I forced myself to keep moving, nerves tingling down my legs.

I reached Tomás's tent and bent an ear close to listen. His deep breaths ended in long, rumbling snores. I moved on to the tent he'd come out of, pushed the slit in the cloth open, and stuck my head inside. It smelled of dust and mildew and stale sweat. Shafts of light shone through various-sized holes in the threadbare canvas, sprinkling Carlos with a constellation of silvery dots. He lay on his side, taking up most of the floor space, knees curled up to his chest. I bent over, shuffling sideways along his back to squat down by his head. Swallowing a gulp of musty air, I gently placed my hand over his mouth. His eyes shot open, and my fingers tightened, muffling his cry of surprise.

"Shhh, it's all right, Carlos," I said softly.

His head jerked sideways. He looked up at me with wide, terrified eyes.

"Please be quiet," I whispered. "Remember me? Sarita?"

His brow scrunched up in confusion, but he nodded. I removed my hand. He pushed himself up, sighing through clenched lips. I jockeyed around in the small space, sitting down cross-legged, facing him. Up close, his nose looked even worse; smashed and shoved sideways from hitting the ground so hard. Most of the blood had been wiped off his face, but black crust circled both nostrils, and violet bruises hung below his eyes. The gash across his forehead needed stitches. He kept one arm around his waist as if his ribs might burst apart.

"How much pain are you in?" I asked.

"I think my ribs are broken," he replied. "My head hurts so bad it's hard to focus ... Alicia ..." Her name came out of his mouth like a strangled gasp. He rubbed his hand across his eyes as if trying to scrub the images away.

"I know," I said.

"I told her not to get involved," he croaked, anger slipping into his tone as he focused on me. "Did you bring her here?"

"No. She found out you were hurt and came by herself."

His face fell with a weight I recognized.

"We need to get out of here," I said. "Now."

He shook his bowed head, slumping over as if resigned to die in the tent. I grabbed his arm and pulled him back up, ignoring his pained wheeze.

"Look at me, Carlos."

He slowly raised his face, dull and defeated.

"Alicia risked everything to try to save you," I said, using the tone I'd often taken with JJ when I needed him to do something without questions. "Javier will come back soon; he will beat you until he thinks you've told him everything he wants to know. Then he'll kill you, and your sister will have died for nothing."

His head bobbed slightly.

"You and I are not going to let that happen," I said. "We're going to get you out of here. For Alicia."

"There's no way." Carlos clutched his rib cage.

"I have two horses tied up not far from here," I went on. "It's going to hurt like hell, but all you have to do is get in the saddle."

I reached into my pocket, taking out a pencil-sized stick I'd found and the little bag of herbs Griselda had given me. I handed him both. "Put a pinch of this stuff in your cheek, like snuff, then bite down on that stick and try with all your might not to make a sound."

Carlos regarded me for a moment.

"You're going to get killed too," he muttered.

"No, I'm not." I pushed the bag and stick at him. "Neither are you."

He shook his head but shoved a big wad of herbs along his gum, his protruding cheek adding to his misshapen appearance. He placed the stick between his molars, bit down, and scooted to the front of the tent. I crawled around him, peering through the slim opening in the flap.

"All clear," I whispered and slipped out.

He slid on his bottom in jerky movements until he was outside. With the .45 in one hand, I wrapped my other arm around his upper back, grabbing him under the armpit, and lifted. The stick snapped in his mouth before he made it to his feet. His face contorted, sweat beading along his hairline, but he didn't scream.

"The horses are just there, in the trees." I pointed the gun at the bushy juniper I'd tethered them to. "Go as fast as you can."

My eyes swept the camp, hugging Carlos close as we hobbled forward. He moved more quickly than I'd anticipated, muted grunts barely audible, but his shallow, fractured breathing gave away his discomfort. How was he going to gallop down the mountain on a horse? He'd have to summon every ounce of willpower he possessed and hang on for dear life.

We left the clearing. Ten more feet. Eight more feet. I began to believe we were going to make it when I heard the crunch of footsteps. I twisted my head around, looking over Carlos's shoulder.

"What is it?" gasped Carlos, rotating his body out of my hold to see.

Tomás stood behind us. I lifted the gun, aiming it at his chest. He stared at me, recognition bursting across his face.

"*Señorita Rubia?*" he whispered, using Javier's label for me.

Tomás looked at Carlos, then me, as if trying to figure out the connection. My thumb rested on the hammer. I didn't want to shoot him; the noise would bring the *tequileros* running.

"*Qué haces?*" he asked, bewilderment folding his scraggy brow.

"I'm taking him," I answered.

Tomás turned toward the camp. Was he going to yell for Javier? Run to get the others? I grabbed Carlos's arm.

"Please," I said, backing away, "just let us go."

Tomás swiveled back around to face us. His eyes traveled across Carlos's battered face then met my glare. A look, an agreement, a reckoning—something passed between us.

"*Ándele,*" he whispered, then walked away.

I didn't wait to see where he went. If I'd misinterpreted the moment, if it was a trick and he was going to rally the others, I wanted to be on the horses by the time they came after us.

"Hurry," I hissed, stumbling along with Carlos like a couple in a terrifying three-legged race.

The cover of the trees filled me with relief, as if I'd walked off a stage into obscurity behind the curtain. Carlos smothered his cries as we went, teeth tightly clenched around the broken stick. When we reached the horses, I made a snap decision to put him on Rat. Rat had experience. He'd be the safest ride down the trail. I had no idea how the mare would do.

"This horse is huge," Carlos remarked through short breaths. I stopped myself from picturing Alicia as she'd tried to climb onto Rat's back.

"Use my hands as a step. I'll help lift you." I stuffed the revolver in my waistband and bent down, lacing my fingers together to make the shape of a stirrup. Carlos placed his right foot on them and grabbed hold of the saddle. I lifted, straining against his weight as he fought to pull himself up. He wasn't as tall as I was, but he was much heavier. Just when I thought my fingers would rip apart, he got his left foot into the stirrup.

"Okay," he rasped, out of breath.

I stood, giving his rear end a push. He balanced there, one foot in the stirrup, holding tightly to the saddle horn, the other foot hanging in the air.

"Okay," he repeated, then lifted his right leg as high as he could. As he swung it over Rat's back, I heard a sharp snap, like something giving way deep inside him.

"Ahhgghh!" he cried out, the stick flying from his mouth. He dropped heavily into the saddle, his scream trumpeting through the air. I could imagine Javier tilting his head at the sound, sniffing the wind, eyes glowing.

"Shit!" I yanked Rat's reins free, threw them over his ears, then looped them around the saddle horn.

"Give him his head," I said to Carlos. "Don't let go of the saddle horn."

His face was white, sweat coursing down his cheeks. Yanking the saddlebag open, I pulled out my bandana and shoved it in his hand. "Stuff that in your mouth. Don't yell again."

I untethered the mare and leapt into the saddle. She skipped sideways as my weight settled.

Please let her be a sprinter.

I jammed my heels into her sides. She jumped forward just as Danté and Rojizo stampeded out of the bushes in front of us. The mare shied and tried to run the other way. I wrenched her head around, kicking hard into her sides. She lunged right at Danté. He dodged to the side, fumbling to unholster his gun. Rojizo rushed at us, grabbing hold of the mare's reins and yanking hard. Her head snapped to the side. She pulled him several feet before bouncing to a stop.

I reached back, yanked out the Colt, and cocked it. As the scared horse skittered around underneath me, I aimed and squeezed the trigger. Rojizo screamed, letting go of the reins to clutch his arm. I'd only grazed him. If I'd hit him full-on from such a short distance, he'd have fallen to the ground.

I whipped the mare around, gaining distance, and located Carlos. He was still in the saddle, but Danté held Rat's reins in one hand and a revolver in the other.

"*Estamos aquí!*" Danté shouted, his focus turning to the camp. "*Rápido! Tiene una pistola!*"

"*Viene!*" one of the men yelled back from the camp.

Horses crashed through the woods in our direction. We'd soon be surrounded, our chances of escape slim. Gripping the .45 in one hand, I gathered the reins. Danté wouldn't have time to aim if I rushed right at him. I lifted my heels, but before I could drive them into the mare's sides, Rojizo charged us, howling at the top of his lungs, blood dripping from his sleeve. The mare reared up, pawing the air in a frenzy. Rojizo couldn't stop. His boots skidded across the loose rocks, throwing him under her thrashing legs. With a crack, one of her hooves smacked his forehead. He swayed then dropped to the ground like a stone.

I grabbed for the saddle horn, holding tight as the mare

descended, her feet slamming onto the ground. My forehead smashed into the top of her neck. I shoved off her shoulders into the saddle. Punching my heels down, I aimed the gun like a lance as we bore down on Danté.

The head-on assault surprised him. He was looking at Rojizo, lying still and bloody, not watching me. Danté stood his ground, mouth gaping, but forgot to aim and fire. At the last second, I yanked the reins to the left.

"Hang on!" I yelled at Carlos.

As I passed, I slapped Rat's hip hard, making him jump like he had in the Rio Grande. Danté had no chance of holding on to the strips of leather connecting him to half a ton of leaping horse. He let out a surprised yelp, the reins ripping out of his fingers. As Rat shoved past him, the stirrup caught Danté's necklace, breaking its string, beads flying everywhere as he fell.

Carlos and I bolted through the trees as the first shot rang out behind us.

Thunk!

A tree trunk shook next to me. More loud cracks punched the thick forest canopy, a hail of bullets slicing through the air, ricocheting off rocks around us.

"Don't look back!" I called to Carlos. "Just hang on!"

The mare dodged through the trunks and bushes, not as sturdy or intentional as Rat, but even nimbler than I'd hoped. I could feel the *tequileros* nipping at our heels, but the dense woods kept them from getting a clear shot. I had no idea where the switchback path I'd taken up to the campsite was. I couldn't waste time searching. I shoved the Colt into my waistband and angled toward the stream. It would be steeper going straight downhill, but it would be faster.

Rat stayed on the mare's tail as we tore across the rocks and dirt. I caught glimpses of water ahead, shimmering in narrow spaces between the trees. Another volley of shots rang out. I hammered my heels into the horse's sides, but the saddle suddenly shifted beneath me, her hooves sliding as if she'd stepped on sheer ice. We slipped down a steep embankment, pebbles and loose soil kicking up behind us. The mare tried to regain her footing. I looked down the hill and gasped. We were heading right for a tractor-sized boulder. It would break our fall, but broadsiding it at full speed would also break the horse and probably my leg.

There was nothing I could do to control her or stop her momentum. As we skated toward the massive rock, I braced for impact. If Rat and Carlos were behind us, they'd smash into the boulder too. Or into us. The mare's legs pumped like pistons, her head bouncing in odd circular motions as she tried to stay upright. I had to jump off. Inches from slamming into the boulder, I yanked my feet out of the stirrups but felt a sharp jerk as her hooves caught firm ground. She jolted forward, flinging me back against the cantle. The rough surface of the boulder scraped against my thigh as we galloped past.

On sturdy ground, I got my feet back in the stirrups, pulled the mare up, and looked around for Carlos. Rat was trotting along the top of the ridge; he'd been too smart to follow our free fall down the mountainside. I watched him pick a safe path and descend. Carlos leaned back in the saddle, counter-weighing the pull of gravity, his eyes half-closed, both hands clasped around the saddle horn. The tail of my red bandana trailed out of his mouth.

As we rode down into a light mist, I realized the gunshots had stopped. I couldn't hear voices or pounding hooves, just the water bubbling next to us. Had the *tequileros* given up? Maybe they'd decided Carlos wasn't worth it. Maybe packing the *tequila* was more important.

The mist grew heavier, engulfing us in a wet cloud. I was grateful for the cover but stayed close to the waterway so we wouldn't get lost. Finally, the ground began to flatten. The river turned in the direction of the waterfall as the fog thickened into what JJ would've called pea soup. Deer loved a thick brume, feeding under its blanket of protection late into the morning. The heavy air made it hard for most predators to hear or smell, but JJ used the cover to stalk up close enough to game to be deadly with his bow and arrows.

I heard splashing, the waterfall appearing like a long-awaited signpost. I slowed to let Rat move up beside me. Only one of Carlos's hands gripped the saddle horn now; the other was flattened against his waist. His head hung loosely, chin grazing his chest. I was wondering if he was conscious when he melted out of the saddle, landing in a heap on the ground.

"Carlos!"

I jumped down next to him. He rolled onto his back; his face screwed up in an expression of pure pain. It was a miracle he'd stayed in the saddle as long as he had. I removed the bandana from his mouth and held the canteen to his lips. He took a swallow, spitting the wad of Griselda's magic leaves out in the dirt.

"What happened?"

"You passed out," I said. "Do you think you can get back on the horse? We have to keep moving."

"It feels like fire when I breathe," he replied groggily. "I need to sleep."

"Not here," I said, reaching down for him. "They could easily creep up on us in this fog."

As if to prove me right, the dull thud of hooves rustled through the undergrowth. I swirled around, yanking the gun out and aiming at the noise. Adrenalin knit into my veins as I pulled back the hammer. I expected Danté and Javier to burst through the mist. Instead, the silhouette of a single horse took shape. As it loped closer in an awkward, dancing gait, I realized there was no rider, not even a saddle. The small horse wore only a halter. I took in the chestnut coat, the long, slender legs and four white socks. Then I noticed the white star on its forehead. The back of my neck prickled.

"Twister?"

He trotted directly to the mare, nudging her hip right

below a brand. I hadn't noticed the marking in my haste. Now I stared, mouth open. The Rocking A of the Arrowhead Ranch was burned into the mare's hide.

"Bluebird," I whispered in disbelief. I'd ridden out of the camp on the mare JJ had been breaking in when he'd encountered Javier. My entire body tingled as she turned her head and touched her nose to Twister's.

A good horse isn't led; he follows.

Twister had been following Bluebird the day Javier killed JJ, and he was still following her. How had he gotten away from the *tequileros*? Maybe they'd realized JJ had been right—he was too young to be of any use to them. He wasn't saddle broke; he'd have pitched a fit if they'd tried to load anything heavier than a flea on his back.

My heart swam in the sweet, unreal surprise of him. Holding my hand out, I clucked my tongue the way JJ had. Twister turned his head to me. I ran a shaky finger down the side of the halter. JJ had bought it with his own money, racing into the tool shed to stamp the name he'd finally chosen into the dark brown leather. Never very good at planning ahead, he'd run out of room after stamping the "e" in Twister, so he'd hand-carved a tiny "r" at the end with his pocketknife.

Twister had been the last thing JJ thought about. His name had been the last word he'd spoken. I could almost hear his joyful hollering raining down from Heaven.

Carlos had managed to sit up. "You know that horse?"

"He's JJ's." Twister nuzzled my palm, his soft lips searching for a treat. "Javier stole him."

"How—"

"I don't know."

I pushed my emotions aside and handed Carlos the bandana, which he stuck back in his mouth. I helped him to his feet, his moaning hard to ignore.

"Can you get back on the horse?" I asked.

He nodded but swayed against Rat. I bent down as I had

before, braiding my fingers, waiting for him to place his foot in my hands. Instead, he sank to the ground as if his muscles had turned to jelly.

As he lay still at my feet, I was forced to acknowledge just how bad off he was. His nose had started bleeding again, a red trail slithering into the bandana stuffed between his dry, cracked lips. The bruising under his swollen eyes had darkened to an angry purple. His chest rose and fell in quick, shallow spasms.

I'd hoped we could gain enough distance to safely reach Laredo, get Carlos to a hospital, then find the Rangers and give them the gun, but there was no way he'd make it that far. For all I knew his ribs were broken and poking into his lungs, causing more damage. He needed to lay down and rest. He needed water, medicine, and a support bandage around his chest. He needed Griselda.

CHAPTER 24

By the time I managed to get Carlos back on Rat, the first hints of daybreak had pinked the edges of the sky. I climbed up behind him, wrapping an arm around his waist so he wouldn't fall off. He wavered in and out of consciousness, his head leaning against my collarbone. I led Bluebird, her reins looped over my saddle horn. I didn't have a lead for Twister, but he trailed the mare like a gosling following its mother.

It seemed like forever before I saw Santa Rosa's twin *campanarios* rising out of the low clouds. As we rode into Múzquiz, I stayed on the outside border to avoid attention. I wanted to get to the church as far in advance of the *tequileros* as possible, but I didn't dare go faster than a slow walk. Any more jostling than necessary could make Carlos's injuries worse. Each time I took the bandana out of his mouth for sips of water, his tormented sounds twisted like screws into my heart.

His rescue had gone terribly wrong. If only I could have stopped Alicia. In my heart, though, I knew nothing would have changed her mind. Once there, seeing Carlos beaten with her own eyes, she had not been able to stop herself from trying to save him. She'd run at Javier with such determination, as if all the frustration she felt about doing nothing had culminated in that one fateful act.

Steam rose from Rat's neck into the cool morning air. Cream-colored foam flecked Bluebird's shoulders. The horses had worked hard to get us down without tumbling head over heels. I hoped the risk had been worth it. We'd gotten away from the *tequileros* only to end up exactly where they were headed. As a tremor rippled through Carlos, I knew I'd had no other option.

I shifted in the saddle, locating Twister a few steps behind us. His jaunty step showed none of the other horses' fatigue. He was young and not weighed down by a passenger and a saddle. He really was a pretty thing with his lengthy, elegant legs and shiny coat; just the sight of him lifted my mood.

I thought of JJ's wonderment as he'd watched the wild mustangs run across *La Isla Grande*. Maybe he'd never have broken Twister, preferring to let him stay wild—as wild as a pet horse could be. A grin pulled at my mouth. That would've caused a hell of an argument with Papa. He would've made JJ put a saddle on the colt sooner or later; he wouldn't have been able to abide an animal not paying for its supper in some way.

Thinking of my father kindled the ever-present urgency in my gut. I sent a silent message to him—*I'm coming, please wait for me.* Maybe he'd improved. Maybe Dr. Andrew's tonic had made him better. Maybe Maude had bullied him into going to Corpus. He was tough, I reminded myself; maybe he'd willed himself to get well. Maybe he'd died yesterday. *Stay strong; please stay alive.*

We reached the back of Santa Rosa. I listened for galloping horses but only heard the chuffing of our own. The *tequileros* would have had to reorganize themselves after chasing us then finish loading the bottles. Leading the mule train down the mountain would be no easy feat. It would take time.

The sun hadn't crested yet. I'd worried people would be milling about the mission already, either arriving or leaving, but the churchyard was oddly quiet. Esperanza and Flora were gone. Griselda's wagon was where it had been, gifts still surrounding it like a pine tree on Christmas morning. I pulled up in front of the water trough. Bluebird and Rat stuck their snouts in and gulped. Twister trotted up and copied them.

I carefully dismounted, not wanting Carlos to fall off without my support behind him. Coming out of his daze, he looked around with red-rimmed eyes.

"Santa Rosa?" he croaked, realizing our whereabouts. "Why are we here?"

"Griselda is inside," I answered.

I reached up to help him off, but he didn't move. Confusion and fear leaked into his glassy stare.

"We can't be here," he wheezed. A cough shook him, and he clutched his chest.

"We don't have a choice," I replied. "Your injuries are too bad to go on; you need Griselda's help."

"This is where they're coming," he said. "Did you drag me out of the camp just so Javier can finish me off here?"

It took strength to be scornful—maybe his injuries weren't as bad as I'd feared.

"Why hasn't he already killed you?" I asked.

"I know things. He needs me," he said, then smirked. "Until he doesn't."

He wobbled in the saddle. I had to get him down before he fell out of it.

"You need to hide," I said.

"Hide where?"

"In Griselda's wagon."

"You want to get *Tía Abuela* killed, too?"

"We don't have much time, as you pointed out," I said. "You want to keep arguing, or you want me to help you off that horse?"

"I'd rather get shot than stay on this horse," he huffed.

Getting him off the saddle wasn't as difficult as getting him in it had been, but just as painful judging by his waxy face and high-pitched whines. We hobbled over to the wagon, and I helped him crawl into the bed.

"I'll cover you with some blankets, then find your great-aunt," I said.

Carlos grabbed my wrist.

"The woman who runs the church," he said, voice strained from exertion, "the one without a nose. Don't tell her I'm here."

"Dove?" I hadn't planned to tell her anything if I could avoid it.

"Yes," he rasped. "She has an agreement with Javier."

I was tempted to ask Carlos about the guns, but his eyes closed. His head lolled to the side. He seemed to be falling asleep or passing out. Every breath he took ended in a whimper. Moving quickly, I surrounded him with some of the gifts left by Griselda's patients, covering his shivering body with a few blankets. Then I fashioned a canopy by draping one side of a towel on a box and tenting it over his face. He was hidden but had air.

"Whatever you do, Carlos, keep quiet," I said, though I was certain he was unconscious.

I hid the horses in a thick bunch of trees. Jackson would recognize Rat, and Javier would know Twister. As I rushed to the closed double doors of the mission, I dreaded what I'd have to tell Griselda. Alicia was dead, and Carlos might be dying.

Pushing one side of the entry open, I noted the queer quiet. A few muffled groans moved through the dank air; a baby's mewling was immediately hushed. The lanterns and candles that had provided light before had been squelched. It was too dark to make out much more than shapes, but I felt the weight of eyes upon me.

At the far end, Dove and Griselda stood in front of the altar, illuminated by a cylinder of pale, dusty light leaking through the big, round window.

"Are you alone?" asked Dove, her firm voice carrying across the space.

"Yes."

She waved her hand. People began moving around and whispering, as if she'd released them from a spell. I hurried through the nave. Griselda stepped toward me, but before I could say a word, a loud ruckus punched through the door I'd left open. The people hushed again as the braying of donkeys and whoops of several men echoed off the mission walls. The *tequileros* had arrived.

"Get out of sight," Dove hissed at me. Her cheeks were flushed, pink spots flanking the cavity in her face, her breath coming in uneven bursts. "I don't have time to explain what a white girl is doing here. One look and they'll either kill you or haul you up that mountain."

Griselda moved closer to me. "Alicia?"

I blinked, lids stinging as if they'd brushed against sandpaper. I didn't want to tell her in front of Dove; I had to protect Carlos. I didn't want to lie either. If Griselda had told Dove what we'd agreed, then she thought Alicia and I had gone to Sabinas for supplies.

"She didn't come back," I whispered, "but what we went for is in your wagon. You should tend to it as soon as you can."

I watched Griselda's dark eyes fill with worry and sadness.

"Stop talking and get under there." Dove pulled up a side of the burlap cloth covering the altar.

I obeyed, heart banging as I shoved the boxes out of the way to make room to sit. A gray bar of light shone along a space between the bottom edge of the cloth and the floor. I rearranged my legs and laid down so I could look through the crack.

I sensed, rather than saw, someone enter Santa Rosa. The air changed, as if there'd been a collective silent gasp. A form marched through the sanctuary toward us. Griselda's beaded moccasins moved to the side then disappeared. She'd shuffled around behind the altar, as if it might protect her. I'd never seen her back away from anything. I could only imagine what must be going through her mind. My words had been ambiguous, but she'd caught their meaning. She knew something terrible had happened at the camp. She'd have to erase the knowledge and face Javier.

The sun finally breached the horizon outside, its golden glow leaking into Santa Rosa through the high windows. As Javier approached, a shaft of light impaled the opening in the rear wall. The beam caught in the fringe of red hair beneath his hat, making it glow. He came closer and closer until all I could see were the bottom half of his black leather leggings and his scuffed, square-toed boots. I stayed as quiet as possible. I would've stopped my blood from flowing if I could have.

"There are people here." Irritation cut through Javier's voice.

"We blew out all the candles to provide some cover," Dove explained, "and I've told the few people here to stay out of the way when your guests arrive."

"That is not what I asked," Javier snapped. "You were to empty the church."

"I couldn't turn out the worst cases," Dove replied. "They risked everything just to get here. Making them leave would be a death sentence."

"After all I've done for you?" snarled Javier. His feet moved closer to Dove's frayed woven sandals. I could imagine those cold, hard eyes boring into hers.

"Throwing people out to die in the street would've raised more attention than just letting them stay," countered Dove. "These are poor peasants. They don't give a damn who comes in and out, or why. All they want is the *curandera's* help."

"You better pray to your crazy saint that you are right," said Javier. "You cross me too often and I will burn the whole *pinche* place down. *Entiendes?* Then where will all your *invalidos* go?"

"You've made that clear enough," Dove answered. Her strength was impressive, but her long skirt vibrated as if her legs were shaking.

"You, *Señora Curandera*," Javier said.

I stopped breathing. Did he only know Griselda by reputation, or did he know that Carlos and Alicia were related to her? Was he about to tell her what had happened at the camp? Blame her somehow? He hadn't recognized Alicia. Jackson had told him she was Carlos's sister. Surely, Javier was too busy to bother memorizing the family trees of Hidalgo?

"*Vas a ayudar la gente*," he said. "*Allá.*"

He wanted her out of the way. I watched Griselda's feet move. Her gnarled hands reached down to pick up some supplies then she shuffled away.

"*Jefe!*" a voice called from the front of the church. "The men are here."

"*Bueno*," Javier replied.

Light poured in through the open doorway at the far end of the church. Several black figures glided across the threshold, silhouetted against the glow.

Dove's skirt shifted out of my line of sight. I watched through the slit as the figures came closer, their features taking shape when they left the sun's glare. I recognized Danté first, wearing the black cowboy hat he'd had on at the camp. He'd restrung his necklace. What I'd thought were long beads were actually the canine teeth of an animal. He had a limp he hadn't had before Rat knocked him down. Rojizo walked next to him. He was still wearing his jacket, a bloodied rag wrapped haphazardly around the arm my bullet had grazed. A dark purple bump glowed like the eye of a cyclops on his forehead where Bluebird's hoof had clipped him.

Jackson strode up the sanctuary a few feet behind them, straight and tall, his mouth set in an inscrutable line. He'd cleaned his hands, but I'd never be able to banish the image of Alicia dying in his arms from my memory.

The *tequileros*—including Jackson in that description only gave me the slightest pause—escorted three other men. Each had removed his hat, as any good Catholic would when entering a holy place. Men looked different without the frame of a hat, but something sparked my memory as I studied the faces. My eyes traveled down to the bandoliers crossing their chests, the pearl-handled revolvers on their hips, and the apprehension I already felt doubled.

They no longer wore the faded olive-green uniforms or tricolor armbands, but they were the same three *Villistas* we'd encountered on our way to Sabinas. Álvaro, the one who'd had the prayer card stuck in his hatband, the one who'd harassed Alicia and asked for the syphilis treatment, stepped ahead of the pack. He marched straight for Javier until he saw Griselda.

Álvaro came to a dead stop in the middle of the nave. His sallow face glistened. Alarm bells rang in my head as I remembered what Alicia had said the syphilis treatment would do. Griselda's back was to him—she had no idea he was glaring at her as she squatted next to a shivering child I recognized as Esmé, the little girl with measles. The child must have taken a turn for the worse and returned with her mother.

I bit my lip, wanting to call out a warning as Griselda stood. When she turned, she was met by Álvaro's stare. She nodded a greeting but said nothing. Breathlessly, I waited for him to call her out, to accuse her of making him sicker instead of curing him. If he started talking about his encounter with Griselda, he might bring up her two companions, the blonde Anglo and the girl in the form-fitting Levi's. There weren't too many young women matching those descriptions in this area. Would Javier put it together? He knew what Alicia had looked like, and Danté and Rojizo had most likely described me to him by now. Had Tomás told him who I was?

Seconds ticked by. Álvaro remained as still as a post. Rojizo stepped away from the group and approached Griselda.

"*Necesito tu ayuda,*" he said, unwrapping the bloody rag from around his arm and gingerly taking off his jacket.

Griselda glanced at the bump on his head, then pulled a pair of scissors out of her pocket. She cut the sleeve of his shirt and began examining the flesh wound in his bicep. Álvaro watched for a moment, then exchanged a harsh look with his two *compadres*, which I interpreted as a warning not to start their taunting again.

I sucked a long stream of air in. Most of the people in the mission had information the others would find interesting at the very least. Only one domino had to fall for connections to be made, causing a chain reaction that could lead to three discoveries: me, the missing gun, and Carlos.

The group, except for Rojizo, continued forward until I could barely see the tops of their heads.

"*Buenos días.*" Javier greeted the three *Villistas* in a genial but steely tone. "It is my pleasure to present *Señorita* Dove, *la doña de Santa Rosa.*"

Pancho Villa's men all seemed to notice Dove's missing nose at the same time. Two of them stared for a minute, then looked around at anything but her face. Álvaro's gaze, however, did not wander as he wiped a line of sweat from his brow.

"Morning, gentlemen." Dove's voice remained cool and calm, though her skirt still quaked. "Follow me."

She led the men through the clutter in the transept as I felt the blood drain from my head. Their footsteps sounded like gunshots resounding off the vaulted ceiling. They rounded the corner, heading for the steps to the crypt. Were they taking the .45s now? Would they inspect every single crate to be sure all five hundred were there?

It took all my willpower not to crawl out from my hiding place and bolt. Rojizo sat on the floor only yards away, cursing while Griselda cleaned out the trench in his arm. The one I'd put there. I couldn't get past him. He'd call out and they'd hear him through the grates in the floor. I had to stay put, waiting for the guillotine blade to drop.

The space under the altar grew smaller and smaller as time dragged. Finally, footsteps signaled the group's return. No angry words had spouted from the floor. I watched as everyone except Dove and Javier filed into the transept. Why were the two of them lagging behind? The others walked all the way to the apse, and still there was no sign of them.

The *tequileros* and *Villistas* made their way down the steps into the nave. Danté sauntered over to check on Rojizo. Ramón and Leandró continued toward the entrance. Jackson and Álvaro stopped several feet in front of the altar. Álvaro placed a hand on his stomach.

"You feel all right?" asked Jackson.

"*Sí, sí.*" Álvaro inhaled deeply.

"The men out front should be just about done loading the *tequila* into your wagon," Jackson said. "Where do you want us to take the other items?"

"Canutillo. It is a few miles from Sabinas," replied Álvaro. "We will send word when it is time."

"How long do you think?" asked Jackson.

Why was Jackson making the arrangements? Why was Javier still in the crypt?

"Only three, maybe four, days," Álvaro answered, wiping his brow again. "You will have *el cañón* by then, *sí*?"

"The transporter said he'll have it here today," said Jackson. "Wasn't easy to move, took a while longer."

"*El General* will pay nothing until he has it," said Álvaro. "*Es muy importante.*"

"What the hell does he need a howitzer for?" asked Jackson.

"Protection for the new *hacienda*," replied Álvaro. "Once there is an agreement, he will not be able to get anything more."

"After all his rebelling, he's going to retire and become a *hacendado*?" quipped Jackson. Álvaro's expression registered no humor and Jackson's droll smile quickly disappeared. "Don't worry, *amigo*, he'll have everything."

"*Bueno. Vaya con Dios*," said Álvaro, turning to leave.

I watched Jackson's face. Did selling guns to Pancho Villa trouble him at all? Had he really procured a cannon for him? A man his own father and grandfather had fought many bloody battles against. Not only was he dishonoring his family name, but also himself.

As Álvaro crossed the threshold and the doors closed, Jackson's shoulders seemed to loosen. Or maybe I mistook my own release as his. The *Villistas* were leaving without having noticed the missing gun. For all of ten seconds, I thought I'd avoided disaster. Then a splintering crash emanated out of the floor grates.

"*Puta!*" Javier bellowed. "Where is it?!"

Liquid heat flared across my body. Maybe the *Villistas* hadn't realized they were a gun short, but, apparently, Javier had.

"Let go of me!" yelled Dove.

She'd all but seen me take the .45. How long did I have before she told him? Could I get out the door before they shot me? Another crack rang out from below followed by the sound of glass smashing. I peeked under the cloth as Jackson and Danté started jogging toward the transept. Griselda rapidly finished bandaging Rojizo's arm and shuffled quickly to the altar. She bent down, grabbing a jar of ointment from a box.

"*Corras!*" she whispered to me.

But I didn't have time to run; they were already coming.

"*Que pasó, hermano?*" Danté asked as Javier dragged Dove by the arm to the altar.

"Turn me loose, damnit!" Dove said.

A low murmur broke out in the nave as people stood, craning their necks to see. Several of them took a few steps forward, and I wondered fleetingly if they would try to protect Dove.

"What happened?" asked Jackson.

"She has stolen a gun and bullets," hissed Javier. "It is fortunate for us all I was able to hide it from Álvaro. If he had noticed, all trust would have been broken."

"Why would I take something I'm supposed to be guarding?" Dove gave her arm a rough yank and Javier let go. "I need those supplies more than I need a gun."

"If you do not have it, someone else does." Javier gestured to the small crowd, then hollered across the nave. "*Quien tiéne la pistola?*"

"None of those people took your fucking gun," said Dove.

Javier brought his face so close to hers his nose seemed to fill the space where hers wasn't.

"The only way you could be so sure of that," he seethed, "is if you know who did."

The altar seemed to be pushing down, forcing air from my lungs. I couldn't take my eyes off Dove. I expected her to walk over any minute, rip the cloth away and expose me. Wind began to buffet against the outside glass of the round window, rattling like chattering teeth. Dove held her ground, chin up in defiance, her glare fastened on Javier.

"I warned you," said Javier, breaking the silence. "You leave me no choice."

He marched over to the people closest to him, Eudora and Esmé. Eudora moved in front of the pallet where her daughter lay. Javier shoved her aside and drew his gun.

"*Amigo!*" Jackson called out. "That's just a sick kid. She didn't take anything."

Javier ignored him; his gleaming eyes locked on Dove.

"I will kill your people one by one until you tell me where it is." He pointed his revolver at Esmé's small, bare chest.

My mouth went dry. Dove would tell him now; she wouldn't let Javier kill her people. I gritted my teeth as she started moving. Instead of coming toward the altar, though, she rushed at Javier with swift strides full of strength. Rojizo stepped in front of her.

"*Detienes,*" he barked, his hand resting on the revolver holstered at his hip.

Dove tried to rush by him, but Rojizo caught her around

the waist with his good arm.

"Don't you dare hurt that little girl!" Dove yelled, her usually cryptic expression filled with angst.

Javier sneered as he pulled the hammer back. I knew he'd do it. Esmé meant nothing to him. I'd known I might cause risk for others by taking the gun, but witnessing the reality of it was different. I couldn't watch an innocent person—a child—die because of me. I ducked out from under the altar.

"Here's your damn gun!" I called out, raising the Colt .45 in the air.

Javier twisted around, pointing his revolver at my head.

Jackson jumped in front of me.

"Don't shoot!" he yelled, ripping the gun from my hand. "I got it."

Jackson set the revolver on the altar. Javier's arm lowered a bit as he studied my face. I'd never been this close to him. He still wore JJ's buckle. With some satisfaction, I noticed a large scab on his cheekbone where it had hit him when JJ threw it.

"*La Rubia*," he said slowly, his mouth twisting, those eyes lighting up. "It was you at the camp, *verdad*?"

Jackson shifted his weight. Was he trying to obstruct Javier's aim?

"*Amigo!*" said Javier, sarcasm lacing the word as he squinted at Jackson. "Why do you protect a thief?"

"There's a lot riding on this deal," Jackson answered, voice hard and steady. "I don't think we should fuck it up now by doing something rash. The *Villistas* can't be far away. They'll turn around if they hear gunshots, and then you'll have to explain why you covered up the fact that a gun was missing."

Javier stilled, digesting Jackson's words.

"All right. We will wait until they get farther away, then we will hang her, *los rinches* style." Javier turned to Danté. "Hold her."

Danté pushed past Jackson and grabbed my arm.

Rojizo, blood already leaking through the bandage Griselda

had applied, had been so surprised by my appearance that he'd let go of Dove. He looked as if he wanted to walk over and strangle me himself. Dove's blue eyes bore into mine as she moved closer to Griselda. She could now place full blame on me for the missing gun and save her people from Javier's wrath. By confessing, I'd absolved her of the guilt of outing me.

We stood surrounding the altar as if waiting for communion—Jackson, Danté, and I on one side, Griselda and Dove on the other, Rojizo just beyond them. Javier stood in front of us all. Expectancy settled heavily over the mission as his eyes swept the group. He was evaluating his next move. I met his glare. I would not give him the satisfaction of seeing me recoil.

If nothing else, he was a man of his word. I had no doubt he would drag me outside and hang me, as the Rangers had hung his people, but that would be better than other possibilities. I thought of Flora's haunted face, her ravaged body, the torture and violation she'd endured at the camp. I'd rather have a noose around my neck than Javier's hands on my body.

I stole a glance at Jackson. Turbulence raged across his face, but I'd so completely lost faith in him that I didn't know the source. Was he angry, scared, frustrated? Would he try to stop Javier from killing me? Jackson knew that if this ended with me gasping for air at the end of a rope, my father would have lost both of his children to the monster he called 'amigo.'

A loud bang resounded down the nave, shattering the suspended moment. Startled, I looked at the entrance. The doors had been thrown open. A shape shadowed the opening then moved into the church, boot-heeled steps ringing out like strikes of a ball-peen hammer. Light bounced off the brim of a ten-gallon hat.

"Y'all waiting on me?" the man said, white teeth glistening in a wide smile. "Got your howitzer outside."

He took his hat off and wiped a hand across his forehead. My knees rocked. Dove inhaled sharply and sidled closer to the altar, hate spilling from her eyes. She raised a hand to the jagged crater above her mouth. An avalanche of connecting pieces nearly took me down. I remembered her words in the crypt, the poison that had soaked them.

Her fingers left her face. The .45 I'd stolen lay on the altar where Jackson had placed it. Dove's hand darted out and snatched it. A blast exploded. Startled screams boomeranged through the church. I covered my ears, expecting another shot. The *tequileros* ducked and crouched.

Burr Archer clutched his chest.

CHAPTER 25

Santa Rosa erupted in chaos. Burr squirmed on the ground, his single voice a screeching choir in the cavernous church. Javier hurried to him, shouting for Griselda. Rojizo and Danté charged at Dove, who backed deeper into the apse, pointing the Colt out in front of her, grip firm. Jackson stood in stunned silence, eyes darting back and forth as people in the church withdrew like ripples radiating from the center of a pond.

I ran.

Bursting out of the doors, I nearly crashed into Pancho Villa's cannon. It sat in a cart, its barrel tilted up at the sky. Beyond it, Tomás and another man were surrounded by mules and donkeys. They'd been coiling the ropes they'd used to secure the *tequila* bottles but must have stopped when they heard the gunshot. Tomás's eyes caught mine. I didn't wait to see what he'd do. I kept running until I reached Griselda's wagon.

"Carlos!" I leaned over the side rail, whispering loudly. "Stay put, they'll be out here soon. Tell Griselda to meet me at the javelina tree."

I heard a rustle under the towel.

"Did you hear me?" I hissed.

"Yeah." His voice was weak, but he was alive and conscious. "I thought they'd shot you."

"Remember, tell her the javelina tree by the river," I said.

"Griselda needs the mare to pull the wagon. She and the colt are hidden in the bushes."

Twister shied away from Bluebird's side as I rushed up, but he followed when I led her deeper into a mott of aspen trees and low piñons. Rat's ears stood up straight, a soldier at attention. I threw the reins over his head and shoved my boot into the stirrup. Rat was running before I got my leg across his back. I leaned over the horn, hovering above the saddle as he lunged beneath me. Exhilaration and fear drove us forward, moving as one, flying over the rugged terrain.

Staying off the main road to avoid the *Villistas*, I concentrated on the ground ahead, not guiding Rat so much as helping him avoid holes and rocks. Questions circled above me, following, waiting for me to stop so they could descend like blackbirds on a scarecrow.

My eyes watered, irritated by wind and dust. I blinked them clear and turned in the saddle to look behind us. Rat sensed my weight shift and slowed. Not seeing any movement, I faced forward and drove my heels down, urging him on. My thighs burned, pumping with Rat's jackhammer gait. JJ's Stetson flapped behind me, the cord biting into the skin of my throat.

Had the *Villistas* heard the gunshot and gone back? Even if they hadn't, I must have already passed them. Traveling with a heavy wagonload of *tequila* would slow them down.

We'd run several miles when I recognized a large camel-back-shaped hill we'd passed on the way to Múzquiz. In front of us, a deep arroyo zigzagged like a lightning bolt through the terrain. I pulled Rat back, easing him down into it. The walls rose ten feet up on either side at the bottom, protecting us from being seen. Clouds hung above, heavy with unspilled rain. I prayed they'd hold. The arroyo could fill with water in a storm more quickly than I could climb out of it. How does a cowboy drown in the desert ... it sounded like the beginning of a joke, but it was deadly true.

We slowed to a trot. I dropped into the saddle, legs tingling with relief. Pulling the cord of the hat forward, I crammed the Stetson on my head. The tension of the string had raised a welt across my throat in the same place Javier's knife had sliced Alicia's open. I squeezed my eyes shut against the image and sent Alicia up to circle with the questions, a white dove among the crows.

At the end of the arroyo, we scrambled up the steep incline. Not much later, Rat told me we were getting close to the water. He didn't break stride, just lifted his head higher, ears twisting back and forth. I spotted the tops of the tall cypress trees strung together in a curving line, relieved to have put some distance between myself and Santa Rosa.

Burr had cut off Dove's nose. Even now, it was hard for me to believe he'd done something so gruesome, so cruel, but there'd been no confusion or doubt in Dove's eyes or in her steady grip when she'd pulled the trigger. It was a pity her bullet hadn't been fatal. It might have broken Burr's collarbone or shoulder, but from what I'd seen, it had been too high to pierce his heart or lungs.

I'd instinctively disliked him, but I'd had no idea what kind of savage hid behind that smile. Jackson had warned me to stay away from Burr, but Jackson was working with him. Burr was their 'transporter.' I doubted he'd seen me. More than likely, he'd been too busy squirming in pain to notice me rushing out of the mission, but soon enough, he'd find out from Javier, or maybe even Jackson, that I'd been there. What would he do with that information? My gut constricted into a hard ball. Had I put my father in a new kind of danger?

What were the threads that connected all this? The pieces came together, then scattered apart as Maude's voice trilled in my ears: "*Too many coincidences to be coincidental, sugar.*"

Rat bobbed his head and snorted. We'd reached the riverbank.

"It's okay, boy, we're not going in."

I patted his neck and turned him upstream to the javelina's big cypress. The tree seemed haunted by Alicia's laughter. As we pulled up next to it, my heart swelled with so much sadness it should have exploded into a thousand pieces. Tears funneled down the crease of my nose. I let them flow. Rat stood patiently while I sat on his back, lost in grief.

I wiped my face, clearing my eyes to look around for a good place to wait. I had no idea how long it would be. Would Carlos be lucid enough to tell Griselda where I'd gone by the time she disentangled herself from the turmoil in the mission? Would he be alive?

So much had changed, blown apart by what I'd seen and what I couldn't figure out. The meaning of it all, the details, kept blurring. Except for one crystal-clear thing—Carlos had to live.

CHAPTER 26

I woke sometime later with a start, a strand of hair tickling my nose. The wind had stiffened, smearing gray clouds across the sky. Rat and I were in a copse of trees near the water with the big cypress in sight. I'd found a root resembling a bench to sit on, leaning back against a trunk. Eventually, my brain had shut down and I'd fallen asleep. I wasn't sure how much time had passed. Judging by the light filtering through the clouds, it was late afternoon.

I walked over to Rat and took the canteen out of the saddlebag, drinking deeply. Rat huffed, letting me know he was tired of standing around. I was anxious to move on too, even though fatigue had invaded every vessel in my body. What if Griselda never arrived? How would I know what had happened? I could not chance going back to Santa Rosa. What was taking her so long? Had Javier found Carlos? Had he hung him instead of me?

A skunky smell drifted my way. The sow trotted out of her tree den. Her three babies followed, all of them heading for the riverbank where several other javelinas were already milling about. I was watching them drink water when the entire pack lifted their heads and looked toward the road. They held stock-still, then, at some silent signal, they all jogged into the undergrowth and disappeared.

Rat turned his head as well. My pulse quickened when I

heard the sloshing of water. I crouched down and moved just far enough out of the trees to get a good view.

Álvaro was riding across the stream. He stopped his horse in the middle and removed his *sombrero*, plucking the prayer card out of the hatband. After sliding the *tarjeta* into his shirt pocket, he leaned way over sideways and dunked the hat upside down in the water. Using both hands, he lifted it out by the wide brim then turned it over his head like a bucket. Water poured down his face and shoulders. He still had fever. I would've smiled at his discomfort if I hadn't been so scared.

What did his appearance mean? I assumed he was on his way to give Pancho Villa a report about the guns, but what had taken him so long? Had he heard Dove's gunshot and returned to Santa Rosa? Where were the others with the wagon full of *tequila*? Had they passed by while I slept?

I sank back into the trees, thinking Álvaro would refresh himself then keep moving, but moments later a series of loud splashes erupted. I stood to look. He'd fallen out of the saddle into the river. His spooked horse was trotting to the other side. I held my breath, waiting for him to stand and go after his ride. Nothing happened. My eyes were glued to his body, which seemed to be moving with the slow flow of the stream. Had he passed out? The water had only been about three or four feet deep when we'd crossed, but that was deep enough to drown in if you were unconscious.

I'd been anxious for Griselda to arrive, but now I prayed she wouldn't. If Álvaro wasn't dead, if there was a chance he'd wake up, I needed to stop her. He might demand her help. There was no telling what he'd do if he found Carlos in her wagon.

I took a few cautious steps toward the water. His *sombrero* was drifting in front of him. I searched the road for other riders then moved closer. He was floating on his back, but his face was barely out of the water. I walked down the bank until I was across from him and stood on tiptoe to see better. Was he dead? His eyes were closed. And then they weren't.

Álvaro gasped, lurching out of the water. Before I could run, his head turned my way, eyes narrowing as he caught his breath.

"I know you," he said in Spanish, voice quaking as shivers shook his body. "You are the *gringa*. The goddaughter of *Señora Curandera*."

I recognized the contradictions in his statement. I was Anglo and therefore an enemy, but I was Griselda's goddaughter, which might shield me—if he believed it. He looked the other way, probably realizing at the same time I did that his horse was gone. I glanced over at Rat. He was barely visible through the trees.

Álvaro moved toward me through the water. I started backing away.

"Stay," he barked, gesturing at the revolvers on his hips. The heavy bandoliers no longer crossed his chest, but the bullets loaded in his guns would be more than enough to take care of me.

As he stepped onto the bank, he stumbled over some rocks, caught himself, then clutched his stomach. The cold water might have temporarily revived him, but he was very ill. His color was off, his eyes puffy and bloodshot, and he was shaking. He turned his gaze to the woods and found Rat.

"I need your horse," he said.

My instinct was to race for Rat, but Álvaro stood between us. If I tried to get past him, he'd have plenty of time to shoot. He headed for the trees. I followed several feet behind.

Before he got very far, he veered drunkenly, putting out a hand to brace himself on a trunk. He was breathing hard, almost panting. He pushed off the tree and walked a few more steps until his foot caught on a root. He fell to the ground. He was still for a second, then he rolled over onto his back.

"The medicine, in my pocket," he rasped. "You make it for me."

He placed a hand on the butt of one of his guns.

"*Ándele*," he croaked, eyelids drooping.

A red-hot wave engulfed me. I was tired of being told what to do; of men taking what they wanted. I was tired of being threatened. I'd seen enough. I knew how this would play out. I'd make his tea, then he'd kill me and take my horse.

I yanked my pant leg up, unsheathed the Bowie knife, and knelt next to Álvaro. Using my body weight, I plunged the point into his chest, pushing it deep between his ribs. When it would go no farther, I jerked up with all my strength. The blade stuck then released with a wet sucking sound. Álvaro's eyes popped open, hands dropping to his sides. His chest quivered. I placed my lips by his ear.

"I need my fucking horse."

His body convulsed, blood pouring from the slit I'd made. I reached out and wrenched the revolver from its holster.

CHAPTER 27

I backtracked down the middle of the road, wanting to leave what had happened behind but not willing to risk missing Griselda. I slowed Rat to a walk. It had started drizzling, and the temperature had dropped. I lifted the flap of the saddlebag. When I pulled Papa's coat out, the Bowie knife came with it, dropping onto the dirt by Rat's back hoof. I'd shoved it into the saddlebag as I'd hurried away from Álvaro's body. I stopped Rat and dismounted, bending down to pick it up. A streak of blood had dried on the blade. I looked at my hands. They were clean.

I'd killed a man. An ill man. I'd thought of a hundred alternatives as we'd galloped away, but each idea was a bad one. In this world, no one could afford to wait and see what happened—it was never something good. I had to grab my moments where I could; missed opportunities were deadly. Perhaps that was why Javier killed first and asked questions later.

I should feel something—guilt, remorse, sorrow—but there had been only one way to get rid of the threat of Álvaro. When he'd had a vulnerable moment, I'd taken advantage of it. The *tarjeta* he'd put in his pocket had done nothing to protect him; my blade had sliced right through it. I scanned my conscience but found only one regret; I should have taken both of his guns.

I put on the jacket then led Rat off the road. Sitting down on a rock, I wiped the blade clean on my sleeve, pulled off my boot, and slid the knife back into its sheath. I was shoving the boot back on when I heard the creak of wood and jingle of tack.

Hitched to Griselda's wagon, Bluebird resembled a child wearing grown-up clothes, but she was pulling like a champ. Something close to happiness sparked through me at the sight of Twister following a few yards behind.

In my eagerness, I stepped out of the brush too quickly and scared the mare. She shied, jerking the wagon forward. A muffled cry of pain came from the wagon bed.

"Woah," said Griselda, tightening the reins. After she got Bluebird under control, she turned to me with a cheerless smile. "I am relieved to find you, *m'ija*."

I peered in at Carlos, alarmed by the deathly pale of his face. Rain and sweat beaded across his forehead as he struggled for air through the bruised slash of his mouth.

"He's worse," I said.

"He needs more medicine, *pronto*." Griselda quickly climbed back to him. "You have water?"

I handed her my canteen.

"Hot would be better, but there is no time to make a fire," she said.

She poured water into a cup and mixed in some leaves, letting them soak for a bit. Carlos whimpered as she lifted his head and placed the mug to his lips. He drank, some of the tea dribbling out the side of his mouth.

"Is there a way to get to Laredo without going through Sabinas?" I asked.

"*Sí*, but the road is rougher, less traveled. It goes through a village called La Capilla."

"We should take it," I said. "I think the *Villistas* are in Sabinas."

"Did you see them?" she asked.

"Álvaro," I said quietly. "He was going to take my horse."

Our eyes met. She did not ask for details.

Carlos's labored breathing began to calm. His eyelids flagged, the anguish on his face dwindling to discomfort. Griselda began adjusting the blankets around him, tucking them in to keep him from rolling.

"Did he tell you what happened to Alicia?" My voice was a cracked whisper.

She stopped, sorrow pouring into her face.

"I'm so sorry," I said.

"She did what she had to do." Her chin trembled, her eyes filling. "It was her choice."

I nodded, swiping at my own tears as Griselda got back onto the bench seat. She picked up her sunbonnet, soggy from the light rain, and put it on, her misery disappearing beneath its visor.

"It is about half a mile back to the cut-off," she said, turning Bluebird around and reining her into a trot.

Backtracking even more was counterintuitive, but at least we wouldn't have to pass the javelina tree and what lay under it. When we reached the detour, I realized Griselda's description had been generous. The road was two narrow wheel ruts with a strip of grass in between. The fading light made it even more difficult to navigate. I cringed each time the wagon creaked over bumps and banged into holes, but Carlos didn't make a sound; the medicine had knocked him out.

We kept as fast a pace as we could. Luckily, the sky cleared up and the road wasn't muddy enough for the wagon to get stuck. Twister would wander off for a while, then jog up next to Bluebird and nudge her hip—a little boy checking in for reassurance. The landscape changed in reverse, becoming less like the mountainous area and more like the desert. It would probably look like home by the time we got to La Capilla, though home felt farther away than ever.

When the road widened a bit, I brought Rat up next to the

front of the wagon. Griselda handed me some beef jerky.

"How bad was Burr Archer hurt?" I asked, chewing hungrily.

"The bullet hit his collarbone and went out. I had to treat him before we could leave; it took a long time."

I braced myself. "And Dove?"

Griselda's bonnet pointed ahead.

"Javier hung her outside Santa Rosa."

The jerky soured in my mouth. I'd hoped Dove had escaped somehow. She'd said she would give up everything for revenge. Ironically, the gun I'd stolen had given her that chance. The unjustness of Burr's survival burned like acid.

"Do you think Javier will send someone after Carlos and me?" I asked.

"They are already coming."

CHAPTER 28

"We have to stop for water," Griselda called out.

During the night, we'd pulled over for a few hours so she could rest. Then I'd tried to sleep while she stood guard, but it had been futile; ghosts and bloodhounds had invaded my thoughts.

We'd been back on the road since long before dawn, leaving the cool air behind. Now the sun blazed down, heating everything in its path. Carlos had to be roasting under the blankets. The effects of his most recent dose of medicine were wearing off; his whimpering grew more and more intense.

I stood in my stirrups. Papa had taught me that the tallest and greenest trees always grew near water. Hunting for stray cattle, we'd scan acres and acres for clumps of live oak rising above the brush line.

"If it were a hundred degrees and you were a fat little heifer, wouldn't you want to be in the shady cool of a mudhole?"

Papa had taught me a lot about ranching, and about the land. I wasn't sure he'd meant to, but his love for it flowed from him the way light came from the sun. He could sit on a horse for hours, traveling across the caliche and through the thornbush, watching birds hunt and game feed. How would he survive letting it go? The ranch was so much a part of him; he was so much a part of it.

Burr Archer was a brutal criminal. He did not deserve

what my father had poured himself into. I had to make sure he never owned La Barroneña.

I spotted a string of cottonwoods. We turned off the road, coming upon a wide creek slinking through gray-green trunks. The temperature dropped at least five degrees, cooled by the water and mottled shade. In my former life, it would have made a nice place to picnic.

"Whoever Javier sent will be moving faster than we are," I reminded Griselda.

The *tequileros* had seen me at the mission but not Carlos; they didn't know if we were still together. When I'd left Santa Rosa, I'd ridden through the woods then down the arroyo. It would be hard for them to follow my trail, especially after the rain. But, if they did manage to track me, they would find Álvaro. They'd see my footprints around the body. They would find Rat's hoofprints leaving the area then joining the wagon wheel tracks. They could figure out I was with Griselda. They might even guess Carlos was in her wagon. We needed to keep moving.

I slid off Rat, my legs stiff and rubbery, and led him to the water for a drink. He must have been thirsty; he didn't balk at stepping into the stream. Twister followed us, splashing in up to his knees. He took a long swallow then pranced back to the bank, wandering off to sniff around a patch of tall grass.

After Rat drank his fill, I looped his reins over a branch and stepped to the back of the wagon to get a bucket. Griselda had already given Carlos some water from her canteen and was examining the wrapping around his ribs. His face was so bruised and swollen he bore little resemblance to the boy I'd known in Hebbronville.

"Hang in there, Carlos," I said. "We'll be in Laredo before too long."

His head swiveled toward my voice.

"You." He struggled to sit up. "You got her killed."

His anger took me by surprise. Griselda gently pushed on

his shoulder until he laid back down.

"*No, no, m'ijo,*" she soothed. "Do not upset yourself."

His lids sagged but didn't close.

"His fever is very high," Griselda said to me. "He does not know what he is saying."

She was probably right, but I couldn't help dwelling on his words. Was there any truth in them? The guilt would pound me into the ground so far I'd never claw my way out. Alicia and I had agreed to go to Múzquiz together—dangerous enough—but we'd never planned on going to the camp.

Carlos's face squinched up, tears rolling into his hair from the outside corners of his eyes.

"I told her to stay away from me," he cried as Griselda placed a wet rag on his forehead. "Why did she come?"

To help him. Of course, he knew that. He couldn't have stopped her any more easily than I could have.

"I should have run far away," Carlos sobbed, his words slurring. "He made me ... I didn't want to help ..."

As Carlos drifted off, I remembered what he'd said about Javier needing him.

"He was just packing tequila," I said to Griselda, "wasn't he?"

"Javier can't read," she replied. "Pancho Villa sent written messages in code, in English. Carlos said he read them for Javier."

Comprehension caught in my breath.

"Why would Javier trust Carlos with something like that?"

"He was disposable," she said.

If he was translating their correspondence, not only would Carlos know about the guns, but he'd also know details about Javier and Pancho Villa. Details that could cause them both a lot of trouble. Carlos had gone from a boy they could get rid of when they no longer needed him to a dangerous silo of information. Carlos was evidence.

I felt a new level of anxiety as I walked into the creek. I filled the bucket for Bluebird, sparing the time it would take to untether her from the wagon. She was lathered, but her pace had stayed steady. JJ had trained her well.

As I headed back to the bank, a loud buzz stopped me short. I recognized the sound instantly. I whirled around, catching sight of Twister, his muzzle down a large hole. Ice plunged into my veins.

"HEY-YA!" Dropping the bucket, I charged the colt with both arms flapping. "Get away from there!"

Twister's head jerked up just as the rattlesnake struck. It missed his nose, hitting him right below the knee. The colt let out a surprised whinny and jumped to the side. The rattler slithered from the rabbit burrow and coiled, ready to strike again. A snake can lunge up to two-thirds of its body length; Twister was too close. I scoured the ground for a weapon, not wanting to risk someone hearing the gun fire. I picked up a baseball-sized rock, lifted it over my head, and chunked it at the center of the snake's thick body.

It writhed around, rattle shaking so fast it blurred. Blood welled from a gash in its middle, but it was still struggling to draw back into a spring and launch itself. Twister seemed to be in shock. Instead of running away, he stood completely still.

I found a bigger rock, got as close as I dared, and heaved it down on the spade-shaped head. It landed with a gratifying crunch. The rattlesnake squirmed, its diamond-patterned scales rippling. The black-banded tail stayed erect, but the three-inch rattle slowed to a quiver. The snake's nervous system would take a while to shut down, but with its head and fangs smashed under a rock, it was no longer a threat.

Twister came to life, stamping his foot and tossing his head up and down. I moved to him slowly, grabbing his halter in case he spooked. Rattlesnake bites were a major concern on cattle ranches. As I racked my brain for everything I'd learned or heard about treating them, Griselda appeared at my side. Talking softly, she ran a hand down Twister's leg. His skin twitched at her touch, puffs of air bursting from his nostrils.

Two fang marks cut deep into his shin, each almost an inch long. If the snake had hit him in the nose, the colt would be much worse off. When cows got bit on the nose, Papa had to put them down. Otherwise, the swelling slowly suffocated them. Twister was still in trouble. The venom would swim through his blood system, destroying tissue and muscle like meat tenderizer. If the fangs had punctured a major artery, he'd die within minutes. Whatever was going to happen, it would happen fast.

"*Agua*," requested Griselda.

The bucket was floating downstream. I retrieved it and filled it with water. Griselda tied a bandage tightly under Twister's knee to slow the flow of poison to the rest of his body. She washed his leg off, then picked up a small pocket-knife. I clutched his halter as she sliced into his flesh, making an X across the puncture holes. His head bobbed up, eyes wide, but he didn't pull away.

Griselda placed her mouth over the wounds, cheeks collapsing as she sucked. She spat his blood on the ground, tilted the canteen to her lips and rinsed her mouth out several times, then repeated the process.

"Is there a lot of venom?" I asked when she finished.

"It is hard to know," she answered.

If the snake had recently swallowed the rabbit whose hole it had been in, it might not have had enough time to store up more venom. Weighed down while the meal digests, snakes can't move as fast after they've eaten. They were most likely to strike then instead of crawling away from a threat. Or from the nose of a curious colt.

Griselda pulled a powdery substance and some herbs out. She tossed them into a small stone bowl, added a little water, and ground the mixture with a pestle.

"What is that?" I asked.

"The fangs might carry *el tétanos*. It is infection that kills most times, not venom."

Mama had said getting bit by a snake was like being vaccinated with a vial full of bacteria.

Griselda smeared the paste onto a long strip of gauze, and then wrapped it around Twister's shin.

"The bandage will need to be changed often," she said. "The wounds need to be washed and more medicine applied."

I looked at Twister's sweet face, and my heart fluttered. He stood quietly, too quietly, his head drooping. The tip of his hoof rested on the ground as if he were trying not to put any weight on the leg that had been bitten.

"Can he walk?" I asked.

"It would be best for him to stay still for a while to keep the venom from spreading," Griselda said. "He is young and strong. If there was not much poison and it does not get infected, he should recover quickly."

I glanced at the wagon where Carlos lapsed in and out of consciousness. His lungs could be filling with fluid; he could be bleeding to death from the inside. He was in a great deal of pain. Making him wait was not an option. Also, we needed to stay ahead of the *tequileros*.

"We have to keep going," I said.

Griselda climbed into the wagon.

"Do you have something I can lead him with?"

Twister had been happy to trail us when all was well, but he might not now. Griselda pulled out a rope, which I tied to the halter's O-ring under Twister's chin. I retrieved Rat, then took up the lead.

"Okay, boy, come on," I said from the saddle, clucking my tongue. Rat started walking. The rope stretched out from Twister's halter until it was pulled tight. The colt's head ducked, and he hobbled forward then stopped. I faltered at the sight of his leg. A patch of blood had already soaked through the bandage and his shin appeared to be swelling. I couldn't force the colt to limp faster. He was hurt, not being stubborn like Rat at a water crossing.

"Damnit!"

Griselda had tied on her bonnet. She was ready to go. Leaving Twister behind would be the prudent thing to do. I couldn't prioritize a horse's life over a boy's life. But, as incomprehensible and ridiculous as it was, the thought of abandoning him felt like abandoning JJ.

"Go on without me," I said. "Get Carlos to the hospital."

Griselda paused, watching as Carlos fought to breathe even in his sleep.

"You are sure?" she asked.

When I nodded, she quickly gathered some things, shoving them into a cloth *bolsa* with a few clean bandages. I took the bag from her, along with an extra canteen.

"I'll let him rest for a bit," I said. "If he doesn't get any better, I'll ... catch up."

"I know this horse means something to you," Griselda said, "but it is not worth your life."

Twister hadn't been worth my brother's life either. I'd been so angry at JJ for choosing to fight for him. Now I was making the same choice.

Griselda crawled to the front of the wagon.

"Do you have any kind of weapon?" I asked.

Alicia had taken the knife Griselda had worn on her belt, and her pocketknife wouldn't protect her against anything bigger than an armadillo. The famous *Curandera Jorobada* had never needed to be well-armed, but she'd never been carrying a living time bomb either. As frustrating as it would be to lose another gun—and wishing again that I'd taken both of Álvaro's—she needed the revolver more than I did. She and Carlos wouldn't be able to get away if attacked. I could at least take off on Rat. I'd have a chance.

I reached around and pulled the gun from my waistband, holding it out to Griselda. Her eyes widened at the sight of it, but she didn't ask where it had come from.

"No—" she started to protest.

"To protect Carlos," I said. She leaned over and took it.

"When you get to the bridge, tell the border patrol Carlos smuggled guns for Javier Salsito de Ortega and Pancho Villa, say those two names. Tell them he wants to make a deal with the Texas Rangers," I said. "Hopefully, they'll take you to the hospital and protect him until he can answer questions."

Griselda popped the reins. Twister made no move to follow Bluebird. I watched them go, clouds of dust closing in behind them. As the noise of the wagon grew faint, a forlorn feeling settled over me.

No matter how seldom traveled the road was, standing in the middle of it would be a mistake. I got off Rat, holding his reins in one hand and pulling Twister forward with the other. The colt limped behind me, dragging his injured leg. I tried not to look, because when I did, his big, luminous eyes begged me to stop. We settled behind the first screen of scrub we came to.

I forced myself to wait for what felt like an hour, then tried walking Twister again. He barely hopped forward. I gave up and focused on the gory bandage. Sitting on the ground next to him, I removed the ingredients from Griselda's *bolsa*, mixing them with water from the canteen then smashing the powder and herbs together. The paste smelled like syrup and chalk.

I started to unwrap the gauze around Twister's leg, but the edges stuck to his skin and hair. I pulled harder, stomach clutching when the strip came away. His flesh was as red as hot cinders and so engorged it glistened. Blood and yellow pus oozed from the gaping holes.

This is hopeless. What the hell am I doing?

Hot air tickled my ear. I jerked in surprise. Twister's nose hovered at my shoulder. He reached out and nuzzled my neck.

"Okay, boy," I whispered, hugging his hot cheek to my head.

I picked up the canteen and soaked a piece of gauze, wiping it gently over the wounds until they were clean. Then I spread the paste on a strip, reapplying the dressing before the cuts could start weeping again. The unnatural heat of his skin quickly warmed the bandage.

"Let's give it another try," I said and stood.

I took several steps forward, encouraged when Twister followed. Rat walked at my side, looking back as if telling the colt to keep it up. We forged ahead, winding through the brush. I pushed the calculations of how long it would take to get to Laredo out of my head. If Twister was willing, I'd keep going.

Suddenly a loud *clunk* rang out and the lead rope ripped out of my hand. I turned, my heart splitting. Twister had stumbled over a large rock. He'd gone down on his good leg. I rushed to him, grabbed the rope, and pulled.

"Up, up!"

He struggled to get off his knee, but his wounded leg gave out when he put weight on it. His back legs buckled, and he went to the ground, rolling onto his side, head flopping down in the dirt.

"No!" I yanked the lead, lifting his head, but his body didn't budge. When I released the rope, his head dropped without resistance. His eyelids lowered until only a crescent shone below them. He'd tried, but he was wasted and suffering. Forcing him on would be cruel.

I tethered Rat, reached inside my boot, and jerked the Bowie knife out of its sheath. I'd boxed myself into this; it was time to be practical. Animals had to be put down on ranches all the time—steers broke their legs, horses foundered, cow dogs got lockjaw. The worst thing I could do would be to leave Twister to die a slow death alone.

I crouched down and placed the sharp edge of the knife at his windpipe. I'd have to cut through it to hit the main artery. I took a deep breath and started to press. Something rustled in the undergrowth behind me. I stopped and looked around at the grass blowing in the hot breeze. Sweat rolled into my eyes. I blinked, rubbing them with my sleeve.

Concentrate. You can do this.

"I'm sorry, JJ," I whispered, tightening my grip.

"*Qué pasó?*" asked a familiar voice.

CHAPTER 29

I leapt up, pointing the knife out in front of me. Tomás stood in the waist-high brush, holding the reins of his horse. I scanned the landscape behind him, certain more *tequileros* would charge out any moment.

"Who's with you?" I demanded.

"Nobody," he said, holding out both hands, palms up, as if to show he meant no harm.

"Did Javier send you?" I asked.

"They send me ahead to track you for Rojizo and Danté," he said. "I want to help you instead."

I scoffed. Now he wanted to help. What about when JJ had lain in the dirt bleeding to death?

"I don't need anything from one of my brother's murderers," I spat.

He bowed his head and removed his *sombrero*. Soft waves of white hair tumbled past his shoulders.

"We were only supposed to take the horses," he said so softly I could barely hear him. "I tried to stop him."

"But you didn't," I countered.

His face contorted, but I couldn't resist going on.

"Javier keeps killing, and you do nothing," I hissed, my face on fire. "You are a coward."

Tears coursed through the deep gullies pressed into the old man's cheeks. I savored his pain.

"*Es la verdad*," he said, hat shaking in his hands, "but let me help you now. *Por favor*."

I paused. As good as it felt to hurt him, he was not the devil. Tomás was a follower.

"How are you going to help me?"

"I will hide you," he said. "Then lead the brothers off a different way."

"Why would you do that?"

"*Perdón*," he answered, his clear eyes holding mine.

Forgiveness.

My anger stuttered. I understood the need to be forgiven. It had been powerful enough to drive me into Mexico. Tomás moved closer to Twister.

"He stepped on a rattler?"

"Stuck his nose in a hole," I said.

"The boy and the *curandera* kept going to Laredo?" When I didn't respond, Tomás went on. "The boy is hurt bad."

He'd tried to take care of Carlos at the camp, I couldn't deny that. When he caught us leaving, he'd let us go and had not sounded the alarm. He bent down and placed a hand on Twister's forehead.

"*Pobrecito*," he said, gently stroking the colt's white star. "They try to make him carry *tequila*, but he kicked and bucked. I worried they will hurt him. I set him free, but he stayed with the mare."

"He meant a lot to my brother," I said.

"*Sí, yo sé*." His voice trembled.

Of course, he knew. He'd watched JJ fight for Twister and lose his life.

"I have someone who can make your brother's *caballo pequeño* better," he said.

I stared at him, letting the irony sink in. He was offering to save my brother's horse when he'd done nothing to save my brother.

"He won't budge," I said flatly.

"He has too much heat."

Tomás pointed at the dark patches of sweat on Twister's neck and behind his front legs. Before I could argue further, he squatted and stuck two fingers deep into Twister's nostrils. The colt's eyes flew open. His long legs floundered about as he gathered himself. Tomás kept the colt's nose plugged, only removing his fingers after Twister blundered to his feet.

"I thought he'd given up." My mouth twitched with relief. "How did you know that would work?"

"He cannot fight the need for air," Tomás explained. "Horses breathe through the nose, not the mouth."

Twister held his head up for a few minutes, but he wilted like a morning glory when the shot of adrenalin subsided. I patted him while Tomás retrieved a canteen from his saddle. He dumped water over Twister's head, rubbing it down his neck. Then he poured the rest of it across the colt's back before handing me the lead rope.

"I think now he will walk," he said. "You come with me, *sí*? It is not too far, but we need to go. The brothers are searching. I want to lead them away before they find the boy."

I skimmed the few choices I had. I could take the chance that Tomás would lead Twister and me to safety, and then keep Javier's brothers from finding Carlos and Griselda. Or what? Cut the colt's throat and race to catch up with the wagon, hoping I wouldn't blunder into Rojizo and Danté on the way?

I decided to trust him.

"Where are we going?" I asked as we rode slowly out of the brush and onto the road, Twister limping along behind Rat.

"The house of my grandson," answered Tomás, "in La Capilla Lavanda."

Griselda had mentioned the road went through La Capilla, which gave me some reassurance that Tomás wasn't leading me to some bandit's lair. I tried to picture what sort of family he had. Was his grandson an outlaw? Did he work for Javier too?

"The girl, Flora, she is all right?" Tomás asked.

I took in the frank concern on his face. Flora had said something about old Jesus, *viejo Jesús*, saving her. At the time, I'd thought she'd been referring to divine intervention, but looking at Tomás's long white hair and flowing beard made me reconsider.

"She lost the baby, but she is safe and with her mother," I said. "Did you get her out of the camp?"

"The things they did ..." His voice cracked. He turned away, wiping his eyes on his shirtsleeve.

Had Flora been the last straw for Tomás? Had her torture led him to start turning away from Javier? Maybe even cowards had their limits.

"La Capilla," he announced after a while, pointing down the road.

The small *pueblo* looked like many of the other villages I'd ridden through in Mexico. People crisscrossed the grass-patched center square, shoppers went in and out of a grocery-and-feed store, groups of men loitered, smoking on the porches of bleached adobe buildings. What set La Capilla Lavanda apart was the beautiful old chapel sitting on the far side of the plaza.

A round piece of stained glass sparkled like an amethyst in the center of the small chapel's façade. Carved stones had been embedded in the clay surrounding its open doorway, through which I could see a simple wooden retable at the back of the room. Each of the thick walls, except for the back one where the altar stood, had two tall, arched windows. They'd been left open, giving the church an airy feeling, like a beautiful birdcage. Even more unique, the adobe of the chapel was the same soft purple color as the tiny *coquina* shells I'd once found on the beach in Corpus Christi. The people who'd built it had somehow turned the dull tone of mud and clay into a pretty shade of lavender.

As we passed by, I glanced up at the round window. I was hoping for a closer look at the design, but the angle of the late-day sun caught in the purple glass, sending a bright beam into my eyes. I squinted against the harsh reflection, black dots swimming through my view like tadpoles.

"*Cuidado!*" Tomás exclaimed.

My eyes flew open. A figure on horseback had risen from the earth like a specter, blocking our path. His features blurred in my sunstruck vision, but my gut told me to run.

I let go of Twister's lead and drove my heels down, jerking the reins sideways as Rat leapt. Tomás spurred his horse. The rider charged in front of us. I yanked Rat's head back. His hooves slipped in the loose dirt, but he caught his balance and changed course as a second rider rounded the buildings in front of us.

There was no chance of getting by them. I spun Rat around, sprinting for the chapel door as an explosion split the quiet air. A bullet hissed by, thudding into the front wall of the church. I pulled my foot out of the stirrup. Before I could jump off Rat and hurtle through the entrance, another shot rang out.

I heard the bullet whine through the air. Something slugged the back of my left arm, knocking me out of the saddle. I landed hard, my face smashing into the ground. Blood filled my mouth. The door was several feet away. I pulled up my knees, scrambling on all fours.

Shots volleyed around the square. I dove into the chapel, landing on the floor under the front window. Chunks of adobe crashed down. I lay flat on my stomach, gasping, waiting for the next round. Had Tomás tricked me? Led me into an ambush? When no shots came, I pushed up high enough to look out the window.

The villagers had disappeared. Only two people were in

the square. Tomás, no longer on his horse, stood in front of the chapel, revolver drawn. Opposite his barrel, Rojizo sat on an appaloosa in the middle of the square, face blazing with hate under his hat. The right sleeve of his jacket bore a fading crimson stain. His left hand held a gun aimed at Tomás. *His left hand.* Most likely not the one he usually used.

"What the hell are you doing, old man?" Rojizo yelled in Spanish, his voice bouncing off the surrounding buildings. "Lower that fucking gun and bring the girl out here, *cabrón.*"

I had to be ready no matter what Tomás did. Where was Rat? I pushed up onto my knees, the nerves in my arm waking with a sudden, throbbing roar. A hot, wet sensation spread to my fingertips. I touched the place above my elbow where the blow had landed. Pain flared; my fingers came away bloody. I'd been shot. I'd known that, but as reality pushed through my stupor, the small room began to slant sideways.

Do not pass out.

I shook off the dizziness and tried to focus on Tomás. He was standing his ground, not coming to get me. Could I help him? I didn't have a gun; we were outnumbered. Hadn't I seen another rider? Danté? I searched the square. Rat stood between two buildings. Where was Twister? Was he safe?

"You want me to shoot you, *pinche viejo?*" Rojizo pulled the hammer back, working to hold the gun steady.

Tomás turned his head and looked right at me. I fought to clear the fog of pain and shock, returning his stare. Even in my confusion, I felt the deep sadness in his eyes, the melancholy of a man who'd seen too much. He swung his arm in my direction, lobbing his revolver through the open window. Instinctively, I reached out with both hands and caught it. Heat seared down my arm, but I gripped the butt firmly.

Tomás turned to face Rojizo.

"*Ah, chingado,*" Rojizo barked as he adjusted his aim. I held the weapon now, not Tomás. He pointed the barrel at me and pulled the trigger.

Tomás launched himself into the line of fire, arms spread wide apart. As if in slow motion, I saw the bullet hit him. He folded, staggering backward, but managed to land on the bottom ledge of the window. He sat up, still trying to shield me. Rojizo shot again. There was a wet thud and Tomás slumped to the ground.

Rojizo spurred his horse, galloping toward me. Gritting my teeth, I stood, raising the revolver with both hands. I cocked the hammer and aimed; my finger found the trigger. I squeezed at the same time a gunshot blasted from somewhere else. The recoil jerked my hands up. Rojizo's hat flew off. He reeled backward out of the saddle, landing face down in the grass. His horse veered away.

A startled burst of energy raced through me. Wasn't the other rider Danté? Why would he shoot at his brother? Or had he been shooting at me? I leaned out of the window just enough to see next door; there was no one there. I focused on Rojizo, half expecting him to jump up, but he lay still. Had I killed him, or had the other shooter? I caught a glint of metal on a rooftop across the square. There was a flash; a gun fired. I hit the ground. Slugs banged against the church walls, one flying over my head and piercing the wooden altar in the back. A spate of return fire broke out.

There was a third shooter.

A thunderous barrage ensued, so many shots I couldn't tell where they came from. A sharp *clang* rang out behind me. A large silver cross fell off the altar and clattered to the ground. I clung to Tomás's gun, pressing my body into the floor. The stones underneath me were slick and sticky. I looked down and gasped. The floor glistened, smeared in blood.

My blood.

I started to shake. Shrapnel pelted the chapel like metallic rain. A loud snap crackled above me. I leapt to my feet, stumbling for cover under the thick entryway as the round window burst apart. Violet-colored shards showered the ground where I'd lain. Head swimming, I leaned against the threshold. My arm was a throbbing stick of fire. My breath wailed like a siren in my ears.

The shots ceased. A lull.

Reloading. They must be reloading.

Black splotches glided back and forth in front of me, five times bigger than tadpoles, blocking most of my vision. I had to move. I was exposed in the open doorway. I took a step. My foot slipped in a puddle of blood.

I'm bleeding too much.

A black wave surged in front of me, pulling my legs like a riptide. I waited for the hard smack of the floor, but instead, firm arms wrapped around my waist.

"Get back inside." Jackson's voice cut through the haze like a hatchet.

He shoved me against a wall. I slid down until my butt hit the floor. My vision kept doubling. He moved to the front window. More reports rang out. A bullet whizzed in front of me, the high-pitched zip momentarily clearing my head. Jackson was sitting up on his knees, returning fire.

How ...

I couldn't form a complete thought; they kept slipping away, like the blood flowing from my arm. He fired two more times then sat back. Emptying spent cartridges, yanking bullets out of an ammo belt, shoving them into the open cylinder. My gaze drifted out the window. A figure on foot, charging us. Jackson's head bent over his gun. Still loading. Tomás's revolver in my hand. Aim. Pull the trigger. The kick hit me with the force of ten mules. A white wisp curled from the end of the barrel as I fell into blackness.

CHAPTER 30

Floating. Weightless. Dark. Swimming up from a bottomless chasm, sounds drifting by like feathers.

"Sarita?"

A deep ache pulsed in my arm.

"Can you hear me?"

I dragged my lids apart. I was lying in a bed. A blurry shape wavered in front of me.

"Hey, there."

The blur formed into a face, hovering a few inches from mine. A handsome face with sea-colored eyes.

"Jackson?" My voice cracked, my lips feeling thick and swollen.

"Thank God," he said, sitting down next to me.

I cleared my throat.

"What happened?" I gingerly touched the bandage wrapped around my upper left arm.

"You got shot."

I shut my eyes, running my memory back.

"Rojizo shot me?" I asked.

"Yeah."

Patches of the gunfight came back to me, along with confusion.

"Did I shoot him or did you?" I asked.

"I think your bullet got there first," Jackson replied with a smile.

"There was someone else. While you were reloading."

"Danté," said Jackson. "You saved my life."

"He's dead too?"

Jackson nodded.

I've killed three men.

An uneasy feeling slunk through me. I wasn't sorry for killing them.

Álvaro had been different, like stopping something before it could happen, but Rojizo and Danté had been a reflex. Shooting them didn't feel much different from killing the rattlesnake that had bitten Twister.

I'd saved myself ... and Jackson. Not JJ, but Jackson.

Maude had said killing a man wasn't an easy thing. Was it a learned thing? A thing I hadn't yet known I was capable of when Javier appeared at our house?

The spiraling thoughts were making me woozy. Something crucial was trying to break through. There was somewhere I needed to be. Someone—

Carlos.

I sat up and scooted to the opposite side of the bed. My head spun as fire snaked around my arm. Clenching my jaw against the pain, I pulled back a blue-and-white-striped blanket to look at myself. A man's nightshirt hung loosely from my shoulders. Where were my clothes?

"Whoa, there," said Jackson. "Where do you think you're going?"

I swung my feet off the bed and placed them on the floor. It seesawed beneath me when I tried to stand. Jackson rushed around and grabbed my good arm.

"Lie back down," he insisted. "You lost a lot of blood; it'll take some time to get your strength back."

I should have been embarrassed to be seen in a nightshirt. I didn't care. I wanted to shove him away, run out the door and find Rat, but my legs were as heavy as lead pipes. My vision tunneled and I slumped onto the mattress. I forced air deep into my lungs, determined not to faint.

"Carlos," I croaked.

"I know he's hurt," Jackson said. "Where is he?"

I looked up at him, trying to focus. His beard had grown scruffier but couldn't hide the features of the face I knew so well. It was his soul I no longer recognized. Why was he here? Why had he helped me? Hadn't Rojizo and Danté been his *compadres*? I wanted answers but couldn't get the questions from my brain to my mouth. Confused, so tired. The abyss was opening back up in front of me. An oasis of oblivion.

"Sarita?"

My eyes blinked. What had I been thinking about? I glanced around the small wood-paneled room. Light streamed through a glass-paned window across from the bed. I looked harder. It had been late afternoon when Tomás and I had been ambushed.

"What time is it?" I asked.

"Around noon."

"Noon? I've been here all night?" Carlos swam into my thoughts again. "I have to—"

"Listen," Jackson interrupted. "Rojizo and Danté are dead. They can't hurt Carlos."

I sank back against the pillow. "But I still ..."

What do I need to do?

Cotton candy was wrapping around my head, muting all my senses.

"Whose house is this?" I asked.

"It belongs to Tomás's grandson, Patricio," he answered. "His wife has been caring for you."

A thud hit my gut. I knew, but I needed to hear it.

"Tomás?"

"He's dead," Jackson said solemnly.

A high price to pay for forgiveness. Who was I to deserve such fatal penance? The cotton candy moved into my brain, wispy strands sticking to my thoughts.

"What are you doing, Jackson?" I whispered, my eyes growing heavy.

"It's a long story."

His words registered then everything disappeared until I felt bites of pain. Something was tugging at my arm.

Jackson?

I turned my head to tell him to stop. A pair of yellow-green orbs glowered at me. Foaming, black lips curled back from jagged teeth in a snarl. My heart thundered as the mouth hinged open. Steel-trap jaws snapped shut, sinking into my flesh. I tried to scream, but my mouth was wired shut.

Jolting awake, my eyes darted around the unfamiliar, dimly lit room. Instead of a rabid coyote chewing on my arm, a woman was bent over it, holding what looked like a pair of needle-nose pliers. She noticed my stare, set the tool down next to a flickering candle on the nightstand, and hurried from the room.

I sagged against the pillow. My arm had developed a beat of its own, hard and fast. I glanced down. The woman had left the bandage open. The back of my arm was red and swollen. I twisted it forward to get a better view; a blazing pain took my breath away. I placed a hand above the back of my elbow and lightly touched the tender skin.

As I explored, my index finger sank into a hole. Every nerve in my body vibrated. I jerked my hand away. My stomach convulsed. I leaned over the side of the bed and retched, yellow foam drooling from my mouth onto the Saltillo tile. There was nothing in my stomach. I couldn't remember the last time I'd eaten.

By the time the dry heaving ceased, my abdomen felt like a hundred fists had pummeled it. I wiped my mouth with the sleeve of the nightshirt, leaving a streak of blood. I remembered hitting my face on the ground after being shot. Was my lip bleeding, or something else? My head throbbed. I'd never felt so rough and beaten.

I'd be stuck here trying to heal for days, even weeks. How long had it already been? The thin linen curtains had been drawn across the window; no light glowed behind them. Had it been hours or days since I'd woken up to Jackson sitting next to me? Had he really been there? Had my imagination conjured him up?

Footsteps approached and a stout young man appeared in the doorway.

"Hello. Glad to see you're awake," he said. "I'm Patricio."

I pointed at the small yellow puddle on the floor. "I'm sorry."

"That's okay," he said with a warm smile. "You've been through a lot."

He grabbed a rag off the nightstand and wiped the floor. The accent in his perfect English reminded me of home. He wore a flannel shirt partially tucked into Levi's as if he'd dressed hastily. His neatly trimmed hair framed a youthful, clean-shaven face made distinct by dark, unruly eyebrows. He looked like a man I'd see walking down the streets of Hebbronville on any given day.

"This is my wife, Katarina," Patricio said with a note of pride.

He stepped aside, and the woman who'd been tending to my wound entered, carrying a mug. They made a curious couple. Katarina's toned frame towered over Patricio's, her smooth angles contrasting with his open curves. She moved to the bed with a fluid grace, a simple leather shift swaying around her body.

"She needs to get the bullet out," said Patricio.

"It's still in my arm?"

"It went in above your elbow in the back, but there's no exit wound," he explained. "Katarina says it probably hit the bone and lodged somewhere."

"My arm is broken?"

"I'm afraid so."

As he spoke, Katarina watched me with onyx eyes set above angular cheekbones. She held the mug out then spoke to Patricio in a language I didn't understand.

"She had to stop the bleeding before she could look for the bullet," he relayed. "She hoped to find it while you were unconscious. She wants you to drink this before she tries again."

I took the cup. An amber-colored liquid filled a third of it. As I lifted the rim to my lips, earthy-smelling steam rose into my nostrils. Thirsty, I took a gulp, gagging on the nasty, bitter flavor.

"What is that?" I choked out.

"Poppy seed tea," Patricio answered.

"Opium?" I blurted. "Why would you give me that?"

"It's a sedative. It will help with the pain," said Patricio.

"I don't want it," I shot back, shoving the mug at Katarina. She looked concerned as Patricio repeated what I'd said to her in Spanish. She replied in what I realized was an Indian language, its nasal intonation interspersed with clicking tongue sounds.

"She made it weak," Patricio said. "It's the only thing she has that will knock you out."

"I don't want to be knocked out." My head was already loose from the one sip I'd taken. "My mother was a midwife; I know what that stuff can do to you. I don't want any more of it, or anything else made from poppies."

"*Haw*," said Katarina, tossing her black braid over her shoulder. She picked up the needle-nose pliers, a small knife, and a flat piece of wood.

"You're going to have to keep very still," warned Patricio. "Okay?"

No, not okay.

Katarina handed me a four-inch-long piece of stripped oak and pointed at the back of her mouth. It was the same pain-coping technique I'd tried with Carlos. Mama had used it when her patients gave birth. She avoided strong sedatives. She had a theory they passed through the mother to the baby.

I'd made my declaration, now I was stuck with it. The bullet had to come out, I knew that. At the very least, chomping down on the stick would keep me from biting my tongue in half. I placed it between my molars, nodded at Katarina, and turned my head away.

She swabbed my entire arm with a damp, cold cloth, my nose crinkling at the astringent smell. I flinched as she carefully cleaned, knowing it was nothing compared to what was to come.

"Hold still," said Patricio, placing a hand on my shoulder. "She's going to open the hole wider so she can find the slug."

The knife felt like a bolt of lightning slicing through my skin. I thought of Dove. Her pain must have been excruciating. She had endured somehow—so could I.

"Now, she's going to use the big tweezers," Patricio announced, as if commentating on a ball game.

I clenched my jaw tighter as the tip of the pliers slid in, burning like a hot poker. Katarina pushed and prodded, the wet, viscous sound reminding me of gutting a rabbit. I stared at the wall, trying to pretend it wasn't my arm she was digging in, but the sharp stabs held my full attention. I fought the impulse to jerk away, clenching my teeth, my back molars threatening to explode from the pressure. Finally, I stopped trying not to scream and roared around the stick.

Just as the wall I'd fastened my eyes to started rolling like the open sea, I heard a tiny clink of metal on metal. Katarina pushed in deeper. I shrieked. She yanked hard. Something gave way then she held up the pliers, a bloody piece of flattened lead pinched between the tines.

"She found it!"

Home run! I thought bitterly. *Thank God she's done.*

Katarina dropped the slug onto Patricio's open palm.

"Now she needs to put in some stitches."

Not done. My head began to float off my neck.

"I think I might pass out," I sighed.

"I'm surprised you haven't already."

A sharp stab followed by tugging. Then again. Two stitches. How many did I need? Another steely prick, the sensation of thread pulling through flesh. Three. Four. Blackness.

"Sarita?"

I opened my eyes. Patricio was sitting on the bed.

"Good news," he said, "she's finished."

The stick had fallen onto my chest when I'd blacked out. I noticed the imprints of my teeth before Katarina picked it up. My jaws complained as I stretched them wide.

I craned my neck to look at the wound. Two inches above my elbow was a four-centimeter circle of glistening flesh. Katarina had sewn up the long slit she'd cut from the edge of the entry site to get to the bullet, but the round hole was still open. I knew geometry; it was impossible to close a circle. The bullet hole would have to heal from the inside.

"It missed the big artery," Patricio said. "The bone should heal, but the muscles will be scarred. The real concern now is infection."

It's always infection. My arm involuntarily recoiled as Katarina packed something into the wound. She made apologetic noises then smeared ointment around it.

As she worked, a soft cloak of wistfulness fell around me. I missed my mother. I missed her reassuring presence, her warm embrace. Before she'd died, I'd focused so much on Papa—what he wouldn't let me do, what he expected of me, or didn't—that I feared I'd taken her for granted. Her love had been unconditional. I hadn't appreciated what a gift that had been.

"Thank you for helping me," I said.

Katarina nodded.

"Is my horse all right?" I asked Patricio.

"He wasn't hurt in the shoot-out. He's in our corral."

"And the colt?" I asked.

"He's here too. That's a nasty snakebite he's got."

"How is he?" I mentally crossed my fingers.

Patricio paused then shook his head, hair falling across his brow.

"Unfortunately, he will get worse before he gets better. The infection and venom must work their way out. The good blood has to push out the bad."

"But Twister will live?" I looked from Patricio to Katarina.

"Kata thinks so. He is young and otherwise healthy." Patricio's broad grin returned. "Why do you call him Twister?"

I paused, a smile slowly forming on my lips.

"There was a bad storm a few days after my brother got him. It rained so hard that it sounded like a herd of cattle stampeding across our roof. Thunder shook the trees and there were big bolts of lightning," I said. "JJ called us over to the window. The colt was running back and forth, out of the barn and into the open corral, like he was scared and excited all at the same time. When the sky lit up, he started spinning around in tight circles. JJ said he looked like a twister, and it stuck."

It felt good to share a happy memory; to talk about my brother and not mention how he'd died. As Patricio related the tale to her, Katarina beamed. The happy expression transformed her features from hard and severe to unusually beautiful.

"She has a soft spot for animals," said Patricio, laughing. "She even names the ones we eat!"

Katarina rolled her eyes as if she'd understood, then asked him something. I listened to the rhythm of her language, trying to understand.

"She found medicine in your saddlebags," Patricio said. "She wants to know where it came from."

"*La Curandera Jorobada.*"

Katarina nodded with reverence and headed for the door.

The mention of Griselda tapped my need to heal quickly.

"How soon does she think I can leave?" I asked.

"We'll see how you're doing in the morning," Patricio said, following his wife. "You try to get some sleep."

"Wait," I said before he stepped out. "Is Jackson Cage here?"

"He's gone." Patricio's friendly expression turned serious. "I know you must be very confused. Tomorrow, we can talk. You need to rest now."

As he looked down at me, I saw the first glimmer of resemblance to Tomás in his sympathetic expression.

"I'm very sorry about your grandfather," I said.

His shoulders slumped. "I am too."

CHAPTER 31

I was jarred awake by a sledgehammer banging against my entire left side. Tossing and turning did no good. I couldn't find a comfortable position. I couldn't cool off. My hair was plastered to my head and the mattress cover was damp.

The curtains hung still in the muggy room. If I could open the window, maybe the night air would give me some relief. I rolled onto my right side and pushed into a sitting position, dangling my legs over the edge of the bed. I waited several minutes to let my equilibrium adjust. When my feet touched the floor, the welcome coolness of the tile sent a tingle all the way up to the top of my head. I shifted my weight, standing halfway, rear end hovering above the mattress. When the ground remained level, I straightened. The room did not spin, but stinging tentacles slithered up my left arm into my shoulder as I shuffled to the window.

I pulled up on the brass handle at the bottom of the sash. It lifted smoothly, and a gust of warm air blew through the open window. I closed my eyes, letting it wash over me. The moist film covering my body soon dried, giving way to goosebumps. At first, I welcomed the break from sweating, but as my skin tightened it pulled at my wound. I walked back to the bed, shivering from head to toe by the time I got there. My teeth began chattering so hard it sounded as if a woodpecker was trying to drill its way out of my skull. I turned to sit. The shaking intensified, and I missed the bed.

Without thinking, I grabbed the edge of the nightstand with my left hand. A thousand red-hot blades sliced my arm. I screamed, clutching my elbow as I landed on the floor. The door banged open. Patricio charged in like a small bull. He rushed over and gently helped me onto the bed.

"What happened?" he asked.

My teeth clacked together. I couldn't stop shuddering. He placed a hand on my forehead.

"Oh," he said, pulling the covers up to my chin.

As he hurried from the room, I worked my hand out of the blanket and pressed it to my face. Heat radiated into my fingers. Katarina swished in, wearing a long cotton nightgown, her black hair hanging loose over her shoulders.

"I used to have hair that length," I heard myself mumble.

She set a bowl on the nightstand, dipping a washcloth into it. The bed sagged as she sat next to me and placed the cloth across my brow. Patricio brought in another blanket and spread it over me. They spoke, but their voices were muted.

"You have a very high fever," Patricio said, leaning close. "There must be an infection."

I know.

I wouldn't be leaving any time soon. I should have been mad and frustrated, but I couldn't work up the steam for either emotion. If Katarina and Patricio had not been hovering over me, I would have cried. Maybe I was crying.

As a child, raw and weepy with fever, Mama would give me a warm sponge bath then wrap me in her *colchas bordadas* quilt. I'd crawl into her lap, sniffling with self-pity while she read out loud from *Little Women* or *Anne of Green Gables*. I'd only been five or six the last time it had happened, yet the feeling of comfort was embedded in me like the deep root of an oak tree.

Katarina was holding a cup to my mouth, liquid moistening my lips.

"It's willow bark, not poppy seed," Patricio said.

The tea tasted of peppermint and lemon, with a tart, woody flavor hovering beneath.

"Drink it all," said Patricio. "Then Katarina needs to change your bandage."

I forced myself to concentrate until I swallowed the last drop. Katarina lifted my arm from under the covers. The layers had warmed me, but a tremor ran across my skin the moment it met cooler air. I clenched my teeth, bracing for the well-intentioned torture. As I watched her busy hands, her serious, chiseled face, she slowly separated into two people. I scrunched up my eyes, but they crossed again. I let go and closed them.

When I woke, the blankets had been folded neatly at the bottom of the bed and only a thin cotton sheet covered me. I wore a fresh, dry nightshirt, and the shakes were gone. My forehead was only slightly warm. I still felt flimsy, but my yearning to curl up and bawl had passed.

I'd slept all day, but what did it matter? It wouldn't help Carlos and Griselda if I keeled over in the cactus trying to get to them. They had the gun for protection, I reminded myself. They should be in Laredo by now. Had Carlos been able to talk to Captain Wright yet? In a perfect world, the Rangers were getting ready to ride out after Javier. I scoffed at myself. What about this world had ever been perfect?

The aroma of cooking meat made my stomach growl. My mother had always said appetite was a good sign. The bedroom door stood ajar. Beyond it, Katarina sang in a high, lilting voice. I wrapped a blanket around my shoulders, taking an absurd amount of time with one hand, and stood cautiously. The nightshirt dropped to my ankles. I had no idea where my clothes were, or how I'd get them on if I found them.

I shambled over to the door, my head bobbing along just above me. When I drew it open, I found a cozy kitchen on the other side. Katarina stood at the counter chopping up zucchini and carrots. A baby squirmed on a thick blanket at her feet. I saw Patricio through the screen door, busy outside with end-of-the-day chores. A dolefulness strummed my heart. Not long ago, my small family would've been doing the same things. Papa and JJ would have been settling the animals for the night, putting away the tools of the day. I would have been preparing supper. The routine had been so ordinary, but maybe that was the essence of a life; the things you hardly noticed.

"You feel better!" announced Patricio, coming through the door. "I'm going to clean up for supper."

He disappeared into a room on the other side of the kitchen. Katarina stopped singing and looked around at me, surprise lighting her face. She wore a linen blouse the color of marigolds and a knee-length skirt of tan suede that flowed over her body. She took my good arm, guiding me to a ladder-back chair, and placed a cup of water on the table in front of me.

Relieved to sit, even after such a short walk, I started to ask about the baby but decided to wait for Patricio. I could speak to Katarina in Spanish, but I wouldn't understand her answers. I slumped against the back of the chair and watched, comforted by her familiar tasks.

"*Buenas noches, Halcón*," Patricio chirped to the baby as he entered the kitchen smelling of sandalwood soap. He'd combed his wet hair and put on a loose, flax-colored tunic with matching pants. He sat down on the floor and lifted the baby into his arms.

"A boy?" I asked.

"*Sí*," he replied with pride.

The baby's round cheeks shone with a healthy glow. His chubby legs and arms stuck out of a simple cotton gown, like the one his parents had dressed me in. He balanced in the middle of his father's crossed legs, his tiny fingers wrapped tightly around Patricio's thick ones, gurgling contentedly through a wet smile.

"How old is he?" I asked.

"Nine months."

"Does 'Halcón' mean hawk?"

"Yes. He's named after Katarina's father, who was called Dancing Hawk."

"Katarina's father was an Indian?" I asked.

"Kiowa."

Katarina said something to her husband as she shucked cobs of corn.

"She wants to know where your people are from," Patricio said.

"Texas," I replied.

He laughed at his wife's response.

"Kata says her people are from Texas too. Maybe you're cousins?"

I chuckled, surprised by her pointed sense of humor. If we could communicate directly, I'd probably have a whole different perception of her.

"I guess she's asking about my heritage," I said. "My mother's family was originally from Spain, and my father's family came from Ireland."

"Her father's people came to Texas from what is now Oklahoma and New Mexico," Patricio said. "Her mother is from Oaxaca, Mexico."

"Are all of her father's people in Mexico now?"

"Most of the tribe moved here when the North became Texas," he said. "They preferred to make new homes instead of living on reservations."

Katarina broke in. Patricio plunked the baby in my lap and went over to the fireplace to remove a roasting piglet from the spit.

I bounced my knee, holding on to Halcón with one hand. He stuck a couple of fingers in his mouth, babbling around them. Drool dripped down my arm. I wasn't one to "ooh" and "ah" over babies, but Halcón was particularly likable. He blinked fawn-like eyes at me, his father's eyebrows wiggling above them like small caterpillars. His other features were soft like Patricio's as well, but a mop of hair as blue-black as his mother's sprouted from the top of his head.

While Patricio carved the meat, placing it on a platter, Katarina put three pottery plates and some pewter utensils on the table, then brought over a large bowl filled with steamed zucchini, carrots, and corn. She set down a plate of flatbread and some sliced prickly pear, then took the baby from me and placed him on his blanket.

The couple took seats on either side of me. Patricio blessed the food, which made me wonder what Katarina's religious beliefs were. Most Mexicans were staunchly Catholic. Would her father have converted, or had her mother learned the ceremonial ways of the Indians?

Rich, delicious smells rose from the dishes. I hadn't seen that much food since my dinner with Josefina and Lancero in Sabinas. Pancho Villa had indeed followed them, as Lancero had feared. I wondered if they'd boarded up their new house and left, despite swearing he would not be displaced again. I hoped they were safe wherever they were.

As we passed the dishes around, it struck me how unusual it was for a Mexican, an Indian, and an Anglo to peacefully break bread. Why was that? What made us think we were so different from each other? Language, religion, culture? Patricio loved his son as much as my father had loved his. He and Katarina spoke two different languages, yet they'd learned to communicate, fallen in love, and started a family. They'd made room for their differences and reached for something bigger.

Patricio thoughtfully leaned over and cut my meat into bite-sized chunks. Tomás's family had taken me in, caring for me as if one of their own. No matter who Tomás had been, his death must have left a void. Halcón would not remember his great-grandfather.

"Jackson told me Javier killed your brother," said Patricio, interrupting my thoughts. "I am sorry. *Los Salsito de Ortegas* are ruthless. We worried about my grandfather every minute of every day."

"Why was Tomás with them?" I asked. "There must be less dangerous gangs for a *tequilero* to join?"

Patricio froze, a full fork halfway to his mouth. He set the utensil down and cleared his throat.

"My grandfather was not a *tequilero*," he stated.

I wasn't sure how to respond. Tomás had died saving me, and the last thing I wanted to do was offend his grandson.

"I'm sorry, Patricio," I said. "I assumed, since he was with Javier."

He took a deep breath, leaning back in his chair, a miserable look on his face.

"For most of his life, my grandfather worked for the Texas Rangers."

"Really?" I was surprised, but then I thought of how uncomfortable Tomás had seemed, how different his behavior had been from the others at the camp. "Why didn't he get the Rangers to arrest Javier, instead of helping him?"

Patricio grew quiet, looking across at Katarina. She left the table, picked up Halcón, and sat in a rocker by the fireplace. The baby nuzzled her chest, his mouth open expectantly. Lifting her blouse with her free hand, she cradled him to her breast, her strong face altered by the sweet smile of a mother in love with her child. I looked away, feeling like the intruder I was.

"I apologize," I said to Patricio. "I have a habit of blurting out questions. As you said, I'm very confused. There are so many things that seem connected, but I can't figure out how."

Patricio regarded me with what might have been a mix of empathy and exasperation.

"You're not wrong," he said. "You've gotten caught up in a big web. I just don't know how much to tell you, or where to start."

"Tell me everything," I said. "Please."

Katarina stood. The baby had fallen asleep in her arms. She whispered something to Patricio then walked into the other room. He watched her go, taking a deep breath when his gaze returned to me.

"Tomás, my grandfather, tracked for the Rangers. *Tito*, as we called him, was one of their best *guias* for over thirty years." A glum look crossed his face. "My father, Benado, grew up with only one ambition—to become a Texas Ranger. When he was sixteen, he started going on missions with *Tito*. At twenty-one, he got a warrant of his own."

"Tomás must have been very proud of him," I said.

Patricio's expression darkened. "About a year ago, *Tito* and my father stopped to make camp on their way back from a tracking expedition. In the middle of the night, *Tito* woke to the cock of a gun. Javier was pointing a revolver at my father's head. He unarmed them then said he wanted to make a deal. He would spare my father, but *Tito* would have to track for him. My father said he'd rather die than see *Tito* work for an outlaw," Patricio continued, his voice husky. "So, Javier pointed the gun at my grandfather, telling my father to walk away or watch *Tito* die."

I could picture Javier's sneer as he made his demands. That sort of one-sided negotiating seemed to be his trademark.

"My father pretended to obey, but as he passed his horse, he pulled the rifle from his saddle scabbard." Patricio swallowed hard. "Before he could turn around, Javier shot him in the back."

I let out a long sigh, though the brutality did not surprise me.

"My father lay in pain on the ground, but Javier was not done with his game." Patricio's face smoldered now. "If *Tito* agreed to be Javier's *guia*, he would let him go to Hebbronville for help. If *Tito* didn't agree, Javier said he'd finish off my father then hunt down the rest of our family, like the Rangers who *Tito* guided hunted down his."

Tomás's face had been full of agony as he'd stared down at JJ bleeding out in the dirt. The sight must have been like a recurring nightmare. A tender spot for him grew in my heart, replacing the hard knot that had been there. Tomás's family had been trapped in Javier's fist; he could not have risked trying to save my brother, a boy he didn't even know.

"Was Tomás able to get help for your father?" I asked.

"Yes," said Patricio, tears sliding into the day-old bristles on his cheeks, "but it was too late. He died before they got him to the hospital."

"I'm so sorry," I said.

"It didn't end there," said Patricio. "In Javier's mind, even though my father died, *Tito* still owed him retribution. He was forced to uphold his side of the agreement and work for the Salsito de Ortegas. Javier reminded him daily that if *Tito* did not do as he was told, he would hang every one of us while *Tito* watched."

No wonder Tomás had reminded me of a beaten dog. He must have been living in a constant state of panic.

"I told *Tito* it wasn't what my father would've wanted," Patricio said. "In fact, it was exactly what he didn't want. I begged him to let me go to the Rangers for help, but he was too afraid." Patricio exhaled in aggravation. "At first, he clung to the hope he could keep the *tequileros* from doing terrible things. At the very least, he thought he could help their victims. He quickly realized there was little he could do."

To have a monster kill your son and then have to watch him—even help him—harm others must have been a crushing weight.

"I was awful to him," I said. "I blamed Tomás for my brother's death. I held him responsible for not stopping Javier. I had no idea of the horrible choices he was having to make." I placed my hand on Patricio's arm. "You should know that he did help people."

"I have no doubt," he replied with an edge, "but he could never balance the scale."

"He told me he wanted forgiveness."

"The vile pact was devouring his soul." Patricio's jaw quivered as he rubbed it. "I don't think he could keep quiet and watch other people's loved ones tortured and killed to save his own family any longer."

I thought of Tomás standing in front of me, arms spread wide, waiting for the bullet he knew would pierce his heart.

"He let Rojizo kill him to save me," I said, my eyes welling with tears.

"He was already dead." Patricio reached out, placing his warm hand over mine. "That unholy alliance was never going to end with *Tito* alive. Saving you gave him an opportunity to do something honorable in the end. For that, I will always be grateful."

I couldn't meet his eyes.

"I called him a coward, but he wasn't," I whispered. "He was so very brave."

Patricio squeezed my hand.

"At least we can give him a proper burial, instead of wondering where his body was left," he said. "He belongs to God now, not Javier. He can finally be at peace."

"What about the rest of you?" I asked, chilled by the thought of Katarina and Halcón falling prey to Javier. "I've put your family in danger."

"The threat existed before you came here," he replied, removing his hand and taking a sip of water. "As long as Javier is alive, we'll be at risk. We cannot succumb to the fear."

"What will you do?"

"We'll harvest as much cotton as we can, board up the house, and go stay with my sister in Alice. We will be stronger all together." He let out a sigh of resignation. "We knew this day would come."

"Javier will realize something is wrong when his brothers

don't return," I said. "Will you have enough time?"

"Jackson will be able to cover for a while. Hopefully, long enough for us to cross the border," Patricio explained. "When we get to Laredo, I'll finally be able to tell the Rangers what happened to my father. That will be a good day."

"Did Jackson know Tomás before he came to Mexico?" I asked.

"Of course," said Patricio. "*Tito* worked with Jackson's grandfather, Captain Cage, for many years."

My whole body tingled. What Patricio could reveal hung before me like the proverbial carrot. Once I took a bite, I'd have no choice but to chew and swallow.

"What is Jackson doing in Mexico?" I asked.

"Looking for Javier's father."

I wasn't sure what answer I'd been expecting, but that wasn't it.

"Who?"

"Ignado Salsito de Ortega," said Patricio. "He killed Jackson's father, Clement Cage, during the Bandit and Border Wars. Worse than that, he made an example of him."

"How?"

"The Salsito de Ortegas had hijacked a train and killed all the white passengers. Captain Cage and his company, which included Clement, went after them," said Patricio. "Clement was injured during the battle that ensued. Ignado took him hostage when they retreated."

I remembered the feeling of loss that had radiated from Gus when he'd mentioned the men he'd lost.

"Captain Cage sent *Tito* and my father to recover Clement," Patricio continued, growing even more somber. "They found him two days later, strung up in a tree. The bottoms of his feet had been burned off. They'd whipped his back until the skin hung in tatters. They'd even sliced out his tongue and hung it around his neck." He paused. "He was still alive when *Tito* cut him down, but by the time Gus got there, he was gone."

I swallowed hard. The details made me physically sick. Losing a parent was traumatic enough, but to have your father's life end in such horror was inconceivable.

"Jackson never told me his father had been tortured," I said.

"He didn't know." Patricio's gaze dropped to his hands, clasped together in a tight knot on his lap. "After Javier shot my father, Gus and Jackson were the ones who tried to help *Tito* save him," he said. "The details of Clement's death came out then."

Something in my chest began to loosen.

"This all happened a year ago?" I asked.

"About that, yes."

Jackson hadn't run away from me. All those months wondering if I'd done or said something wrong had been a waste of emotion. His disappearance had nothing to do with me. I felt both relief and frustration. Why hadn't he told me?

"Does Gus Cage know Jackson's looking for Ignado?" I asked.

"He might suspect, given the timing," said Patricio.

"Did Tomás tell Gus that he'd been indentured to Javier?"

"No. He knew Captain Cage would try to intervene if he told him the whole story," said Patricio. "*Tito* told him that my father had been attacked by one of the Salsitos but didn't mention Javier specifically. A few days after Benado died, my grandfather told Gus he was retiring to Mexico."

Every answer led to more questions. I'd craved information for so long, I wanted to consume every morsel, identify every ingredient.

"Is Jackson looking for Ignado by himself?" I asked.

"Not exactly," Patricio replied. "He met with the adjutant general in Austin. He demanded to know why Ignado had never been brought to justice. He ended up with a silver star and warrant of authority."

I paused, digesting that nugget.

"Jackson is a Texas Ranger?" I stared at Patricio in wonderment. "They sent him after Ignado?"

"Yes."

"The Bandit Wars ended five years ago," I said, still trying to line things up in my head. "Why pursue Ignado now?"

"The Salsito de Ortegas continue to terrorize the borderlands," Patricio replied. "Ignado stays deep in Mexico, but he's still the head of the family. He calls the shots, and occasionally surfaces if the deal is big enough."

"Wouldn't Ignado and Javier know who Jackson is?"

"I doubt he knew Clement's name, only that he was an Anglo Texas Ranger," he said. "If he does figure it out, Jackson has a cover story, which *Tito* had backed up—he blames the Rangers for his father's death and the possible loss of their ranch. There's nothing left for him in Texas, so he's in Mexico to make his fortune."

"Javier's not stupid," I said. "Would he believe that?"

"Jackson gained Javier's trust by providing something Javier needed," Patricio replied.

Suddenly, as if I'd finally read the last page, I saw the full story.

"Javier stole a load of U.S. military guns," I said. "Jackson got a man to transport them into Mexico. They are selling them to Pancho Villa."

Patricio's mouth hung open for a bit.

"Well, if Jackson's goal is to smoke out Ignado," he said, "that should do it."

I'd thought Jackson and I were at odds, but we'd been on the same side the whole time. Why hadn't he trusted me with the truth? He could have made me his partner instead of trying to send me home. Without all the information, I'd drawn terrible conclusions. I'd put him, and others, in danger.

"You must think I'm a fool," I said.

"Not at all." Patricio blinked with surprise.

"I was focused on my own goal," I said, shaking my head.

"I've compromised everything Jackson set up."

"Your goal is no less important than anyone else's," Patricio countered. "My grandfather wanted to protect us, Jackson wants retribution for his father, you want justice for your brother."

JJ had wanted to protect Twister, Alicia had wanted to rescue Carlos, Carlos had wanted to help his mother, and Gus Cage wanted Jackson to come home safely. We'd each had our own objectives, but they'd braided together. What would be the cost of picking them apart?

CHAPTER 32

I woke very early the next morning, no longer feverish. I'd gotten a few hours of sleep between silent recitations of everything Patricio had told me the night before. I'd taken Carlos. I'd taken a gun. I'd compromised the meeting with the *Villistas*. None of that held a candle to killing both of Javier's brothers. No matter what Patricio said, I was escalating the threat to his family by staying there. It was time for me to leave.

I rolled out of bed and went to the window. Katarina was already working in the garden next to the corral, taking advantage of the break of day coolness. Halcón was strapped into a cradleboard on her back. His arms and legs waved up and down like a stuck beetle as his mother picked vegetables and herbs. She was stuffing them in a cloth bag at her feet, then turning the dirt, preparing the garden to lie fallow while they were away in Texas.

Glancing around the farm, I located my clothes on a laundry line stretched between two spindly trees. I pulled my boots on under the nightshirt, almost accustomed to being one-handed, and walked outside. As fresh air filled my lungs, the musty cobwebs began clearing from my head. My stamina wasn't anywhere near a hundred percent, but it would return.

Jackson would not be able to hold Javier off for long. I could only imagine the level of his fury when he learned what had happened to his brothers. What would he do if he figured out Jackson had played a part in their deaths, that Jackson had been fooling him the whole time? As brutal as Ignado's torture of Clement had been, I feared Jackson would fare even worse in Javier's hands.

What had Jackson's plan been? How was he going to signal the Rangers? As far as I knew, Tomás had been his only ally. He couldn't arrest Javier and his men by himself—or keep five hundred guns out of Pancho Villa's hands.

Outside, Katarina stopped gardening and met me at the clothesline, pulling the pins off and handing over my shirt, pants, and underwear.

"Twister?" I asked.

She led me past the corral where Rat was penned and into the small barn. The smells of straw, dust, and horse dung stirred up my longing for home, as so many things about this little farm did. Twister was snacking on a bale of hay in an open stall. He raised his head as we walked in, ears pert and forward.

Katarina handed me a corncob still in the husk from her basket. I tilted my head in doubt, but she waved encouragingly. Draping my clothes over a sawhorse, I held the cob out to Twister. He watched me with bright, clear eyes that made my heart sing. Slowly, he stretched his neck out to take a sniff, nibbling on the silky tassel on the end. Then he yanked the corn from my fingers, gobbling up the whole thing. When he'd finished chewing, I wrapped my good arm under his neck, resting my head against his for a moment, JJ's presence soaking into me.

Katarina squatted down, Halcón's tiny toes touching the ground behind her, and opened the bandage on Twister's leg. I inhaled at the sight. The flesh around the puncture wounds was still so swollen and misshapen it appeared to be inside out, but the color had faded to pink and there were no seeping globs of pus rolling down his shin. Katarina glanced up at me then closed the dressing.

"It looks so much better," I said around the relief in my throat.

She stood, dipping her head in the funny way she'd done before. She pointed to the house, and I picked up my clothing to follow her.

In the bedroom, Katarina took Halcón out of the cradleboard and placed him on the floor. He rocked from his tummy to his knees, crawling a short way before plopping down flat. Almost as helpless as the baby, I had no choice but to let Katarina help me dress. I couldn't even unbutton the nightshirt, much less pull on my pants. I bit my cheek to keep from crying out as she gently worked my injured arm into the shirtsleeve. Once she had me clothed, she took a piece of muslin and tied it at my neck then helped fit my arm into the sling. When she was done, it rested securely at my belly button.

Each article of clothing added a rock to my wall of resolve. In the nightshirt, I'd felt small and broken. I wasn't. The infection was gone, and my arm would heal. I finally had enough information to give the Rangers a full picture. With Carlos to corroborate, they would not be able to ignore me. I wouldn't let them.

I thanked Katarina and hurried out to find my gear. Patricio was in the barn when I entered. He stopped whistling but kept forking hay into a pile.

"You've decided to go?" he asked.

"Yes," I replied. "Twister seems well enough."

"You are both much better."

"I'm so grateful to you and Katarina."

"Kata says the medicine *la Curandera* gave you for Twister made a big difference. If he hadn't gotten care so quickly, he would've been much worse off."

"Katarina did the same for me," I said with a grateful smile. "Would you mind helping me saddle my horse?"

Patricio stopped and shot me a puzzled look.

"I can tack him up for you," he said, "but will you be able to get into the saddle?"

I stopped myself from retorting that of course I could. In truth, I wasn't sure. The bullet wound, the fever, being in bed for several days, had all drained my strength.

"You might have to help me get on, but then I should be fine."

"It's likely you'll have to get off that horse before you reach Laredo," he said with a good-natured snigger. "Why don't you take my wagon?"

"That would just slow me down."

"You think you're going to be galloping with a broken arm?" he asked. "The wagon will be smoother. You can go faster with less pain than bouncing around in a saddle."

He set the pitchfork against the wall. I followed him out of the barn to the other side of the corral, where a hay wagon sat in the shade of a live oak. Two forms lay in the bed, tightly wrapped in white muslin, like rolled up carpets.

"Are those ... is that—" I stammered.

"Rojizo and Danté are wanted men," said Patricio. "Jackson asked me to hand their bodies and effects over to the Rangers when we go through Laredo. I'll move them to the barn, and you can take this wagon. They're delivering a big buckboard tomorrow for us to pack our household things in."

I leaned against the wagon, thoughts dive-bombing. Those weren't just any bodies.

"I'll take them," I said after a moment.

Patricio looked at me as if I'd lost my mind. "Why would you do that?"

"Because if Javier finds them here, he'll have even more reason to kill you and your family," I replied. "Also, I need the Rangers to listen to me. I need them to believe me. Two dead Salsito de Ortegas will help."

"Good points, but I'm not comfortable putting such a burden on you."

"I'll get to Laredo before you do," I countered. "Jackson's going to need help. Javier might begin to suspect him. Not to mention, the gun deal could go through any day."

"And if it does, the Rangers won't have the evidence they need to arrest Javier and his *compadres*," concluded Patricio.

"The Mexican government is negotiating a surrender with Pancho Villa," I said. "If the Rangers tell them he's about to buy five hundred .45s stolen from the U.S. military, they could send troops to Múzquiz. They'd probably get there faster than the Rangers."

Patricio nodded. "Wait here. I have something for you."

He jogged to the house and came back carrying a large feed sack and a gun.

"I believe my grandfather gave this to you," he said, holding out the revolver Tomás had thrown to me in the chapel. The one I'd shot Rojizo and Danté with.

My fingers ached to grab it. "Don't you need it?"

"We have my father's Winchester and his .45," said Patricio. "*Tito* would want you to keep this."

"Thank you." I took the gun and pointed at the bag. "Are the bullets in there?"

He opened the sack and reached in.

"I brought you something else of *Tito's*," he said. He pulled out a leather ammo belt, bullets already in the loops. "Do you mind?"

I shook my head, and he threaded the belt under my sling and around my waist. Tomás had been so slender that it fit me.

"This'll be easier than getting a box of shells open with one hand," he said. He picked up the feed sack again. "The brothers' weapons and bullets were stolen before we got to the bodies, but their hats, boots, and other personal things are here. Including Danté's strange jewelry."

He pulled the necklace out as he spoke and handed it to me. Up close, I saw there were silver spikes and chunks of what looked like bone strung in between the thick fanglike teeth. It was a gruesome piece.

"What kind of teeth are these?" I asked, my finger testing the sharp points.

"Canines of a wolf, I think," said Patricio. "Must have meant something to him. There's a tattoo of a howling wolf on his chest."

My hand jerked as if the teeth had bitten me, Flora's voice whispering in my ear.

El Lobo.

CHAPTER 33

The odd sensation of an experience about to repeat itself gripped me as I drove the wagon toward La Capilla Lavanda. Thankfully, all I encountered were shooting rays of morning sunlight. Deep divots marked the lavender walls of the chapel like chickenpox scars. A man stood on a ladder at the front, nailing boards over the round space where the pretty stained-glass window had been. A second man knelt inside the entryway, scrubbing at a large copper-colored stain on the floor. I glanced down at my arm and urged Rat into a fast trot.

Twister, his leg wrapped in a clean bandage, jogged along beside the wagon almost as if nothing had happened. At least my getting shot had given him time to rest and heal. I let myself feel happy he was all right, instead of dwelling on all the things that had happened after I'd decided to try to save him.

The two tightly wrapped bodies in the wagon bed resembled the Egyptian mummies I'd seen photographs of in a *National Geographic* magazine. Katarina had covered them with a brown-striped *serape*, but every time I glanced over my shoulder I half-expected them to be sitting up, staring at me.

The feed sack containing the brothers' belongings sat under my seat. I supposed the Rangers would give it to their families, along with the bodies. Who would mourn them? Their father and Javier, of course, but did the men have wives?

Children? Danté had kidnapped and raped Flora then mutilated her. How could a man harm a child if he had one of his own? Or abuse a woman if he loved one? Did their mother know what beasts she'd raised? Did she love them despite it? Or were the women in the family oblivious to all the terror their husbands, fathers, brothers, and sons inflicted on others?

When I'd killed him, I hadn't yet known that Danté was *El Lobo*. I'd shot him to save Jackson. Now that I did know, I was glad I'd killed him. It wasn't a feeling of joy—like seeing Twister recover; it was a sense of things being put right. It was the feeling I wanted my father to have.

Had Jackson been able to cover for Tomás? The image of Tomás taking a bullet meant for me had stitched itself into the quilt shrouding my conscience. I desperately wanted his family to be safe.

Rat nickered as a roadrunner darted out in front of him. Roadrunners could fly short distances but weren't very good at it. They hunted for lizards and snakes on the ground. Once, Papa and I had watched one race in front of the truck for more than five miles, veering off here and there but coming right back to be chased. I hadn't been much different from that bird, running down someone else's path. It had been easier than fighting for my own choices.

A low, whining call rang out. I looked up at a kettle of turkey buzzards, circling in the white-stippled sky. I'd thought of vultures as ugly freebooters, but Papa described them as skilled opportunists, feeding on carrion because they weren't able to kill their own food. They were scavengers, not birds of prey, and had to rely on well-honed survival skills. Unlike roadrunners, they flew long distances without stopping, soaring on the wind's currents. They had strong beaks and a keen sense of smell. Buzzards could locate rotting remains from thousands of feet above the ground. Papa called them nature's janitors.

I'd been jiggling around on the bench seat for a while. My

rambling thoughts and birdwatching could no longer divert my attention from the fierce jabs in my arm. I pulled Rat to a stop and dug through Griselda's *bolsa*. There were a few crumbs of the pain-relieving leaves left in the pouch. I scraped them out with my fingernails and sprinkled them inside my cheek.

Patricio had given me a tin cup and a pail of water covered with an oilcloth to save me from struggling to unscrew the canteen top one-handed. As I filled the cup, Twister stuck his muzzle into the wagon, nosing the bucket. I took a few sips then poured some water in my palm and held it out to him. He slurped it up with his thick tongue, nudging my hand. After giving him some more, I climbed down and offered a palmful of water to Rat. He raised his chin and snorted at me.

"I know, pulling a wagon is beneath you," I chuckled, "but you're doing a great job."

When we started off again, I noticed the roadrunner hadn't stuck around and the V-shaped wings of the buzzards no longer dotted the gathering clouds. A few minutes later, though, the big black birds reappeared when we came around a curve in the road. Five or six of them were roosting in the bare branches of a dead tree. As we drew closer, their bald, red-dipped heads turned, beady eyes sizing us up.

Rojizo and Danté had been dead for several days; they'd probably begun to rot. Could the buzzards' sense of smell penetrate the blanket and muslin shrouds? Would they pounce on the bodies as we passed? It was a creepy thought. The loaded revolver was holstered in Tomás's gun belt. I tucked the reins under my knee and pulled it out just in case, but the vultures only watched as I drove by.

Downwind from their perch, the stench of decay caught in my nose like a hook. Was it the buzzards that smelled so bad? Or did they have a kill nearby? The smell grew stronger; I took shallow breaths through my mouth. Twister raised his snout, moving as far to the other side of the road as his lead would allow. I popped the reins.

As Rat broke into a canter, my eye caught on something fluttering ahead in a tall, wispy retama next to the road. The material blended in with the tree's yellow blossoms. I might not have seen it at all if a breeze hadn't been blowing. When we got closer, I noticed tiny red rosebuds scattered across the fabric and jerked Rat to a stop.

At first, all I could do was stare, wishing it would change into something else. When it didn't, I holstered the gun and reached out. Fingers trembling, I carefully untangled Griselda's sunbonnet from the thorny branches. My heart thundered, engulfing the sound of the wind, the rustling of the grass, the songs of the grasshoppers. I swiveled to look back at the buzzard-laden tree.

Please. No.

I set the bonnet down on the bench and lowered myself to the ground, examining the dirt for signs as I backtracked. I didn't have to walk far. Before I reached the buzzard tree, I found smooth lines in the sand, like those left by wagon wheels, hoofprints stamped down the middle of them. Walking back farther, I spotted the tracks of another horse crossing the road then following the wagon into the brush. The prints were deep; the horses had been running. A path of bent and broken branches led me on, and I was soon drowning in dread and the growing odor of something foul.

Griselda's wagon stood in a small clearing, its contents strewn all over the ground. Bluebird was gone. A few feet away, two buzzards perched on a body, their sharp beaks tearing off strips of flesh. I forced myself to walk closer. My head spun with recognition; my stomach seized with disgust.

Her thick black and gray hair had blown across her face, hiding it. Her embroidered blouse was bloodstained and dirty, her skirt bunched up around her knees. One of her beaded boots was missing, the big toe of the exposed foot gnawed to the bone. A gust of wind pushed the putrid smell of her into my nose and down my throat. My gut turned inside out, knocking me to my knees.

When the convulsions stopped, I staggered to my feet.

"Get the hell off her!" I yelled, waving my arm at the buzzards.

Their wings opened, but they waited. I started to reach for the gun but thought better of it. If I killed the two buzzards, others would just take their place. It wasn't worth the risk of someone hearing the shots. I picked up a handful of gravel and threw it at them. They took off as pebbles showered Griselda's body.

I walked to the side of the wagon, bracing myself, and peered into the bed. Relief and alarm rained down on me. Carlos was not there; only the blankets he'd been wrapped in remained. Griselda's things—her cures, powders, and herbs—had all been tossed about. I climbed in and moved the pile with my foot, uncovering the small pocketknife. The blade was brown with dried blood. Whose blood? Where was the revolver? Where was Carlos?

Back on the ground, I found the tracks of two horses heading away through the brush. I dodged around the cactus and cenizo, following the trail until it merged with the road several yards ahead of where I'd tethered Rat and Twister. One horse had followed the wagon into the brush, but two had left it. Whoever had attacked Griselda had probably thrown Carlos, dead or alive, onto Bluebird and led him away. A common thief wouldn't go to all that trouble. The person who'd taken him had either guessed somehow that Carlos was valuable or had been sent to find him.

I walked back to Griselda's body. One buzzard had returned. It stood on her chest, head jerking up and down as it shredded the skin of her neck. Anger plowed through me. I picked up a long stick and charged. The buzzard lifted its bloodred head, a low, guttural hiss coming from its hooked beak. I swung the stick, just missing as it took off.

"Stay away, you fucking bird!" I screamed.

Griselda deserved better than to be mutilated by vultures and torn apart by coyotes. She'd ministered to hundreds, maybe thousands, of people. Hers should be a burial full of dignity, where people gathered to give thanks for the generous way in which she'd shared her gifts.

My heart ballooned with a sense of injustice. The two criminals I was carting to Laredo would be treated better than the *Curandera Jorobada*. Their families would have the opportunity to give them a funeral, bury them properly, but Griselda, a woman revered and respected, would rot in the middle of nowhere.

I held my breath and bent down. Taking hold of her arm, I tugged, trying to walk backward, but she was surprisingly heavy. I wasn't strong enough to drag her through the brush and get her into the back of the wagon with one arm.

I can't leave her like this. I won't.

I rushed about the clearing, gathering sticks and dried grass and stacking them around Griselda's body. The drumbeat in my arm banged harder each time I bent down. Each time I had to gasp for air, I gagged on the stench of decomposing flesh. I'd never get used to it. The fact that it was coming from someone I'd cared about made it even worse.

I dug through the bags and boxes that had been thrown out of the wagon, collecting anything that would burn and tucking it under Griselda. I pulled one of the blankets out of the wagon and flung it over her. It landed across her body, but her head was exposed. The gust produced when I'd dropped it lifted the hair from her face. I spun away, but not before glimpsing black craters where her kind, knowing eyes had been.

I don't know why, but I needed to cover her face. I swallowed hard, locked my gaze on my good hand, trying to see as little as possible, and got the blanket over her head. Sweat and tears burned a trail down my face. I struggled to spread the cover across the rest of her.

How could the life of someone who'd overcome so much, who'd devoted herself to others, end in such an unceremonious way? I heard Papa's words like an omen from the past.

What's it all been for?

Death hung so thick on me I might never be able to wash it off. The smell, the loss, the waste of it. There was no rhyme or reason. Good people died and bad people lived; God seemed to choose at random. Or did He leave the choosing to us? Was there no grand scheme, no divine plan? Were we all just trying to survive each other?

I struck a match against a rock and lit the funeral pyre, the best end I could offer a woman who warranted so much more.

"Thank you," I said, walking away as the kindling caught.

I untied Rat and Twister and climbed into Patricio's wagon. Griselda's yellow sunbonnet had fallen to the floor. I placed it in the *bolsa* before snapping the reins. I turned one last time as we trotted away. A black column twirled toward the clouds. In my mind, Griselda's spirit rose with the smoke, arms wide as she flew free from the bonds of her body, soaring up into heaven, where a long line of grateful people waited to embrace her.

CHAPTER 34

I followed the two sets of tracks until they veered left at a fork in the road. They weren't headed to Laredo; they were headed to Hidalgo. Carlos was going home, but not in the way Alicia had wanted. He wouldn't be escorted into his family's embrace. If he was still alive, he'd be handed over to the *tequileros*, or to Javier himself. I slapped the long reins against Rat's back.

Griselda's stature as a healer had not been enough to protect Carlos, or her, in the end. Whoever had killed her either hadn't known who *la Curandera Jorobada* was, or hadn't cared. Maybe the killer was white. Anglo-Christian culture did not have much reverence for Hispanic and Indian beliefs or customs.

The two people I'd worried would go after Carlos were the only two who could be ruled out. They shimmied about in the back of my wagon, bound up tight in their own *tules*. If they'd found Carlos and Griselda, would they have respected *la Curandera* enough to leave her alone? Maybe not if she'd pointed a gun at them. I'd thought the revolver would protect them. What had happened?

I lost the hoofprints among all the others pressed into the sandy dirt of the main road as we closed in on Hidalgo. In the distance, the outline of small adobe homes glowed in a bloom of orange that would soon wither to twilight. When it was dark enough, I'd steer the wagon to *La Fonda* and park it in the shed. People were accustomed to seeing a wagon there. The bodies would be hard to discern in the dark. Twister and Rat would be safe in the corral. Guests of the inn kept their horses in there all the time. Then I'd find Carlos.

Rat slowed, his ears jockeying about. I heard the rhythmic clop of hoofbeats coming up behind us. I tucked the reins under my leg and shoved my hat down. I drew the gun and placed it in my lap. As a rider pulled up next to me, I stared straight ahead, easing Rat back to let the man pass. He slowed to match my pace.

"Howdy," said a friendly voice.

I kept my eyes on the road, acknowledging his greeting with a terse nod. He moved his horse closer to the wagon.

"Miss Gibson?" he asked.

Tingles raced to my fingertips. I turned to face him. He had long black hair tied back under a beaver-felt hat. Below the brim, piercing blue eyes beamed out of a smooth-skinned face, lighting up the corner of my memory.

"I know you," I said.

"Wagley. Wagley Phillips," he replied, touching his hat rim with two fingers. "We met at your house. The day after your brother got killed."

The young tracker who'd come out to the ranch with Captain Wright's company, the one whose eyes had reminded me of JJ's. He'd been the only one of Wright's men to express sympathy for my situation. Now I realized he'd probably known that Jackson was imbedded with Javier's gang.

"What are you doing out here, Miss Gibson?"

Should I tell him anything? I didn't want him getting in my way.

"You go first," I shot back.

"Well, I'm tracking someone for the Rangers."

"I thought you couldn't do that sort of thing by yourself." I hoped he caught the barb in my tone.

"I do whatever Captain Wright tells me to," he replied with a shrug. "Is your arm all right?"

If I admitted I'd been shot, he might never leave. He seemed like the type of young man who'd feel obliged to help.

"It's fine."

"Why'd you cut your hair off?" he asked, a smile deepening the cleft in his chin.

"It was getting in my way."

"It's shorter than mine!" He chuckled, showing no sign of riding off. "What'd you say you're doing out here?"

My armpits grew damp. I had no time for this. "I didn't say."

"This road goes to Villa Hidalgo," he said. "You know, it can be a real rough place."

For God's sake. "I'll be fine."

"What happened to the colt?" He pointed at Twister's bandaged leg.

I swung my head around to tell him to shut up and leave me alone, but his wide-open gaze disarmed me. Had JJ's eyes really been that big and blue, or had my memory become distorted already?

"He got bit by a rattler," I said. "You ask a hell of a lot of questions."

"Yeah, Captain Wright says the same thing," Wagley frowned, "but my grandfather taught me curiosity is the best way to avoid stupidity."

He leaned over his saddle and looked at the striped *serape* in the bed. I shot him a warning look, daring him to ask. To his credit, he didn't.

I tightened the reins until Rat was barely moving. We'd reached the outskirts of Hidalgo and I needed to get rid of Wagley. A wet trickle ran down between my shoulder blades as he pulled his horse up too, his eyes pointed at my face.

"Have you heard any news about your brother's killer?" he asked.

Was he really going to continue that farce?

"Why don't we cut the bullshit."

Splotches of pink bloomed on Wagley's cheeks.

"What is it you're trying to figure out?" I demanded.

"Well, I—"

"Tell me the truth, Wagley."

"All right, Miss Gibson." He reminded me of a puppy caught peeing on the floor. "You're right. I ain't been forthcoming with you."

"How do you mean?"

"Well, ma'am," he said. "You got a lot of people stirred up when you left."

My mind spun until it landed on his meaning.

"I'm the person you're tracking?"

"Yes, ma'am."

The Rangers were looking for me? Who had told them I was missing? My father? Maude? I was surprised they'd actually sent someone to find me, even if he was barely more than a boy. Maybe his youth was to my advantage. An older, more experienced Ranger would've been harder to deal with.

"What do you plan to do now that you've found me?" I asked. "Drag me back home?"

"I got a feeling that might be difficult," Wagley said with a dash of chagrin. "Mostly, I'm just glad you're all right."

"When did you start looking for me?"

"Day before yesterday," he replied. "Captain Cage told us you've been missing for going on a week or more."

Gus must have realized his ploy to lure Jackson home had failed. Had he gotten worried about me, or was that giving him too much credit?

"He said you'd gone to Hidalgo, so that's where I started," Wagley continued. "From there, I was heading to Sabinas when I saw smoke. There's a bad scene several miles back."

"It's … terrible," I said, unable to cleanse my voice of grief.

"Did you build the pyre for the *curandera*?" he asked.

I nodded.

"I thought so. The bartender said you'd left Hidalgo with her, and also with his cook."

"Alicia."

"Excuse me?"

"Her name was Alicia."

He noted my use of the past tense, his gaze traveling over my face. After a pause, he asked, "Who killed the healer?"

"I'm not sure."

"Were you with her? Is that what happened to your arm?"

It seemed unlikely he was going to leave me alone. I glanced down at my arm, resting uselessly in the sling. Wagley hadn't been much help before, but he could be useful now.

"Griselda was attacked by someone who wanted the boy traveling with her."

"Why's this boy so important?" he asked.

"He's been working for Javier, and he knows too much."

Wagley's face filled with confliction, his mouth moving with words he wasn't sure he should say.

"I told you to stop the bullshit," I remarked. "I know about Jackson going undercover to get the Salsito de Ortegas. I just wish I'd known it from the start."

He looked surprised, then relieved.

"I was sworn to secrecy." He bowed his head, looking at the ground. "I felt terrible leaving you and your father with no answers." When he lifted his eyes, they were full and glistening. "My mother was killed by horse thieves. They weren't ever caught."

"That's awful. I'm sorry," I said, pausing for a few seconds. "I could use your help, Wagley."

As Wagley listened patiently, I told him about the shootout and whose bodies were in the wagon bed. I told him about the stolen guns and Pancho Villa. I told him Carlos was hurt and I needed to find him. I told him Jackson was in danger and needed the Rangers' help. I told him everything. It felt good to unload it all on someone. He didn't question me; he didn't try to talk me out of anything.

"There's a big patch of yuccas not too far back," he said when I was done. "It'd be a good place to hide the wagon and safer than driving it into town."

We rode to the spot. He tethered Twister then helped me unharness Rat.

"The saddle is in the back," I said.

Wagley hauled it out and tacked up Rat. He held him next to the wagon, and I got into the saddle from the bench without much trouble. When the sun's color burned out, we rode into Hidalgo together.

CHAPTER 35

I chose a narrow side street through a quiet neighborhood. Yellow candlelight glowed from a few windows, providing a dimly lit path. Shadows danced and flickered within the small houses as people settled in for the evening. Night had been the only time Mama had to herself. I used to peek out my bedroom door to watch her read or do her mending, a peaceful look on her face. This night felt anything but peaceful.

Stray dogs watched us pass without bothering to get up or bark. A flock of chickens scattered lazily in front of the horses, clucking softly. A cat leapt off a roof, landing on silent paws next to Rat before slinking into the darkness. I startled at every movement, as if I'd entered a cave crawling with vipers.

"What's so special about Hidalgo?" I asked in a hushed voice. "Why'd the smugglers choose to ruin this particular town?"

"It's close to the border, a straight shot from here up to San Diego where they sell the *tequila*," Wagley replied. "Mostly, though, they've got protection from the locals, including the mayor."

Soon the raucous *fiesta* noise from the plaza rippled over us.

"This is close enough," I said.

Wagley jumped down and helped me off Rat. I had to admit it would've been hard on my own. The short horseback ride on top of the long trip in the wagon had lit up my arm. It felt like someone was holding a blowtorch to my bones.

We tethered the horses by a water trough. I checked the bullets in the revolver and shoved it back into the holster. As we hurried through a maze of alleys, the noisy din of the square grew louder and louder. Music, singing, people calling out to each other—all happy sounds that set warning bells ringing in my head. Hidalgo appeared to be a jovial place, but scratch the surface and another, darker, layer emerged.

By the time we reached the back door of The Mad Rabbit, I'd worked myself into a lather. Wagley disappeared around the corner of the building. I'd never hated a place as much as I hated the *cantina*. I leaned against the wall and tried to slow my heart rate. Just as I began to settle, footsteps whispered down the breezeway and Wagley reappeared.

"That was fast," I said.

"I wasn't going to stay any longer than I had to." He was a little breathless, his eyes shining with something close to fear, reminding me how young he was. "There's a mess of bandits in there."

The back door burst open, startling us both. Wagley threw himself in front of me, hitting my wounded arm as he flattened me against the adobe wall. I bit off a howl of agony as Mozo walked outside. When he spotted me, a relieved smile spread across his face.

"*Señorita!*" he said. "I am so glad to see you. I have been worried."

He pushed Wagley aside and folded me in an embrace so comforting tears pricked the corners of my eyes.

"You are hurt," he said when he let go. "What has happened?"

"I got shot," I said, then paused, gathering my thoughts. "Alicia ..."

His face filled with anguish. "I know."

"And Griselda ..."

Mozo nodded solemnly.

"To kill a woman who did nothing but help people is the devil's work," he said.

"How did you find these things out so quickly?" I asked.

Distress swam across Mozo's face before it was replaced by raw anger.

"Mr. Hank," he hissed.

At the mention of his name, the blood drained from my head, my fingers finding the outline of the scratches across my chest.

"He killed Griselda?" I asked. "Why?"

"She tried to protect the boy," said Mozo.

"Hank has Carlos?"

Mozo let out a frustrated growl. "I tried to talk him out of giving him to Javier. I told him the Rangers would pay more."

"Carlos would sure be safer with the Rangers," Wagley said.

"Did Hank agree?" I asked.

"Javier is already on his way," said Mozo. "I am afraid it is too late."

I heard a quick intake of breath. Wagley's eyes seemed to have doubled in size.

"If Javier is headed here, I need to let Captain Wright know," he said.

"You're not doing anything until we have Carlos," I said. "Where's Hank keeping him?"

"In the barn at my uncle's house," Mozo replied.

"How do we get there?" I asked.

We scurried along the backstreets out of the hub of Hidalgo, then took the shortcut Mozo had suggested through some pastures. Javier was coming to Hidalgo; what had happened with the gun deal? Had it already gone through? Was Jackson safe?

I looked across a wide cotton field to a two-story plantation-style house glowing like its own universe. At least twenty windows were lit up from within. We circled behind the mansion, around a large corral, and through some cattle pens.

A single electric light shone on top of a tall pole in front of the barn, which was twice as big as my entire house. A pair of sliding doors stood open on either side of the yawning black hole of the entrance. I started toward it, thinking only of getting to Carlos, but Wagley grabbed me. He pulled me back behind a patch of tall verbena, pointing at a horse loping up the road from the house.

The rider pulled up just shy of the yellow circle cast by the pole light. I couldn't see who it was; too many bushes blocked my view. I removed the sling, ignoring the sharp stabs in my arm, and crept along the fence line of the corral. Wagley's short breaths stayed on my heels as we crawled behind a large, rock water trough.

The man dismounted, taking off his hat. His scar glistened as he walked into the light. Hank's fistfight with Jackson had not improved his looks. His nose had been flattened, his jaw was lopsided, and the remainder of a shiner hung below his one eye. A white bandage was wrapped around his hand.

"I do not see the boy."

Wagley and I both jumped. Javier's voice was coming from the shadows at the far side of the barn. He sauntered into the light, the brim of his black hat hooding his face.

"He's in there," replied Hank. "First, I want to talk about my payment."

"The price was for both," Javier said.

"The girl wasn't there," Hank complained. "Just the kid and the woman. Old witch was armed, too. Shot my hand before I got the gun away."

"I want to see him." Javier's voice was like static in the air. "He better be alive. I will pay nothing for a corpse."

If Pancho Villa already had the .45s, why would Javier care if Carlos was alive?

"*Ja, ja,*" Hank huffed, "but we are not done discussing this."

He disappeared into the barn for a few minutes before

leading Bluebird out. She was hitched to a hay cart like the one Flora had been in. Hank stopped the mare next to Javier then went around to the back of the cart and lifted a pile of burlap.

"Get him out," said Javier.

"*Scheisse*, you can just—"

"Get. Him. Out," Javier commanded.

Hank dropped the burlap on the ground then reached into the cart. Carlos bellowed as Hank dragged him out and let him fold to the ground.

"As you can hear, he is not dead yet," Hank quipped. "Now, about the money—"

"*Cállate*," growled Javier.

Hank had the good sense to shut up. Javier walked over to Carlos and grabbed a fistful of his hair, jerking it back. It felt too much like what had happened at the camp, as if there had been an intermission and now Javier was going to finish the act. Wagley's hand closed on my leg, holding me in place.

"We meet again, *niño*," Javier said in a low voice, glaring into Carlos's face. "You have made a lot of trouble for me, *entiendes*? The only reason you are still alive is to answer one question."

Javier yanked up. Carlos let out a pathetic squeal as he was pulled to his knees.

"Where is the girl with the yellow hair?"

Air squeezed from my lungs. If Carlos heard, he said nothing. His eyes were thin lines, his lips chalky and dry. He barely seemed conscious.

"Cat got your tongue?" asked Javier. "I will cut it out unless you tell me where she is."

Carlos made no response. Javier threw his head down and Carlos toppled over.

"Do you know what she has done?" Javier squatted next to him, glaring. "She has killed my brothers."

He knows.

Blood raced from my head; my face went numb.

"Do you hear me, *niño?*"

He stood, pushing Carlos's side with his foot. I could only imagine how much it must have hurt, but Carlos didn't make a sound.

"He passed out," said Hank.

"No matter," said Javier, unholstering his revolver.

No, no, no.

"What the hell are you doing?" yelled Hank, placing a hand on the butt of his own gun. "You cannot kill him until I have the money. The Rangers will not want him dead."

Javier shook his head like a disappointed parent.

"You bring me one and expect me to pay for two," he said. "Then you threaten to sell him to my enemies. You are too greedy."

Before Hank could get his gun out, Javier's revolver exploded. The bullet grazed Hank's leg. He cried out, stumbling back several steps, still fumbling for his weapon.

"Stop," Javier said coldly. "I have not killed you only out of respect for the man you work for," he gestured at the mayor's big house, "but I will if you make me."

Hank held both hands up in surrender. Javier turned his focus back to Carlos.

"If you cannot tell me where *la rubia* is," he said, lowering the gun to Carlos's head, "you are finally of no more use to me."

I leapt to my feet, leveling the revolver, pulling back the hammer. Hank's eyes jerked my way.

"Watch out!" he yelled.

Javier spun around, hat flying off. His lips curled. His eyes glowed. I pulled the trigger. His body jerked back. I cocked the gun again, my whole being streaming into it. Javier stumbled sideways, a look of shock contorting his face. He looked down, clutched his chest, and sank into the dirt.

Hank's gun banged. I ducked away, senses now on fire.

Wagley shot from behind me. His bullet went high, clipping Hank's shoulder. Hank cried out but held steady, aiming at Wagley.

I fired. Hank dropped to the ground, screaming in pain.

I stepped around the water trough, holding the revolver out in front of me with both hands, finger on the trigger.

"Careful, Sarita." Wagley came up next to me. "I don't think either of them is dead."

I kept my aim on Javier. "Check the other one."

Wagley walked over to Hank.

"He's hurt bad but alive," he said.

Javier lay on his side, facing away from me, blood spreading out from under him. I could see his ribs moving. I could hear his labored breathing. As I came up behind him, he rolled over, still gripping his gun.

"*Rubia.*"

"Don't make me kill you," I said.

He tried to aim, the revolver shaking in his weakening grasp. I kicked the gun out of his hand. His coyote eyes burned white-hot as I leaned down and leveled the bead between them.

"I miss him every day." I pulled the trigger.

CHAPTER 36

I ran to Carlos.

"Hang on," I said, crouching next to him, relieved to see his eyes flutter open. "I'm going to get you to the hospital."

Wagley stood over me, the weapons he'd removed from Hank and Javier glinting in his hands.

"They will have heard the gunshots at the house," he said. "The mayor will probably send someone to check."

"Help me."

We lifted Carlos into the cart as quickly and carefully as we could.

"Is Hank dead?" I asked.

"Not yet," he replied.

Tremors—of rage, of relief—quaked through me. Hank twitched on the ground like a worm. His scarred face twisted with each wave of pain. My bullet had hit him in the stomach.

"What do you know about the gun deal with Pancho Villa?" I asked.

He squinched his eye open. "Nothing."

I placed my boot on his stomach, pressing down until he squealed.

"Called off," he sputtered.

The agreement had fallen through? I removed my foot, not wanting to cause so much pain he couldn't talk.

"Where's Jackson?" I asked.

Hank whimpered, tucking his legs up and wrapping his arms around his middle.

"*Mein Gott.* Please ... get it over with," he pleaded.

I tapped the toe of my boot against his side.

"Tell me what's happened to Jackson Cage or I'll drag you into the bushes where no one will find you. It'll take days to bleed to death, unless the coyotes get to you first."

Hank swallowed.

"Ignado ... he came for the deal."

"Ignado has Jackson?"

"Holding him." Hank coughed, blood splattering his lips.

Panic zipped through me.

A long, pitiful moan rose from the cart. I left Hank crying in the dirt and rushed over to Carlos.

"Is your arm okay?" Wagley asked, coming up next to me and placing a hand on my shoulder.

I ran my fingers down my sleeve. It was warm and sticky. The wound must have opened. I tugged the sling over my elbow. As my muscles relaxed into the support, the cutting pain returned.

I covered Carlos with the burlap then looked across the corrals and pens at the mayor's mansion. No one appeared to be racing over, but it was only a matter of time before someone decided to investigate.

"Go, I got this." Wagley waved his hand around the barnyard. "I'll meet you in Laredo with your wagon and the horses."

He helped me onto Bluebird.

"What do you want me to do about him?" he asked, gesturing at Hank.

"Leave him, kill him, drag him to Laredo behind the wagon," I answered. "I don't give a damn."

The ride to the river was a blur, my focus on making Bluebird pull the cart as fast as she could. The border patrol officers only gave us a swift once-over when we crossed the newly built bridge into Texas. They were mostly worried about

Asian immigrants, outlaws, and smugglers, and we didn't appear to fit the mold for any of those. I'd wrapped a gunnysack around my shoulders to hide my blood-soaked sleeve. Carlos had passed out. In the predawn glow he appeared to be sleeping.

I pulled Bluebird to a stop in front of Mercy Hospital and dropped ungracefully out of the saddle. The sack fell to the ground as I hurried up the front steps. I got across the doorway of the big, red-brick building before my legs filled with water and my vision wavered. I'd been so determined to get there; now that I'd made it, the past several days loomed over me like a hammer.

A desk in the front lobby blocked a long white hallway. A blurry form in black and white rose from behind it.

"There's a boy ... in the back of the cart." I couldn't catch my breath. My lips felt swollen. "He's badly hurt. His ribs ..."

"Oh dear, what happened to your arm?" a woman's voice asked.

"No, not me." Antiseptic smells engulfed me, cold sweat beading up, rolling down my forehead.

"Captain Wright with the Texas Rangers." I forced the words out, fighting to stay present.

"Is that a bullet wound?" The voice was getting farther away.

"I need to tell him, tell him. Ignado ..." My tongue was numb. "Jackson Cage in danger. Please ... tell Captain Wright."

The bright, gleaming walls folded in on me.

I woke in a narrow bed, wearing a light blue hospital gown, my arm securely wrapped in a clean bandage. It hurt, but the feeling was removed, like it was drifting around next to me.

Everything was white—the walls, the iron bed frame, the sheets. The window across the room framed the only color, a deep blue sky. I heard a sound and turned my head. A nun was taking the temperature of the patient in the bed across from me.

"Excuse me," I said, my voice scratchy.

She turned, her habit swirling around her feet as she drew a white curtain divider across the room.

"Hello, there. I'm Sister Barbara," she said. "Welcome back."

"I brought a boy here," I said. "Can you tell me how he is?"

Her face went blank.

"I don't know about a boy. I just came in this morning."

I pushed myself up on one arm. The bed became a merry-go-round.

"I need to know if he's okay," I said, blinking against the movement. "The lady at the front desk last night, did she give Captain Wright my message?"

"Lie back down, dear," said Sister Barbara, gliding toward the door as if she had no feet. "I'll get Dr. Elliott."

Carlos had to be alive. The thought of him surviving everything only to die in the hospital was unbearable. I tried to focus on the doorway, but my eyelids drifted together, and I melted into the mattress.

A bright light flew toward me. I dove out of the way. I was underneath the big live oak, by Mama's cross of roses. A new white cross had been planted next to it. JJ's? I placed my hand on it. An ice-cold shaft blazed up my fingers into my heart. Another cross pushed out of the ground. Papa's? I backed away, more crosses springing up, one after another until I stood in an orchard, not of mesquite and live oak, but of grave markers, stretching out as far as I could see.

Footsteps brought me back into the hospital room. A tall man with wire-rimmed spectacles was striding through the doorway. His white coat matched the walls, and his head seemed disconnected, hovering above me.

"Good morning. How are you feeling?"

"A little woozy," I replied.

"That's the ether, it'll wear off," said Dr. Elliott. "You lost quite a bit of blood, but the bullet missed the major arteries. Must have happened several days ago, correct? There's no exit wound. Someone got the bullet out for you?"

I nodded.

"I tried to reset your humerus without much success. The wound looks as if it was reopened after it had begun to heal. I did a debridement of the damaged tissue. You'll have a nasty scar and some significant loss of motion in that arm."

He wasn't saying anything Katarina and Patricio hadn't already prepared me for.

"Carlos?" I asked. "The boy I brought in with the hurt ribs?"

"Right." Dr. Elliott nodded. "Is he a relative of yours?"

"No," I answered, my heart contracting. "He's the brother of—he's a close family friend. Is he okay?"

"Was he hurt in the same incident in which you suffered that bullet wound?" he asked.

"No."

He waited for me to go on, but I didn't.

"I see." The doctor stared at me over his wire rims. "In any case, he's a lucky young man. No punctured lung or ruptured aorta. He has two broken ribs and several that are badly bruised, which kept him from taking deep breaths. His lungs are full of fluid, and he's got a very bad infection."

"He'll live, though?" I asked shakily.

"He's a hearty young fellow. He should recover. He'll need to stay here for observation and rest until his fever's gone. His nose was broken as well. I tried to straighten it, but I'm afraid it had already set. My nurse says it'll add character to his face."

Dr. Elliott shrugged as if apologizing, but a crooked nose was nothing. An ugly scar on my arm was nothing. We were both alive.

"Can I see him?" I asked.

"Not until the infection clears up," he said. "He's in a vulnerable state and we don't want him exposed to anything else." He paused for a moment, glasses sliding down his nose. "Captain Wright came by yesterday. He insisted on questioning the boy. He talked to you too. You'd already been sedated so you might not remember."

I couldn't recall anything after talking to the woman at the front desk.

"What did I tell him?" I asked.

"Something about a cage in Múzquiz, and Pancho Villa buying guns," replied Dr. Elliott. "Sounded like a hallucination to me. I told the man you were under the influence of ether, but he listened to every word you uttered then took off."

Worry lifted from my body. Whatever I'd said, it had gotten Wright moving.

"You're to go to the sheriff's office as soon as you're released," the doctor added.

"When will that be?"

"I'd like you to stay one more day. You could've lost your arm if that infection had spread." He headed for the doorway. "Whoever cared for you did a good job."

I silently thanked Katarina and Patricio. And Griselda for caring for Carlos. She would have been so happy to know he was alive and in good hands. Her grandson had survived. I sank into the pillow, taking in the moment of gratitude.

As I began to relax, Javier invaded my thoughts as he had so often. This was different, though. I no longer needed to worry about where he was or who he was hurting. I no longer needed to pray for someone to stop him, to bring him to justice; I had done it. His days of spreading terror were over.

CHAPTER 37

Laredo was the main gateway between Texas and Mexico. Since childhood, I'd watched the city grow as the Mexican Revolution brought in countless immigrants, swelling the population to over twenty thousand. In the past, when I'd come with Papa, I'd found the mix of people, the shops and cart vendors, the automobiles, and bustling streets exciting. Now the city overwhelmed me, the commotion pounding the raw nerve endings of my arm. I pushed through the crowds in San Agustín Plaza and headed to the sheriff's office.

Unable to sit still any longer, I'd talked Sister Barbara into letting me leave. Before discharging me, she'd looked at my pile of soiled clothes and bustled off. She'd returned from Lost and Found holding a long-sleeved shirtwaist with a wide collar and a pair of jodhpurs. The white blouse was too big, but it was clean. Sister Barbara had cut the left sleeve so my bandaged arm would easily fit through and helped me with the small pearl buttons down the front. The jodhpurs she'd found were too short, but I'd tucked them into my cowboy boots. I pushed the Stetson on over my dirty, shorn hair, then placed my arm in a new sling, certain I looked like an escapee from an asylum.

As I approached the sheriff's office on Flores Avenue, I saw Twister, Rat, and Bluebird in the corral next to the low limestone building. The sight made me grin. Wagley had not let me down. He'd even found Bluebird in front of the hospital. Patricio's wagon was parked behind the pen, its bed now devoid of Salsito de Ortega bodies.

A cluster of men stood in front of the building, which also housed the jail. A sheriff's badge was pinned to one man's leather vest. The other three wore the drab green uniform and high riding boots of the Mounted Inspectors, guards on horseback who patrolled the border. I made my way toward the sheriff.

Before I reached him, the group of lawmen turned to watch two riders, each leading a string of loaded pack mules. The sheriff stepped off the porch and opened the gate to the pen. The Customs Officers followed the mules into the corral.

"Excuse me," I said.

The sheriff appeared to be in his late sixties, but slender and athletic-looking.

"Can I help you?" he asked as he closed the gate.

"Captain Wright said I was supposed to come by."

His face brightened. "You must be Miss Gibson!"

"Yes, sir," I said.

"Well, now," he said with a smile. "You've been quite the talk around here this morning."

His even tone didn't indicate whether he was poking fun at me or giving me a compliment.

"Sheriff Tim Bennett," he said, removing his cowboy hat. "Pleased to make your acquaintance."

"Nice to meet you," I replied, shaking his outstretched hand. "Is the captain here?"

"Well, no, ma'am," he said as if surprised I'd asked. "He and his men took off for Múzquiz after visiting you and the boy in the hospital."

My knees swayed as tension in my shoulders released.

"You okay, Miss Gibson?" asked Sheriff Bennett.

"I'm relieved," I said, steadying myself.

Bennett replaced his hat. His gaze stayed on me as I tried

to decipher his expression. It looked like respect.

"Danté, Rojizo, and Javier Salsito de Ortega," he mused. "That's quite a trio of dead bandits young Wagley brought in for you."

"Yes, sir, I suppose it is." I'd killed those men—bad men— but it wasn't something I felt boastful about.

Bennett placed a hand on my shoulder, as if sensing my disquiet.

"You've done a good deed, I assure you. If Javier had been allowed to complete his transaction with Pancho Villa, there's no telling how many more people would've been endangered, both in Texas and Mexico." He lowered his voice. "Ignado Salsito de Ortega ran a ruthless and vengeful operation. With his three sons dead, he's got no one to take over. Once he's caught, it'll finish off that regime."

His praise left me speechless. If Jackson succeeded, it would mean that together we'd ended the reign of *Los Diablos Pelirrojos*.

"I need to process this batch of mules," the sheriff said, glancing at the corral. "Wagley's inside doing paperwork. I'll need your written statement."

Bennett walked into a corral full of proof that I might've stopped the Salsito de Ortegas, but I hadn't put much of a dent in *tequila* smuggling.

I entered the sheriff's office, grateful to get out of the relentless sun. Wagley sat at a desk, pencil in hand. He looked up when I closed the door.

"Sarita!" he exclaimed, rushing over to me. For a moment, I thought he was going to hug me, but he seemed to remember himself just in time.

"I'm real glad to see you," he said. "Are you all right?"

"I will be," I replied, pointing at my wounded arm. "Doctor says it could have been a lot worse. Thank you for getting the wagon here, and the horses."

"Of course." He walked over to a table and retrieved my

saddlebags, handing them to me.

"Have you heard anything from the Rangers?" I asked.

"Captain Wright sent a scout back," he said. "He told the sheriff they've got several prisoners they're bringing in, and two deceased."

I'd been so happy that the Rangers had gone to Santa Rosa that I hadn't thought about what would happen when they got there. Had Ignado been waiting to ambush them?

"Did the scout say who's dead?" I asked.

"We'll find out soon enough," Wagley answered. "You know, you've surprised a lot of people. Nobody thought a girl would go after Javier, much less kill him."

"I'm just a person who was looking for justice."

"Well, you're braver than most people," Wagley said with a wide grin. "Captain Wright told me to telephone the sheriff's office in Hebbronville. I talked to Deputy Cage."

"Did he happen to say how my father is?"

"No, I'm sorry," he replied. "He did say they're sending someone to get you." His eyes went to the open windows. "Looks like a crowd's gathering."

We walked into the growing horde of people in front of the sheriff's office. A bystander announced that Captain Wright's company had been spotted riding across the bridge. The hum of excitement rose. Within minutes, Wagley and I watched the traffic part as the mounted posse headed up Flores Avenue. I strained to see over all the bobbing heads, searching the riders.

Wright rode out in front, leading a rotund man who'd been handcuffed to his saddle. People called out as they recognized him.

"*Es el alcalde de Villa Hidalgo.*"

"The mayor of Hidalgo!"

"*Señor Mayor Hinojosa!*"

The mayor wore a three-piece suit, as if he were going to a bank meeting instead of to jail. Beads of sweat rolled off his bald pate. His flaccid face glowed red. He had none of Mozo's friendly traits.

"There's Jackson," said Wagley, pointing to the middle of the pack.

My eyes found him as the noise of the crowd swelled. Bloodstains marked his shirt, but he sat straight and tall in his saddle as if unharmed. His lead rope was attached to a horse carrying a prisoner, hands tied to the saddle horn. Under the man's black, flat-crowned *sombrero* was a stern face with a gray-flecked auburn mustache, the ends of which had been waxed and curled up into a point. His black riding coat was dusty, and worn over an unbleached shirt. He had a red silk kerchief knotted neatly around his neck. He held his head high, scanning the crowd as if riding in a parade. I found his eyes—a dull, faded version of Javier's.

Ignado didn't look like the patriarch of a gang of outlaws, murderers, and rapists. He didn't look like a man who would torture others out of spite. Mostly, he looked like the *hacendado* he'd started out as before politics changed his country, corruption took his land, and blind prejudice killed his people. It was possible to find sympathy for him—if you didn't take his crimes into account—but nobody was gifted a life free from tragedy and injustice.

"Do unto others as you would have them do unto you" had been planted in my mind as a child. It seemed simplistic. Once you broke the Golden Rule, was there any going back? Was it like eating sugar cubes—I've had one, I might as well have three? I've killed one person, what difference does it make if I kill another, and another? Was it only a matter of intent? My intention wasn't to kill, but now I knew I would.

Captain Wright had told my father that wrongdoing didn't go unpunished for long. At the time I'd thought those words trite, but now I understood that evil people, who do evil things, keep doing evil. A man who would kill a boy in cold blood would commit other atrocities, and sooner or later they'd be his end. It was the collateral damage in the meantime that raked my soul.

People began to "boo" and "hiss" as the rest of the company trotted into view with their prisoners. I spotted Burr Archer astride a horse led by one of the Rangers. His smile had vanished behind a grimace of pain. I located the place Dove's bullet had penetrated his shirt on its way through his shoulder. I hoped it left a misshapen and ugly hole; I hoped the muscle and sinew and joints around it burned until his dying day. I hoped he would forever be reminded that there had been a woman who'd said no.

Cheers mixed with jeering rang out on either side of the road as five more prisoners and two dead bodies passed by. Speculations about multiple hangings further energized the throng of people. I'd never been to a public hanging; never wanted to. They'd been banned in bigger cities, but in South Texas they were still something of a spectator sport. I had a feeling I'd be seeing my first one soon.

Jackson rode up to the hitching post in front of the corral. People pressed forward, vying for a good look at his prisoner.

"They seem captivated by Ignado," I said to Wagley.

"He's a legend, but not in a good way," Wagley agreed. "Captain Wright called him the 'epitome of infamy.' Not many people have laid eyes on him and lived to tell it."

"All right!" Sheriff Bennett called out to the bystanders. "Y'all need to disperse and give us room to do our jobs."

He motioned for Wagley to push the mob back, while he and his deputy assisted the Rangers in getting the bandits off the horses and into the jail. I looked over at Jackson, thinking he might grab Ignado and yank him out of the saddle, perhaps even rough him up a bit. Instead, he left the old man sitting on the horse, walking away without a backward glance.

It was me Jackson's eyes were locked on. It was the first time I'd seen him since learning the truth about why he'd disappeared. In my mind, I'd thought he would look more like he had before he left home, as if the person I'd seen in Mexico had gone back into hiding. Watching him walk toward me, I realized that was ridiculous.

Jackson reached my side, removed his hat, and folded me gently in his arms. His embrace felt warm and comfortable, but I couldn't bring myself to hug him back. It wasn't the way he looked; it was the things I associated him with now. I stood like a dead fish for a moment, saddlebags folded over my good arm, then took a step away. There was an angry bruise on his cheek and a deep cut above his eye that was bleeding. I felt something soften, surprised by my desire to wipe the blood off.

Captain Wright stepped onto the porch, spurs jingling as he walked across to us. I wondered if he was going to apologize for his behavior at our house, or maybe offer some sort of explanation for his brusque treatment of my father.

"Miss Gibson," he said, all business. "I'll need you to come back here in the morning."

No amends then.

"I've already given my written statement," I said. "I have to get home to my father. He fell ill after you and your company rode off."

Wright's face remained indifferent. I wanted to make him listen to all the horrible things that might not have happened had he told us the truth that day, but it wouldn't make any difference now. He'd had his orders; it had been his job to follow them.

"The governor will be arriving tomorrow before noon," he explained. "He'll need to speak with you before his meeting with Mexico's interim president."

Home was so close. I could feel the pasture breeze on my cheeks, taste the caliche dust on my lips, hear the bobwhites' call in my heart.

"Deputy Cage has already sent someone from Hebbronville to take me home," I said, wondering if Wright could order me to stay.

"It's just one more night, Sarita." I felt Jackson's hand on my back. It was all I could do not to shake it off. What was wrong with me? My feelings for him wormed in and out of my heart like larvae.

"It's imperative that you relate to Governor Hobby what you know." Wright's voice was full of authority and finality. "Several Mexican citizens have been arrested and several others are dead."

Some of those "others" had died by my hand. That responsibility meant something; I had to stay. Captain Wright tipped his hat to us and walked off.

"I've got to help get this mess settled, but we need to talk," said Jackson, eyes begging me to dive in. "You should probably stay at the Hamilton Hotel. I can meet you in the dining room for dinner around seven. Would that be all right?"

He'd assumed command of the situation. I agreed to meet him, if only so I could leave. I walked across the street and headed for the yellow-brick hotel on the corner. The closer I got, the faster I went, anxious to use their telephone to call Dr. Andrew.

Please, please let Papa be all right.

The image of crosses springing up in our pastures like bluebonnets haunted me. I wanted to tell Papa that Javier was dead to his face, not to his grave marker.

An automobile horn blared, making me leap to the side of the street.

"Sarita Gibson!"

I turned to find Maude Langley leaning out of her roadster.

"My, my, aren't you a sight for sore eyes!" she exclaimed.

"Mrs. Langley?" Her sudden appearance jarred me, as if I'd been inhabiting another world and had suddenly run smack into my real one.

"I've been searching all over tarnation for you, sugar," she said.

"Did Clyde send you?"

"He did! Drove as fast as this tin can would go."

She looked me up and down, pausing a moment on my short hair and the sling holding my arm.

"You look like an unbridled filly!" she declared. "Where you headed in such a hurry?"

"The Hamilton," I croaked, her face and voice swaddling me in the familiar. "The Rangers need me to stay until tomorrow."

"Well, stop gawking at me and hop in," she said.

I climbed into the roadster. The only question I wanted to ask her sat on my lips like a bubble I was afraid to burst. She ground the gears, swinging the Ford around several horse-drawn buggies as we bounced down the street.

"Hotels are sprouting up like corn stalks in this city." Maude chattered away as if we'd just seen each other yesterday. "I still prefer the Hamilton, been staying there for more than fifteen years. They're planning to add several floors soon. That'll make it the tallest building in Laredo, I reckon."

She looked over at me.

"You don't give one single cent about that, do you?" she said, patting my hand. "Your pa is still with us. He's hanging on by the skin of a hare's tooth, but he's alive."

My heart floated in my chest, tears pooling in my eyes.

"Dr. Andrew tried and tried to get him to go to Corpus," she said. "John insisted he wasn't budging until you came home. If stubbornness could cure a bad heart, he'd never have another spell."

We pulled up to the hotel and parked. A bellman took Maude's small carryall and my dusty saddlebags. Maude's heeled bootsteps echoed across the lobby as she marched to the front desk, demanding the largest suite. We swept past the sitting area and into a small elevator. Maude closed the folding gate and pushed a button.

On the top floor, I followed like a lamb as she led me down a wide hallway to a pair of double doors where the bellman waited with our things. He escorted us into the most beautifully decorated room I'd ever seen. Done up in blues and golds, fleur-de-lis printed wallpaper covered every wall. Billowing silk drapes framed a pair of French doors, which opened out onto a balcony. A warm breeze fluttered over two canopied beds. Their linens looked like puffy white clouds.

I'd escaped misery and landed in the middle of luxury. The complete and sudden change was disorienting, and I felt myself detach, unable to navigate the gap between the barbarity of the past several days and the extravagance I stood in.

"Sugar," Maude said after the bellman left. "I don't mean to offend you, but you are in dire need of a bath."

Hot water and perfumed soap wouldn't wash away all I'd seen and done, but maybe it would snap me out of my stupor. Maude went into another room. At the sound of running water, I began to itch all over, as if the dirt were trying to dig in deeper.

"All right, come on," Maude called out.

In the bathroom, she removed the sling for me, undid the buttons of the shirtwaist I wore, then loosened my pants.

"There now, you take a long soak," she said after taking my boots off for me. "There's a scrub brush on the vanity. Might take some elbow grease to shine you up. I'll be in to help after a while."

The room was a cool, sterile cave of blue and white tile. I finished undressing, a new sore or scratch or wound revealed each time I took off a piece of clothing. I had no idea bruises came in such an array of colors. My body was a light yellow to deep purple timeline of injuries. The gash on my shoulder from my trip down the Rio Grande had not healed well. It would leave an ugly scar. The contusion on my hip had shrunk but left behind a baseball-sized knot. My knee was almost back to its normal size, but the skin was rough and pitted. The scratches across my chest had faded. In an odd way, I didn't want those to disappear completely. They were a reminder never to let myself get into a situation again where I was not in control.

Bites from unknown pests peppered my torso, and my pants had rubbed raw spots around my waist. Even my heels were red and patchy with layers of blisters and dead skin. None of the injuries held a candle to the gunshot wound, though. I left the bandage on. Sister Barbara had just applied it that morning. It was the only clean thing about me.

My toes sank into the steaming water, the temperature wonderfully almost too hot. I slid down into the deep porcelain tub, resting my hurt arm on the rim to keep it dry, and closed my eyes. Lovely, heavenly, exquisite—words I never thought would describe the simple act of bathing filled my mind. As warmth enveloped me, my pores seemed to open, releasing the filth that had accumulated in them.

I was almost asleep when the door clicked. I heard Maude whisk in. She set a ceramic pitcher on the floor next to the tub and gathered some things from the vanity, then pulled a stool over and sat down. I felt her amber eyes on me and opened mine.

"Did you find the man who killed John Junior?" she asked, running her fingers through my tangled hair.

I knew she'd been resisting the urge to ask a thousand questions. I took a deep breath, rising from the lull of relaxation.

"Yes."

"And ..."

"He's dead."

Maude nodded. "Is that a bullet wound in your arm?"

"It is."

"You might have taken my advice a little more seriously than I intended," she said, but a proud, pleased look played on her face.

I sat forward so she could pour water over my head.

"Cage thought you might have run into Jackson," she said, lathering shampoo into my short hair, the exotic smell of coconuts seeping into the moist air.

"He's here, in Laredo."

"Are you going to see him?"

Uncertainty flowed through my mind. I'd learned a lot from Patricio, but I wanted to hear Jackson's own words. There were things lurking in the corners of my mind only he could clear away.

"I'm meeting him here for dinner tonight," I replied.

"Hmph." Maude finished washing my hair, then picked up the brush and soap, scrubbing my back gently. I had not been given a bath since I was a toddler. It was a surprisingly soothing experience, administered by Maude in such a straightforward way that I forgot my modesty. I could never have done such a thorough job with one hand.

"Let me see those fingernails," she said, picking up a file to smooth the jagged edges.

Finally satisfied with her work, she handed over the washcloth and left me alone.

The room grew quiet again, except for the plinking of drips from the faucet. The experiences of the past weeks sat on my chest like a sealed trunk. Things squirmed inside, vines searching for an opening, desperate to be aired, to find the light. I exhaled a long, jagged breath, blowing the lock open. My lips stretched apart, and I made no attempt to squelch the howling wails. Maude was the only one near enough to hear, and she would understand. Tears, and more tears, tumbled into the bath, a waterfall of anguish and frustration and loss and grief—and, finally, relief. When the sobs calmed, I leaned my head back against the warm porcelain and closed my eyes. I saw my father's face and smiled.

While drying off with a thick towel, I realized my forearms hadn't just been dirty; they were tanned and speckled from the sun. Mama would've chided me for not keeping them covered. I picked up a hairbrush, my reflection slowly appearing as the steam cleared from a large mirror hanging over the vanity.

The short hair was not completely unflattering. I could have the beauty shop shape it into a fashionable bob. The back of my neck and a V-shape down my chest had been burned red by the sun. The Stetson had protected my face somewhat, although my complexion had darkened, and my nose sported a new smattering of freckles. Hollows beneath my cheekbones told of lost weight, but there were no real outward signs of some metamorphosis. I looked like someone had beaten me up and left me outside to roast.

There was a soft knock on the bathroom door. I got the towel wrapped around myself and opened it.

"I ran down to the little shop next door and got you some things," said Maude. "A nightgown, some clean day clothes—I'm not sure where that outfit you were wearing came from—and, well, although I prefer britches, I thought you might like a dress to wear to dinner tonight."

"That was very thoughtful," I said, hugging her with one arm. "Thank you for taking care of me."

"Well, sugar," she said in an unusually soft, emotional voice, "God didn't bless me with children, but if I'd had a daughter ... well, I'd have been proud to have a daughter like you."

As I looked at the woman standing in front of me, I saw love in her expression and realized she had been a mother to me over the past two years in the only way she'd known how. My eyes swam with gratefulness.

"Now," said Maude, sniffling back her own emotion. "Let's get some clothes on you. I'm anxious to know all that's happened. Especially how you ended up with that hole in your arm."

She helped me put on the clean undergarments she'd bought, then I stepped into the dress, carefully pulling the loose sleeve over my bandage. Modern in style, it was as light as air, made of black silk chiffon with a pink and blue floral print, delicate black lace trimming the elbow-length sleeves and neckline. It was the prettiest thing I'd ever worn.

Maude buttoned the back. The dress hung loose from my shoulders to the ruffle of the handkerchief hem swirling above my ankles. I stepped in front of a tall oval-shaped mirror in the corner of the room. The weight I'd lost made me a little scarecrow-like, but the dress complimented my tall, slender frame. When I moved, the light fabric flowed with my body, making me feel like a butterfly—a bruised, battered butterfly with a broken wing.

"Now look what a dip and a brush-out will do for you!" Maude said, pleased with herself. "You look like a fashion plate, not the ragamuffin I plucked off the street a few hours ago."

My cheeks grew warm at her compliment, but it was strange not to be wearing JJ's vest and boots. I felt a bit like a tortoise who'd crawled out of its shell to try on a grander one. It was beautiful, but I wasn't sure it suited me.

CHAPTER 38

In the elevator on the way down to the first floor, I determined I'd listen to Jackson and try not to interrupt until he got his story out. Exiting the small, motorized cage, several people stopped to watch as I walked to the restaurant. Had I gotten something wrong? Was the dress hanging crooked, or had I forgotten to buckle the black T-strap shoes Maude had given me? Maybe it was the bandage and the sling around my arm. When a man smiled and tipped his hat, it occurred to me that perhaps they were stares of appreciation for the way I looked.

Jackson sat waiting at a table covered with a white cloth. A candle flickered on a silver tray in the center next to a crystal vase holding one yellow rose. He stood as I entered the high-ceilinged dining room, and I was relieved to see I wasn't the only one who'd cleaned up for the occasion. He'd been to the barber. His hair had been neatly cropped around his ears. His beard was trimmed and shaped to complement his face, which shone with a healthy glow. One cheek was slightly swollen under the bruise I'd noticed earlier, and he'd gotten a few stitches in his forehead, but compared to what I'd feared Ignado would do to him, he was surprisingly undamaged.

The structured jacket of a tweed sacque suit hugged his broad shoulders. His silk necktie had a narrow diagonal stripe of navy that picked up the accent colors of the tweed, which made me doubt he'd picked the outfit out himself. I'd never seen him so dressed up. He looked older and somewhat sophisticated. Then I noticed his beat-up cowboy boots and smiled.

"Sarita," he said. "You're beautiful."

I felt the heat rise in my cheeks and turned to look around the room, hoping he wouldn't notice. The compliment pleased me and disturbed me at the same time. I'd gained something through my experience, something I couldn't put my finger on but did not want to lose. I'd saved Jackson's life; I couldn't let a dress and kitten heels diminish that fact.

Jackson pulled a chair out for me. The waiter appeared as soon as I sat, covering my lap with a white cloth napkin. He filled our water glasses and placed a basket of warm, divine-smelling bread next to me, dropping thick pads of butter on small plates. Then he told us, in detail, about the chef's recommendations. When we declined his offer of a wine list, he finally stopped fussing and went off to retrieve our first course, leaving an uncomfortable silence in his wake.

I suddenly regretted accepting Jackson's invitation. The dress, the restaurant, the circumstances were all wrong. Jackson wasn't talking, and I had no idea where to begin. How were we going to have an honest conversation in a situation that wasn't natural to either of us? The evening should have been a chance to reconnect, but we were playing parts. Too much hurt, anger, and misunderstanding hung between us to discuss over roses and candlelight. The farce made our previous relationship and everything we'd gone through—together and apart—seem small.

Jackson's pleasant, if tense, smile evaporated and he cleared his throat.

"Maybe this wasn't the right idea," he said, tugging at his necktie.

My clenched fists relaxed. He felt it too.

"That's a very handsome suit," I said, trying to poke a hole in the tension. "Did you pick it out?"

He looked a bit embarrassed. "I ran into Mrs. Langley earlier. She told me you're staying with her, then she gave me a piece of her mind. In the end, though, she recommended I wear this getup for dinner."

"Looks as if we have a fairy godmother," I said, chuckling.

"A regular matchmaker," laughed Jackson.

The light moment dwindled. Did we need a matchmaker? Not so long ago, we'd matched ourselves. Were we so different from those two people?

"Sarita, I—"

The waiter pushed a cart next to the table, and Jackson fell silent. The dinner began, and the chance to abandon the folly passed. My mouth watered as the most amazing aromas rose from the dishes in front of us. I was starving after days of eating whatever I could find or was offered. I abandoned thoughts of meaningful talk and gave in to the pageantry.

The server started with a bowl of brothy soup, adding cubes of avocado and chopped Bermuda onions, and layering fried *tortilla* strips on the top. It was delicious and salty. I forced myself to eat slowly, glancing up at Jackson.

"Why is your grandfather's horse called Rat?" I asked, grasping for conversation.

His face softened with amusement. "Have a little trouble crossing deep water with him?"

"As a matter of fact, I did."

"Well, that's how he got his name," he chuckled. "A rat can swim; it just doesn't want to."

I laughed and started to tell him about crossing the Rio Grande the first time, but the next course arrived. The waiter moved the vase and candle aside, placing a stemmed crystal bowl of pink Gulf shrimp in a red sauce in the middle of the table. I watched Jackson, noticing how his blue shirt complemented the color of his eyes. He gestured for me to go first, and I focused on stabbing a shrimp with a small fork.

We ate every plump bite, even dragging pieces of crusty

bread through the tangy, spicy sauce. Jackson appeared to be as hungry as I was. Occasionally, I caught him gazing at me, a bemused look on his face. What was he thinking? Was he grappling with his emotions as much as I was with mine?

A slice of beef tenderloin arrived next. The waiter cut it for me.

"It's cooked perfectly," said Jackson, his knife slicing through the meat. "The Captain always says it should be done on the outside, but barely dead on the inside."

I felt a twinge of something at the mention of his grandfather. My feelings about Gus Cage were yet another riddle I'd have to solve.

The dessert was called *flan*, a delicious egg custard topped with caramelized sugar. As we ate it, the waiter wheeled a coffee service cart to the table.

"Have you ever tried putting cream and sugar in it?" asked Jackson as the coffee was poured into delicate porcelain cups.

"I haven't." It seemed wasteful to use such precious things in a bitter, barely tolerable drink.

Jackson gave the server a nod and he poured cream from a tiny silver pitcher into my cup, then added a cube of sugar. I stirred it and took a sip. The concoction was warm, sweet, and delicious. When I looked up, Jackson was watching.

"It's wonderful," I said, my heart flitting about of its own accord as he grinned broadly. Over the past year, his face had settled into itself, a man's face instead of a boy's. It made him even more attractive. I reminded myself that looks weren't everything—in fact, they weren't anything without a heart and mind equal to them.

"Will there be anything else?" the waiter finally asked.

When we said no, he informed us that Mrs. Langley had paid for our meal. A sweet smile passed between us, a moment of common thought, but I was no more enlightened than I'd been before the meal had started.

"Are you game for a walk?" asked Jackson as we stood.

The coffee had perked me up, but I was still sore and achy.

"Or maybe a sit?" he said, noticing my grimace as I took a step. "There are some benches in the park across the street."

If I left him now and went to bed, where would our relationship stand? We would have to have a real conversation at some point.

"All right."

Jackson held my good arm as we crossed the street. I had to concentrate on not limping, my worn-out muscles objecting to every step. Being next to him felt as comfortable as a worn-in pair of boots, and as new as my kitten heels.

Tall electric lamps lit the perimeter of the large square. We sat down on a wooden bench, watching couples stroll along the path in front of us, the younger ones trailed by chaperones. The bells of the cathedral began to toll, marking the hour with nine loud bongs.

"Sarita, I do owe you a real apology," Jackson said when the bells grew still. "My leaving must have been bewildering for you." He paused, eyes filling with grief. "I found out some things about my father."

I didn't want him to have to go through the pain of telling me the details.

"Patricio told me what happened to Clement."

Jackson's expression changed to sad relief.

"I had to go after Ignado," he said.

What had happened to Clement was horrific—any son worth his salt would've done what Jackson had. What I wanted him to explain was why he hadn't told me. I thought back to before JJ had been killed, when Jackson's sudden disappearance had felt like the worst tragedy of my life. I'd counted on the future we'd planned together. He'd put it on hold without a word to me.

"You did the right thing by your father," I said, "but you didn't do the right thing by me."

His face fell.

"I'm so sorry, Sarita. I wasn't sure how to explain it." He looked away for a moment, as if still filtering through what to tell me. "I haven't felt whole since my father died. There was this empty place deep inside that needed to be filled. When I was with you, I didn't feel it so much, but when we were apart, it felt like water running out of a hole."

"You should have told me," I said. "Maybe I could've helped."

"It wouldn't have been fair to expect you to make me whole when, in the end, I knew you couldn't."

"I wasn't enough for you?" I bit my lip to keep from saying more, remembering my pledge to give him the chance to speak.

"No, that's not it." He rushed his words, reading my face. "What I mean is, even though I didn't feel as empty when I was with you, I knew the void was there. What if we got married and it grew? What if I began to resent it so much that I started to fill it with bitterness and anger like my mother did, or started to push people away like my grandfather? What if I took it out on you?"

I sank into the hard bench. He was talking about concerns he'd had even before he'd learned the truth about his father. I'd been angry about him leaving, thinking that had been the whole issue, but now it seemed he'd had reservations all along; doubts he'd never expressed to me.

"Damnit, I'm not saying this right," he said, standing.

He walked in a circle in front of me, raking a hand through his hair. I'd never seen him so tangled up in his own words. Part of me wanted to help him put them in order, but I had no idea what he would say next. He came back and knelt in front of me.

"I was always coming back for you, Sarita," he said, taking my hand. "My hope was that when I did, I'd be offering you a complete person with nothing from the past to suck me in. I wanted our life to be ours. I wanted the for-better-or-worse to be in our hands."

My heart was not made of stone—his words and his earnestness touched me.

"Is the empty place full now?" I asked.

"I think so."

"And you still want a life for us together?"

"More than ever."

We both grew quiet, not the awkward quiet like during dinner, but a thoughtful one. He was saying the right things—things that made me believe he still loved me, no matter what might have changed—but what he'd said about not being complete stuck in my mind. Was I a whole person? If not, what did I need? At one point I'd thought I'd find whatever it was as Jackson's wife, but I knew that was not enough. Jackson had never been the answer to my unhappiness.

Jackson had his resolution, but my journey wasn't over. I hadn't had a chance to decipher what the past weeks meant. I didn't know if Javier's death would fill the hole that had opened when JJ died. Maybe nothing would. I didn't know how Papa would react when I told him what I'd done. I didn't know the fate of La Barroneña or what it would mean for me. I had changed, but I didn't know how yet.

"I'm not the same girl you left," I said.

Jackson flashed a smile. "I know who you are."

"Do tell," I said, irritated by his presumption, but curious.

"You're the strong, capable, beautiful woman who was always there waiting for the right time to come out," he said. "When you had to, you took matters into your own hands and saw it through."

"Just like you did."

He cocked his head, smiling the smile I knew was mine. "I guess so."

I understood his mission, but there were things that haunted me. Like Tomás, Jackson had stood by as Javier tortured and killed others. I could see the line he'd walked. Looking back, his casual warnings to Javier, the way he'd tried to redirect him, took on new meaning. Still, there was an ambiguity to his actions I could not shake.

In the end, who the hell was I to judge Jackson? He'd gone about things in an organized fashion, with a plan and the backup of the Texas Rangers. I'd lit out like a cat with its tail on fire. I'd made mistakes that would plague me forever. People I loved and cared about had lost their lives.

I could feel his eyes on me, those beautiful eyes. I was not ready to let him go, but I wasn't ready to recommit to him either.

"I'm not sure where we go from here, Jackson."

"Back to Hebbronville," he replied, hope dancing on his words.

"You know that's not what I mean." I looked up at him and smiled.

"Yeah," he said, growing serious. "I never stopped wanting to marry you, Sarita, but I realize you might need time to trust me again."

He didn't have all of it right. I did need to figure out if I could ever trust him, and if we could truly be partners, but mostly I needed to understand where I stood in the world.

"I don't want to make any more choices based on what I think I can't have," I said.

Jackson held his hand out to me, and I stood to face him.

"Sarita," he said softly. "You should never have to settle for anything."

CHAPTER 39

In the suite, I lay on the bed and closed my eyes, still feeling the soft pressure of Jackson's good night kiss on my mouth. Maude had refrained from peppering me with questions when I'd come back. She'd helped me change the bandage around my arm and put on the nightdress, then all but tucked me into bed. The mattress lived up to its promise of softness. I drifted off, my mind unusually clear.

When I woke hours later, the room was awash in a golden glow. I tiptoed through the French doors onto a balcony over-looking a courtyard. Tilting my face to the early morning sun, I breathed in the sweet smell of the honeysuckle twin-ing around the wrought iron banister. Footsteps clicked below as a maid passed by with a breakfast-laden tray. My stomach rumbled, even though I'd eaten more the night before than I'd ever eaten in my life.

"You all right, sugar?"

I turned to find Maude sitting up in bed, propped against several pillows.

"Sorry if I woke you," I said.

"Oh, you didn't wake me," she replied. "My body just natu-rally rises with the sun. All these years of ranching, you know, can't waste a minute of daylight."

"What's it like?" I asked.

"Ranching?"

"Being a woman who owns her own ranch," I said.

"Oh, well." Maude smiled. "Hard, frustrating, downright demoralizing, but worth every drop of sweat and blood, and every tear of vexation."

"What makes it worth it?"

Maude peered at me from under sleep-tousled hair.

"It's mine and I'm proud of it," she said. "I don't think that's different from any other woman. Whether it's a home well run, or children well raised, there's a satisfaction in doing your best and being pleased with the result."

I walked over to sit on the end of her bed.

"You have the freedom to be good at what you love," I said.

"You think so?" asked Maude pensively. "I suppose you're right, although it doesn't always feel that way. There are not a few people, of both genders, who don't take kindly to a woman doing business. They consider it a man's territory. I've had to do things I never thought I would." She paused for a moment. "I guess you know how that feels now, don't you?"

I turned, looking through the French doors at a pigeon sitting on the balcony railing. The bird let out a series of soft, drawn-out coos, and another pigeon landed beside it. Their heads bobbed at each other, iridescent green and purple throat feathers glimmering, then the first pigeon took off, the claps of its wings echoing across the courtyard. The second pigeon cocked its head sideways one way then the other, bright black-bead eyes looking into the room. After a moment it turned away, flying up into the deep blue square of sky.

"Sugar, there's something I should tell you before we head home," Maude said, her tone serious. "About your father."

I faced her, cold fingers wrapping around my heart.

"He's not doing so well," she continued. "I sent one of my maids to stay with him while I came over here to fetch you."

"I see." My voice quivered.

"Now, now," Maude soothed, patting the space next to her.

I scooted closer, tears rolling down my cheeks as she wrapped her arms tight around my shoulders. I'd been feeling a newfound confidence, a kind of belief in myself and my ability to cope, to learn, to adapt, but the mere mention of my father's ill health had reduced me to a sniffling child.

"After several days passed and you weren't back, your father asked me to put the word out," Maude explained. "I knew from your note that you'd gone to see Gus Cage, so I eventually went out to his place. He told me you'd most likely crossed the border and he promised to alert the Rangers. When I drove back out to La Barroneña the next day to tell your father, well, he'd taken a turn."

"Why didn't he go to Corpus?" I asked.

"He's waiting for you to come home."

Is he waiting for me to come home so he can die?

"There's another thing," Maude went on. "The undertaker had to go on and bury John Junior. He's under that big oak tree next to your mama. The grave's unmarked thus far since he didn't have any instructions about what y'all wanted. I doubt your father has even looked out there."

The orchard of crosses flashed across my mind; the urge to rush home shoving at me.

"We can leave as soon as Jackson and I talk to Captain Wright and the governor."

"Of course," said Maude. "I'll have everything packed up and ready."

I got dressed, relieved when Maude took a pair of cotton twill trousers, a leather belt, and a chambray shirt out of the wardrobe instead of another dress and some heels. She helped me into the clothes then I pulled on JJ's boots.

Neither of us spoke on the short drive. I had been nervous about the meeting, but now I just wanted to get it done so I could go home. When we arrived, several automobiles were already parked in front of the sheriff's office. Maude pulled up farther down in front of the jail. I climbed out of the roadster, slamming the door a little harder than I meant to.

"Don't give Governor Hobby too hard a time, sugar," Maude said with a wink. "He seems to be a modern man; supports women's voting rights and all."

As I stepped onto the front porch, the office door swung open, and Burr Archer walked out. His hands were cuffed behind him, his shirt unbuttoned enough to show the top of a bandage wrapped around his chest. Wagley came out behind him, taking hold of his elbow.

"Morning, Sarita," Wagley said, tipping his hat. "I'll tell them you're here after I escort Mr. Archer back to his cell."

Burr stopped short, staring as if seeing me for the first time ever. Wagley tugged his arm, but he held fast.

"Seems I underestimated you, Miss Gibson," he said, trying to look amused instead of pissed off. "You'll have to forgive me."

I fought the urge to punch him.

"For underestimating me? Or for partnering with my brother's murderer?"

"Now, see," Burr said, his grin wilting. "Javier was just supposed to steal your horses. Shake y'all up a little."

Breath stuck in my chest, Tomás's voice in my head: "*We were only supposed to take the horses.*"

"What do you mean?" The words came out in an exhale.

"Sarita—" Wagley started, but Burr interrupted him.

"I've got my shortcomings, Miss Gibson, but I'd never sink so low as to send someone to kill a kid."

My legs turned to lead. I felt Wagley's arm around my waist. He pushed me onto a wooden bench. Burr was still talking, his voice distorted, muffled.

"That's enough, Mr. Archer." Wagley gave Burr's arm a rough jerk, pulling him toward the jail.

I leaned back against the rock wall, staring blindly at the porch ceiling.

Javier had not happened upon our home. Burr Archer had sent him.

I had assumed Javier had argued with JJ because it was

his nature, the way a cat plays with a mouse before inevitably killing it. Javier could have ridden away without Twister, his job done. His ego wouldn't let him lose to a boy. So, he'd killed him.

Footsteps thumped up the front stairs. I lowered my eyes to see Jackson standing in front of me.

"Did you know?" I asked.

Confusion crossed his face.

"Did you know Burr Archer sent Javier to our ranch that day?" I'd begun to shake with the kind of anger and pain that promises more to come.

Jackson's shoulders slumped. He lowered his head for a moment.

"I suspected he might've," he said, meeting my eyes. "He'd been using whatever means he could to buy up land for oil exploration. That's why I knew he'd run Javier's guns for the right price."

"Was it part of the deal you brokered between him and Javier?" I asked. "That Javier would harass my family?"

Jackson's eyes opened wide, flooding with hurt.

"I swear, Sarita, I knew nothing about it until we talked at La Fonda."

I fought to stop the thread from unspooling; the thread that connected Burr to Javier, and Jackson to them both. I believed Jackson would never have endangered my family on purpose, but the unease I'd felt began to sharpen to a point.

I'd told him Javier had murdered JJ; I'd told him Burr Archer had been trying to buy our ranch. At the time, those two pieces of information were not connected in my mind other than Burr taking advantage of my father's grief. Jackson had known the connection, and he'd kept me in the dark.

The door to the jail banged closed. Wagley approached, eyes flitting between Jackson and me.

"I'll see if they're ready for you," he said, skirting around us and disappearing inside.

Silence screamed in my ears. I thought of Jackson's willingness to return to our engagement as if nothing had changed. Everything had changed. I stared at him; all I saw were those lines he'd talked about crossing, coiling around him like serpents.

Wagley opened the door to escort us into the office. My core vibrated as I battened down my emotions.

The governor stood to shake our hands. I'd expected an older statesman, but he looked to be in his late thirties or early forties. He had a kind, thoughtful face. His well-tailored suit separated him from the lawmen and Rangers in the room.

Before answering any questions, I asked for assurance that Carlos would not be sent to jail and that he would be safely returned to his grandmother and mother in Hidalgo. He was young and had been a victim of circumstances, I explained. He would cooperate fully with them against the *tequileros.*

"I have another request," I added, glancing over at Jackson. "Carlos's sister, my friend, Alicia Polanco, was killed by Javier at his camp in the Sierras. I believe Jackson knows where her body is. I want it retrieved; I want her taken home to her family. She should not have to spend eternity in that hellhole."

A reverent hush filled the room for a moment.

"Of course," Hobby agreed; the compassion on his face led me to believe him.

He and Captain Wright asked their questions then. I gave them as much detail as I could remember. Jackson told them that the chaos in Santa Rosa had made the *Villistas* nervous. In addition, one of their men turned up dead by a river between Múzquiz and Sabinas. Javier's explanations had not satisfied them. When Ignado arrived, Pancho Villa refused to meet with him. Ignado had been furious. He had indeed recognized Jackson's surname, focusing all his ire and suspicion on him.

In the meantime, Javier had raced to Hidalgo to meet with Mayor Hinojosa, who had helped Burr get the guns across the border by threatening rail officials and bribing customs inspectors. The *tequileros* needed to sell them to someone else quickly. Javier had brought a crate with him to show potential buyers. The guns had been in the mayor's barn when his property was raided.

"I was lucky Wright's company arrived when it did," Jackson concluded with a nod my way.

"Thank you for your service, Miss Gibson," Captain Wright said as the meeting came to an end. "We will need you to testify at the trials."

"About that," I replied. "Among other atrocities, Burr Archer is responsible for the murder of my brother."

The men all looked at each other in surprised silence. I turned to Jackson.

"You explain it to them."

I let the door bang shut behind me. The interview had taken over an hour, and my concern for Papa had grown with each passing minute. Maude was waiting for me in the roadster, our belongings stashed in the boot. As I started to get in, I heard my name called.

"I thought you'd want this," Wagley said, jogging up to me. He held out something wrapped in a piece of chamois cloth. I took it from him, my heart guessing what it was even before I unwrapped it.

"I saw his name on the back," said Wagley.

I held the warm rectangle of silver against my chest. Wagley pulled a chain out from his shirt collar, rubbing his finger over a coin-sized medallion.

"My mother's St. Christopher," he said. "I can bring Twister and the mare out to your place in the next day or so if you'd like."

I glanced over at the corral. It held several horses and mules, but Twister, Bluebird, and Rat stood off to the side in their own little clump.

"Just a minute," I said to Maude.

I jogged to the pen and ducked through the fence. Rat

lowered his head as I approached. I scratched his forehead, then wrapped my good arm under his neck.

"Gus Cage was right about one thing," I whispered in his ear. "You are the finest horse I ever met."

CHAPTER 40

The old wooden gate to La Barroneña could not have brought me any more joy had it been made of diamonds and gold. A hummingbird fluttered in my chest as we drove through, threatening to break free and race ahead. The chalky smell of dust and the bright scent of buffalo grass were so famil- iar that, for a moment, it felt like I'd never left. The windmill spun in an age-old rhythm, red cows still dotted the pastures, and the dirt road rose and fell in the usual places.

The acres spread out around me, a mottled green ocean, live oak islands reaching through it for the sun. The sight filled my soul, gripping me as it had my father and his father before him, and my mother and her people. Land could pro- vide a bounty never imagined, or suck the life out of you. It could never truly be controlled, tamed, or destroyed, even though we crossed it with fences, scarred its soil, and sucked its veins dry. Land was a living thing; people were only tempo- rary caretakers. It would survive long after all of us were gone.

Maude stopped the roadster in front of the house. Her maid came outside to greet us. She hugged the widow and then caught me off guard by embracing me.

"*Su papa,*" she said. "He is asking for you."

I hurried inside. Papa's chair sat empty by the fireplace, but I heard his uneven breaths. I walked into his bedroom. Dim light filtered through the blinds, casting him in a gray shadow. His head, small and bare without his cowboy hat, lay lightly on a pillow. The outline of his body was barely discernable under the *colchas bordadas* quilt, but he'd always be a giant in my mind.

"Sarita?" he said.

"I'm here, Papa."

His head turned my way.

"That really you?"

"Yes, sir."

I stopped at the side of the bed and took his hand. Weathered fingers wrapped around mine. His strong, workworn grip had seemed harsh at times, but he'd always kept me safe. He'd always loved me.

"Did you find him?" he asked.

"Yes, Papa, I did."

"Is he dead?"

"Yes, sir."

"Graveyard dead?"

"Graveyard dead."

His head lifted, the line between his brows deepening as he noticed the bandage around my arm. Then his gaze fell on the silver buckle at my waist. When his eyes lifted to mine, they were clear and sparkling. He stared so long and hard it felt as if we were soldered together. Finally, he sank back against the pillow, a long sigh escaping his lips.

"Good," he said, his voice a wisp of smoke. "That's good."

"Papa?" I squeezed his hand, pulling him back to me. "I want your blessing."

"About what?"

"I want to carry on our legacy here, on this land our family fought so hard to keep," I said. "I want to run La Barroneña."

A weak smile moved across his lips.

"Well," he said, gripping my fingers tighter. "I don't know who else you thought was going to do it."

ACKNOWLEDGMENTS

I'd like to thank my husband, Drew, for his endless support and patience. Never once did he discount my desire to finish this project. He believed in *Sarita* from the first sentence until the last, and during all the years in between. OX

Thank you to my family and friends for their continued encouragement and support, and for not cringing (at least not in front of me!) every time the subject of my book came up.

Thank you to the following for editing, reading, teaching, developing, encouraging, mentoring, and/or dreaming with me: Todd Allen, Amanda Alvarez, Suzanne Frank, T. Kirk and Karen May, Asata Radcliffe, Harry and Amanda Werksman, David Marion Wilkinson, and Katie Zdybel.

ABOUT ATMOSPHERE PRESS

Founded in 2015, Atmosphere Press was built on the principles of Honesty, Transparency, Professionalism, Kindness, and Making Your Book Awesome. As an ethical and author-friendly hybrid press, we stay true to that founding mission today.

If you're a reader, enter our giveaway for a free book here:

SCAN TO ENTER
BOOK GIVEAWAY

If you're a writer, submit your manuscript for consideration here:

SCAN TO SUBMIT
MANUSCRIPT

And always feel free to visit Atmosphere Press and our authors online at atmospherepress.com. See you there soon!

ABOUT THE AUTHOR

NATALIE MUSGRAVE DOSSETT grew up in San Antonio, spending a great deal of time on family ranches in deep South Texas. A seventh-generation Texan, she was raised on tales (some of them tall) of the Wild Horse Desert, a place her great-grandmother referred to as an "aquired taste." Her love of history and writing was nurtured by wonderful teachers at Saint Mary's Hall and strengthened while earning a BA in History at Vanderbilt University. She lives in Dallas and enjoys a large, growing family with her husband.